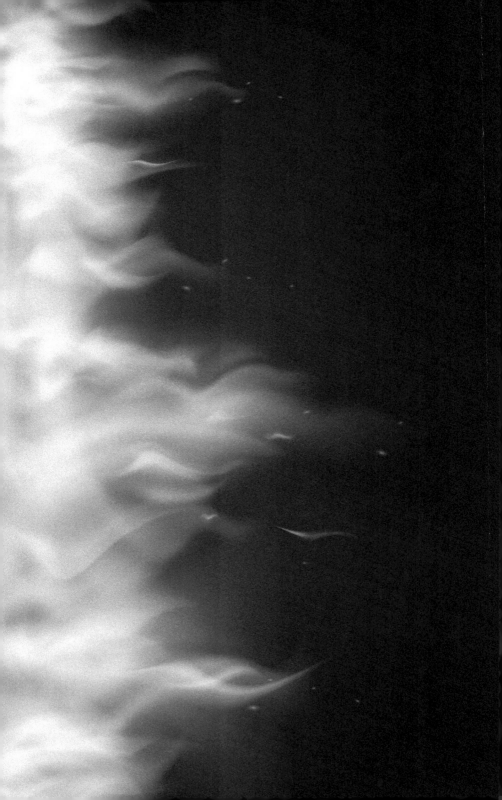

EMMIE MEARS

HEARTHFIRE

A STONEBREAKER NOVEL

INDIGO

Livonia, Michigan

Editor: David M. Johnson

HEARTHFIRE

This book is a work of fiction. The characters, incidents, and dialogue are drawn from the author's imagination and are not to be construed as real. Any resemblance to actual events or persons, living or dead, is entirely coincidental.

Published by Indigo
an imprint of BHC Press

Library of Congress Control Number:
2017945133

ISBN: 978-1-947727-51-9

Visit the publisher:
www.bhcpress.com

Also available in
Softcover (ISBN: 978-1-946848-52-9)
Ebook (ISBN: 978-1-947727-52-6)

For those in transition, who know that sometimes
we need to find rebirth within ourselves to truly live.

AN INTRODUCTION BY
EMMIE MEARS

Dear Reader,

Welcome to the Hearthland! This world is one I have been building for the past four years of my life, and I am so excited to finally open the doors wide to you.

Being a writer is a chance to play god, in a sense. Whether we are reimagining the world we occupy on Earth or spinning a new one from scratch, what comes out is a manifestation of our subconscious and conscious awareness alike.

This book came to me very much by accident. A stray line in Patrick Rothfuss's *The Name of the Wind* about how the weeks in that world were eleven days long set my mind spinning. We build time based on so many factors—the cycle of the moon, the movement of the earth around the sun, the turning of the planet to see the sun and then look away.

My brain ran with those thoughts until it came to a what if question: "What if a land were so bountiful that one day in five was a feast day?" I spent the next eight hours thinking out exactly how another world might be different in how they structured time and seasons, how the basis of society (agricultural, hunter-gatherer, industrial) shapes our perception and use of time structures. Running through all of that was the soul of what would become this series: what would someone in such a bountiful land do if they discovered that the abundance they enjoyed came from draining the life from the earth itself? Could a person live with that? And what if there were consequences for deciding one couldn't live with that knowledge? I wanted to explore an epic fantasy parallel of climate change and its human impact through the lens of magic.

The characters of *Hearthfire* met me there. A young man bullied relentlessly, his feelings minimized and undermined. A young person who has built a place for herself but is not certain she has chosen the right path. A young genderfluid person (hyrsin, in the book) who knows who they want to be, but whose desire to affect change will come at a steep cost. And another young woman, whose path is laid out for her in certainty and who will do whatever she must to keep her homeland safe and fruitful—no matter the price in blood.

You'll notice that there is a different set of pronouns included in this book (sy/hys/hyr/hyrself). Those pronouns are, in-world, the ones used by people who in our world would be non-binary. They can be genderfluid, bigender, agender—in the Hearthland world, they define hyrsin as people who are "both and neither, all and none." Children embody that potential, and in this world, children all use those pronouns until they are fifteen, when they declare to their village who they are. Some then declare that they are men or women (cis or trans, to us), and others move from hysmern (children) to hyrsin.

Hearthfire is a book that surprised me. It's a book about confronting humanity's impact on the earth and recognizing that hoarding resources hurts people, about the price of doing right, and it's a book about consequences. It's about power—and how the uses of power, whether intended for good or ill or personal profit, can cause unexpected repercussions. About how what we throw into the ocean will return on the next tide—or wash up on someone else's shore. And most of all, it's about choice—how we always have a choice, even when it's not a good one.

Thank you for exploring this world with me.

Emmie Mears

HEARTHFIRE

1

THERE WAS something, Carin always thought, in the way Dyava's skin caught the sunlight. The whole of him soaked it up as if he could make magic of it. Light revealed, darkness concealed, and with the rays that fell upon his face, Carin saw only love.

"If you keep staring at me," he said, "I might turn to dust before sunset."

"If I don't keep staring at you, how do you expect me to still remember your face when I return?" Carin teased. "High Lights is some time away."

Her tone was much lighter than her heart felt, but Dyava knew her, and she knew him, and neither of them would give way to the weight of tomorrow when today was here now.

His eyes, warm and brown, twinkled as he smiled at her. Dyava reached out to take Carin's hand, kissing it. His long black hair tickled the side of her arm. He even smelled like sunshine.

For a moment, Carin allowed herself the thrill of it and the wicked moment of remembering the youth Dyava had been only one cycle past. Dav, he had been. Before he set out on the same Journeying she herself was about to, returning to Haveranth new-named. Dyava. Her Dyava.

Carin caught his hand in hers and turned it over, kissing his even as he'd kissed hers. "I saw Jenin heading toward Lyah's roundhome," she said. "They'll be together these next moons and still they steal moments today."

"You're jealous," Dyava said. He pulled Carin close to his chest. "I suppose there's no hope for it. I'll have to join you lot."

Carin let out a laugh that was almost a snort, even though her heart soared suddenly at the idea of Dyava by her side for the Journeying. "Merin would have you trussed to the village hearth-home, possibly on a spit."

"Good point."

The silence that followed threatened to sink lower. Carin pulled back to look at Dyava. His face was quiet, with the stillness of a forest pool. As if he was suddenly miles away. Carin thought she knew what he was thinking. Jenin and Lyah had been inseparable since they had all been hysmern, children with no appellation of their own. Carin had not understood it, then, though as Dyava's Journeying had approached the cycle before, she had found herself dreading his absence. When he returned days before High Lights, thinner and quieter and stronger, Carin had known nothing like the relief she felt. She had struggled to catch even a glimpse of him for the days that followed, until the sun claimed its longest day and the village toiled under its heat and that night, oh, that night. Exhausted and aching as always, Carin had taken her cup of ashes and turned at the sound of Dyava's soft voice addressing her.

"I failed you, Carin," he had said. "In all those moons walking, each step reminded me that I had forgotten to make something clear between us. I hope you will forgive me."

"Forgive what?" Carin's hands had nearly dropped her cup.

"Simply that I care for you," said Dyava. "More than simply for a friend. I should have told you sooner."

Carin had dipped her whole hand into her cup, covering her palm with ashes that stung her skin. Without speaking, she placed her splayed hand over Dyava's heart and met his eyes. The next morning, with the whole of the village nude and covered in the ashes of forgiven wrongs, Dyava and Carin leapt into the Bemin River together, the cold-flowing water reviving them anew. Carin thought that until that moment she had never been alive at all.

Now, no ashes coated her palm or Dyava's tunic-clothed chest, but she looked him in the eye and knew he remembered.

And, true to Dyava, he smiled, kissed her, and changed the subject. "Once you return, we will have to prepare for the High Harvest."

Any other person would simply mean preparations for the feasts, the dancing, the festival in which villagers from Cantoranth and Bemin's Fan would arrive and set up colorful tents surrounding the whole of Haveranth for the whole waxing and waning of Harvest Moon. This time, though, Carin knew what he meant.

"I'm not sure I can think about that yet," she said, "or if I will truly do it."

Carin had chosen her appellation at her fifteenth cycle, like everyone did. But for some time it had not set well for her. She had gone from being child to woman, just as Lyah had, but now, two cycles past and on the verge of true adulthood, Carin could not be sure that she had been true to herself. High Harvest would be the time to make it right.

At her trailing silence, Dyava seemed to come back to himself, pulled her closer. "Sometimes people need to leave something behind to do what is right. Be you," was all he said.

He did not use her name, and in that moment, Carin loved him for it. Tomorrow she would go search for the name her village would know as her true name forever, but today she was trapped in now. Carin el Rina ve Haveranth. Was that who she was?

In the warmth of the arms around her, she had no need of a name at all.

The sun sank toward the horizon, and after a time, Carin bade Dyava a bountiful night, knowing he went to his parents. Jenin's parents, too. Dyava and Jenin were sahthren, born of the same blood a cycle apart.

Dyava gave Carin no lingering goodbye, only a flash of a grin as he turned back toward Haveranth, leaving Carin to slowly turn back herself.

RYD AL Malcam va Haveranth hated being sat on.

It may have been one of the unfortunate effects of being smaller than everyone else, but the other village children seemed to think it was a fine past time. Never mind that he was due for his Journeying and only two harvests away from being a full adult. Never mind that the rumps pressing into various parts of his body belonged to squeaks ten harvests his junior. Never mind that even the grown folk in town found it amusing.

Ryd didn't.

He struggled against the weight of six bodies—a giggling *whump* of new pressure made it seven—pinning him to the lush blue grasses.

"Geroff!" he hollered.

No one listened. They never did.

Ryd looked overhead through the wiggly cluster of sweaty children, catching glimpses of the bone-white halm tree's trunk. Against the blue of the sky, the halm was dotted with deep red buds that would soon open to the sun. A knee punched into Ryd's side, bony and probably covered in dirt.

This is it, Ryd thought. *This is how I die.*

A startled squawk from one of the children cut through their giggles, and suddenly the weight of seven squirmy bodies vanished. Ryd gulped a breath of the warm spring air, scrambling to a sitting position just in time to see the kids—carpenter Stil's brat wouldn't even pay for hys idea of a joke at home later—scamper off into the town square. None of those squeaks had even reached the age to declare their appellation, and no one cared that Ryd was on the cusp of becoming full-fledged adult, with a place and a name and a purpose.

"You're welcome." A whoosh of air brought Carin's muscular frame down hard in the grass beside him. She plopped an apple into his lap, its skin redder than the halm's leaves and as shiny as the sun on the Bemin River.

"You don't always have to rescue me, you know," Ryd said. The words came out more cross than he meant them to, and Carin sniffed.

"You're right. I don't. Want me to call them back?"

He shook his head. In spite of her joking, Carin had the look in her eyes that said she had just come from Dyava. Half dreaming, half present. Even half present for Carin was enough to send the village hysmern scrambling away from their usual hobby of sitting on Ryd, though. Ryd thought he should resent that they fled her presence and laughed at his, but he couldn't.

Ryd took a bite of the apple, licking the juice from the skin where it seeped out around his lip. It danced on his tongue with a slight tartness that quickly vanished into the silken sweetness of candy or syrup. They were called Early Birds because the trees that bore them flowered with the first frost and offered their slow-growing fruits just as the spring's daffodils opened their golden trumpets. This was the first Ryd had eaten this season, and perhaps the last before the Journeying. The thought soured his next bite.

"You're thinking about it, aren't you?" Carin's voice was quiet, punctuated only by the ringing of the blacksmith's hammer on an anvil across the square. The rest of the village had gone silent in meditation for what would come on the morrow, but apparently the children had decided sitting on Ryd escaped the cause for solemnity.

"How can I think of anything else?"

Carin didn't answer, but she took a crunching bite of her own apple. A trill rose from the halm tree. A whitfinch with its *trr-dee-trr-dee-dee-dee*.

Carin pointed past the town square where the road rose toward the foothills. The hills themselves wore the deep blue of spring, blazing bright in the yellow sun. The road curved around Kinnock's Rise and vanished, but Ryd could have drawn the map of the route under the darkness of the Veiled Moon with the stars hiding their faces from the night.

"Speak for yourself," Carin said softly, letting her hand drop. They sat with their bodies touching in easy friendship, but somehow Carin was leagues away.

Ryd still looked where she had gestured.

Past Kinnock's Rise to Haver's Glen. Up the cleft of the glen along the banks of the Bemin to its source, a high and shining lake known simply as the Jewel. Skirt the shores of the Jewel to the west and climb, climb, climb the Mistaken Pass to the Hidden Vale where the Hanging Falls floated, dripping crystalline drops hundreds of feet to water the grasses beneath. Beyond the falls, on the westernmost slopes of the vale, was a cave.

It was to that cave he was supposed to journey tomorrow. Not just a journey. The Journeying. To seal his passage into adulthood. To mark his growth. To find his name.

By harvest time, he and Carin and the others would be starting their trades, new-named and ready to prove themselves to the village. Not quite full villagers, not until their twentieth harvests, but closer. Named. Respected.

Ryd linked his elbow with Carin's, and together they looked into the west.

When he found his name, he wouldn't let anyone sit on him again.

ON THE banks of the Bemin, far from the sun-warmed grasses over-looking Haveranth's surrounding hillocks, Lyah el Jemil ve Haveranth wove her fingers through her lover's hair. Jenin's dark locks flowed over Lyah's lap, lustrous and shining in the light of the setting sun.

"*Suo vo dyu, dyu vo suo,*" Lyah murmured. Light from darkness, darkness from light.

"Spoken like a true soothsayer." Jenin teased, but hys eyes lit with pride. Lyah had been apprenticed to Merin, Haveranth's soothsayer, at the last Night of Reflection—a celebration of her reaching her seventeenth harvest and the coming of her Journeying with the following spring. She'd known for some time that Merin would take her as an apprentice, but it was finally official. Lyah would one day be soothsayer. As such, she'd taken to learning the lore of the village and found herself uttering proverbs even when she didn't mean to. As the first apprentice Merin had chosen in her three hundred cycles of long life, Jenin couldn't often disguise the pride sy felt at Lyah being the one chosen.

And Jenin's pride in her made Lyah glow like the backlit maha trees that dotted the horizon, their leaves glowing deep blue with the gold of the sun behind them. Jenin went still beneath Lyah's gentle touch on hys hair.

"Tomorrow," sy said after a long pause.

Tomorrow was the Journeying. Lyah tried to disguise the skip in her heart that came with the thought of being off with Jenin for turns on end as they traveled. Of course, Carin and Ryd would also be there, but that wouldn't stop Lyah's excitement. Carin and Lyah were *fyahiul,* pillow-friends, practically family without sharing blood. Ryd would tag along, as he always did. Like a bug clinging to a falling leaf. Both Carin and Ryd seemed apprehensive about the Journeying, their thoughts rotting with the fear that they wouldn't find their names and would be cast out of Haveranth as Nameless, but Lyah had no fear on that score. Nor had Jenin, but the tension in hys shoulders, even as Lyah ran her fingers through hys hair, told Lyah that perhaps something had shifted.

Jenin's chin was stubbled with whiskers, and sy turned to lay hys head on Lyah's knee, the roughness of hys chin through the thin fabric of her leggings sending a tingle of excitement through her. Jenin fell silent, hys posture tensing as sy lay across Lyah's lap. A question hovered in hys eyes, but sy didn't speak. Instead, Jenin's dark eyes searched hers. For the space of a breath, it looked to Lyah as if Jenin's eyes bore the weight of a thousand mountains, quashing their dark warmth with nothingness. After a moment, sy blinked and smiled and reached out hys hand to touch Lyah's face.

"Why do we have to go on the Journeying?" sy asked.

"To find our names and join the village as adults," Lyah responded automatically.

"That's all?"

"The Journeying proves us worthy to join the village. It's arduous but necessary."

Jenin broke eye contact, hys gaze focused on Lyah's midsection. Not in the way Lyah hoped; there was no lasciviousness in Jenin's face, only a quiet vulnerability that made the tingles of excitement in Lyah's stomach turn sour.

"Jenin?" Lyah placed her hand on Jenin's chest, her fingers seeking out the solidity of Jenin's flat planes and strong muscles that came from hys toil in the fields. For all sy came from the same womb as Dyava, Jenin could turn serious with the changing of the wind.

"I have to tell you something," sy said. Hys eyes darted to the skyline of the village, the low curved roofs of the roundhomes clustered at its center. A breeze ruffled Lyah's hair, pulling long strands from her hasty plait that stuck to her lips.

The sour nervousness in her stomach grew, like fermented plum juice gone past enjoyment. This was not what was supposed to happen on the eve of the Journeying. "Jenin," she began, putting all the love she could into the speaking of hys name, only to have it die on her lips as she remembered that sy would only shortly bear it, that the name she'd come so accustomed to speaking in love would be eschewed for a new one. Now

Jenin yl Tarwyn vy Haveranth—then who? Who would Jenin be in three moons' time?

Jenin scrambled to hys knees and took hold of Lyah's shoulders, sensing her discomfort. "It's not about us, fruit of my heart. It's more than us. More than the Journeying."

Alarmed, Lyah felt her breath come faster into her chest, even as the breeze rose to become well and truly wind around them. "What is it?"

"I can't say yet." That weight returned to hys gaze.

"Then why say something now?" Lyah's tongue felt dry like the clay that caked her mother's worktable.

Jenin's hands tightened on her shoulders. "I ought to have kept quiet. I've not spoken of this to anyone, but I've learned things and—"

The bell tolled in the village, one loud, reverberating note that spread out through the fields and hills around Haveranth. Sure enough, the sun had dipped below the horizon to the west, its rays following the Bemin to the sea where it bid farewell to the folk of Bemin's Fan before sleeping in darkness for the night. To the east was Cantoranth, where only the slightest haze of smoke betrayed the presence of their neighbor-village. Strange that this cycle no one would join them from Bemin's Fan or Cantoranth for the Journeying; no others came of age. There were whispers in town that fewer folk had been born in recent cycles, that two thousand cycles back the Journeying had brought as many as a score of young folk searching for their names. Now there were only four, all from Haveranth.

For the first time a true vine of fear spread through Lyah's core, writhing like a worm at the center of an apple. Someone called out from the village, and Jenin, whatever sy'd been about to say lost, rose to stand, pulling Lyah to her feet.

"One day," sy said. "One day, I'll be able to explain to you. Don't worry on it."

Lyah felt that spoiled pit in her stomach grow heavier and sourer. "Jenin," she said.

"*Ahsh*," sy said, hushing her. "Remember one thing for me."

"Always."

"There is always the choice. As children, we choose the things we love and the village nurtures them. As youths we find ourselves and declare our appellation to our families, man or woman or *hyrsin,* declaring not just who we are but who we will become. As adults there will be the choice as well. I've made mine. *Lu dyu, pah, artus lu suo dyosu suon.*"

Sy smiled as if to say sy could quote proverbs too, but it didn't reach hys eyes.

"I choose you," Lyah said, her voice full of a vehemence she didn't know she possessed.

"And I will never be far from you," said Jenin, kissing Lyah's lips with softness like down. Sy left Lyah on the banks of the Bemin, the rushing of the water over its time-smoothed stones not full enough to make the proverb Jenin'd spoken less hollow.

In darkness, birth. Light reveals all for good or ill.

CARIN'S THOUGHTS as she watched the shadows lengthen arm in arm with Ryd had less to do with getting sat on and more to do with trepidation.

By the time she removed her arm from Ryd's—her own was now cramped at the elbow and sore to the shoulder—she gave serious thought to plunking right back down in the grass where their twin rump-marks had left double dents in the early spring growth.

She bid Ryd a bountiful night and made her way home to her round-home, though it wasn't hers yet.

The lamp was not yet lit, the shutters not yet open. This night was the last she would spend with her mother in their house. When she returned from her Journeying, she would be new-named and free to pursue her trade. Whatever that might be. Whoever she might be.

Its rounded walls curved back from where she stood, inviting. She could picture the wide central room, its hearth and chimney painstaking-ly constructed from the Bemin's smooth stones and mortar she'd mixed herself. Carin looked up at the domed roof, its clay shingles kiln-fired and glazed by her own hand.

Her fingers closed around the door's latch, the handwrought metal curving gracefully out from the polished wood that she herself had shone to its current warm gleam.

The windows she had framed and set herself as well, the panes of round glass snug in their encircling bands of wood. Carin could still feel the strain of the wet maha as her fingers closed around it, warping the wood with its grain, molding it around the metal template, binding it with clamps so it would dry snug and tight.

She had made this home with her hands. As much as Dyava had wanted to help, she had not let him, though she had acquiesced to him bringing her fresh pockets of curried goat in soft bread and dried berries in conu juice. Her home had needed to be hers alone. Now, though, she wished some mark of Dyava's had worked its way into the building of it. Her fingers trailed away from the latch, the metal now warmed by her heat.

Carin walked the path to her mother's home, unable to help but notice that she already drew a dividing line to show that her ownership of that home had lapsed.

It hasn't yet, she thought fiercely. Try as she may, though, she could not bring herself to think that she was going home.

She only hoped that when she returned from her Journeying, she'd think herself home in the house her hands had raised. Perhaps someday Dyava would make his home there with her. Perhaps.

Grey smoke piped from her mother's chimney, bringing with it the scent of herbs and spice. Two figures showed silhouetted through the window as Carin approached, and she knew without closer inspection that one would be Merin. The eve of a Journeying. It was seldom these days that four villagers were to make the trek in one season, and tonight Merin, the village soothsayer, would pay respects at each home.

Carin felt a chill that spread from the metal latch on her mother's door shoot through her hand to the top of her spine where it sent tendrils down her back and up her skull. Merin knew all their names.

What if I can't find mine? Every child asked that question at least once, and the adults always laughed. Every Journeyer found her name. There were no Nameless in the Hearthland, and there hadn't been for cycles. Entire High Harvests had passed since the last, each five cycles apart.

Every child asked that question, but not on the eve of the Journeying. Perhaps they all kept their asking only within the confines of their skulls.

Carin pushed down on the latch and opened the door. A gust of warm, spice-scented air greeted her, and she closed the door behind her before turning to face her mother.

"Favor find you," Merin said first, her crackly voice reaching Carin's ears from the direction of the hearth.

Carin paused, doing her best to wipe any apprehension from her gaze. When she turned to face the soothsayer, she had made sure her eyes were relaxed and open, coaxed a small smile into tugging the corners of her mouth. "And you, Merin. May the planting this Harmonix eve bear bounty for the good of Haveranth."

The old woman's face folded into a knowing grin, as if Carin's careful rearrangement of her own expression could not fool anyone.

Carin's mother was nowhere to be seen, but after a moment, she came bustling in from her bedchamber with a long parcel in her hand. She set it on the trestle table and turned to face her daughter.

Rina ve Haveranth was built for her smith's trade. Standing of a height with Carin, her broad shoulders drew her out to double Carin's width. Where Carin's muscles were lean and long, her mother's were short and strong. She didn't often show emotion, but when she looked over the trestle table at her near-grown daughter, Carin was almost sure she saw Rina's eyes glimmer. She wore a furrow between her brow, and she didn't look away from Carin's face for several long moments. Finally, Carin forced herself to turn, embarrassed at her mother's stare.

At the hearth, Merin clunked a wooden spoon in the cook pot that burbled there. "If the two of you are done staring at each other like a couple cats, why don't you set the table?"

No one else could have gotten away without a skinning telling Rina ve Haveranth what to do in her own home, but Rina and Carin both took deep ceramic plates and heavy clear glass goblets from the open shelves on either side of the hearth and placed them dutifully on the table. Carin tried not to look at the long parcel. It took up nearly half of the sturdy wooden table, a table that had always been far too large for only Rina and Carin. As Carin laid the last spoon and fork next to a plate, her mother caught her arm.

Rina said nothing for a moment, but her callused hands dug into the bare flesh of Carin's forearm. When she pulled back, pale white impressions quickly faded from the bronze of Carin's skin. Carin was so transfixed by the strength of her mother's grasp that she almost missed the shining tear that escaped Rina's right eye, captured quickly by Rina's left hand and obliterated into the dark blue woolen folds of her tunic, to be remembered only by the blue-black smudge it left behind.

"That's a good child," Rina said. Her voice gave away no clue of the tear, nor any acknowledgment that any such liquid had ever spilled from her eyes.

Those were the final words spoken until the stew spilled from Merin's ladle into the deep plates and Rina splashed deep blue iceberry wine into the goblets. It shone like twilight stone in the light from the hearth, and the colors it cast on the table turned purple-bright against the polished red cast of the wood. The glassworkers of Bemin's Fan had come to Haveranth for the Night of Reflection and exchanged the goblets for Rina's expertly forged knives and kitchenware. Merin hung the pot back over the hearth, her movements as sure as if she shared the home and wasn't simply a guest.

The older woman sat down first, looking expectantly at Carin and Rina until they joined her at the table. The stew steamed in Carin's plate, the scent sweet and spicy. Dots of purple oil from the cave chilies speckled the creamy white surface, and Carin breathed in the humid warmth. She was a dismal cook. This might be the last home-cooked meal she got before the Reflection Vigil on the darkest night.

She ran her hand along the edge of the table. Strong wood. Dense wood. The same maha she had used to frame the windows in her new roundhome. Tooled into the edge were runes of home and hearth. Carin would miss this table.

"I've never known either of you to lack for words, Carin and Rina ve Haveranth. If one of you doesn't start eating soon, I'll switch out your tooth scrubs with mashed cave chili seeds." Merin picked up her spoon and slurped a mouthful of the spicy-sweet conu broth. "Carin may have gotten her wits kissed out of her, but you, Rina, ought to be joyful on the eve of this Journeying."

Rina said nothing, only dipped her spoon into her soup herself.

Carin hurriedly followed suit, plucking a chunk of white fish from the stew and popping it into her mouth. "Thank you for sharing your cooking with us, Merin."

Merin waved a hand. "Are you ready for tomorrow, child?" Oddly, her eyes were on Rina as she said it, though not even Merin could get away with calling Rina "child."

If there was anything Carin looked forward to without any accompanying anxiety, it was returning from the Journeying to never being called "child" again. She swallowed her bite and washed it down with a sip of wine.

"Ready as one can expect," Carin said.

Merin's eyes still held Rina's, but she broke the look to give Carin a tight smile.

Something seemed to pull the air in close and tight. Carin's shoulders had drawn in with it, whatever it was, and she tried to relax. Her mother's expression, still stamped between the eyes with her worry, was not the way a mother ought to look on the eve of the Journeying. Proud, nostalgic, fierce—but not troubled. The question rose again in Carin's mind, bubbling to the top like water just about to boil.

Rina reached over and picked up the long parcel and handed it to Carin.

Confused by her mother's action, Carin set down her spoon to take it.

The parcel was long and bulky, wrapped in thin, rust-colored wool and secured with leather thongs in surprisingly intricate bows. Carin tugged on the thongs to untie the bows, almost sad to watch as the loops shriveled into kinked strands. The wool was good quality, and there was enough of it to make a cloak.

Or perhaps it already was a cloak. Carin turned over one edge to reveal a hood and a lining of soft, cured leather. She sniffed at it—pimia oil. Very rare and expensive, but excellent for waterproofing. Carin looked up at her mother in shock. The cloak was a gift suitable for the High Harvest, not a Journeying. The High Harvest wouldn't come for half a cycle yet; every Harvest Harmonix was special, but this one would be different. Only once every five cycles did the Harvest Moon share the sky with its satellite and the sun, the three orbs dancing across the sky as one. This would only be the third High Harvest Carin had ever seen. If she was getting such a gift now, what might her mother have in store for later?

Her fingers had stilled on the oiled leather, and Rina's barked command jerked her out of her thoughts.

"Keep on," Rina said, voice gruff.

Carin pulled back the sides of the cloak. And again. There was something stiff beneath the folds of wool and leather. Her first glimpse was of a white, gleaming curve. She followed that curve as it bent beneath the leather, her hand chasing its smoothness. A gut string brushed her knuckle. She pulled back the final fold of wool and leather to reveal a glorious bow, a recurve crafted from fine white halm. Halm was a sacred tree, a powerful tree. Dense and strong and enduring, yet resilient. This bow could be a day old or a thousand thousands. Unable to speak, Carin ran her hands along the length of it.

It was a gift out of legends. And it was hers.

MERIN LEFT shortly after, saying nothing about the bow or the cloak, only bidding Carin and Rina a bountiful night. But to Carin, formulaic though the farewell was, something seemed to lurk beneath it, flickering between the old soothsayer and her mother. Something that deepened the crease between Rina's eyes. Telling herself it was all in her mind, Carin watched Merin cross the pavilion that housed the village hearth-home and knock soundly on Ryd's door. Jenin and Lyah tended the fire; Carin could see them in the central village hearth, their faces lit with flickering light, not paying Merin any heed as she walked by them. At high night, Clar el Novah would come to take over the tending of the fire—how she would do so all cycle was a mystery to Carin.

Merin vanished into Ryd's home, and Carin closed the door. All those undertaking the Journeying would play host to the village soothsayer that night. Rina took her leave only moments later, leaving Carin alone to wash up and wonder how her mother had come across such a gift. Both gifts. Even now, they sat in a sturdy chair across from where Carin washed the night's dishes. The bow she'd laid across the chair's arms, and the fire cast pale orange flickers across its length.

Just before her mother had closed her bedchamber door, Rina had produced a leather hip quiver full of halm arrows. The wood was dense enough that no heads were needed. Honed to a deadly point and barbed at the sides, each arrow could pierce flesh or rend bone. Carin felt a prickle of unease, compounded by these items coming into her possession. She had never heard of such splendor given to Journeyers. Not for the last time that night, she wondered what would come of her if she could not find her name.

Her mind would not quiet, nor would her thoughts be calmed that night. Carin tidied the kitchen, polished the trestle table, and banked the fire for the evening, each domestic movement a shadow of her own future when the roundhome down the path would be hers. She shuttered the windows, as was proper for the home of Journeyers.

When she finally retired to her bed, the woolen coverlets felt at once familiar and foreign. Tomorrow would dawn in only a few short hours. The rest of Haveranth would rise early; Carin had seen it before. They would rise before the sun and begin their work. Planting Harmonix, the day when the sun and moons danced equally through the turning of the earth. Night and day gave way to one another, and the planting for the cycle began. The Journeyers would set forth without fanfare, while those in the village plied their trades and skills to work the land just as every other day.

If Merin was correct, the Discovery Moon would be well overhead as the sun rose, her sister beside her, always present, always circling.

And Carin would leave Haveranth behind her to set off into the Mad Mountains to find her name.

An insistent tapping at her window made Carin jump in her bed. She rose on warm feet that shied away from the cold of the wooden floor and unshuttered her window.

Lyah leaned on the sill, an impudent smirk lighting her face. Carin threw the window open.

"Get in before someone sees you," she hissed.

Lyah wore only her night robe and leather-soled woolen house clogs, and she leaped the sill with the practiced ease that came with having done the precisely same action at least once per turn for twelve cycles of the moons. She doffed her clogs and shuttered the window again herself, turning to face Carin. She was taller than Carin by a knuckle's length. Her eyes were green-flecked gold, and her dark hair was a ratted mess, carelessly plaited over one shoulder. She smelled of spring and the river grasses that told Carin Lyah had spent her day by the banks of the Bemin as always, most likely with Jenin at her side. Woven over those scents was the smoke from the hearth-home fire. The dark gold in Lyah's eyes was almost the precise color of her skin, which gave her an almost unnerving sense of cohesion about her. The rest of Lyah, however, assuaged any fears of being too together. Her hair was always only half done; her eyes held that glimmer that said mischief was only moments away. She seldom wore shoes, and she was the best fisher in Haveranth with a spear.

Now she hefted herself into Carin's bed with her usual familiarity, and after a bemused moment, Carin followed.

"Pull the coverlet up," Lyah said. "It's always so cold in here."

Carin pulled the coverlet up higher and nestled into the mattress. Silence crept through the chamber, long enough that Carin thought Lyah had gone to sleep straightaway.

The bedding gave and rustled, and Carin felt and heard Lyah's sigh at the same time, a puff of vanilla-scented sweetness from the resin she chewed at night to clean her teeth.

"Are you frightened?" Lyah asked.

Had anyone else asked her that question, Carin would have turned her face to a mask and answered in the negative. "Yes," she whispered instead. She'd forgotten to clean her own teeth, and she could smell the spiced conu broth souring already on her breath.

Lyah didn't seem to notice. "As am I."

"You?"

"Yes, me." Lyah turned and snuggled into Carin's shoulder. "Jenin said something today," she trailed off, shaking her head against the pillow with a rustle of fabric Carin heard rather than saw. Carin felt a pang at the mention of Jenin.

You're jealous, Dyava had said. Another three moons without him, watching his sahthren with her friend grow closer in love with every day spent walking.

Carin tried to shake the feeling off and laid her cheek on Lyah's hair.

After a moment, though, Lyah propped herself up on one elbow. "Are you still thinking about the High Harvest?"

Carin held the breath she had just inhaled. There it was again. High Harvest. It was a day of feasting and ceremonies, for villagers to declare new bonds, new bulging bellies of coming babes, new appellations.

That last had never seemed like such a momentous thing, though she had seen others do it, their faces relaxing with some profound relief. Carin had hinted to Lyah some turns before, but she had immediately regretted it. It was too much to think of on the eve of the Journeying. With Dyava she could simply *be.* It used to be so with Lyah, too.

Carin let out the breath and simply said, "No." She knew Lyah would know the lie and the reason for it.

There was no light in the room with the window shuttered, but Carin knew Lyah's expression would be consternation, her straight eyebrows pulled together as though stitched at the center of her forehead, her mouth tight and a little lopsided. After a moment, Lyah moved back to the subject of the Journeying.

"Ryd and Jenin said Old Wend told them about the last Nameless in Haveranth, back when our parents were children. They said he'd been a favorite, that he was a charismatic leader and a master woodsmith by the time he chose to abjure the syr form. Overnight they shunned him, forced him out of Haveranth. They loved him one day, disowned him the next. Only the elders remember him. Jenin said sy tried to ask Tamat about it while sy tended the fire and Tamat went silent and said there had been no Nameless that cycle. What if we don't find our names? What if we return Nameless? What if they forget us?"

We won't, is what Carin ought to have said, would have said if anyone else were present. But with Lyah... "I don't know."

The last Nameless to leave Haveranth had gone cycles ago. Carin was familiar enough with how Nameless were treated, but she hadn't known any details of the last. If one came back from the Journeying having not found her name—or reporting the wrong one; Merin always knew—they were exiled. Some went north, back toward the cave, into the Mad Mountains to wander and die in the hundreds of leagues of peaks. Others would travel south, past the plains and into the other range of mountains beyond.

None ever returned.

It was said in the Hearthland that if one traveled far enough to the south, through the wildlands of plains and past the southern unnamed mountains, the sea would greet you as it did at Bemin's Fan to the west. But those were only stories, and the folk of Haveranth never traveled far enough to the south to discover its truth. The older villagers sometimes spoke of lands across the sea, where the earth went on far enough for the land to grow warmer, then cooler again if one traveled across its length from south to north. All had ventured to the foothills of the Mad Mountains for the Journeying, but there it is colder, not warmer, and thus most believed these tales to be naught but falsehoods and spun sugar stories.

Carin didn't know what happened to the Nameless or to where they wandered. All she knew was that they never came back.

"It won't happen to us," she said finally, her voice cracking in the stillness of the night. She thought she heard a hitch in Lyah's breathing, but it may have been the shifting of the sheets on the mattress.

"It won't," Lyah echoed. She lowered herself back down to the bedding, pulled her pillow close to Carin's. "Will you braid my hair tomorrow? I want to look presentable when we leave."

"Of course." Carin knew exactly why Lyah wanted her hair to look nice, and it wasn't for the benefit of the villagers. She thought of the way Jenin had looked at Lyah over the winter fires and how sy'd shared the first of the Early Bird apples from hys tree with her. For a brief moment, Carin wondered what that would be like. Then she sloughed off the thought and turned over. She had far more pressing things to fret about.

Their breathing became slow and deep, but an hour passed before either could drift into the realm of sleep.

THE FIRE of Jenin's family hearth lay banked and ashy, giving off little warmth. Hys parents, Silan and Tarwyn, each clasped one of Jenin's hands in their own. Something wild and raw and full of storms gathered in Jenin's breast. Hys time of tending the village hearth-home's fire had ended, turned over to his cousin Clar, who would spend the next cycle tending the village hearth in ignorance, as she should. Dyava had gone home, as was expected, for he no longer shared their home.

Hands held tight to hys parents, Jenin felt as if sy were alone on all the earth. Sy wished Lyah could be there.

Jenin felt a pang when sy thought of Lyah's own ignorance, but sy could not allow hyrself to pursue the emotion. Time for that had long passed. What would happen would happen.

The windows sat shuttered, so there was little need to fully bank the fire, but Silan had said that they could not allow the chimney's smoke to show their continuing wakefulness. Not now, not this night.

It whispered through the air in the roundhome, the prickles of magic that Jenin now recognized. It had been the same for turn upon turn now, but tonight was different.

Silan's usually gentle face grew determined and set like the slow hardening of clay in a kiln. He grasped Jenin's hand tighter, as did Tarwyn, her angular features every inch as sure of what she did. Merin's visit that night had hardened them, fired their certainty, burned away any remaining doubt they might have had about what they meant to do. Jenin had hardly been able to bear it.

The prickles crept through Jenin's hands like the needling sensation that followed a sleeping foot's numbness. At hys shoulders, Jenin took one last clear intake of breath as the prickles wove like vines through hys chest and stifled his exhale, turning it shaky.

Jenin had chosen this. This was hys to bear.

Jenin concentrated hys thoughts on the hearth, on the stones that sy had pulled off one by one to inscribe their insides with runes, replacing them with new power of cloaking, for no one outside this roundhome could know what the family did, or what awaited the village on the morrow. They had to be surprised. They had to believe.

Even when the sun rose and the Journeyers departed, they would not know.

But by then, Jenin knew that the first unfurling tendril would greet the dawn—for sy would be the one to make it.

With the Journeyers' first unknowing steps toward the mountains and their names, Planting Harmonix would bring true seeds of change to sprout in Haveranth.

Jenin had seen to it, and tomorrow it would be hys choice that changed the world.

ONLY FOUR times in a cycle did the great bell toll out the morning, and on the morn of Planting Harmonix came the first for that cycle. The bell struck three times, and its resonant hum hung in the crisp morning air. Carin sat straight up in bed, brushing a lock of Lyah's hair from her face.

"Lyah!" She poked the still-sleeping young woman with her forefinger. "You have to go. We're not supposed to see each other until the Journeying!"

"Tosh," Lyah muttered. "They'll never know."

"That was the third bell!"

Lyah bolted out of the bed so fast that she tripped over her clogs where she'd left them. "Third already?"

The fourth bells began to ring through the village.

"Rot." Lyah threw her feet into her clogs and scooped up Carin's hands in hers. "I will see you in the hearth-home."

"Go out the kitchen door—Mamo might not be awake yet."

"I will."

Lyah flung open the door to Carin's room and slid across the floor in her clogs. Carin closed her eyes and tried to steady herself. She felt as though the down from her coverlet had crept into her skull over the few short hours she'd slept.

"Morrow, Rina." Lyah's voice came out like a squeak, and Carin heard the slide of Lyah's leather clogs on the floor as she skidded to a stop.

"You're not supposed to be here, child. Get to your home. This isn't a day for bending rules."

"Yes, Rina."

To Carin's surprise, Lyah actually sounded contrite.

Poking her head out her door, Carin met Rina's glance. The older woman's face was sober, unamused.

"Joyous Journeying, fruit of my womb," she said, sounding as though she believed nothing of the sort. Rising from her chair by the fire, she set down a cup of steaming red bush tea that smelled of honey and spice. "You had best get ready."

The new woolen cloak was folded neatly on the edge of the table, the new bow strung and sitting next to the cloak. As Carin filled her ceramic mug with tea from the kettle, her new possessions tickled at the corner of her eyes.

There was not much she could do to prepare. Journeyers were allowed only weapons, a waterskin, and a bundle of clothing and provisions. No pack animals, no coin. She gathered up the gifts from her mother and returned to her chamber, mug clasped in her free hand.

Three cycles before, Tilm al Hadeer, who had been injured in a hunting accident at nine harvests, had been carried in a litter by the other two Journeyers who left with him. That cycle had been a somber one, a fearful one beneath the smooth surface of the villagers of Haverath. Everyone had tried not to show their apprehension—would Tilm return Named or Nameless? Would they return by High Lights? Would he return at all?

The days of spring had marched forward. Seeds sown burst through the loam and snaked upward, budding then blooming then bearing fruit as always. As the days continued toward the longest light, the High Lights ritual of atonement and amends, the tension had grown like a new bowstring pulled to its notches. Tilm's parents, Hadeer and Almin, stared down anyone who looked their way as if daring their neighbors to suggest their son would be branded Nameless.

But then, on the third day of the Stem turn under the Toil Moon, one day before High Lights, one day before Merin would have to declare Tilm and his fellow Journeyers lost and Nameless, a young shepherd spotted them in Haver's Glen as they descended the Mistaken Pass.

Three Journeyers, all on foot. The litter was nowhere to be seen.

Tilm al Hadeer va Haveranth strode into the village on two healed legs. While whispers made waves through the people gathered around the central village hearth, Merin closeted herself in her roundhome with the three Journeyers for three hours. When they emerged, no one had said a thing until the Naming at High Lights, when Tilm had become Tillim va Haveranth, Named and welcomed home.

No one spoke of what had happened on his Journeying, or how the legs that had kept him from walking for eight cycles sparked once more to life, but strange things happened on a Journeying.

Carin shuddered at the chill that snaked up her spine, and she drained the remainder of her tea. In her reverie she had piled half her clothing on her unmade bed. With anxiety-numbed fingers, she sorted her belongings. Three sets of hose, two of brown bavel and one of soft leather. One pair of wide-legged trousers of a thick weave. She pulled on one pair of bavel hose and a light linen tunic with sleeves that fell to her wrists. Carin belted the tunic with a wide leather strap, adding her sheath to one side and a pouch of fishing line and hooks to the other.

She bundled the remaining clothing into her leather rucksack. After a moment of chagrin looking at the quiver, Carin discovered that her mother had gotten Jemil—Lyah's mother must have done it, for Rina herself couldn't stitch a single swatch without sewing her own finger into it—to sew a pocket onto the side of the rucksack. The quiver fit into it perfectly, and two leather buckles held the quiver firmly in place.

With her rucksack on her back and her bow slung across one shoulder, Carin quietly made her bed and returned to the kitchen, knowing she would find it empty.

She washed her mug. She took a long look around the home of her mother.

And Carin el Rina ve Haveranth left home behind.

I T WAS an eerie thing, watching the village ignore her, Lyah thought. There was Malcam, her sacks of seeds belted to her expanding middle as she trotted off to the south to sow her fields. No one looking would think her own son Ryd was about to embark on a Journeying that would span the next three moons or more. And there, Rina. Rina who had bid her good morrow without scolding her for breaking the village rule and visiting a fellow Journeyer on the eve of their departure. Rina had a hammer in one hand and hefted a bundle of ingots in the other, and she too did not look Lyah's way.

No sign yet of Jenin or hys family, but they lived on the far side of town and were known for their lack of punctuality as much as for the conu orchard they tended to perfection. Lyah's hair fell into her face, unbraided. Had she woken at first bell, Carin could have fixed it. Lyah supposed she might as well leave Haveranth with it in a state of disorder; it looked like this every other day anyway. Perhaps leaving on her Journeying with it properly tidy would have been a sort of lie.

A clatter of a latch reached her ears, and Lyah turned to see Carin walking toward her, her face set in that square expression Lyah had learned cycles ago meant she had a storm raging in her gullet but would die before she let anyone see it. Over one shoulder, Carin wore a shining white bow. Halm, it was. It had to be. Lyah tried to stop herself from gaping. Great Toil, where had she gotten that? Carin stared straight ahead, and Lyah wondered what it would be like to leave knowing any sight of one's beloved would be soured by the beloved ignoring one's very existence. Lyah did not think she could deal with such a thing. She pitied Carin and Dyava both for this parting.

The hearth-home was full of a quiet bustle. Market stalls open, the whistle of an ihstal here and there, the soft clicks of their padded hooves on cobblestones. And yet Lyah and Carin—and Ryd, who came round the corner just then—were excluded. Quiet solemnity eddied around the three of them.

This, too, was part of the ritual. Until they returned with their names, they had ceased to exist.

Ryd and Carin reached Lyah at the same time, Ryd looking as unnerved as Lyah felt. His eyes, pale green in the morning light, darted back and forth as if tracking a pendulum that hovered right in front of his face. His normally rich brown skin looked pale and sallow. Carin never looked sallow, even now when Lyah knew her friend had barely slept. No, her face had a healthy golden glow, and her eyes, which were the color of the Bemin's deeper pools, a dizzying sapphire blue—those eyes showed no redness or bags.

There they stood.

The hearth-home was Haveranth's direct center. Haver's Road ran north and south through the middle, with Cantor's Road spreading east and west. It was to the north they were to go.

The scent of fresh smoked goat and baked eggs wafted past, but Lyah made herself ignore it. She saw Ryd take a deep breath and then exhale.

The spears strapped across her back chafed already under the weight of her rucksack. Looking over at Ryd next to her, she wondered what weapon he'd brought. No swords hung from his belt, and no spears or bows to be seen either. A cook pot and a shallow pan clanked against each other when he moved. Ryd was small, almost a head shorter than she, and she hoped he'd brought something other than a frying pan that could do some violence.

None of them spoke, only stood in wait for Jenin to come scampering down the street. Any moment now sy'd appear. Lyah tried to suppress her excitement of spending whole moons with Jenin at her side. She'd hoped for some time that when they returned properly Named, sy would give her some clue of whether they would join in the bonding ritual or not. They wouldn't be allowed until their twentieth harvest anyway, but she wanted to know.

No one came. Minutes stretched by, and the sky colored itself lighter and lighter with each passing moment. Soon the sun would peek above the horizon, and then they would be off. Shadows formed on the westward side of buildings and stalls, still as bleary with sleep as Lyah felt, still no sharpness to be had of them until the sun crested Cantor's Road and cut a golden line down the center of Haveranth.

Jenin ought to be here by now. Ryd's foot tapped with anxiety—Lyah knew him well enough to know that there was no way it could be excitement when a gaggle of children frightened him enough to go hiding in his parents' roundhome.

Carin's face was inscrutable, and one hand absently stroked the bottom curve of the bow over her shoulder. Such a bow. Lyah again marveled at it. For a moment, Lyah thought of Carin's quiet "No" the night before. She knew her friend was feeling at odds with herself, that possibly Carin might be hyrsin instead of woman, but it would do no good unless Carin admitted it to herself and let the light shine on it.

A loud yell made Lyah jump. Ryd, too, from the sound of the clanking pots on his rucksack. Carin and Lyah exchanged a nervous laugh. Someone probably walked by the wrong side of an ihstal and got a start and a bite.

But the yell was followed by another, a curt shout, the words unintelligible at a distance.

Lyah looked up the road to her right, toward the east where the sun had sent burning golden clouds ahead of itself to announce its coming to the sky. It was almost time. They could ask no questions, receive no answers. Only wait until the dawn signaled them to go.

Another yell, closer this time. The three Journeyers waited as the yells grew closer, like a relay race at Harvest Harmonix, they passed from voice to voice, person to person until they entered the hearth-home where several villagers had gathered next to Old Wend's coopery stall.

She wanted to ask, wanted to yell herself. Make someone speak up. Whatever this news was, it was racing the sun.

"Where is Jenin?" Lyah said aloud.

Neither Ryd nor Carin answered, both focused across the pavilion at the tumult that seemed to spread from the small knot of villagers. Someone took off at a run to the north, someone else to the south, directly at the three Journeyers.

Mag—or was it Meg?—from the south side of the village. Not yet fifteen and known for keeping to hys own company, Lyah had perhaps spoken to hyr once on a festival day. As sy ran by Lyah, clearly struggling to ignore their presence, Lyah wanted to grab hyr and ask hyr what had so tightened hyr face and why something wet splashed Lyah's arm as sy passed.

"Something's wrong," Carin said. "Where is Jenin?"

Ryd's face took on an even more sallow cast. "Sy said sy'd be early today. Seemed so determined about it."

"When did you see hyr?" Lyah asked, eyes still on the knot of villagers across the hearth-home. They weren't to talk, weren't to act as though this was their village. This wasn't their village until they returned with their names. But something made her disregard etiquette. "Ryd?"

Ryd's shoulders jerked, but he didn't answer.

Clar el Novah, Jenin's cousin and neighbor, stumbled into the hearth-home to tend the fire. Or so Lyah assumed until she looked closer. Even in the non-light of just before dawn, Lyah could see Clar's hands from where she stood.

Clar's hands were covered in blood. Clar fell to her knees at the knot of villagers, and Old Wend flew to her side with an agility far younger than his many harvests should have allowed. Lyah strained to hear, willed her ears to pick up what they were saying, begged her heart to quiet itself and stop filling her head with its thudding.

The first ray of sunlight hit Lyah's face.

"No," she said. "Not yet." She looked over at Carin and Ryd, both of whose eyes remained trained on Clar's crumpled form. "We can't leave without Jenin!"

"You must go now, children." Merin's voice cracked through the air like a splitting paving stone.

Lyah turned to see the soothsayer, framed by the first light of dawn. "Not without Jenin!"

"Jenin is dead. And if you three want to remain on this side of the soil, you must go. Keep to the west side of the river. Do not forget." Merin waited only a moment, as if absorbing their indecision. When none of the three moved, frozen to the ground in shock, Merin took a step toward them. The golden sunlight washed her body, lighting her hair from behind like a halo. She almost seemed to grow larger, and something lurked behind her eyes. "Go or be made Nameless. Go now or be forced out to never return. Go now, children. *NOW!*"

Her final word punched through Lyah like a hot poker.

Carin reached out and grabbed one of Lyah's arms. "Lyah, come on!"

"No," she whispered.

Ryd grabbed her other arm and yanked her forward with more strength than someone his size ought to have. Fear spiked through her, and Lyah's feet jolted forward. She turned once to look at Merin. Merin's face was beautiful and terrible and powerful. In that instant, Lyah forgot about Jenin, forgot about the future and possibility she'd allowed herself to imagine at hys side. Forgot fishing by the river, forgot the rumble of hys laugh, forgot the loamy brown of hys eyes. In that instant, all she saw was Merin's face and the flicker of fear that passed over it and vanished.

They fled.

I CAN'T RUN anymore," said Ryd. His arm ached from pulling on Lyah's, and his lungs burned from breathing dust. They were just beyond the edge of town, and Ryd forced himself not to look back.

He closed his eyes for an instant and opened them again immediately. Behind his eyelids, Clar's blood-spattered face and red hands lurked. Jenin's blood. Jenin was dead.

Just last night, Ryd had sat with hyr at the village hearth-home, help-ing hyr tend the fire before being called away to have tea with Merin. Just last night. And now Jenin was dead. Murdered.

Merin would have said it was an accident if it was.

When was the last time there had been a murder in Haveranth? Not in Ryd's lifetime. There was the odd brawl or drunken fight down at the village hearth-home in the market, but as far as he was concerned, that wasn't really violence.

Dyava. Great Toil, Dyava. Ryd's gaze shot to Carin, who stood silent. Surely Merin would have said if Dyava had died too. His round-home was close to his family's. He tended the same stock, grew food from the same fields.

Lyah's face was ashen, but she stumbled forward, her feet walking in a sort of calculated trudge. Carin still supported her, face set.

"We're barely out of Haveranth, Ryd," Carin said. "We need to keep moving."

"I know; I just can't run."

Had Jenin tried to run? Was Dyava alive? Ryd covered his mouth with his hand but felt nothing. His blood throbbed in his veins.

"Maybe we should get off the road." Lyah's words surprised him, and Ryd turned to look at her.

She swallowed, her throat bobbing. Lyah pulled her arm from Carin's and folded it against her other one.

"What do you mean?" Carin asked.

"If someone killed Jenin on the eve of hys Journeying, maybe we're not safe either."

Ryd felt a flash of shame that he hadn't thought of that. He met Carin's gaze and nodded. "She's right."

Merin's face before they left had filled him with terror; Ryd had never seen the old woman like that. She'd brought all four of them into the world. She was the village wise woman, its healer and its teacher. Ryd was a fool to forget that she was also its soothsayer and its Namekeeper. Merin knew all their names. The intensity with which she had sent them from town had frightened him then, but it frightened him now all the more.

How much a few minutes could change.

His stomach turned, thinking of Jenin, thinking of Dyava and Tarwyn and Silan and how the family could possibly face today. Would they ever know what had happened to hyr? Strange things happened on a Journeying.

Not for the first time, Ryd wondered if he would return.

Carin pointed off the road, to the spring cajit grove. Like the Early Bird apples, these cajits bore an early harvest. "If we cut through there, we can skirt Kinnock's Rise and catch the mouth of the glen to the west. Besides, we'll need provisions."

"Carin," Ryd said, staring at her hardened expression.

She held up a hand with a sharp gesture and a tight shake of her head. Ryd went silent, then made his feet start off toward the cajit grove.

Journeyers were set off without any food, only a full waterskin and a weapon. Ryd was fairly certain they wouldn't be the first to pillage this grove.

He pulled his rucksack off his shoulder and rummaged in the top for a large handkerchief. He tucked one side into his belt and cinched the belt a bit tighter to hold it. They set off into the grove. They worked quietly as they walked, Lyah shaking a tree and Carin and Ryd quickly gathering the nuts that fell.

When his handkerchief was full and bulging and both Carin and Lyah had bundles to match, they stuffed them into their rucksacks. The morning quickly grew warm as they walked, and by the time the sun shone down from its peak, a thin sheen of sweat covered Ryd's brow. Kinnock's Rise was visible to their right, poking up above the tree line opposite the orchards. The cajit grove behind them, there was no more food to gather. Ryd had spent little time worrying about how they would feed themselves, but just now the thought of dinner churned his stomach.

Ryd sipped from his waterskin as they walked. It was half empty before he remembered that he couldn't fill it from the Bemin—not with the herds to the north by the quarry. They'd have to wait until they passed the quarry—or reached Haver's Glen, another ten leagues to the north. There, waterfalls striped the glen's walls, clean and pure water for the taking. Nearly a turn's walking, maybe more.

He turned and looked to the south. The smoke from Haveranth's chimneys colored the tops of the hills behind him, grey-blue and hovering. As they followed the west bank of the Bemin north, passing the sheer cliffs of the west edge of Kinnock's Rise, Ryd felt farther from home than he'd ever been.

Carin and Lyah walked beside him in silence. There seemed to be an empty hole in their group, three where there ought to be four and a gaping question besides. Jenin should have been there with them. Instead sy was dead in Haveranth, never to reach adulthood. How had sy died? Ryd realized that he had been assuming someone killed hyr. Maybe it *was* an accident. Maybe the blood on Clar's shaking hands had been from trying to save Jenin from a fall. Maybe sy'd been gored by the family's breed ram—the creature had horns that were fierce-sharp. Maybe Merin's terrifying urgency had not been because Jenin had been murdered.

Ryd allowed hope to kindle for only a moment. The sobering memory of Clar's stricken face, the panicked air of the villagers—accidents happened and were met with grief. Not fear.

Who had murdered Jenin?

For the first time, Ryd wondered if perhaps he were safer out here.

TREES BEGAN to appear, slowly as though creeping down from the mountains themselves. Carin, used to the order of the orchards and groves of Haveranth, couldn't help but feel unnerved by the way the trees chose their own pieces of earth here. The hills grew steeper on either side of the Bemin, turning from the knolls and hillocks of the plains to the true foothills of the Mad Mountains, which even now spiked above the horizon beyond, impassive and imperious both.

The trees here, far from implying that they simply didn't know their place, captured her attention with the idea that no, she didn't know her own. There were great halms with white trunks and branches as gleaming as the eggs laid by the horn-legged cluckers at home. Here and there a maha challenged all its fellows, growing wider and taller than any of the others around it. Halm and maha were the common hardwoods, dense and powerful. Like Carin's new bow. The hardwoods weren't easy to work. It took a master of the craft and a person of enormous strength to form halm to one's will.

The other trees, the hawthorn and ash, hazel and sycamores—those daunted her somewhat less. But still, as she walked, Carin wished there were a straight path, something that went directly from where they stood to where they were headed. Somewhere she could see what lay ahead. The Bemin to the south grew wider and cut a swath through the plains, separating the foothills from the fields. But here, where it wound its way from its source, gathering tiny tributaries on the way, it was only as wide as a village street and half as decisive.

And still, it wasn't working. As much as Carin tried to think of her surroundings and not the sight of Clar's hands covered in Jenin's blood, it wasn't working.

Dyava had to be safe. Merin would have told them. Merin would have told her. Carin closed her eyes for a bare instant and thought of Dyava's face soaked in sunlight, trying to believe.

Something crackled in the distance.

Carin opened her eyes and almost stumbled.

Ryd halted, reaching out to touch Lyah's arm. He pitched his voice low. "Did you hear that?"

"It's probably a saiga. They're starting to come up from the plains." Lyah spoke as though the words were pulled out of her.

This was something she could do. A path. Carin pulled her bow from her shoulder and nocked an arrow. "I can't promise I'll hit it on the first shot with a new bow, but I wouldn't say no to meat with our cajit nuts."

"Which way was it?" Lyah peered into the woods.

Ryd pointed.

They made their way through the trees toward the sound, pausing every minute or so to listen. An occasional crackle guided them, and Carin silently thanked her mother for her training in how to walk silently, rolling her feet forward with each step. After several minutes of walking, Carin spotted movement.

She raised her bow, still not drawing the arrow back. Her heart beat loud enough in her chest that she thought it would alert the animal of her presence.

The saiga antelope nosed its way past a thicket, pausing to bend and nibble at some new spring growth. Carin moved forward slowly, waiting to draw the bow. Her fingers grew moist on the smooth halm arrow. She could do this. She could help keep her friends alive.

The saiga didn't seem to notice them. The air was still, and even if a wind were to rise, it would likely come from the north, keeping them safe from their scents spooking the beast. Its horns, ridged from base to tip in concentric circles, caught a dangling twig, and the saiga twitched its tube-like nose.

Beside him, Carin breathed in, then slowly out, drawing the bowstring back to her cheek. She released the arrow in a smooth motion, and the saiga cried out and burst into a flurry of movement. The bow responded as if it had been made for her.

Carin, bow in hand, took off running with a whoop. The saiga squealed and ran into a halm, leaving a smudge of red on the tree's smooth white trunk. The animal hit the ground with a thud. Its hooves scrabbled against the tree's roots. Carin reached it first, pulling her belt knife from its sheath. She fell to her knees next to the animal.

"Thank you, for your life," she murmured, and the words felt too big in the air. Carin pushed Jenin and Dyava from her mind. She plunged the knife into the saiga's neck at the base of its skull. It flailed once and died.

About the size of a large goat, the saiga didn't look like much, but it would feed them for several days. Carin pulled rope from her rucksack and wrapped it around the animal's neck. She threw the rope over a branch and hauled it into the air, silent. The smell of blood was hot like the metal of her mother's forge. Carin nearly choked on it.

No one helped her.

It took her several minutes to figure out why neither Ryd nor Lyah made a move to assist her. Carin was a hunter, taught by her mother. Lyah could fish with the best, but Carin doubted that she'd ever so much as snared a rabbit. And Ryd, well. His family was farmer folk. He grew new life; he didn't end what already existed. At their hearth, one was more likely to find stews of yams and curried plums than meat. Ryd himself shifted uncomfortably. Carin looked down. Her hands wore blood just as Clar's had.

Lyah turned away after a spell, her face ashy under its brown hue.

It was already done. The saiga was dead. Carin felt a wash of shame that touched at the edges of her grief and fear. She couldn't go back. Only forward.

Carin worked on, her brow set and her lips as tight as the rope holding the saiga's feet. The offal she piled under the tree.

"Did anyone bring any waxed canvas?" Carin asked the others, breaking the rhythm of her wordless work. She kept her gaze fixed on her task, but she knew the set of her shoulders said she knew what Ryd and Lyah were thinking.

Ryd looked at her for a moment, then dug through his pack and produced a tightly folded length of the cloth, spreading it out on a mossy area near where Carin worked. He didn't seem to want to watch, but he stared as his Carin cut the haunches from the animal, piling the feet next to the offal. She skinned it like an expert, hanging the hide over a branch while she sliced off hunks of meat. When she was finished, she untied the rope from around the animal's neck and piled the carcass on top of the offal. Carin wrapped the meat tightly in the waxed canvas and bound it with the rope, hefting it with one arm.

"We'll have to take turns carrying this," she said. "Can you do that?"

Lyah looked over for the first time and nodded, and Carin saw the glimmer of tears in her eyes. The sight made her own eyes prickle. She didn't want to think of Jenin. Couldn't, or she would collapse. How Lyah wasn't a heap on the ground, Carin did not know. Dyava.

A tear escaped her eye, and Carin ignored it.

It was better when they kept moving.

"We should get moving again," Ryd said, reading Carin's thoughts and looking embarrassed when his voice cracked.

Lyah motioned to the pile of still-warm saiga. "We need to put some distance between us and that. There's more than just saiga in these foothills."

A shiver went through Carin at the thought, knowing Lyah was right. She ought to have thought of it herself. Wolves. Coyotes. Kazytya, the wild cats that used their intelligence to hunt as much as their other senses. The occasional tiger. All of them would be more than happy to discover meat for the taking. None of what Carin had left on the ground would go to waste.

The warmth of the meat soaked through the waxed canvas she held, like life dying in her arms.

Ryd reached out and took the bundle of canvas from Carin. It easily weighed three stone, and her arms felt oddly buoyant without the weight.

She almost asked for it back, to make the heaviness in her arms match the heaviness in her heart.

CARIN FELT thankful that Ryd had taken the meat from her not long after. Lyah's silence felt heavier than the bundle she carried, and as the blood dried on Carin's hands, all she wanted was to get back to the banks of the Bemin so she could wash. A tiny spot had dripped onto the hem of her tunic.

When the rushing of the river grew louder and the ground finally dipped away at its bank, Carin trotted on ahead with relief. She heard the clank of Ryd's pack behind her—though he'd made some effort to quiet it, she noted—but she concentrated on washing. Scrubbing her hands with a stone, she rubbed until they were pink instead of red and then held them in the water, letting the current cleanse away the remnants of blood.

She thought of Dyava and herself, naked in the dawn after High Lights, washing the ashes from their skin.

Now she washed away blood, and Dyava's own family had a gaping hole where Jenin had been.

Ryd and Lyah had scarcely met her eyes, and only once Carin had washed off the blood did they look up.

She understood. She wasn't immune to the image. Jenin's blood on Clar's hands, reflected in the saiga blood on her own. But they had to eat, and their destination was turns away, and then they would have to come back over the same distance to a village still reeling from a murder.

Jenin was gone. Forever.

Carin could not quite feel anything but guilt, for each time she heard Merin's words again, her mind went straight to Dyava. She knew she should trust Merin, that Merin would have said if Dyava was gone, but Carin could not know for certain.

So she scrubbed her hands as if it would accomplish something. Anything.

Beyond that, the scrubbing dampened the growing sense of being watched. She didn't think the others felt it, but to her, the sense of eyes on her was like walking through the woods with a spear to her spine. She could get used to it until she made an unexpected move, but then the sense returned, and it was all she could do not to continually scan the trees around her for whatever had her in its sights.

Suddenly the water on her hands was more cold than cool. She pulled them out, shaking them in the warm afternoon air.

A splash made her turn downstream to see Lyah pulling her spear from an eddy, a flopping tilapia about twice the length of her hand. Lyah's eyes met Carin's, and the other girl nodded once as if to say, *I may be grieving, but I can still help.*

Carin watched as Lyah speared two more in quick succession, stringing them on a line of gut.

"They're drawn to the blood," she said.

Carin nodded.

The three continued upstream until the sun began to filter through the trees to their left, dappling them in the golden hour's orange tint.

The sky was still and cloudless. High overhead, Discovery Moon floated, waxing gibbous with her sister by her side. There would be no rain tonight. When they came across a small clearing, Carin stopped.

"How about we make camp here for the night?"

Neither Ryd nor Lyah offered any resistance, and Ryd set out immediately digging a fire pit and gathering wood. As the flames grew, Carin
opened the canvas bundle and hauled a large flat rock from the river to
begin slicing up the saiga meat into thin strips.

The evening ought to have been full of anxious laughter and giddiness. Instead the three Journeyers set about their tasks with a single-mind-
ed focus. Lyah took Ryd's cook pots and spread out batches of cajit nuts to
dry near the fire, rotating them every few minutes. Their work was punctuated every so often by the popping of a cajit shell as it dried enough to
open. Carin propped up her rock next to the smokiest part of the fire,
then spitted three remaining cuts of meat and held them out to roast in
the flames.

Although exhaustion set into her almost immediately, Carin
couldn't bring herself to go to her bedroll. Instead, she and the others
sat up by the fire, first quietly eating saiga, then shelling dried cajits. The
green-purple nuts looked almost black in the deepening twilight. Lyah
cooked her fish next, placing them between the cook pots when she finished to have for breakfast the next morning.

"I'll take first watch," Carin said when Ryd yawned widely.

The first hour was marked only by Lyah's quiet sobs. As much as
Carin wished she could go to her, a hard kernel in her heart kept her by
the fire, eyes on the surrounding woods. Somewhere deep down she felt
like part of herself had died with Jenin and another part, a rawer part,
would not leave her be until her arms were about Dyava again.

She thought there should be tears, but none came. Only the sizzling
of saiga meat on its rock.

THE MOON appeared to perch atop a maha tree, her sister sitting
at her feet on the next lowest branch. Carin wished she had a knack
for drawing; the image felt like something out of another reality. The stars

above glittered, the Tiger in Repose constellation lounging between two treetops with the tip of its tail pulsing in the dark.

Carin looked down to the fire, then got up, stretching her back and legs. She carefully turned each strip of meat on the rock. By morning it would be passably dried and smoked for travel. They could do another batch after they made camp again.

Something moved behind a tree.

Carin froze, one finger on a strip of meat until it brushed the hot rock and she pulled it back, sticking it in her mouth.

Not wanting to wake the others in case it was only an owl or a passing halka, she raised herself from her crouch and walked toward where she'd seen the movement.

A blurring shape passed another tree, just out of the circle of firelight.

She tracked it, waiting for it to emerge again. Her heart jumped twice before resuming a steady, albeit faster pace.

A figure stepped into the firelight.

No. It can't be.

Jenin.

For the span of several heavy heartbeats, all Carin saw was hys face. Hys loam-colored eyes flickered in the light from the flames as sy advanced on her, the same eyes that shone out from Dyava's face, but Jenin's laughing lips did not curve upward.

Carin took an involuntary step backward, the heat of the fire on her back. Then she looked closer. Brown blood had dried in a macabre collar around hys neck where a gaping wound flapped open.

Watching the ghastly shape of her friend, Carin knew without any whisper of doubt that she was seeing how Jenin had died. Throat slit from ear to ear. This could have been no accident.

She took several steps back, and her foot clanked on one of Ryd's pans. Neither sleeping form stirred.

"Ryd! Lyah!" Carin yelled.

Neither moved.

Jenin walked toward her.

Sy had none of the shambling gait children whispered about in stories at High Lights, of bloated corpses oozing in the punishing heat of the longest day. Sy looked like Jenin, except that sy wore dried blood like a necklace beneath hys death wound.

"Jenin," Carin said. "Jenin, stop."

Sy didn't.

Carin wanted to run away, run back toward Haveranth and flee until the sight of her dead friend left her eyes, but something rooted her to the ground. Sy advanced on her, one hand reaching out to her in the flickering firelight. Hys fingers were caked with hys own cracking blood. Sy'd had time to clutch at hys throat before death.

Carin closed her eyes tight for a moment, taking a breath to slow her now-frantic heart. Her backside felt numb from the hours of sitting by the fire, but her legs beneath her were steady. Opening her eyes again, she hoped for one blazing moment that the visage of Jenin would be gone. Still sy stood, even with the fire now.

Two more steps brought Jenin within arms' reach. Hys hand touched hers.

Carin.

Jenin's voice sounded like a kazytya's scream in her mind.

Carin.

Hys hand on hers was cold and stiff and dead, but still sy moved, still hys body swayed, hys shadow rocking back and forth on the ground with the dappling of firelight.

I died.

Jenin paused, frowning as if something were wrong. Carin almost choked a laugh; everything was wrong.

I did not die, but I died.

Carin's breath hissed out of her mouth. Jenin was so close she could see the lips of the wound on hys neck, hys brown skin parted by an expert hand.

"Who did this to you? Dyava—is Dyava alive?" Carin made herself speak, somehow trusting more in this specter's answer than in Merin's omissions.

Jenin did not answer.

For the first time since the morning, tears welled up in Carin's eyes. Nothing but blank death reflected back from hys. Jenin should have been asleep beside Lyah, wishing they could sleep closer still. Sy should have been here with them, laughing and poking fun at how many children would be asking forgiveness of Ryd at High Lights for sitting on him so often. Jenin should have been on this Journeying with them, not cold and dead in Haveranth.

For you. I did this for you.

Hys words came like a death rattle in Carin's skull. They nestled into her mind like burrowing worms.

And then sy was gone. The grip of hys fingers vanished from her hand.

Ryd and Lyah stirred. After a breath, Lyah sat bolt upright in her bedroll, tears streaming down her face. Ryd jerked once and scrambled to his feet, chest heaving and eyes just as wet.

Carin looked down at her hand. Flecks of dried blood stood out plain and solid on her palm.

THE WORLD felt pale and dim, muted by magic and death.

Jenin struggled to keep hyrself present, felt too keenly the blade at hys throat and the stillness of the body sy had sacrificed. Not even hys body, not truly. An illusion, but one Jenin had been bound to. A necessary binding. And yet it had meant that sy felt the blade, the blood. Heard Clar as she screamed for Dyava's help.

For what? The thought was as dim and pale as the world, as the forest in which hys friends dwelled.

Sy had been warned about this, of the blur that would surely take hyr, the constant fight and struggle it would take to remain. The why was important. Jenin could not forget it.

And there it was, a hard seed in a soft night.

Jenin had wanted to tell them. The truth. Anything. But to be solid took energy sy needed to save, and the words had blown away on the night's wind. Any shape sy took came at a cost.

Tarwyn and Silan had assured hyr it would grow easier, that they would help.

For now, Jenin dwelled in the between-places, listening to the sounds of the trees and holding tight to the hard seed. Hys body lay masked beneath hys parents' roundhome, cool and silent, stilled by magic, but alive, alive, alive.

Hys spirit, though. Hys spirit was free. And hys task now was to strengthen hyrself and to bide, bide, as long as need be.

It was begun.

LYAH'S FINGERNAILS dug into her hand. She pushed herself to her feet, feeling as though she'd slogged through the mud of the Bemin's flood plain after the spring thaw. Carin stood on the opposite side of the fire, staring at her right hand as if it had somehow betrayed her. Ryd swayed on his feet, looking like he was about to sick up.

"I saw Jenin," Lyah said. Her voice sounded like a thin piece of metal hit with a fork. Tinny and raw and jangled. She felt something wet trickle down her palm and ignored it.

Carin shuddered and looked toward her. "You saw hyr too?"

Carin had seen hyr? Confused, Lyah took a staggering step toward the fire. "Sy...was here. Next to my bedroll. I woke to see hyr there, saw hys hair unbound. But sy wasn't breathing." The memory rushed through her, and Lyah fought to keep the tears from starting to fall again. "Sy still turned toward me. Sy looked at me. Hys eyes were dead. And hys neck..."

Ryd's voice was like stepped-on bark. "Hys throat was slit."

All three nodded, and rather than the confirmation causing relief, Lyah felt her fear crystallize.

"Sy threw a pebble at my head," said Ryd. "Just like sy used to do to get my attention when Old Wend was teaching us to read."

A breeze began, cooling the liquid on Lyah's palm. She held up her hand and forced her fingers to obey and open. Cupped in the hollow of her palm was a lock of hair bound with grey thread and a carved heart of halm. Jenin's hair. A lover's token. A crescent of blood stood out near it, where her nail had cut her hand.

Her fingers tightened back, closing tight around the hair.

"What did sy say to you?" Carin asked, her voice pitched so low that the breeze almost whisked it away.

Lyah closed her eyes. She didn't want to answer that.

"Sy said sy died." Ryd answered for her.

Lyah waited, somehow sure Carin was doing the same thing.

"Sy said sy died for me."

There was no sense in attempting sleep. They passed the remaining hours until dawn shelling their cajits while the strips of saiga continued to dry and smoke by the fire. Carin saved every shell.

"They will be useful tinder in the mountains," she said.

The fish Lyah had caught made a good breakfast, but the flakes of tender meat felt like sawdust in her mouth.

When they were done breaking their fast, Lyah opened a small pocket on the inside of her rucksack. There she tucked the lock of hair. How a dead friend had come to them, how sy had left something behind for them—Lyah saw Carin continue to wipe her hand on her leggings long after she had gone to the river to wash the flakes of dried blood from her skin—there was no knowing.

What was this magic?

As Merin's apprentice, Lyah had learned somewhat of magic, learned the names of the powers that could be woven together to alter the course of nature. But she had never heard of anything like this.

The early morning air held a chill that sifted down through the glens and vales of the foothills. It smelled of snow and jagged ice.

It was said strange things happened on the Journeying, but no one ever spoke of how or what that meant. Every sound from the forest made Lyah want to jump. She felt as though she'd been playing a game of dice her whole life and suddenly discovered that someone had changed all the rules and shifted the pips around.

She looked upriver at the curve of its banks. She knew what lay ahead but, for the first time, felt uncertain of what that familiar landscape would hold.

• • • • •

They broke camp an hour before dawn, just as the muddy light from the rising sun swathed the sky in grey. Funny, Lyah thought, how the manner of one's waking could color the entire day.

Carin had had no sleep, but still she shouldered her pack and the canvas bundle of remaining saiga meat with an easy kind of stoicism.

Lyah tried not to think of what Jenin had meant when sy said sy'd died for her. Or had sy meant all of them? Or both? There could have been any number of things sy meant, but Lyah's certainty that someone out there wanted them only grew with each step they took along the river. Jenin had told her sy had learned something before sy died. Someone had killed hyr for it. And yet Jenin had also said sy hadn't died.

At midday, she saw the hawk.

It soared above the trees, calling out in joyous shrieks against the azure sky. Larger than the birds she was used to, it spiraled far above their heads. It would have been of no note other than its size had the bird not tracked them for the rest of the afternoon.

More than once, Lyah caught Carin gazing up at the sky, her hand caressing her bow as if her fingers itched to nock an arrow and shoot the bird from the sky.

Carin wasn't one for trophy hunting, but Lyah understood the impulse. The farther they walked through up the banks of the Bemin, the more the bird's continued presence bothered her like the pinion of a clucker feather sticking through a pillow.

The ground rose steeply around them, and Lyah could feel the air thinning with each league they covered. Her legs burned from the exertion of walking, and her neck and back felt woody and tight with weight.

They stopped for a short lunch of cajits. The oils of the nuts would be enough to sustain them until supper. The Bemin eddied there, and the trees around them had begun to wear needles more than budding leaves. All that

remained this high were the pines, firs, cedars, and a few silver-barked doubloon trees that were just beginning to bud. The hawk still circled above
them. Carin had turned her strategy to pointedly ignoring the bird, but
Ryd's eyes found it every few minutes, his expression troubled.

Something blue glinted across the river, flapping and splashing in
the water. A blue-eared kingfisher, its head shining like metal and its
breast bright as wet rust in sunlight.

"That should not be so close to the mountains," Lyah said quietly,
motioning at the kingfisher. She spent time near the waters of Haveranth,
fishing with her parents. She knew the birds of the Bemin's pools and
ponds, and the bright fisher bird was a familiar sight—one that ought not
be here in the foothills. Not past Kinnock's Rise. In fact, she'd only ever
seen them south of Haveranth itself.

She rose from the rock upon which she sat, her hand still half-full of
cajits. The blue-eared kingfisher had caught a small bass and was beating
it against the rock where it perched.

The river was full of spring life. A short moment spent watching
showed Lyah a pouch of frog eggs in a still eddy. Beneath the surface were
schools of new-spawned fry fish. Downstream, a pair of emerald-cloaked
ducks swam surrounded by fluffy chicks. Everything was in place, as it
should be. Except the kingfisher.

Perhaps this one was just confused. Lyah took another long look
around the river.

At the next bend was a second kingfisher. Lyah kept it in her sight.
Yes, it was a different bird. The first had killed its bass and had set about
eating it. Downstream was one more; she caught the flicker of bright red
and blue through the needles of a fir.

She turned back to the others, feeling as though a hundred eyes were
aimed at her back.

"Can we move on?" The hawk still circled above, its wings outstretched on some higher breeze, barely flapping in the air.

Beads of perspiration budded on Lyah's forehead. She picked at
a hangnail.

"What did you see?" Carin asked.

"Things that should not be here," Lyah said.

She thought the watched-feeling would abate when they began to move again. She had not thought of the hawk above, still rending the air with its cries. It flapped ahead, then circled back. Lyah lost her footing on a rock and stumbled.

The kingfishers remained to her right.

There was no accounting for the behavior of the birds. Lyah's irritation at the hawk above slowly banked its first flames and turned to embers of resentment.

Everything felt wrong here. It took several leagues and the sun sinking enough to brush the tops of trees for Lyah to circle the why. The woods were silent.

The river was not; it burbled like a river ought. The fishes and birdlife went about their business there—though not all the birds belonged.

To her left, growing around the base of a cedar tree, a bush of iceberries flowered. It was then Lyah stopped. There were no bees, no bugs at all. She hadn't seen bloodsuckers or the tiny biting white socks. No earthworms or beetles.

She looked back to the river, where the water teemed with life. How were all the fish eating if there were no bugs?

The hawk cried out, high above.

OTH OF the girls seemed to be taking the appearance of Jenin's death mask far better than he. Even Lyah, whose stony-faced grief had cracked for an instant, regained her composure as soon as she tucked something into her rucksack.

Ryd felt as though he might come apart at the seams and leave bits of himself behind on the trail.

He never thought the Journeying would be like this. He thought it might be like the jaunt to Haver's Quarry he'd taken with Jenin and hys family when they reached their twelfth harvest. They had brought a pack mule and canvas tents and used the campfire to melt brown sugar into syrup to pour over White Lace apples. He had thought it would be a celebration. A long one with no sugar, but surely not the kind of anxious trek he now found himself engaged in, dreading each curve of the Bemin.

Soon the river would curve to the northeast, taking them into Haver's Glen. Ryd's apprehension increased at the thought of the glen rising up on either side of them, walling them between its steep faces where only goats tried to climb.

He noticed that Carin kept her face turned toward the north, on their path, refusing to acknowledge the circling hawk above any more than she already had. Her right hand held tight to the end of her bow. Lyah kept glancing toward the river with a troubled expression, but he didn't ask why. They needed no reason to be troubled after last night.

On the other side of the river, a lamp-lighter bug shone bright orange and then vanished from view. The sun's rays had long since deserted their path, though the tops of the trees to the west glowed, dimming visibly as he watched. They would stop for the night soon. The morning would bring Haver's Glen and the next leg of their journey.

Lyah noticed the mist first. She gave a small cry, and Ryd soon saw why. The mist rose from the river and spread in grey-white tendrils from the banks as if it were hands seeking out structures in the dark. Unlike the sleepily rolling fog that blanketed Haveranth in spring and autumn when the nights were chilled, this mist moved and changed, searching, wandering.

"We should leave the banks," he said. The fingers of white sent ice into his veins, and Ryd shivered.

"No," Carin said. She'd stopped and stared at the river as if it had come to life in front of their faces.

"That mist," Ryd protested. He didn't want to be near it. He couldn't explain the aversion he felt. He did not want those tendrils of mist to touch him.

Lyah's eyes were locked on the far bank of the Bemin, and Ryd saw several more lamp-lighter bugs flicker on and off across the water. For some reason, the sight made Lyah shudder.

"It's only by the river. We have to get away from it."

Carin shook her head, her face stony. "No. We stay by the river and follow it to the Jewel. That's what we do, Ryd. That is the journey."

The mist snaked out from the rapids of the river toward its shore, fingering rounded rocks in the falling twilight.

A tin taste filled Ryd's mouth. He fought the sudden urge to flee to the west, away from the fitful fog.

"How far are we from the glen?" Lyah asked suddenly.

Panic rose in Ryd, but he forced an answer to tumble from his lips. "A league and a half. Maybe two."

The girls exchanged a glance.

"Do you think the mist is dangerous?" Lyah asked.

Yes, Ryd wanted to say, but the word this time escaped his tongue before it could give it voice.

"I don't know," said Carin. Her eyes sought out the hawk above. It still circled, even now in the twilit dimness of the forest. It flapped on north then, almost out of sight, then returned to dip above their heads.

The mist crept up the bank of the river, and Ryd took a step away.

"Let's move," Lyah said.

Two leagues would take them another two or three hours. Ryd's legs ached, and his head buzzed with thirst. He had thought they would make camp outside the glen, that he would have at least one more night outside of the steep-walled confines of that deep welt through the hills. He pushed his feet forward, draining the last sips from his water skin without thinking.

They walked another hour and a half, Carin setting a brisk pace that made Ryd's lungs feel as though they would burst. The mist on the riverside slowly inched away from the water until Ryd thought he could reach out with his right hand and skim it with his fingertips. He instead took another step away from the river.

Darkness fell, but the mist seemed to light the way with an odd, greyish non-brightness. It did nothing to calm the rising tide of panic in Ryd's chest.

"The glen," Carin said. She pointed upriver to Haver's Gate, the stark edges of pale grey rock barely visible. Only fifteen minutes now.

Lyah screamed.

Her right arm was wrapped in a white tendril of fog. Ryd hesitated, frozen by the sight of the mist around his friend's arm. Carin rushed to her side, taking hold of Lyah's midsection and hauling her to the other side with her whole body's weight.

To Ryd's shock, the mist relinquished its grasp, but its now-empty fingers seemed to grasp at nothing, working their way out closer to where Carin held a shrieking Lyah on the ground.

His eyes stayed trained on the moving mist.

"Lyah. Lyah!" Out of the corner of his eye, Ryd saw Carin grab Lyah's arm. Lyah screamed again.

"We have to go," Ryd said.

The mist, sluggish at first, now snapped and roiled in front of his eyes, pulling away from the river with more speed as if it had found its mark.

Perhaps it had.

"We have to go!" Ryd bellowed the words, pointing at the mist.

Carin finally saw it, and she took Lyah's free arm and jerked her to her feet. Both her hands went to either side of the taller girl's face. Lyah's eyes locked to the mist, and she cradled her right arm close to her body.

"Lyah. Look at me. Look at me!" Carin spoke low and quiet. "We have to go. We have to get to the glen. Can you run?"

Lyah raised a shaking hand to her face and brushed back her tangled hair. "By all sustenance, yes."

They ran.

The mist behind them seemed to gain speed. Ryd took up the rear, afraid Lyah would stumble back into the white fog. The light around them felt like the touch of dead Jenin's flesh, and as much as Ryd wanted to put on speed and fling himself to the west, he repeated Carin's words in his head. This was the journey. They could not leave the banks of the Bemin, not now, not so close to the glen.

Even with the eerie unlight of the living mist, the ground felt as though it had grown new rocks and roots beneath Ryd's feet as he ran. His throat burned, and he knew there was no more water to be had from his skin. Only in the glen. He skirted the mist where it jutted out from the bank, once narrowly missing a finger. When Haver's Gate loomed in front of them, Ryd almost sobbed in dual relief and trepidation. The glen could be their savior or their tomb.

A wide swath of mist suddenly surged into their path.

"Carin, stop!" Ryd shouted.

She skidded to a halt, throwing Lyah behind her. Carin had some-how thrown the rope-bound bundle of saiga meat over her arm, and it dangled from her elbow, making her arm droop with the weight. Sweat slid down her straight nose, but it was the only sign of her tiring that Ryd could see. The mist curled back in on itself, forming a crescent like a scythe waiting to fell them like summer grain. Just beyond, the glen's entrance waited.

"We have to go around it," he said.

Lyah made a soft keening sound, her right elbow tucked tight into her middle, but she took a steadying breath and nodded.

The three of them darted out around the mist, which tracked them to the left. Carin and Lyah cut past it, and Ryd leaped to the side.

Not enough. A searing pain tore into his right arm just above the elbow, pulling a scream from his lips. It froze him to the spot, the pain spreading from his bicep up to his shoulder and down to his elbow. He heard himself almost as he had heard Lyah, distant and frightened, his voice somehow disconnected with himself. The pain tethered him to where he stood, and a fierce bright light filled his eyes, painful and shin-ing through his skin, down to his marrow, down to—

Lyah tore him away from the mist, Carin at her side.

"Run," Lyah urged through gritted teeth.

He ran, stumbling forward. His arm felt as though it had been dipped in molten metal from Rina's forge. It hung at his side, limp and flopping as he ran. He couldn't bend it to pull it inward. Fear spiked his heart, and his breath came quickly like grains tumbling through Old Wend's mill.

"The river," Carin said, gasping.

The mist covered the Bemin River. Ryd's eyes could make out only a white, undulating sheet that even now grasped for them. And the glen...

"The gate." Ryd pointed with his good arm. Haver's Gate, which should have been still directly in front of them, now stood a hundred yards to their right. *Carin was right,* he thought. *She was right.*

We never should have left the riverbank.

"Can we make it?" Pain held Lyah's voice captive, tight.

"I don't know," said Carin.

To the west held survival, but they would return to Haveranth Nameless and be shunned forever.

"We have to try." He started forward at a jog, then broke into a run. His knees protested, and his arm was a burning knot of pain at his side.

The gate was still unobscured by the fog, and he aimed himself at the gap in the rock. The gap was wide enough to allow the river through, and that was nearly it. Aside from a ten-yard strip of gravely bank on either side, there was no getting around it. Legend said once the Jewel had been a shining inland sea until a giant punched a hole in the rocky grey promontory and set the Bemin free. Ryd ran, wishing that giant was handy to pluck them up from the ground and deposit them inside the glen.

He was not sure the glen was safety; perhaps this mist would fill the enclosed valley with burning death. Still he ran.

The edge of the gate appeared before them just as the mist lurched from the river. "Go!" he yelled.

Lyah flung herself past the edge of rock with Ryd and Carin fast on her heels. Ryd stumbled forward, tripping over a rock but keeping upright enough to recover his gait. He kept running until the darkness of the glen consumed him. It was the darkness that stopped him.

He collapsed in a heap on the banks of the river, the rushing sound of the glen's hundreds of waterfalls a trickling, tinkling music counterpoint to his heaving breaths.

Darkness filled the glen. No unnatural light. No eerie tendrils of mist. His arm still felt as though it had been smothered in pimia oil and set aflame, but he plastered his body to the ground, pressing his face against the coolness of the pebbled beach.

Safety.

A hawk's scream rose in the night.

THE SKY above her suspended stars from its dome, glittering purer than Carin had ever seen. She lay on her back, the dampness of knobbly gravel cooling her, turning the perspiration cold against her skin. Ryd and Lyah sat back to back, both cradling an arm to their chests. Carin could see them out of the corner of her eye, could watch the still-heavy rise and fall of their breathing.

She made herself get up. Lyah started to rise as well, but Carin held out a hand to stay her. "You both wait here. I'll be back."

She gathered their water skins and stepped around them, following the lighter spattering of water she heard to her left, the rushing of the Bemin on her right. Not ten yards up the glen was the first waterfall, barely more than a rivulet—but it would do. Carin put her face directly under the stream for a moment, her body jolting at the cold shock. The water itself was icy and sweet with the slightest mineral hint from falling hundreds of feet over the sheer face of the glen's wall. When she had drunk her fill, she held each skin under the stream until they bulged in her palm.

There would be no fire to last the night; this part of the glen was too rocky and narrow for trees to grow, but at least there was water to be had. The moons had not yet risen above the crest of the glen, and only starlight lit its darkness.

Carin returned to Ryd and Lyah, handing each of them a bottle. "Drink," she said. "I'll fill them again once you've finished."

They drank in silence, each holding their water skins gingerly as if holding it in their uninjured hands could somehow add to their hurts.

"I wish I could see it," Ryd said after wiping his mouth on his sleeve. "It's too dark."

"It still burns," Lyah said. She held her arm away from her body, trying to straighten her elbow in vain. She winced and drew it back in. "It feels like I did the day I swam naked in the Bemin as a child all day just after High Lights. When it blistered after, but worse. Much worse."

"What was that?" Ryd asked. "I've never heard of any such thing."

Even if he had tried to keep the fear from his voice, Carin would have felt it. She shook her head, unsure if they could see the gesture. "I wish I knew."

They spent an uncomfortable night at the mouth of the glen. Carin thought she would surely sleep, but instead sat watching the mist swirl just beyond the gate. Its tendrils still sought entry into Haver's Glen, as if driven by some sentient being. They tested each edge, each crumble of rock, each corner. Thus, she passed the night, discomfited by the steady, too-quick beating of her heart and the fear that the mist would find a way through.

Grey dawn came late, the sun taking too long to peek its face above the ridge. By unspoken agreement, they waited to begin their trek, instead using what few small sticks they had brought to simmer the saiga neck in one of Ryd's cook pots to make a weak stew just before the fire died. Carin found feverfew growing in the clefts of the glen's rock faces and dropped a handful into the stew. The herb would help dull their pain.

They examined their wounds in the growing light. Webs of white overlaid the bronze skin on both Ryd and Lyah's arms, rimmed by angry red. Both looked as though the webs had grown outward from a spiral shape around their arms as if a large snake had wound its way from hand to shoulder.

"Does it feel any better today?" Carin asked.

Lyah gave an uncertain nod, followed by Ryd a moment later, but neither allowed their eyes to meet Carin's. She instead wet the scrap of towel she had brought in the Bemin and packed it with more crushed feverfew, wrapping it around Ryd's arm. "Lyah next," she said.

When the sun finally shone bars of light into the glen, the rocks around them seemed to burst into millions of tiny sparkles. Ryd gasped at the sight, sloshing his stew over the edge of his wooden bowl.

For a moment, Carin imagined Haver's Glen as it may once have been: grey-white stones covered in the deep blue water of the Bemin, filled to the high crest above their heads and hundreds of feet deep. Perhaps the Jewel truly had been so large, a huge blue eye in the land.

The wonder filled her only seconds longer until the miles of water she imagined suddenly weighed down upon her where she stood at the would-be bottom of a sea. A chill filled her that had nothing to do with the early morning coolness.

"It's back," Lyah said, eyes trained on the sky. One hand held Carin's towel wrapped around her arm, and her bowl of stew sat steaming on a rock.

The hawk had returned, resuming its circling above their heads. "At least the mist is gone." Carin didn't want to step outside the Haver's Gate to prove herself right, but she had watched those burning tendrils recede as the sky grew lighter. She hoped never to see something so horrifying again.

In spite of her injury, Lyah insisted on spearing several more fish before they departed. Though it took her longer and sweat beaded her brow, she returned with a string of six fish. "The glen will keep them cool enough until we stop for the midday meal," was all she said.

As they walked, Carin repeated their path directions in her head. She brought up the rear, allowing Ryd and Lyah before her, and each time one of them shifted a shoulder or winced visibly from the pain in their arms, Carin couldn't help but fear the road ahead, knowing they'd only just begun. She looked up at the hawk once, staring at the circling raptor as if she could force its secrets from it with her will alone.

LYAH SAW Jenin again on the third day after they reached Haver's Glen. The glen had widened enough for trees to grow, and though now she cursed every buzz of every bloodsucker to light upon her skin, she'd almost cried with relief when she saw the first bee bustling around a few spring buttercups blooming on the banks of the Bemin.

The hawk still circled above, and it screamed once on that third day, swooping low over a hazel tree where Jenin sat, leaning against the bark. Lyah started and cried out, turning to alert Carin and Ryd, but when she looked back, sy was gone. She feigned pain in her still-burning arm and walked silently for the rest of the day.

When she saw hyr again that night, she said nothing. And again the next day as the glen widened still more and they took their midday meal on a rocky spit that jutted out into the river's expanding girth. She saw hyr yet again when she woke in the early hours the next day to relieve herself.

She said nothing to the others. Sy never approached or spoke. When sy appeared, sy seemed to busy hyrself with mundane tasks, sharpening hys belt knife or whittling pegs for the furniture sy liked to make. The more often Lyah saw the face of the lover she'd always thought she might take to name, the more she believed hys presence a simple, if mad torture of her own making.

The glen soon began to bustle with the life Lyah had noticed lacking outside Haver's Gate. Tiny picas chirped in the rocky outcroppings of the glen, sometimes bathing themselves in its many waterfalls. Sometimes Lyah would hurry ahead, jogging for a short time to outstrip Carin and Ryd until she found a waterfall herself. There she held her wounded arm under the icy water, shivering at the contrast of the cold on skin that still felt like it had been set aflame. The daily compresses of feverfew did little to numb it; the white webs across her brown skin did not fade, but stood out like bone beads on leather.

When the others caught up, she would pull her dripping arm back from the water and continue. She sometimes saw Ryd doing the same, and their eyes would meet in understanding. Carin strode grimly on without acknowledging neither the inspiration nor the attempts to treat it.

On the eve of the new moon, they set up camp at the head of the glen. There, cliffs rose higher than the glen's walls that had hemmed them in on either side for the past turns. A smattering of grasses invaded the glen there, rough scrubby blue stems that stood stark upright in the gravelly floor and yellowed at their tips as if they had only managed to draw enough nutrients from the earth to rejuvenate part of the way from the winter's dormancy.

Lyah volunteered first watch. The morning would see them on a climb—even in the fading golden light of the setting sun, she could make out the rough-hewn path that cut to the left and began to switchback across the edge of the hill ahead. It would lead them to the Jewel, and from then to the Mistaken Pass.

Carin and Ryd fell to sleep before long, both snoring lightly in the quiet of the night. Here the crickets didn't sing so loudly yet; spring started sluggish in the higher foothills.

"Lyah." A soft voice behind her made her turn.

She already knew to expect hyr, and there sy stood.

"You can speak."

Hys gaze darted upward, but then Jenin stepped forward to meet her. "I haven't time."

"You're dead. You have nothing but."

There it was then, a hint of a smile around her dead would-be lover's lips. Lyah felt something clench tight in her chest, something that fused her ribs until she wanted to double over and rend the ground with her fists. Instead she held herself steady and made her eyes meet hys.

"Why do you come to torture me?" Her voice was only the lightest wind in the night. She should ask about Dyava, if he was all right. Carin would want to know—

"I've not come to cause you pain. Only to give a warning."

The tightening in her chest loosened, and Lyah stifled a laugh. "A dead friend's warning. What could you have to say?" *Ask about Dyava.* Lyah could not make her mouth form the words, too afraid of what the answer might be.

"That not all paths are what they seem to be."

"That sounds like the warning of the dead," Lyah said, feeling the bitterness of her words as if she'd bitten into a cajit without removing its husk. Vague, like a soothsayer's words. Like Merin's endless proverbs. Lyah had never ascribed undue meaning to Merin's pronunciations before; why should she listen to the dead now?

Jenin's body tensed, and sy looked around hyr. "I cannot tell you more. Names are as much choice as they are discovery. And some magics cannot be forever sustained. They rot, just like fruit."

"What does that mean?"

Hys face, harshly grey in the dim starlight and still cast with the pallor of death, grew panicked. Sy stepped forward and cupped Lyah's face in his hand. "It would have been you," sy said.

Then sy was gone, leaving her alone with the night.

TWO DAYS trekking up the face of a cliff took their toll on Ryd's arm. The exertion of climbing made him perspire, and the sweat that beaded on his arm felt like cave chili juice poured into a cut. Lyah had gone silent during the hike up the mountainside, and Carin hadn't been much more talkative. She stumbled once on the climb and scraped her right palm on a sharp rock, but she refused to stop even to bandage the wound.

This Journeying had turned to a grim business.

Ryd wasn't sure what he'd expected. In his mind, the Journeying had always been a key to his freedom, a marked transition from being the scrawny child all the younger kids sat on and knocked over into a respected adult. When he returned he could ply a trade, earn a living, grow up. In two more cycles, he would join the village in full. He had thought that he would embark on the Journeying with a full heart, not with a hole of grief growing wider in his chest and an arm that was nearly unusable for the pain. There was no soothsayer to consult, no answers to be found. Only the road ahead.

And back, he reminded himself.

A thought slithered into Ryd's mind, making him wonder if things would really change when they got home. His expectations for the Journeying had been so fully thwarted and covered with death. Perhaps when he got home, everything would remain as it ever was, with Ryd being hounded by children half his age and the only difference being what name they called him when they did it. Could he bear it, if this were the whole of his life?

Even the sight of the Jewel could not cheer him. The lake itself was all it was meant to be. It appeared as a glittering blue pool of pure beauty against the jagged backdrop of the Mad Mountains beyond, the size of an egg in the distance even though were he to stand on its shore, the whole of Haveranth would fit comfortably into its waters twice over. Sharp white peaks stretched as far as Ryd could see, but they did nothing to settle the anxiety in his belly.

The saiga meat was long gone, and they lived only off the fish Lyah caught. Too early for berries or fruits, the glen had been devoid of any wildlife to hunt. Pikas were mostly too fast to catch, too smart to be snared, and not worth the effort besides.

Thus the days continued. The Jewel glimmered in and out of sight through the trees and ridgelines of the foothills. Ryd's arm throbbed with every step, pulsing with the beat of his heart and footsteps alike. He tried to ignore its nagging just as he pretended not to feel the gnawing knot of hunger in his belly that increased each day. Each night, fish. Each morning, fish. And not enough. The swiftly moving currents of the Bemin's infant waters harbored only tiny fry fish and fresh-spawned climber fish. Lyah pointed out these depressions in the gravelly banks, filled with eggs that had yet to hatch.

If Ryd ever returned to Haveranth—and as the days went on, his doubts grew and would not be assuaged—he was quite certain that he'd not touch another fish until three High Harvests had come and gone.

It was in Carin he first noticed the changes. She stripped on the Bemin's banks one day, her back to him as she crouched in a sandy hollow to splash water on her underarms and neck. Her back was lean and powerful. She'd always been muscular—an affinity for wood and metalworking was not for the weak—but her body now resembled a rock snake coiled to strike. Any hint of fat had been worn away; her legs bunched beneath her like springs, the lines of her sinews and muscles clear to his eyes.

He looked down and pulled up his shirt. The planes of his stomach had flattened—and beyond, the constant hunger had made his belly almost concave.

Ryd pulled his shirt down and turned away from Carin, wondering what else was changing besides their bodies. Who would they become?

• • • • •

Two days later, they reached the Jewel just as the sun passed its zenith in the sky.

Its banks were pale grey rock, its beaches pebbly. The water itself shone in the midday sun like the deepest of blue topaz around the edges and darkened to rich cerulean in the depths, clear and clean.

A surge of hope filled Ryd's chest, ballooning his lungs. He held his breath without realizing it, stripping his scuffed leather boots and tunic and stumbling toward the water. His injured arm dangled at his side, sore and swollen. He splashed into the cold water, not caring that his trousers were soaked immediately. Wading deeper, he reached chest level before he stopped, letting out his breath with a gust of air that rippled the water in front of him. So clear. Ryd could make out the pebbles under his toes. They massaged his aching feet, and though the temperature made him shiver and gasp, he filled his lungs again and sank under the water.

It was said that the Jewel's purity was healing. Some of the older villagers made pilgrimages to the Jewel to take the waters, saying they were good for the heart and the blood. And so Ryd let his arms fall to his sides, hovering under the water with his knees bent and his head bowed, the tiny bubbles of his slowly releasing breath tickling his nose.

He hung suspended until his lungs burned from the need for fresh air and his skin burned from the cold of the water. He exploded to the surface, spitting water and coughing. Snot trickled from his nose, and his eyes watered.

His injured arm looked the same.

Disappointment tugged him downward, irrational but heavy nonetheless. He trudged back to the bank, shivering. No healing from the Jewel's waters after all. Ryd ignored Carin and Lyah's curious stares and sat on a large rock, staring back at the path from whence they'd come.

Hungry, hurt, tired.

Now also cold and wet.

LYAH'S STOMACH chastised her loudly. Though the others didn't know, she'd had no food for two days, opting instead to split her portion between Carin and Ryd. Though her body said she was hungry—said it with vehemence—she could not bring herself to eat.

Ryd had yet to move from his perch atop the wide white rock on the banks of the Jewel after inexplicably dunking himself in the glacial water. He'd stopped shivering only because Carin, after two hours of whittling a stick and watching Ryd's back remain uncovered and shaking, had built a fire a few feet from him where the warmth would reach him even if he decided never to turn around.

They passed the evening that way, no one speaking except their stomachs' churning growls that gave away their hunger. Carin at last pulled out the last handful of cajits and divided them into two piles. She handed one to Lyah.

"Eat these. If you don't eat something today, you may not make it through the pass tomorrow."

Startled, Lyah met Carin's gaze. The flicker of firelight danced with the golden remnants of sunshine, weaving across Carin's face. Lyah looked to the west almost involuntarily, toward the Mistaken Pass. Why it was called that, she didn't know, but the path itself was obscured by jagged peaks. If she didn't know the pass existed, she would never see it there. It was there they had to go, and Carin was right. She took the cajits and shelled them, making a tidy pile in the cleft between two stones at her feet. The nuts, usually sweet with a light hint of spice to them, tasted like charcoal in her mouth.

Carin watched her until Lyah ate the last of her portion, then nodded, turning to Ryd. "Ryd, your turn."

Ryd didn't answer.

Lyah brushed fragments of cajit shell from her knee and stood. "Ryd?"

She rose to her feet and walked past the fire to where he sat, back to them. He didn't turn, but shining tracks of tears glinted in the light of the moon. His injured arm stretched out in front of him, he tried to bend it at the elbow and winced.

"I don't know if I can keep going," he said.

Lyah and Carin exchanged a glance.

Carin frowned, looking from Ryd to the Jewel. Its waters matched the sky in the last vestiges of dusk, the small waves quietly lapping the shore. "You thought it would heal your arm, and it didn't."

Lyah started, flexing her own injured arm. She hadn't even thought of that possibility, and now, looking at Ryd whose trousers had dried in stiff folds and whose skin was littered in gooseflesh, she was glad it hadn't occurred to her.

"I don't think it's that easy," she said.

"I thought that Tillim—"

Tillim. He had left Haveranth on the shoulders of his fellow Journeyers and strode back into the village on two healed legs. Of course Ryd would think of Tillim.

"We don't know what healed him," Carin said. Her voice held a hushed apprehension rather than the awe Lyah might have expected.

Lyah understood. So many unknowns on the Journeying.

Suddenly the air felt colder and too quiet. Lyah sat facing Ryd. His rock wasn't big enough for the both of them, so she sat in front of him, looking up. "You can do this. You have to. We all do."

She looked northwest at the blue-white peaks of the pass. Lyah couldn't have said if she thought they'd find healing beyond those mountains or just more pain.

CARIN INSISTED on bringing up the rear the next day as they began the ascent to the Mistaken Pass. Once she hung back enough to shoot a rabbit, still sluggish in the spring air that was slower to warm the higher altitudes. She cleaned it and scraped the hide while Ryd and Lyah stopped to drink from their water skins, then wrapped the small steaks in the waxed canvas for later, preserving the organs as well. She was tying the bundle when Lyah came up to her with a handful of green onions, nodding once over her shoulder at a mulchy hollow. She tucked them into Carin's pack without a word, and they continued on.

Soon they would climb past the snow line, Carin knew. Those onions could be the last fresh food they would find. That night they looked at their meager food stores and counted out the days they could afford to eat. After a night with empty bellies, the three Journeyers woke with somber eyes and the thought of their hollow stomachs being drawn out for turns to come. Together they picked through the hollows and gathered more onions and yarrow. The first shoots of spring were all that could be found, peeking pale blue and green through the loam and undergrowth. Pricklebush grew early, and they picked it, mindful of the stings of its leaves. Lion flowers sprouted, bearing no blooms yet, but they harvested the early greens. Ryd climbed trees to raid the nests of birds, gathering eggs to boil in one of his cook pots. Food became their first priority, to ensure they would survive the remaining turns' hard walking to the Hidden Vale beyond the Mistaken Pass. For three days they foraged out around them, the need for food outweighing the press of time upon them.

On the third day, it rained through the sun's arc across the sky, turning to sleet as the sun set around them. All three worked to harvest as many plants as they could, to save them from freezing in the night.

Carin kept her bow always at the ready, and Lyah and Ryd made sure their fire was always tended, to smoke and dry the meat from the rabbits and even a few pikas she shot and snared. Lyah speared fish on the banks of the Jewel, and in those three days, their bellies rumbled even as they amassed a hoard of foods to carry with them. When they finally set out on the fourth day with grim looks all around, they each chewed a strip of dried rabbit and a bunch of cold cress from a marshy pond they found near the Jewel.

The mountains rose on either side of their path. The trio of Journeyers threaded through the Mistaken Pass, the trees shrinking around them until Carin felt as though she and the others had simply grown to dwarf them, like giants. They had left the Bemin behind at its source, but runoff from the Mad Mountains cascaded down through the foothills even here. Though the steep slopes on either side of them looked like mountains to

Carin, she knew that these were merely anthills compared to the peaks beyond their destination. Five hundred leagues of impassable mountains lay to the north.

That was why it was called the Mistaken Pass, she knew. From the lush plains and rolling hills to the south where Haveranth and Cantoranth grew on the Bemin, prosperous and flourishing, the Mistaken Pass looked like it would cut through the mountain range to the north. But it ended at the Hidden Vale, an alcove of rocky caves and strange stone formations to which every villager from the Hearthland's three settlements Journeyed to come of age.

There was no pass through the mountains, no avenue of travel to whatever lay on the other side.

As a child, Carin had sometimes wondered what existed beyond. When she had asked her mother, Rina had responded, "Not land nor sea, nor journeys three." It was vague enough that Carin had walked away feeling rankled, and after a time, she'd never brought it up again. As she grew older, Lyah once traveled to Bemin's Fan by the sea and came back to Carin with tales of a seafarer who had crashed upon the rocks to the north where a jutting promontory protruded under the waves. There were just the mountains and no telling of what could lay beyond.

The days passed, became turns as first five sunsets, then ten, then fifteen pushed them deeper into the mountains. Snow dotted the hills around them, creeping closer to their path with every new step.

When the path rose sharply between two rough outcroppings of rock one day, Lyah and Carin met each other's eyes. Here was the Mistaken Pass, the last major hurdle between the Journeyers and the Hidden Vale. They walked on silent feet between the jagged stones. The air became cold where it had been cool, and Carin pulled her cloak around her, raising the hood to cover her head and conserve her warmth. She noticed Ryd and Lyah doing the same, but still the three shivered in the alpine air. Any fat they had carried with them out of Haveranth had sloughed away, carved off their bones by the lack of food and the constant trek into the highlands.

The hawk cried out above Carin's head, startling her.

In the days that had passed since they entered Haver's Glen, Carin had almost forgotten about the hawk. But still it circled, soared, swooped above their heads with each passing day.

It seldom made noise, but with that sharp piercing of the high mountain air, all three of them stopped short, their feet scuffing on the trail that was now more rocks than soil.

A rush of air sounded up the mountain, like the flap of wings but loud like the fabric from a canvas tent snapped in the sharp wind of a storm.

"What is that?" Lyah's hands fell to her belt knives, her thumbs on the hilts as if ready to draw them.

Carin slowly removed her bow from where it lay slung across her shoulders. She fingered the now familiar string, pulling it a few times to loosen it in the cold air. Nocking an arrow, she took a few steps ahead.

It came again, the loud flapping sound. Ryd looked up the mountain and pointed. "It's coming from up there."

"I don't see anything," Lyah said. She unsheathed her knives, one in each hand. The blades were honed to expert sharpness, and the glint of the sun on the metal's sharp edge brought to Carin's memory the *ritch-ritch-ritch* of Lyah's whetstone on the blade as they sat around the fire at night.

Carin shook herself out of the thoughts, forcing herself to concentrate on the sound instead of picturing her friend's face as she honed her knives. A flicker of apprehension licked through Carin's chest as she looked around at the empty mountainside.

The pass was silent, the lack of sound somehow viscous and sticky as they waited for the flapping to return.

Still high above, the hawk circled.

Lyah took several steps forward, her body tense and muscles drawn. "It has to be watching us."

"What is it? If it's a bird, it's massive." Ryd looked to and fro over the mountainside.

Carin did the same, seeking out any hint of movement. Nothing showed itself to her. "I haven't heard of anything like that living up here," she said, knowing that didn't mean nothing did. Had Dyava heard this sound? Had he seen the creature that made it?

Would Carin ever get the chance to ask him?

"There!" Lyah pointed to a rocky promontory high above them. The flapping sound came again.

Ryd looked around wildly. "I don't see anything!"

"Just a flicker, there!"

Sure enough, up the side of the rocky mountain, the very stones seemed to ripple with the sound of enormous wings. It was the ripple Carin watched as it skirted the side of the mountain, the sound growing fainter. When the ripple reached the mountain's edge, it vanished into a low-hanging cloud. The beating of wings grew faint, then disappeared into the quiet whisper of the wind.

Her fingers numb from holding the arrow against her bow's string, Carin relaxed them, taking the arrow into her hand.

"What is it?" Lyah asked, her voice low and fearful.

"Did you see it?" Carin turned to Ryd, unsure what her own eyes had beheld.

"No," he said.

"It looked like the rocks themselves were moving," Lyah said. "I've never heard of anything like that at all."

"Nor have I," said Carin. Her eyes sought out the part of the mountain where the ripple had vanished into the cloud. "Whatever it was though, it didn't want to be seen."

THAT NIGHT, the three Journeyers slept huddled in a small cave. Lyah pulled her cloak tightly around her, resting her head on her rucksack. Her stomach gnawed itself, unsatisfied still with the two strips of rabbit and the bunch of boiled greens they'd eaten, even though it had felt like a feast at the time. Ryd had even brought out a packet of salt he had tucked away in the depths of his rucksack.

She didn't like the idea of creatures out here that she'd never heard of. There was a reason she stayed close to Haveranth and the Bemin. As Merin's apprentice, she'd heard many stories of the dangers outside the Hearthland's haven of safety. Sea monsters that could swallow whole fishing boats. Packs of kazytya that were intelligent enough to hunt people. And now, invisible beasts that flew.

Lyah rolled over onto her side and stifled a gasp when Jenin's face appeared directly in front of hers.

"Did I fall asleep?" she asked.

Jenin simply smiled at her, reaching out a hand to caress her face. Hys hand felt cold as it always did, but there in the Mistaken Pass beneath the waning gibbous Quicken Moon, the wind whistling over stones, Lyah could almost imagine that the chill in her skin was the product of the mountains and not the touch of hys death upon her.

Almost.

It was the first time Lyah had seen hys face in three turns. The turns had come and gone, fives upon fives of days. What in Haveranth was broken every fifth day by rest and rejoicing, here on these steep paths was only endless walking. She'd last seen hyr on the shores of the Jewel as Discovery Moon hid her face for another cycle, giving way to the tiny crescent of Revive, which had waxed and waned and waxed again as Quicken. Lyah had kept track of the passage of moons, feeling the coming of Bide, which would be followed by Toil. They had to reach the Hidden Vale, and quickly, or they would not return for High Lights at the peak of summer.

For a long while, Lyah looked into Jenin's eyes, barely noticing hys neck wound anymore. It had become a part of hyr, awful though it was, and she did not wish it away.

"You're almost there," sy said, and then hys face and the touch of hys hand vanished into the welcoming dark.

• • • • •

Lyah awoke with a start, the tiny ticks of snowflakes on her leather rucksack rousing her. The sky was dim and overcast, and Carin already stood beside her, stretching her arms in the morning.

Lyah rose and relieved herself, not speaking of Jenin or anything else. Shame filled her, to keep something like that from Carin and Ryd, but Lyah knew also that to speak of it would change things. Perhaps Carin and Ryd still saw Jenin's face and perhaps they did not. Perhaps Carin saw Dyava's but could not bring herself to speak word of his death. Lyah knew death had claimed Jenin, though, that by now the fire had burned hyr to ashes scattered where worms and beetles could return hys body to the earth, bringing hyr back into the cycle of life, but she would not wish hyr gone from her memory. No, Lyah would keep Jenin with her as long as sy appeared.

They walked through the morning without much talk. The path turned downward, sloping almost imperceptibly at first, but then steeper, curving to the west. As they walked, the air grew warmer and the sharp tiny snowflakes that fell turned to large, mushy flakes that melted almost as soon as they touched stone. Midafternoon, the flakes became rain, and the path and stones smelled like one large cavern.

"We've got to be nearly there now," Ryd said. He'd taken to looking around them often, his eyes darting over rocks and ridges, then upward at the hawk that still paced them above, then back. Lyah didn't blame him.

Carin pointed up ahead, at a flash of blue-green struggling through the rocky ground. "You're right."

The tiny sign of life renewed their steps, and Lyah found herself pushing her feet to walk faster, chasing each new sprig of plant life on the path. The steep sides of the mountains that had encroached on their steps gave way to a wider basin, spreading out around them in a growing return to life.

When the first shrubs and trees appeared, Lyah wanted to shout, to run toward them. Instead, she sipped from her water skin and continued their brisk pace down the slope.

Just before sunset, the misty rain and clouds around them parted, revealing the descent into the Hidden Vale.

Lit by the deep gold of the waning daylight, the vale shone like a sea of cobalt. The sun made the deep blue grasses sparkle after the rain. Far below, delicate spires of stone seemed to grow out of the land itself, pale grey and shining in the sunlight. They rose into the air, as tall as three roundhomes stacked on top of one another. Higher. At their zeniths, the stones fanned into odd circles, from which water flowed, trickling and cascading over the edges to fall to the ground some thirty feet below. Some rose even higher, and Lyah stopped short on the path to marvel.

"The Hanging Falls," Carin murmured. Her eyes were as wide as the circular windows of her home, and Lyah was sure her own had done the same.

Ryd, too, stopped, affected by the sight of the Hidden Vale's most mysterious feature.

The vale lay in a bowl, and beyond it the peaks of the Mad Mountains were just starting to appear through the mist.

Without discussion, they set up camp and watched as the last hour of sun burned away the mist to reveal a nest of life and early summer surrounded on all sides by the harsh rock of mountains.

Lyah knew part of it was the sheer beauty of the place, of having the chance to see the sun paint the sky with red and gold and fire itself over the deep blue of the vale's grasses and the green-blue of the maha trees' leaves. It blended with the scarlet of the vale's halms, which bridged the land from earth to sky, white trunks as bright as pearls in the sunset.

But part of it was what lay at the far side of the vale, beyond the tinkling falls and the lush foliage that lay unspoiled by the hands of Hearthlanders and beasts alike.

Lyah knew that at the farthest reach of the vale, there was a cave, and in that cave was her name.

RYD WASN'T surprised when sleep evaded him that night. He took third watch from a dozing Carin and sat facing the Hidden Vale as the sun crept toward the horizon.

He had never seen such a place of beauty as this—from the way the first rays of light turned the Hanging Falls to fountains of diamonds to the scent of spring wildflowers that spread out from the vale on the breeze.

And yet with the hawk still spiraling above them, the memory of giant wings flapping unseen against the slopes of a mountain, Ryd couldn't help the trepidation that filled him top to bottom, hair to toenails.

All the walking and starving and foraging had led them to the crest of this hill and to the vale that lay beyond, and Ryd fought every impulse in his marrow not to simply stand up, brush the gravel and grass from his backside, and begin the long walk home to face exile.

He couldn't stop thinking of Jenin, about the words his friend had used. Jenin had said sy died for them. Had Jenin died in their place, or to protect them? Had only one of them heard those words from the mouth of the dead, Ryd would have dismissed it immediately. But all three had heard the same thing. Jenin saying sy died for them.

Carin stirred a few feet away, her waking as fitful as her sleep had been. Ryd met her eyes as she woke. She met his gaze and swallowed. Ryd wished he could go to her, hold her tight and give her some comfort, the way she had always done for him. He didn't think she would let him, though. So he simply looked back at her until she looked away. Not far away, Lyah still slumbered, curled into a ball far smaller than it seemed her lanky form should make.

Ryd got up then, not to flee back to Haveranth, but instead gently shook Lyah's shoulder.

She opened her eyes, first with fear ghosting across her face. After a few moments, it faded into recognition, and Ryd noticed that her fist was tightly closed around something. A wisp of faded grey poked out between the folds of her fingers, and when Lyah caught him looking, she quickly spirited her fist away into her cloak. When her hand emerged a moment later, it was empty, though her palm bore imprints of curved lines.

Ryd didn't pry. The three of them each ate a boiled egg and a side of dried fish, washing it down with cold water from a nearby spring.

Camp broken, they set off down the path, which sloped steeply downward into the vale. Birds chirped as they descended, the sound of birdsong strange in Ryd's ears after the days in the Mistaken Pass with nothing but the sound of the wind and the mysterious creature to break

the silence. A valepip tweeted a merry tune from the branch of a doubloon tree, and another called a response from a perch on one of the stone
towers of the Hanging Falls. The water that fell from the Hanging Falls
provided its own music in the vale, and to Ryd's ears, the new additions of
noise quickly became almost overwhelming.

Haveranth was never silent, of course, but it struck him strange how
quickly one could become accustomed to the quiet of a rocky pass. For
turns they'd seemed to walk backward into winter, and now the din of late
spring surrounded them.

The vale was just as lovely up close as it had been from afar. The
thump of hooves met their ears as they wove between the Hanging Falls,
and Ryd looked to the west to see a herd of wild ihstal, their slender necks
outstretched as muscular legs drove them forward. Ihstal were indepen-
dent beasts, but a few folk in the Hearthland had managed to tame them,
to train them for riding or the pulling of carts to bring wares down Haver's
Road from Bemin's Fan on the western coast to Cantoranth in the east.
Ryd had never seen more than two or three at a time, and here the herd
shone in the morning sun, their coats varying between the pearl grey of a
cloudy morning to the light beige of sand from the shore. They vanished
after a time, their long gait taking them off the vale's plain and into the
surrounding forest. The ihstal whistled to one another, long necks dipping and rising as they slowed and ran, slowed and ran. Padded, cloven
hooves beat the grasses.

Looking up, Ryd watched the water drip downward from the Hanging Falls. The path they took between the stone towers wove around pools,
the dry land upon which they walked formed into a natural trail by the
water from the falls. At the base of each towering waterfall, a pool spread,
clear and deep. The falls formed the center of the vale, surrounded on all
sides by a meadow that slowly became forest, weaving into the crevasses
of the mountains. From the vale's floor, Ryd could only see the front most
mountains, but he knew how many scores of leagues they stretched to the
north. In his mind's eye, he pictured the mountains as they spread, spread,
spread northward into...what? Ryd didn't know. No one did. Merin had
always told the children the mountains were all there was, endless and

vast, and that they were fortunate for the bounty of the Hearthland, its lush fields and clean wells and orchards and herds.

It took the better part of the morning to cross the vale, and they finally stopped at midday in front of a sheer stone face that dripped run-off water like tears from thousands of tiny rivulets. There, back to the right, shaded by the slope of the hill that climbed until it became a mountain, was the cave.

Had he guessed, he would have thought the cave would be in the very center of the cliff. Instead, there it was, off center and strange. Waiting.

No one spoke while they ate.

After they finished and wiped the dried meat's grease from their fingers, all three looked in the direction of the cave.

"We've only two moons to return to Haveranth," Lyah said quietly. "Less. One moon in full, three turns beside. No more. Getting here took more than half our time."

Ryd wondered then if any from the villages of the Hearthland had ever tried to simply stay in the Hidden Vale, to build a life in this shining place.

It didn't look like it, to his eyes. Next cycle more Journeyers would come, and this place would never be anything but a reminder of exile.

They left their rucksacks in a small stack by the mouth of the cave, the meager supply of remaining food left on a small rock a few spans away in case any scavengers came by.

"Should we go in together?" Carin asked. She swayed from foot to foot, looking around them as if expecting something to appear. Ryd thought it was the first agitation she'd displayed since they left Haveranth. He didn't blame her.

Lyah nodded. "Together."

The cave entrance was about the size of one of the gates on carpenter Stil's farm in width, and though it was tall enough for them to enter without bending, the darkness within made Ryd feel as if he were about to squeeze into a rabbit hole.

His breath came faster in his chest, a slight wheeze with each inhale.

The three linked arms and stepped into the dark.

I N THE dark was safety and warmth, and it embraced Ryd like the heat from a crackling hearth fire on a winter day.

He was shrouded. He was safe. And he was alone.

In the dark grew a whisper and a hum. It rose around him, lifting his spirits and his body until he floated like a drop of dew at the center of a weaver-leg's web.

Ryhad, the whisper said, *ryhadryhadryhad.*

There it was. So simple and so close to what he was already called, but for Ryd it felt like pulling off a set of tight shoes he'd worn so long he'd thought they were simply broken in, only to pull on new ones the cobbler had made just to his measurements and lined with wool or bavel.

Ryhad.

This was why he had come here. Ryd exulted in the knowledge, tucked the name *Ryhad* into his heart where he knew he would keep it until he returned home to Haveranth. Until he could declare it to Merin at High Lights and be renamed in front of the village. Until it would make him whole. For the first time in the passage of many, many moons, Ryd felt hope.

A light bloomed in the dark.

L *YARI.*
 Lyarilyarilyarilyarilyarilyari.

Lyah heard the name pulse through her like her blood flowing in her veins, so much was it hers. It ran through her body with the force of a wailing gale of wind, but it left in its wake warmth and security instead of cold.

But still something evaded her, there in that welcoming dark.

Three entered where there should have been four. Jenin's lock of hair, hys token for her, sat at her middle, held by her belt against her waist. She had brought it with her because a piece of Jenin needed to be in the cave.

It was only as her own name thundered around her, sounding at once rich and foreign and right, that Lyah understood why she had brought it.

Her hope withered like the skin of an apple in the hot sun of Toil.

Bringing something of her lover had not conjured hys name.

She would never know who sy was meant to be, and nor would anyone else.

Hot tears fell from her eyes and did not touch ground, but fell, fell, fell into the void.

CARIN FELT the darkness swallow her and longed for it to keep her. It breathed around her like a living being, her skin taking in the feel of it, and for a time she simply was.

Her sense of self vanished into that welcoming blackness. There was no Haveranth or home or hearth there, no Ryd or Lyah or Carin.

No *she*. Nothing.

Just dark.

And then it came.

Caryan.

Carin shuddered with the force of it. The name seared her, branded her, bereft her.

Caryancaryancaryancaryancaryancaryan.

She held tight to the cocoon of enveloping blackness. She tasted it on her tongue like iceberry wine. She heard it like the low drone of a halmer's horn.

Too soon, too soon, too soon came light.

• • • • •

The light shone on faces, and Carin searched for those familiar to her. There were none to be found. No Ryd or Lyah in the brightness that burned. It chased away the comforting dark and left Carin alone in a bright sea of strangers.

There in the faces was an echo of something she knew. A pair of eyes like her mother's. A build like Lyah's, lithe and quick.

But Carin knew them not.

Her feet *became* again, and on staggering legs she walked down a tunnel of light. On the ground were stones, five of them, heavy and immovable, each bearing runes. As Carin drew near to them, she felt a pull as if they wanted her.

She pushed past them and farther, past the faces that weren't quite known to her. Beyond them was a child.

The child did not see her, and sy did not look up. Instead sy knelt in dirt and coughed like Rina did when the smoke from the forge-fire blew in her face. The child coughed, and hys body convulsed. A harsh rattle came from hys lungs. Carin watched, horrified, as the child spit a gob of green onto the dirt, splattered with the bright red of blood.

Sy vanished.

The scent of salt air filled Carin's nose, and the sound of waves rushed around her. She blinked, and in front of her was a band of folk, their bodies gaunt. Between them was a string of scraggly fish, half the size Carin was used to, but the people praised them as if they were precious pimia oil or a flute of halm.

Half a fish went to each person, and Carin watched as they ate slowly, taking small bites, savoring the flakes of fish on their tongues.

Again the people disappeared, and something flew by Carin's ear with a sharp whistle. An arrow erupted from the chest of a man, the blood spreading from the wound to drip upon the ground. He fell to his knees, and from behind Carin, a trio of people with swords ran forward. One slit the man's throat with a motion so practiced it seemed reflexive, and they moved as a single unit to relieve the dead man of his purse, his water skin, and a fine halm knife that hung at his belt. His rucksack they also took, rifling through it to remove a packet of dried meat, a carved wooden bowl, and a lump of weathered red glass.

Carin wanted to look away, but the scene drew her gaze. Her tongue felt coated in dust, and it stuck to the roof of her mouth like she'd eaten too much brown sugar candy with nothing to drink. Try as she might, she could think of no reason to kill a person for their food. Such a thing was an affront to the bounty of their land. Who could do such a thing?

When they faded with the next burst of light, Carin began to wonder if this was indeed her land she saw. Sand spread out in front of her as far as she could see. Her mother kept a glass bottle of sand on the mantelpiece, brought from the beaches of Bemin's Fan where the river ran to greet the sea. But here the sand went on in every direction, dry and pale and hot like midday on High Lights.

A huge cat prowled the sand, its shoulders bulging and muscular. A kazytya, far larger than any Carin had ever seen. It had no tail like the tigers Carin had glimpsed in the woodlands north of Haveranth, but instead only a nub at the base of its spine. Stripes in shades of beige made the cat blend in with the sand around it, and Carin scanned the horizon to see what it might be hunting. But there was nothing, only the sand: the dry, endless sand.

The sand around her changed. From a pile of rocks, a spring burst forth, the water trickling out into the thirsty land around her. Sprigs of blue and green sprouted from the ground, then spread, then the trickle of water became a rivulet, then a stream, and finally a river flowed beside her. Carin blinked to see trees, some with heavy fruits, to see birds flitting from branch to branch. Strange birds. Unfamiliar birds. The land changed, and with it, Carin got the sense of time bearing down on her, pulling her backward from a land parched and hungry to one flowing with water and fruits.

And she saw people, the same she had seen in the bright tunnel before. She saw them bent beneath coils of leather that licked at their backs and stung like a switch. She saw them cast out of camps, chased away.

She saw one of them bend to the ground in her fury, and when the woman rose, fire leaped from her palms.

Five pairs of people stood in a circle around a large rune stone, with all their hands red with blood to the elbows, and the stone dripped with it, red rivulets flowing down the side. The people wore the blood like a hog wore mud, as if they'd bathed in it. They stood surrounded by others, clean and dry, all who watched in silent approbation and beneath that, something more fierce and angry and wild. Carin could not put a name to what she saw in them, feeling again their cries as they bowed under whips and the shame and rage at their mistreatment. And now this fiery approval for those wearing dripping red. Bodies lay beyond the stone, piled in a heap. She had never seen so many dead.

She felt them, the dead. They screamed through her in betrayal and fury. They had—she grasped for the words—they had trusted their killers to deliver them from their torment.

They had trusted that those who promised them freedom meant they would live to see it. Instead...instead...

Carin herself watched as the five living pairs placed their bloodied hands on the rune stone, and from the ground came a terrible roar that shook her teeth in her mouth and sounded like rending rocks. The people surrounding the stone were tossed to the earth, where they covered their heads with their arms, shying from the piled bodies beyond. Carin did not fall, nor did the ten with bloodied hands pressed to the stone's face. Again, she felt the pull toward the stone, as if it wanted her. She stumbled forward toward it, her hands outstretched, drawn to the stone and at once repulsed by its hunger.

The stone felt like Carin's trek-starved belly, and from it came the pull, a force that drew what it desired to it, sucking something from the land, through the land, through the blood that now marked it like a goatherd's brand.

Those with hands already pressed to the stone did not see her. The grasses around the stone began to wither, their blades turning inward as if they, too, felt the pull Carin did, and the color faded from their blades, draining them to the dullness of winter until they turned white and crumbled to dust. Still the stone ravened, awakened by the people's fury and need into a pure, famished draw that Carin felt to her bones.

The stone would never be sated, never full.

The ten people around the stone pulled away, and for a moment, just for a moment, Carin thought she saw a web of light jet out from the stone itself, barreling off to the west and to the east as if seeking something—what, she knew not.

The circle broken, the crowd moved to the south, and when Carin turned to follow, she saw the mountains that rose in the distance, high and impassive, and she knew what she saw. The far side of the mountains she now sat within.

Carin closed her eyes against the harsh light, and she saw it all again. The hunger. The thirst. The land itself desperate for sustenance. She knew why it died around her.

She beat her eyes with her hands, wanting the vision gone, but no matter where she looked or how tightly she scrunched her eyelids closed, it did not abate.

She felt the pull from the stone even now, and although she couldn't explain it, Carin saw the grasses around the stone continue to fade, to die, to turn to dust. The stone drained the life from the land itself.

She watched the crowd of people vanish into the mountains and knew where they went, where the power they had stolen was directed.

Her homeland. The Hearthland.

The people marched to the south, blood drying on their skin until it cracked away before it could be washed.

With them they took the life of the land, and that stolen soul followed them south to a place that would be called Haveranth, a place that would be fed life bought by far-off death.

Through the brightness around her, another name whispered through her.

Lysiu.

Carin fell to her knees.

L YAH STUMBLED into the darkness and tripped over Carin, who knelt almost prostrate just outside the cave. She landed hard on one knee next to her friend. The Quicken Moon shone down upon them, her sister at her side, full and plump and cheery.

The moonlight lit tracks of tears down Carin's face.

Lyah crawled to Carin and took her in her arms, and the two of them wept.

A scraping behind them brought Ryd from the cave, his eyes showing bright in the moonlight.

"What did we see?" Ryd asked, his voice hoarse and grating with pain. He sounded as if he were asking the question of the night.

The cool darkness was a balm on Lyah's eyes, and she hugged Carin tight to her chest, her fingers grasping the soft wool of Carin's cloak.

No one answered Ryd for a long time.

When finally Carin pulled away, leaving Lyah to sit in the grass while Carin slowly gathered twigs and tinder and built a fire, Lyah scooted close to the flames.

"Did Jenin say anything more to you?" Lyah looked at both Ryd and Carin, hoping for some clue as to how they felt. When neither of them answered, she rolled her next words around in her head, wondering if she wanted to give them voice.

"Sy told me our names were as much choice as they were discovery," she said finally.

Ryd's head snapped up, and Lyah thought she heard a whisper in her mind. *Ryhad.*

Her heart gave a thump, and her breath fought the bellows of her chest as she tried to inhale. Had she just heard his name? Motes danced in front of Lyah's eyes, like sparks in front of the fire. She looked at Carin, but saw nothing. Lyah had heard that last breath before the cave expelled her into the night, from brightness to the still darkness of the Hidden

Vale. She had heard the name *Lysiu* and felt it sink deep within her. But she knew even then as she watched her oldest friend and heard no whisper that Lysiu was not Lyah's own true name; Lyari was the name that came upon the tide of magic in the cave. Lyari was who Lyah would become when she returned to Haveranth as Merin's apprentice.

The thought struck her dumb. Merin knew all their names. Lyah was Merin's apprentice. She looked at Ryd and saw Ryhad there. She stared so long at his face that she didn't hear him speak.

"I'm sorry," Lyah said. She stood by the fire and brushed grass and dirt from her breeches. "What did you say?"

Ryd watched her closely. "I asked what you meant, about our names being choice."

Carin did not speak, but her eyes were just as intent, and the light of the fire danced against the deep sapphire blue of her irises.

"I don't know what sy meant," Lyah admitted.

She could still smell the stink of the gob of green the child had coughed onto the ground in the cave. It smelled of death, and from the depths of her memory of Merin's lessons, she drew forth a word. Illness. The child had *illness*. Something twisted inside hyr body that made hys lungs seize up and try to expel poison. Illness and hunger and thirst— that was what existed outside the Hearthland. What their ancestors had saved them from and cast a spell to ensure their safety for all the coming generations.

"What did we see?" This time Carin asked the question, and her words fell like shards of glass through the air, as shattered as a broken vase.

"We saw the history of our people," Lyah told her. "How we came to be here."

"Did you know this?" Carin drew a ragged breath and spat into the fire. Her saliva hissed and jumped on a rock, then burned away into nothing.

"No," said Lyah. One cycle of the moons past, if Carin had been angry or hurt, Lyah would have reached out and drawn her into the circle of her arms. They would have gone to the Bemin and hurled stones into its depth until their muscles ached and the upset was gone. They had done it a cycle past, when Dyava was on his Journeying and Carin's loneliness for the lack of his company had made her short tempered and uneasy. And now Dyava might be dead and it was their own Journeying. Moments before Lyah had held Carin close to her, felt her breathing in rhythm with her own. *Fyahiul.* They had shared their pillows and their hurts both for seventeen harvests. And now, the fire between them felt like they were instead standing on two mountaintops, leagues apart, their bodies cold and uncomforted.

Her mouth sour and dry, Lyah shook her head violently. "I didn't know any of this."

"I thought we were only coming here to find our names." Ryd sat with his legs pulled up to his chest, his arms tucked tightly beneath the crook of his knees.

"As did I," Lyah said.

"You're sure that is our history?" Carin's body was as still as the pond on Jenin's farm at first light. "Our ancestors did this thing?"

"This thing?"

"They starved the land to feed themselves. They starved *people.*"

Lyah started. Her fingers trembled at the question. "You saw the same as I did. They were treated like unruly goats. Worse. Beaten and abused. They found something that could save them from depending on harsh masters."

"By becoming those same masters?" Carin's shoulders shook now, and she licked her lips, the firelight glinting on the sheen left by her tongue. "By becoming worse than abusers and beaters? By..."

Carin's mouth moved as if her tongue tried to find the right words but could not.

"By becoming the sort who would end life to take for themselves," Carin said at last. "Taking what was not theirs. Taking and not sharing."

Ryd looked back and forth between the two of them, his mouth agape. "Carin," he said.

"Everything," she trailed off, and her lips drew together.

Lyah knew the gesture. She'd seen it countless times growing up. Carin would speak her mind no more, but keep her thoughts locked within her.

"I want to go home," Ryd said suddenly.

"Merin knows magic."

Again, Lyah felt surprise at Carin's words. She nodded mutely, feeling as though the bond between her and Carin had been sliced with one of Rina's blades still hot from the forge.

"Do you?" Carin plucked a pebble from the ground. "If I threw this in the air, could you stop it from landing?"

"No. I don't know." The words sounded hollow even to Lyah's ears, and her heart pounded the sides of her head like a stick against a drumskin. Over and over. Over and over. Over and over. She wasn't supposed to reveal what she was taught in her apprenticeship. Her eyes darted to Ryd, but he stared straight ahead, not looking at either of them anymore.

"But you know some magic." Carin pressed. "You know some."

"Some little, yes."

"You never told me."

There was a heaviness in the air like one of the neighboring mountains had decided to lean forward over them, and Lyah felt as though it were leaning specifically on her.

"I couldn't. Merin said—"

"Tell me what you know."

So fierce was the light in Carin's eyes that Lyah couldn't help but respond. She would rebuild the bridge across this sudden rift between them, and if it took sharing this knowledge, what little bit she knew, Lyah would do it or rot.

R YD HEARD the two girls speaking, but he could not bring himself to heed their words. His breath was a thin rushing in his chest, and his mind faltered on the knowledge that swam in his head, competing with everything he knew about his homeland.

He knew Carin was right, that their ancestors had done this thing, this terrible thing. He knew then that his home was built on the bones of children, whose flesh had shriveled with pain and hunger and that horrible seizing cough he could not explain.

But he knew it was his home.

Like Carin, Ryd had built himself a house on the outskirts of town. He'd been careful to pick a plot of land far from Stil the carpenter, whose bratty sprig of a child was often the instigator in the plans to knock Ryd to the ground and sit on him. While he was no halmer by far and no great worker like Carin, he had built a serviceable home. He liked to whittle. His trestle table had heaps of little figurines in the center. Squat and comfortable, with a wide central hearth and a hearthstone he had chosen himself from Haverford Quarry. He had chiseled his runes into it with his own hands, just as Carin had done for her own.

He could not atone for the transgressions of his ancestors; there was no way for him to reverse time and alter their course. Ryd al Malcam va Haveranth was who he was, and he would return home Ryhad va Haveranth, a man of his own making, ready to prove himself to the village and take his place three harvests hence.

Somehow, though, he could not stop his throat from swallowing, over and over.

Standing, he ignored the conversation between Carin and Lyah and walked some ways away into the vale. The pattering and splashing of the Hanging Falls filled his ears, and above him stars glittered in the rich black sky. Quicken Moon hung heavy above, and Ryd looked up to see the constellations that circled the singular hearthstar that even now pulsed with a pale green hue. The Tiger in Repose everyone knew, as they knew the Great Halm, which now seemed to rise out of the mountains on the horizon. Others Ryd had learned himself from Merin's scrolls and books. The Saiga that grazed upon a cluster of three small white stars. The Cookpot, small and faint but resting on two stars that had a reddish glow. And there, a handspan above the mountaintops to the north, the Nameless. Whether no one had named any stars between that figure and the others or whether none could make out shapes in his surroundings at all, Ryd did not know. But the Nameless stood silent and alone, far from the Saiga and the Tiger and the shelter of the Great Halm's branches.

Anyone to return from the Journeying without finding hys name would be exiled, like the Nameless figure in the sky. To stand alone over cold, jagged peaks and circle the hearthstar forever as if chasing after hys fellows.

Ryd had found his name. He was going home to claim it.

"TELL ME," Carin said again. Ryd had wandered away from the fire, and Carin felt the heat of the embers within her chest, each passing second of silence like a pump of the bellows.

Lyah's face showed a helplessness Carin had never seen before, but her words before, spoken with such certainty, had driven a wedge deep into Carin's heart. Across the fire, Lyah was both familiar and alien. Carin knew her messy braid, which even now came undone over one shoulder. She knew Lyah's hand shook like that when she was embarrassed or uncomfortable, and though a part of Carin's soul cried out in protest that *she* was the cause of that trembling, Carin could not shake the churning in her belly. It was like the day she'd eaten iceberries in the moon of Harvest when they were still pale on the vine. Carin's stomach had felt mushed, like potter Ahntin's clay when sy pushed hys hand into it. It felt like that now, looking at Lyah's face across the dancing flames.

Her oldest friend knew things she didn't, and those things were tied to a terrible past. Her people had taken lives, lives of people who *trusted them to lead them to freedom*, spilled them upon a rock, and with that power doomed an entire land to starvation and death. Carin wanted to cry, to flee the circle of harsh light into the safety of the surrounding dark, where her eyes could not see the faces of her friends. Did they not feel this thing? Did they not bear this weight?

Could Lyah have known?

Dyava knew.

The very thought made Carin's breath suck in to her lungs, sharp and harsh.

Dyava knew.

"Magic is energy," Lyah said after a long moment, ignoring the sound Carin's unconscious gasp had made. Her voice sounded wan and lost, but even in its weakness it made Carin focus her attention. "I don't know much; Merin told me she would teach me more when I returned from my Journeying."

"Tell me what you know." Carin met Lyah's eyes, knowing that the fierce yearning in her core would translate only as pleading. She had to know, to try and understand this thing. How her people had made the land do their bidding. "Please."

Lyah picked a blade of grass.

"Energy," Lyah said. "It makes us live, grows the grasses and trees, makes the fire burn." She let the grass fall to the ground. "It makes things fall. It's in the wind and the rushing of the rivers. The heat of the sun."

Picking up the grass again, she set it on her knee. Carin watched as Lyah added a pebble to her other knee.

"Imagine that the pebble is a seed. In that seed is the entire life of a living thing, a plant that will grow leaves, bear fruit, turn to seeds of its own, and someday die. It may grow to be chopped up and burned on our hearths. It may be eaten by a passing saiga or goat or clucker. We don't know what that seed will be, what it will nourish, what its life will accomplish. That is potential energy." Lyah moved her leg and both the blade of grass and the pebble fell to the ground. "Those things fell and made a change in the ground; their potential to do that was always within them."

Irritation rose in Carin. She had heard these things on the village green, but not about magic, simply about life and the nature of things. "That isn't magic. That's the mooncycle. From Renewal through Reflection, by means of Bide and Toil, Harvest and Foresight, and all those between."

"It is magic," Lyah insisted. "It is the hearthstone upon which the fire of magic burns."

Carin had been ready to object, but Lyah's words stopped her. "Then how does one kindle that fire?"

Lyah raised her hands, but not in a gesture of one about to perform a deed. She simply held them up and gestured outward before folding them in her lap. "I don't know."

"You do."

"I know the theory, that is all."

"Then tell me the theory." Carin pushed.

With a sigh, Lyah looked around as if she were expecting Merin to step out of the cave behind them and yank her by the ear to drag her away for a scolding.

"There are five branches of magic. Life, *var.* That is the blood in your veins and the bud opening to the sun. It's the trout flopping on the bank."

Carin felt a ghost of a smile try to touch her lips before fading away. Trust that Lyah would mention fish. She waited expectantly.

"Will, *ryh.* It is your determination and your mind. The intention that shapes the blades in your mother's forge. The way you bend a wood to form the shape of your choosing. Grounding, *pey.* This is the force that pulls the leaf to the ground instead of allowing it to float like a mote of dust in a beam of sunlight. It is what holds you together. Potential, *dyupahsy.* How the seed becomes something new throughout its life. How a child grows to build a bridge or a boat. How this pebble can dent the dirt."

Lyah recited all these things with the air of one who had learned them from a scroll. Carin thought that it was likely Merin's explanations too had found their way into Lyah's speech.

"You said there were five. That is four. What is the last?"

"Energy itself. *Abas.* The lightning or the river that turns the millstones. The wind in the grasses. The fire that warms you." Lyah stretched her legs out in front of her, looking over her shoulder for Ryd, who had not yet returned.

"You've given me five bricks but no mortar," Carin said.

"The mortar is what I don't yet understand. Merin said magic requires a catalyst and that it is different for everyone. The salt that makes the water come to a faster boil. Something to change the person who means to use it."

Carin thought of her ancestors and how their backs bent beneath the coils of leather that licked at them, leaving broken flesh and harsh red lines across the brown of their skin. Could that be such a catalyst? "Can you do it?"

"No." Lyah watched Carin as if she expected her to react in disbelief.

Carin pitied her in that moment, and guilt chewed at her belly. She repeated the words Lyah had spoken in her head, determined to remember them. *Var, ryh, pey, dyupahsy, abas.* And the catalyst that would make them spark.

"How does it work?"

Lyah shrugged, her eyes helpless. "Merin said one day I would know, that those strands could be woven together or drawn upon separately. She said it's like wiggling your ears; once you can do it, you always know how."

Though Lyah had answered her questions—and Carin knew the answers had cost them more closeness, driven them apart all the more— there were so many things left unsaid. How their ancestors had known what to do, why the blood on their hands had made their magic work, how they convinced a stone to suck life from the earth that made it.

L YAH DID not turn back as they crested the hill to leave the Hidden Vale behind. She did not turn to look once more on the glittering beauty of the Hanging Falls in sunlight, nor did she search out the herd of ihstal they had seen grazing in the far meadow as they retraced their path to the slow climb into the Mistaken Pass.

No one spoke as they climbed, and the grass gave way to packed earth and then gravelly rocks. The air grew cooler, and then cold. Lyah pulled her cloak tighter around her body.

As they stepped into the pass, a scream sounded high above. Ryd looked up at the hawk Lyah knew had returned, but Carin and Lyah simply exchanged a glance. Lyah knew Carin was thinking of the talk they had the night before. What magic could send a hawk to follow them, and what had stopped it from entering the vale?

Lyah resolved to ask Merin when she returned, grateful that her apprenticeship could soon begin in earnest. She looked to her right and started, stifling a cry. Jenin walked beside her.

"Lyari," sy said, and that time Lyah did cry out. When Carin and Ryd turned to look, they met her eyes with only concern. Neither seemed to see Jenin at Lyah's side.

"I hit my foot on a rock," Lyah said, the lie springing from her lips. They turned back to the path, and she slowed, bending to touch her foot before continuing up the path.

Jenin was still there, hys wounded neck garish in the morning sun. She looked at hyr, her eyes questioning how sy could know her name.

"You learn much when you're dead," sy said.

For an entire league, sy did not speak again. Yet sy remained at her side, keeping pace with Lyah's strides.

When sy opened hys mouth just as the air began to grow misty with the approach to the cloud line on the mountain, Lyah feared what sy might say next.

"You have a choice." Jenin looked straight ahead. "You have a choice when you return. You have a choice now."

What choice? Lyah wanted to ask.

"You know the answer."

Lyah turned to ask, to risk voicing a question with the others not far ahead, but her lover's specter had already disappeared into the mist.

• • • • •

Though the clouds camped upon their heads as they walked, first up to the zenith of the Mistaken Pass, then down as they had come days before, Lyah felt the waning of the Quicken Moon give way to that breath of dark silence that preceded the birth of Bide. The days passed with footsteps and hungry bellies, with clothing made damp and clammy from the continual mist around them.

She could not see the turning of the moon, but she felt it inside her just as she felt the joints in her body when she moved.

Six turns now. Six short turns of five days each. Thirty days before High Lights.

Three days later, a pika ran beside them on the stones of the pass, chittering loudly enough for the chirps and squeaks to echo throughout the mountains. For an entire league it followed, each sound from its throat as harsh in Lyah's ears as the hawk's cry above their heads. A small animal with grey-brown fur and black eyes like onyx, it scurried from rock to rock, chastising the Journeyers as it went.

When it settled on a rock just ahead of her, chattering and making a sound like the creaking of Old Wend's rocking chair on gravel, Lyah pulled her spear from across her back and threw it.

It flew past Ryd's shoulder, and he leaped to the side with a yell, but the spear hit its mark with a spray of blood.

Carin watched as Lyah retrieved her weapon and cleaned it. Lyah worked, silently and immune to the eyes upon her. The pika's tiny body had little meat, and what there was had been pulverized by the impact of the spearpoint.

"Why did you kill it?" Ryd asked. "It was following us."

"We killed pikas before, on the way here," Carin said, but Lyah felt that the defense was hollow and that Carin knew it. Carin looked off into the distance, and she swallowed, tight-lipped.

"Yes, but—" Ryd frowned. He opened his mouth, but shut it again.

"We need food," Lyah said.

She felt shame fill her, milk poured into a full cup. The creature had bothered her, its noises grating upon her ears. But once skinned and cooked, it would barely fill their mouths twice over, let alone their stomachs. They had two haunches of rabbit left that Carin had hunted in the early morning the day before. Lyah wanted to apologize, though what good it would do, she didn't know.

Carin took the corpse of the pika from Lyah's hands.

Lyah didn't watch as Carin skinned it.

That night Jenin appeared again, this time by Lyah's side as she sat watch.

The clouds had thinned, and above them the sliver of Bide made a faint glow through the misty veil. Lyah watched as it climbed higher into the sky, this glow, trying to make out the smudge of light that was the moon's sister. She could not, and still Jenin did not speak.

"I had to," she said quietly, more to herself than to the form of her dead lover by her side.

Sy didn't answer.

"Will you not speak to me tonight?" Lyah pitched her voice low, watching the huddled forms of Carin and Ryd in their cloaks for any sign of movement.

Jenin said nothing. Hys hair had straw in it; Lyah hadn't noticed before. She moved over to hyr and reached out, wondering if her hands would connect with hys body or if they would encounter only empty air. She didn't get a chance to find out.

Jenin held up hys hands to tell her to stop. "You want to ask me something."

Lyah froze, her hands in midair halfway to hys head. She knew sy didn't mean the question of Dyava's fate. Because Dyava was still alive or because it mattered not whether he breathed or not?

"You wanted to know it in the cave." Hys face had the same stubble that had caught on the fabric of Lyah's leggings as they lounged by the Bemin the day before the Journeying.

The question did not want to form in Lyah's mouth. She made it, telling herself that if she faltered, she may never again have the chance to ask. "You know my name. Do you then know yours?"

Jenin smiled sadly, hys hand going to hys throat where hys fingers brushed the length of the slit.

"Names such as these must be found," sy told her, "and I never had the chance to look."

"Merin knows." Lyah felt hope bloom with the knowledge, that Merin would tell her Jenin's name.

Jenin didn't respond to that, but instead stood. "Sometimes I think I hear it, but it's like believing I understand the way the leaves speak to the breeze."

And with that, sy was gone.

WHEN LYAH saw Kinnock's Rise before them, free of any haunting mist tendrils—her arm still throbbed, unhealed—she wanted to sob with relief. Neither Carin nor Ryd had spoken in two days, and the sight of the familiar landmark meant they were only a short distance from Haveranth.

She pressed ahead of the others when the cajit orchards came into view, her legs burning but her body continuing to stumble forward. The nearly full Toil Moon shone overhead, plump and burning orange in the twilight even as the lamplights of Haveranth appeared in the distance. High Lights was two days hence, if the moon was indication, and Lyah saw the fires of home as darkness fell. Soon she did not hear the footsteps of Carin and Ryd behind her, only felt drawn by the crackling hearths of her village and the knowledge that home was close.

Lyah broke into a run when she passed Jenin's family's farm, the emptiness of grief pushing back against the relief of being almost past the trials of the Journeying. She did not see Tarwyn or Silan or Dyava there, no one. Lyah ran faster than she thought she could, her legs numb but churning against the packed earth of the road. Pounding footsteps beside her made her turn to see Carin there, keeping pace, her face knowing and grim. Once she looked over, toward the roundhome where Jenin and Dyava had grown up. For the first time since stumbling out of the cave in the Hidden Vale, Lyah felt the old connection to her friend, and tears stung her eyes in gratitude.

Old Wend was packing up his stall for the evening, a leather skin of iceberry wine held to his lips when Lyah crossed the invisible line into Haveranth's hearth-home. A gaggle of folk clustered under the shelter around the fire, and they all gave Lyah and the others only a passing glance before returning to their conversations.

Lyah wanted to scream at them, to fall to her knees, to grab a cup of icemint tea and drink until she was sated. Instead, she slowed to a walk.

Her legs felt like the jelly that remained on the bottom of a roasting pan after the meat had sat overnight in a dugout cellar. She felt Carin's hand creep into hers and give it a squeeze, and Lyah swallowed around the dryness in her throat.

They would be okay. They were home. They were almost there.

Hand in hand, the three walked Haver's Road, past Rina's smithy and her own family's home. After the three moons they had spent walking, this final distance felt like being asked to walk to the sea.

Outside Merin's home, dual torches burned to light the way with a deep emerald glow. Whether magic or the fuel Merin kept for only this occasion, Lyah didn't know. Her whole life, Lyah had seen those torches lit on the first day of Toil, and they would burn thus until High Lights when the entire village would be lit by torches. At noon on High Lights, the green of the flames would turn bright white, and thus they would remain until daybreak on the following morning.

Now, with Ryd and Carin at her sides, Lyah pushed herself to climb the shallow grade up the small hill to Merin's door. The evening's dark had dissipated some of the day's heat, but between the green torches, Lyah's skin dripped sweat. Her hands were clammy where they held tight to Ryd's and Carin's, and she dropped their hands to knock.

Merin pulled open the door, relief palpable in the air between them like a cool breeze.

Her hearth was cold behind her, but lamps burned bright on the rounded walls of her central room, filling her home with dancing shadows.

"Merin." Lyah said with a gasp, and she fell into the old woman's arms.

Merin pulled her close, her muscles tight and strong. The many harvests of Merin's life had made her hardy, but her work as Namekeeper and soothsayer had made her kind. Lyah couldn't tell if it was sweat or tears running down her cheeks, and she didn't heed either.

When Merin pulled back after a long moment, she looked over the other two, then out onto the path behind them. Her lips moved as she murmured something Lyah couldn't hear, and she beckoned at the three of them to come into the house.

Three cups of conu juice sat on the trestle table, and three plates of roasted goat with fragrant amaranth and braised plums and apples to the side.

"Sit, children; sit and eat."

They fell upon the food, and Lyah ate with her fingers, her fork to the side of her earthenware trencher plate, forgotten. Plums burst in her mouth, flooding it with sweetness and a hint of curry and brown sugar. The goat was tender and full of fat, and Lyah paid no attention to the dribbles of grease that escaped her lips, caring only for the growing sensation of fullness in her belly, which stretched taut and round as she plied it with hearty food for the first time in moons. The conu juice had a tinge of cinnamon and clove, and Lyah finished her cup before her plate was half empty.

The amaranth she pulled from the glazed dish with sticky fingers, licking them clean and wiping her mouth with the back of her hand. There was nothing but the meal in front of her. When Merin brought a vessel of cool well water to the table and filled their cups anew, Lyah cared not for the melding of water with the dregs of conu sediment, only took deep pulls from the water. It tasted not of minerals and stone, like drinking from the falls in Haver's Glen. It tasted not of leather from her waterskin. Only the sweet, cold delight of home. She nearly laughed, but then Merin brought a plate of sweet summer berries, of preserved iceberries and red drop berries, tiny round beadberries that stained her fingers and tongue deep purple.

She ate until her stomach protruded, full and round and sated. Lyah had never had such a meal in her life.

Still she wanted more, but Merin shook her head. "You may not keep even that down," the soothsayer said, but she did bring more water, filling their cups to the brim.

The room was naught but a golden haze of aromas and flickering lamplight, and Lyah leaned forward on her elbows on the trestle table, blinking eyelids that threatened to stay closed each time.

She didn't realize she had drifted off until Merin's hand on her shoulder gave her a shake.

"Come, child."

Lyah looked up to see that Carin and Ryd were gone, and that two of the doors to rooms off the central hearth-chamber had been closed.

The muscles in Lyah's legs shrieked as she stood, her joints cracking like dry autumn boughs. She followed Merin to a third room, a room she had slept in before after a long night of lessons, and there the feather mattress greeted her and welcomed her to the darkness of sleep.

RYD WOKE to the sense of sinking. He jerked upright in bed, swimming in the depths of the feather mattress that seemed like it was trying to swallow him whole. His belly ached and cramped from too much food, and his mouth tasted of sour berries and cinnamon. Pushing himself to sitting, he braced himself with both hands. The bed was soft, too soft, and days before Ryd would have given his last strip of leathery smoked rabbit for a soft bed that had neither roots nor stones to gouge him. Today though, he couldn't make himself fall back asleep.

Finally, he swung his legs over the side of the bed and stood on aching feet. Still fully clothed, he found a basin of cool water on a table across from the bed and splashed his face. A folded bavel cloth and a larger towel sat beside the basin, along with a square of goat milk and honey soap and a jug of fresh water. Ryd stripped off his clothing—his leggings sagged in the knees and their laces were frayed almost to the point of being scraps. The harsh exercise for three moons had whittled away all his fat and left only tight muscle behind. Ryd's whole body was different, harder. He washed himself with slow, measured movements, massaging the rock-hard muscles in his legs and arms that throbbed and ached. When his body was clean, he washed his hair in the basin twice and poured the entire jug of water over it to rinse it. Cleaner than he had been in the turns since they had last passed the Jewel on the way home from the Hidden

Vale, Ryd dried himself with the bavel towel and took a deep breath of the now sweetly scented air. His dirty clothing he folded neatly and tucked into his rucksack.

Merin had even laid out new things for him. A pair of loose breeches that Ryd recognized as being of Cantoranth make—they grew crops of a plant called vysa that bore long, fine fibers that could be tatted and woven like wool, and the breeches billowed out around his legs as he tied them at his waist. The tunic was the same fine material and the same pale green hue. He belted it at his waist with a leather strap, the buckle for which was stamped with Rina's mark. The soft fabric felt luxurious against his travel-hardened body, like kisses on his skin.

Home.

For the first time since they had crossed over the Bemin and laid eyes upon their home village, Ryd felt a glimmer of excitement rise up in his chest like bubbles in fermented cider. He was home. Tomorrow was High Lights. Tonight they would be welcomed back into Haveranth for the last evening with their old names, and at daybreak on the morrow, they would labor with their families under the demanding fullness of the Toil Moon, sharing the sky with the grueling sun. Their work would be the final burst of their old selves, until they could slough off that husk with the atonement ritual through the night. And when the sun rose the next day, they would greet their village newly named.

Ryd pushed aside the memories of what he had seen in the cave, of the whisper in his ears that was the last thing he heard before he fell out of that chasm and into the vale. *Lysiu*. He was home. He could not change the past, but he could build a future for himself.

He opened the shutters on his room and blinked into the harsh afternoon light. He had slept through the morning and almost to the evening. Storm clouds gathered in the distance, but they would not come over Haveranth, not from that direction. Knowing the natural way of things in his village filled Ryd with pride. This *was* his home. He knew his land and his people.

When he opened the door to his room and stepped into the hearth-chamber, Carin and Lyah already sat with Merin, each with a cup of icemint tea in her hand and each dressed just as he was in vysa breeches and tunic, belted with wide brown leather. Merin stood and poured a cup for Ryd, pressing it into his hand. She gestured for him to sit.

Ryd obeyed, and Merin handed him a bowl of fresh sweet dew melon, its flesh the same green as the clothes he wore. He ate it, marveling that even after stuffing his belly the night before, his stomach hungered and begged for more.

"Once you finish your meal and your tea, you may reenter the village," Merin told them. "You may visit your families and friends. Tonight you must return to sleep here, and with the dawn you will toil with all of us. You now understand why we do so at High Lights, do you not?"

Lyah's eyes darkened, and Carin suddenly became preoccupied with her tea.

"To remember those to the north who toil daily to survive," Lyah said finally.

Merin nodded, a gleam of relief and pride in her eyes. Carin nodded, though Ryd felt sick to his stomach. The dew melon tasted less sweet with his next bite, but he forced himself to chew and swallow the rest of what his bowl held. He thought of the folk on the beach dividing up scrawny fish, and suddenly he didn't want to eat anymore.

Ryd was the last to leave Merin's house, hanging back for nearly an hour after the two strode out Merin's door. Merin sat quietly on her maha stool, watching the sunset. Part of him wanted to hang back, to not venture out into the village until he could do so with his true name. But after a time Merin coughed pointedly and nodded at the door, and Ryd felt he had no choice.

Torches lit Haver's Road into the village, and though Ryd's muscles still ached and burned from exhaustion, he made himself follow the road to the village hearth-home. Between the branches of the roads that made spokes out from the village hearth were crescents of green, and it was there Ryd sat, looking into the south where his family home was. He thought of his parents, his mother who grew the best yams in Haveranth and who could have some cooking on their outdoor hearth, buried in oak chips that would give them a smoky flavor. Ryd thought back to the last meal he had had at home before the Journeying, those yams topped with goat yogurt and coriander and the yellow salt from the small mine near Haverford Quarry at the source of the Cantor River.

Something hit Ryd, sending him sprawling backward onto the grass. Weight landed on his stomach, and the dew melon he had just eaten almost came back up. Within moments Ryd found himself buried under squiggly children, their sweaty little bodies pushing him into the grass. One of them lay across his head, and their giggles muffled. He couldn't breathe. Ryd flailed his arms under the squirming onslaught, but the children just shrieked and scrambled to sit on his arm, too.

Rage boiled up inside of him, sending hot tendrils licking through him. His lungs felt charred from lack of air, and he threw his weight sideways as hard as he could. It loosed his head from the child—Old Wend's grandchild, Onan—and Ryd bellowed with his remaining breath, "GET OFF."

Only more gleeful giggles greeted him, and Ryd found purchase with one hand in the grasses and shoved himself sideways, trying to escape. They knew he hated this, knew it drove him past his patience. Still they persisted, and this on the eve of his naming.

It would never change, he realized.

Adult or not, named or not, Ryd would never escape the ignominy of these rotten children who took such pleasure in humiliating him in front of the entire village. He could hear a burst of laughter from the hearth-home behind him, and the sound of an adult sharing in the children's bullying gave his tired muscles one final burst of strength. Writhing out from under Stil's child—always Stil's child!—Ryd's palms connected with two children's shoulders and he shoved backward as hard as he could.

The two children went flying backward like a pebble launched from a slingshot. The weight of the other bodies quickly vanished, and they ran away, dragging their friends to their feet and vanishing into the twilit dark.

Ryd pushed himself to his feet, straightening the fine vysa clothing that had hung with such elegance from his new, strange body. Now they stuck to him, rumpled and grass stained, blue streaks on the fabric. He turned to see Stil himself sipping from a cup at the hearth-home, a smile dancing across Stil's face.

"Did you have something to say?" Ryd barked, his voice sharp edges like blades.

Stil's smile slipped. "They're only children," he said. His dark hair was streaked with silver over his brow, the only sign of his hundredth harvest past.

"And I am a man nearly grown and named! Keep yours away from me, Stil."

Before Stil could answer with anything more mortifying, Ryd stalked off to the north, in the opposite direction of his parents' home. He didn't know where he was going, but he did know he would venture nowhere that would remind him he had a day left where he would be considered a child.

Behind him, Ryd heard a snort and a chuckle from Stil.

A dark, angry part of Ryd's mind hissed that he would never escape the path that had been chosen for him by that gaggle of sticky children.

CARIN MET her mother at the door of her new home, after being pointed that direction by Tamat at the village hearth-home. Rina held only a stone lamp that smelled of conu oil, and she embraced Carin after setting the lamp down on the windowsill of Carin's roundhome. A sturdy hand slapped Carin's back, and Carin's throat closed around the lump that rose. When Rina pulled away and opened the door without a word, Carin blinked back tears.

She was home, and this was her house, built by her hands. She ran her palm up the doorframe, expecting to feel the thrill of knowledge that she had made this thing. Instead, stepping inside, Carin felt a hollowness in her chest that she tried to push away like an unwanted embrace. It matched the un-lived in hollowness of the roundhome. Her mother led by lamplight and cupped her hand around a beeswax candle as she lit it from the lamp and placed it in a holder.

Carin halted just inside the door as light blossomed in her home.

Her mother's maha table stood to the right of Carin's hearth, polished to a deep red gleam in the golden light of the candle. Carin walked to it as if in a dream, trailing her fingers over the glossy wood, over the familiar runes. *Avar,* revive. *Olvar,* renewal. *Lahmlys,* hearthstone. *Sahla'amvar,* family.

Rina clasped Carin's shoulder. "I thought it belonged with you, in this place you made."

Carin turned and flung her arms around her mother's neck, burying her face in the blacksmith's shoulder. Hard muscles tensed with surprise, but after a moment, her mother pulled her into a tight hug.

"Thank you," Carin said.

"Bridges connect more than banks," said Rina in answer.

Carin took a breath and let it out, then met her mother's eyes. "Dyava," she said quietly. "Is he alive?"

Rina's mouth opened in surprise, then pulled Carin tighter again. "My dear child," she said. "Yes. He is alive. Have you gone all this time thinking he died with Jenin?"

Carin could not answer; she only clung to her mother's strong frame, shaking.

When Carin returned to Merin's that night, she settled into the feather mattress and heard Ryd snoring in the next room over. She thought of her new home and the work she had done for the entire cycle before the Journeying, and something didn't sit right with her mind.

She lay awake in bed as the last dim slit of light from Toil Moon crept in beneath a gap in the shutter. The hours passed in the night, and Carin, naked in the heat of the room except for her underclothes, bare breasted and perspiring, finally understood that it wasn't physical discomfort that was keeping her awake.

The home she had built and the life she hoped for in Haveranth had been built on something that didn't exist. The foundation of kindness and bounty that had brought her up through the eve of her adulthood had been dug into sand and secured with rotting boards and blood.

When she closed her eyes, she saw people, people she had never known and would never know, but whose suffering she ate at each plentiful meal and drank with each sip from a full, clean well.

Worse, every adult she had ever known knowingly added more rot to the pile, all the while smiling at the children and proclaiming things fine. Her mother.

Dyava.

Her love lived, but he had stayed knowing what every adult in Haveranth and the whole of the Hearthland knew.

She wanted to go to him, wanted to climb through his window the way she had done before, curl up beside him in his bed and cry with him over the lies they had been fed with their first milk.

But if she did, would he weep with her, or would he look at her with sad eyes and say only what Lyah seemed to believe?

She could not bear hearing him justify it. She couldn't stomach the thought of hearing Dyava—her Dyava—explain how he could wake each morning and feed the lies to new children. To his own cousin, Clar. As he had done to Jenin for the past cycle. Carin's chest felt so tight and heavy that she thought someone could have dropped the roof on her and it would have made no discernable difference.

Carin thought of Rina's hard, tight hug. The table she had left in Carin's new roundhome. Everything here circled toward High Lights as it ever had, but this year Carin felt herself on the outward spiral, as if she might be flung into the currents instead of drawn into the deep comfort of home.

First light came too soon.

Merin knocked on the door just as the grey slit of light beneath the shutter began to return, this time from the coming sun and not from the full and rising moon on its arc over her head.

Carin rose and dressed, as all Hearthlanders would that day, in naught but a loincloth. She broke her fast on only water, clean and cold.

As the first rays of the sun touched the earth with hot, greedy fingers, Carin and the townsfolk of Haveranth went to work. Carin walked alongside Clar el Novah va Haveranth herself, Dyava's cousin—and Jenin's—and together they lit torches in front of every home. She saw Ryd as they went, carrying wood to stoke fires on hearths. On this day, the day where the sun ruled the sky for longer than any other, all lamps and fires, all torches and braziers would blaze while the villagers toiled.

On High Lights, every villager labored under the sun, brown bodies glistening with perspiration and swaying with thirst. Carin found her place in one of Tarwyn and Silan's fields, tilling the soil with a spade. By midday, she wore dirt from feet to waist. The sun beat down, unrelenting on the people of Haveranth. Not a cloud threatened its dominance; not a breeze stirred its heat. Even though she worked in his parents' fields, though, Carin could catch no glimpse of Dyava. Her stomach grew sourer with each handspan the sun sank toward the horizon.

When sunset finally came, the entire village of Haveranth met at their hearth-home in the village center, where the elders passed out cups of water. Carin took hers and drank deeply until a thought choked her. To pay tribute to those her people drained of life, they worked all day for one day and still were handed cups of clean water at its end. The liquid sloshed in her empty stomach, and Carin stumbled, catching herself on one of the poles of the hearth-home's circular pavilion. The children approaching their fifteenth harvests brought forth metal bins of ashes from the fires that had burned all day in Haveranth's houses. Carin filled her cup with ashes when a child came by her, and stood for a moment in the organized chaos while the rest of the villagers gathered their cups of ashes.

"I have wronged you," a voice said from behind her. Carin's heart leapt until her ears heard who had spoken.

Lyah stood there, her body bare except the simple cloth that clung to her skin at her hips. "I hoarded my knowledge and climbed upon it, using it to look down on those around me, including you. We have been fyahiul since swaddling clothes, and in my arrogance I betrayed you."

Carin stared at her, pain digging between her ribs. "I forgive you," she said, dipping her fingers in her cup of ashes and drawing them down Lyah's chest between her breasts. Over the heart, to show she meant the words. "And I have wronged you in my silence. I have shunned you when I should have been your comfort."

Carin jumped when Lyah's fingers touched the skin over her own heart, the ash leaving black streaks in the sweat Carin still wore from the day.

The darkness fell, cooling the village after the heat of the day. All torches were extinguished, all lamps snuffed out. It was a balm on Carin's sun-brittle skin, and she moved through the crowd of townsfolk, sifting through her memories of the past cycle. Before her Journeying, she had known a list of those she needed to ask for atonement, but now her mind could not recall what slights had seemed important. Stiltedly, she apologized to Old Wend for dropping a hammer on his stall while he worked and scattering his nails all over the ground. She asked forgiveness from Tamat for saying that her curried goat tasted more like curried dung one day. Carin went throughout the crowd, her body itching with the ashes that soon decorated her skin, asking for atonement from some, offering it to others, her fingers dipping into her cup of ashes until it was nearly empty.

But through the night, through the gritty smear of ash-covered fingers on her sweat-drenched body, Carin saw other faces superimposed upon the faces of those she had known her entire life. Who were the people they truly needed to beg for forgiveness? Her skin itched with the burn of the sun and the lye that sank into her.

It wasn't until nearly moonset when she saw him.

Dyava stood at the very edge of the village hearth-home, his body smeared with ash even as hers was. Carin walked toward him on unsteady legs. When she reached him, his hands took hers, fingers clasping each of their held ash cups between them on either side.

"Jenin—" Carin got out, but Dyava's eyes darkened and he shook his head.

"Your mother told me what you told her last night," Dyava said.

Carin went still. "Merin made us leave so quickly, all we heard was that Jenin had been murdered, and you always worked with hyr in the mornings—"

"I know." Dyava took Carin's cup from her and placed it on a stone ledge. "But it was the morning of the Journeying. Jenin was simply gathering what sy needed to leave. I wasn't even on our farm."

"Why?"

Dyava gave Carin a wry look. "I couldn't bear to see you go and have to pretend not to see you at all."

Carin's throat tightened. She thought of her roundhome, of Dyava bringing her food as she built it. Part of her cried out that he had known; everything that so repulsed her in the cave, Dyava had known. And yet he was here, nearly an adult in full in the eyes of the village. He had returned the previous cycle with no seeming conflict.

"I've missed you," Carin said, and then she was in his arms, the ash from both of their bodies mingling, and she pushed all other thoughts out of her mind.

When Toil Moon sank beneath the horizon at last, leaving only the stars to light the village, they broke their fast with cold mutton and smoked fish. Again Carin thought of those to the north, and she could not eat. All her life High Lights had been a hard day, a day of work and an aching back, but never had she understood what it was supposed to be. Now that she did, it fell far short.

Dyava left her in the dark hours of the night as all the others in the hearth-home made their ways home, and Carin stayed, perched on the ledge with her ash cup in her hands.

Villagers were meant to return home and spend the night in contemplation, but instead Carin found herself at Merin's doorstep, her hand knocking on the door before she could stop it.

R YD STARTED when he heard the knock at Merin's door, and he blinked with surprise when Carin entered, her body covered from neck to hips in smeared gritty ash and from hips to toes in soil and bits of grass. Merin made no remark about the grains of lye and dirt that sloughed from Carin's near-naked body, only handed Carin a cup of water and motioned her to sit on the bench next to Ryd.

Only the light of the Toil Moon through the open windows lit the room, and the light was grey and pale, turning the ash on their bodies black.

"You have made it through your Journeying," Merin said to them both.

Ryd nodded, looking at Carin, but she only took one sip of water from her cup, grimaced, and set it on the table. He didn't hear Lyah enter, but a moment later a scrape of the other table bench made him turn. All three, then. He supposed it wasn't a coincidence that all three felt out of place after returning from the Journeying, but of the three, he was most surprised to see Lyah.

"You're troubled," said Merin.

Lyah licked her lips, then spit out a piece of grit into the palm of her hand and wiped it on her loincloth. "These ashes burn."

It was clear she meant something more than simply the ashes, which all three had worn for twelve harvests at High Lights, ever since their fifth harvests. The ashes were not the problem; they were not what burned. Ryd felt bitter tears behind his eyes and blinked them back before they could fall and turn the ash on his cheeks to even more of a sting. Lyah had returned to an apprenticeship with Merin. She would be the next soothsayer of Haveranth. Carin had her home—as Ryd had his—and a successful hand at woodsmithing to start her trade in the village. Ryd could grow conu or apples if he wished, but every day he would have to face the children who sat on him and made him a fool in front of everyone he knew.

"You understand now why we celebrate High Lights," Merin said then. "We know our bounty comes from without our lands. We toil because we need to atone for the wrongs of our forebears."

None of the three responded.

"Every adult in the village knows this," Lyah said suddenly. "Our whole lives, our parents and mentors have all known."

"What then is the point of the Journeying to find our names?" Ryd asked. "If you know our names and everyone could simply tell us of this thing, why make us trek through the wilderness for three moons to see for ourselves?"

Merin had acknowledged Lyah's statement with a slight nod of her head, and now she turned to Ryd. "We wait until your naming day and your seventeenth harvest because we want your childhoods to be free of these burdens. While I know your names," she started but paused, and behind her eyes, Ryd could hear a whisper like the one he had heard in the cave, of *Ryhad,* "they are not mine to bestow, but for you to find. The cave was enchanted by our forebears to also reveal our history; your names you would find on the Journeying otherwise, even without the cave. Had we told you simply to leave the village for three moons and spend that time in contemplation in the foothills of the Mad Mountains, you would still have returned with your names. Your names are yours to have and keep, and you would find them no matter what the task we gave you said."

Carin opened her mouth, but did not speak for a long moment. "Then the Nameless fail somehow, or there would be no Nameless."

"Believe me, child, there are Nameless." Merin's eyes grew flinty in the moonlight. "You three ought to get some rest. The sun will be here soon."

Lyah slid off the bench behind Ryd, and Carin followed after a beat. They were meant to spend the night in contemplation, but the last thing Ryd wanted was to be alone with his thoughts. He left Merin's round-home and wandered through the surrounding fields, noting the progress of the growth of bavel or the way the moon illuminated the puffs of white on the bavel's stalks, painting them silver. He thought of the soil he'd tilled through the day, the weeds he'd pulled, the stones he'd piled to the side for use building walls or cobbling a path. He thought of anything he could rather than dwell on the Journeying or High Lights, and too soon the sun drained the darkness from the sky.

Ryd made his way to the river, slow steps taking him a different path than he had taken ever before. Only Carin was there already, though Ryd could see the crowd of villagers beginning the walk to the banks of the Bemin. Carin sat, knees pulled to her chest. She looked up when his foot broke a twig on the path, her eyes assessing his arrival.

"Today's the day," she said. "Last night. You saw Dyava?"

All Ryd could do was nod.

They came in twos and threes from the village, all the folk of Haveranth in their loincloths and ashes, caked in the grime of the previous day's work. Spreading out along the shallow shore of the Bemin River, no one spoke as the sun continued to make its journey toward the horizon. When a few scattered clouds turned gold with the coming dawn, Ryd saw Lyah off by herself, her lips moving silently. She froze when she saw him, then looked away.

The sun rose on the villagers, its butter-yellow rays lighting the filth on their bodies.

Before, Ryd had always felt purified when this moment came. When the sun exposed their wrongs forgiven. Before he might have looked at old Ramih, the leatherworker who wore only a few smudges across her shoulders, with some distrust, as the lack of markings on her body indicated that she had asked forgiveness of few people and thus felt she wronged few. Those who had nothing to show this day after High Lights were often those with the most to hide.

Ryd, with his body cloaked in ashes—and his fingers still caked with them beneath his fingernails from smearing them on the shoulders of the children who had asked his forgiveness for sitting on him—faced the rising sun with a sinking feeling of unease.

A murmur went through the crowd as the sun finally crested the eastern hills, and with no other needed signal, the people of Haveranth waded into the Bemin to wash themselves clean of the wrongs of the seasons.

The water felt cold on his body, and Ryd stripped his loincloth, tossing it onto the bank. His skin rippled into gooseflesh as he sank into the Bemin, and swirls of grey colored the deep blue-green water, making it cloudy where it once had been clear. He washed himself carefully, scrubbing the grit between his palms and his torso, ducking his head under to let the current toss the dried sweat from his hair. He came up sputtering and cold into the warm morning air, and stood, watching the sun dapple the water with sparkles.

He used to feel clean after this.

Instead, Ryd stood downstream in the water, watching those farther upstream wash. The water flowing past him grew murky, and Ryd shifted his shoulders, unable to escape the sense of being steeped in the wrongs of others.

He stepped out of the river, not sure he'd ever feel truly clean again.

CARIN DRIED herself with a bavel towel, her hands shaking from something she could not describe. Her roundhome was quiet, its walls holding no memories but those of her hands forming them, its hearth cold and not yet lit. Her clothing lay in stacks across her bedroom table, ready to be placed into her wardrobe's shelves. Her rucksack and bow sat at the foot of her bed, and mechanically, Carin pulled everything out, her towel wrapped around her body. Someone—likely her mother—had unstrung her bow, as if to say that she would not need it. That her journey was over, and she was home, and it would wait for her until she had need of it for hunting.

Merin had said that everyone found their names. Everyone. That your name was yours, and it would find you if you looked for it.

She remembered something Lyah had said, something Jenin had told her. That finding one's name was as much about choice as it was fate.

Believe me, child, there are Nameless.

Merin's words rang through her, and she hugged the towel closer around her body.

They kept this from the children to keep them free of the burden, Merin had said. But could that be the whole of it? Carin had never believed that Merin would lie. Yet her words left Carin hollow and cold and certain that the true reason the Hearthlanders were kept ignorant for seventeen harvests was because by then, they would be full members of the village, for all ceremony dictated that didn't officially happen until they reached their twentieth harvest. By seventeen, it was already set. Accepted and loved, bound to their fellows with bonds of friendship and shared life.

Bound so close that the thought of leaving would feel akin to cutting off a leg to rid oneself of a knee with a scrape. Her mother. Lyah. Ryd. Dyava.

The thought sent a new shudder through Carin's body, and her stomach churned. The food she had eaten since returning had made her ill. It felt as if it had been steeped in blood.

And even then they were not to be full adults. Suddenly the remaining seasons between harvests seventeen and twenty made sense. Those intervening cycles made sure the returning Journeyers could stomach the secrets.

Believe me, child, there are Nameless.

Carin thought over the Journeying. All the sense of being watched, the hawk that tracked their movements and vanished once they left Haver's Glen. What if the Nameless were those who simply veered from the path? Keep to the west side of the Bemin, they'd been told. And they had. They had found their names and more in that cave.

A tremor racked Carin's body, and she dressed herself in a new set of vysa breeches and a tunic, this time the pale blue of the sky just before dawn. Those approaching their fifteenth cycle would be preparing a feast to break their fast. Soft boiled pheasant eggs, yam hash with spiced mutton, redberries with goat's cream and drizzled with rilius syrup. They would be giddy, sure of themselves, ready to proclaim to the village who they were for the first time, if they were woman, man, or hyrsin. They would be excited to begin the cycles of study and duties that lead to and through their Journeying, the second half of which Carin should have been preparing for just then. The younger children would prepare the feast for the returning Journeyers, taking care to make the meal rich and sumptuous, to help them regain their strength.

And Carin could not stomach the thought of it.

She left her bedroom for the central chamber of her roundhome, walking toward the kitchen, where herbs hung from hooks over the worktable. A basket sat on the table itself, and in it Carin found parcels wrapped in waxed canvas. Smoked climber fish, its pink flesh almost orange against the canvas. It smelled of honey and hickory. In another a side of mutton. At the bottom of the basket were covered bowls, one containing slices of honeycomb and the other goat curds. Under the table was a corked pair of carafes, goat milk and conu juice.

Her mother had left her food, stocked her larder with some basics.

Carin picked up a goat curd and squeezed it between her thumb and forefinger, watching the whey seep out. No matter that it was a different color, to Carin it looked like blood. This food, this home, this village—all were built on the backs of those who would never offer forgiveness and smear ashes over villager hearts.

A small parcel caught her eye, and Carin unwrapped it. Pockets of curried mutton, the outer crusts brushed with clucker egg and a crisp golden brown. She held the pockets in both hands. She knew Dyava's cooking as well as she knew her mother's.

Her heart beating out a quick rhythm in her chest, Carin carefully covered all of the foodstuffs in the waxed canvas, looking back and forth between the basket and her room, her heart worrying at her ribs like a school of fish at a bit of bait.

She couldn't stay. She couldn't live knowing the prosperity of her people came at so high a cost.

There are Nameless.

Carin thought back to all the tales she had heard as a child, of those who left on the Journeying and returned without their names. Now she knew differently; they had returned, and found the cost of doing so too much to bear.

She picked up the basket and tucked a few bundles of herbs into it and wedged the carafe of conu juice into the corner. In her room, she pushed clothes into her rucksack, followed by wooden bowls and a tinder bag she had put away in her room back when she finished building the roundhome.

Her chest hurt as if the tongs of her mother's forge had squeezed it. Her home. Her mother. Her everything.

All of it a lie.

If she did what she planned, she would never be able to return. She would cut every tie. She would be alone.

A knock sounded at her door.

Carin froze, one hand on her full quiver of halm arrows. She willed her face into a mask of impassivity.

"Come in," she called.

It was Lyah who poked her head in the door, her hair still damp from the river and uncombed. She came in and looked around, nodding with satisfaction. "You did well with this, fyahiul," she said. "But it's too far from my own home. How am I to crawl through your window at night?"

Carin started to say that Lyah could use the door now, but her tongue stuck on the words, and they piled up behind her teeth.

"I brought you something," Lyah said quietly, not noticing the struggle going on in Carin's face. She held out a scroll, rolled tight and secured with a leather thong.

"What is it?"

"It's all I could find in Merin's study about magic. It won't help you learn how to do it without a catalyst, but it's a few bits of history and everything I told you around the fire in the Hidden Vale and a little bit more. About how our people came to be here. I don't want to keep things from you again." Lyah tucked the scroll into Carin's hand, closing Carin's fingers around it.

The parchment was rough against her fingers, and the feel of it was like death.

"Thank you," Carin said. Her voice cracked on the words, and she didn't blink for fear the tears in her eyes would fall.

Lyah gave her a sympathetic look, then looked closer at Carin's face. "Are you okay?"

"I'm...very tired." That much, at least, was true.

"I will leave you to rest before the feast." Lyah put her arms about Carin's neck and kissed her cheek. "Soon we will be named, my friend."

As Lyah closed the door and the latch fell with the heavy clank of metal forged by Rina's hands, inside Carin something broke.

L EAVING CARIN'S roundhome left Lyah with a strange sense of wrongness. She made her way to the village hearth-home, where the children of near-fifteen—only two of them—covered tables with food for the feast. She saw Ryd standing by himself, leaning against a pillar of the pavilion. Walking over to him, Lyah clapped him on the shoulder before moving on to circle around the hearth at the center of the pavilion.

The sun had crested the roofs of Haveranth, and it shone down more gently than it had for High Lights. Village folk milled about, clean and exuberant, and Lyah wished she felt she could join them in their joy. Her mouth tasted bitter from the lie she had told Carin, how she had said she didn't want to keep anything from her friend.

Having made a half circuit of the pavilion, Lyah looked across the hearth-home to where Old Wend was telling a story to a gaggle of the children who usually made Ryd's life miserable. Even now, out of the corner of her eye, she could see Ryd shifting his weight as if preparing to flee. But it was behind Old Wend that Lyah focused her gaze. Jenin watched her back, hys dead eyes glinting in the morning light.

This she had kept from Carin, and she would keep it from everyone.

When Lyah looked at Jenin, the face of her dead lover so steady and unflickering in the midst of the very alive bustle of Haveranth on a feast day, rage bubbled up inside her. Someone in this village had cut hys throat with a knife, and had left hys blood to stain the earth.

Lyah would find out who.

She yearned for the use of the magic she had described to Carin, to be able to make the wind whisper the name of Jenin's killer. For all her yearning, though, there would be no whispers on the wind, no name born from magic. Lyah would have to find the killer another way.

When the first bell tolled throughout the village, everyone gathered at the tables to eat, and Lyah went with them. She noticed Ryd hung back, skirting the main crowds of villagers and only placing a few pieces of mutton and apple with cheese curds on his plate and climbing onto a nearby barrel to look around. As was customary, she moved farther away from him, blending with the crowd without being part of it. Her full reentry to the life of Haveranth was about to happen, and Lyah's feet took her toward where Jenin stood on the edge of the pavilion's green.

Lyah stayed at hys side, unspeaking, for she didn't want to risk anyone noticing her talking to no one. She knew Jenin was not really there, that hys presence was only a specter or a ghost. It didn't matter. Being near hyr was the only thing that kept Lyah focused on the task at hand.

She searched through the crowd for Carin, but didn't see her.

As the sun slowly climbed farther into the sky, Merin made her way to the center of the pavilion. When she spoke, the chatter of villagers died into a buzz, then into silence.

"Three Journeyers set out on Planting Harmonix to find their names," Merin said. "Three have returned to us."

"Three have returned to us." Lyah repeated the sentence reflexively, even though this day she referenced herself. Her eyes fell upon Dyava's face, cast in a shimmer of light reflecting off a glass bauble hanging from the pavilion's edge. She had not spoken to him since she returned, and when she looked again at Jenin, hys eyes were on Dyava as well.

Merin went on, but Lyah didn't hear. She instead broke her gaze away from Jenin and Dyava and searched through the crowd for Carin, yearning to have the comfort of her friend near her and knowing that it was traditional to stand alone for the naming ceremony, to be a part of a village first, other bonds second. Now she understood more fully why. Now Lyah understood why the bonds of village came first.

Carin was first born, so she would be first named. Lyah would be next, followed by Ryd.

When Merin fell silent, Lyah waited. Her breath felt elusive, as if her lungs had to chase the air in order to breathe. Next to her, Jenin still stood, hys face unreadable.

"First born," Merin said. Her voice rang out through the hearth-home of Haveranth, louder than it should have been. Loud like it had been on Planting Harmonix when she made them leave after Jenin's death. Loud like the call of the hawk above their heads on the Journeying.

The silence after felt louder still.

It continued on, and Lyah felt anxiety creep up behind her and perch on both shoulders. Carin should have spoken now, should now have a different name.

Lyah saw Rina then, not far from her, the smith's face ashen like the dregs of her forge.

"No," Lyah said aloud. No one else spoke, all the village folk afraid of what Merin might say. The wind whistled past the pavilion, heedless of custom or ceremony.

Merin's own face did not keep its expression, but sank for an instant into despair. "Nameless," she said.

Lyah's heart plunged into her stomach, roiling there like sick-up. "No," she said again.

"Nameless," the village whispered. "Nameless. Nameless. Nameless."

The people pulsed with the word, their combined whisper blending with the wind. It was not magic like Lyah had imagined speaking Jenin's murderer's name to her, but it found a home in Lyah's gut and burrowed like a worm.

Lyah closed her eyes, willing herself to know Carin's name, pushing at the edges of her apprenticeship to Merin, pleading with everything around her to hear Carin's voice calling out over the din of whispers.

"I'm Lyari," she murmured against that whisper, as if by speaking her own she could summon Carin's. "I am Lyari."

36

RYD HEARD the whispers of the crowd surging before him, but he didn't pay them any heed. Instead, his gaze locked on a lone figure on the far bank of the Bemin, one he'd spent three moons walking beside. The figure wore a rucksack and walked quickly toward the west.

From his vantage point on the north side of the hearth-home, standing on a barrel to be able to see over the crowd, he had no trouble picking her out between the roof of Rina's forge and the frame of Old Wend's coopery stall. Carin was leaving Haveranth.

She had found her name. She was not Nameless. But she was leaving and had been declared so.

A wild flutter took up in Ryd's chest, like the frantic beating of a baby bird's wings.

Where Carin was going, he didn't know.

Here in Haveranth he would always be the one folks laughed at, the one they told to take things in stride. Elsewhere, what could he be? Where was elsewhere?

Ryd thought for only a few seconds more, and then he jumped from the barrel, darting across the road and between roundhomes to run to his own. He ignored the screaming part of his mind that told him he had gone well and truly mad, to be considering fleeing Haveranth into some unknown land. If there was even any land they could get to. A quick glance over his shoulder told him that no one had seen him go—or if they had, they didn't seem to care.

He burst through the door of his roundhome, where his rucksack still sat beside the door, still packed. He dumped the clothes from the rucksack onto the floor and ran to his room, where he grabbed handfuls of tunics and leggings and stuffed them into the belly of the bag. He had no food, nor did he have anything particularly useful to bring otherwise, but he packed an extra water skin and filled it from the pump in his kitchen. He had a roll of carving tools, and he brought them too. They had been his grandmother's, and they were the only things he had of any sentimental value. Seeing them made him remember the old woman's lined face, her still-steady hands and the way she could nevertheless whittle a perfect tiger or kazytya even once her eyesight faded.

As he left the roundhome through the kitchen door that faced to the north, Ryd realized that it had never felt like his. He had built it, but he had not made it his own. He did not belong to it, nor it to him.

He skirted the other homes as he hurried toward the Bemin, his legs still aching from the Journeying and the toil of High Lights, but strong from it as well. Still no one seemed to know he had gone, and the knowledge of that stung him like chili juice poured into a scrape. Even on this, his naming day, he was not missed. He had not even seen his parents as he left the river, though he did not take that to mean they did not care for him.

Tears stung his eyes at the thought of their disappointment in him, to have a son Nameless and exiled, stricken from the village record. In time, though, they would not even remember he had ever existed.

Ryd broke into a trot, then into a run. The bridge appeared before him, all pale grey stone and graceful arches. He didn't look back. Only forward at a future he could not know.

THE WINDS blew hot and dusty from the north, the scent of sand somehow flavoring the air even in the wooded crevasses of the foothills of the Mad Mountains that gave the area its name, and Sart Lahivar stared down the rover who'd barred her way on the road. Annoyance warred with other emotions Sart didn't want to admit to: a tendril of fear, a thorn of rage, a buzz of panic.

"We're in need of a good halmer," he said. Thin and lanky, the man wouldn't be a threat were it not for the densely corded muscles that showed through the gap in his vest—or the pair of worn-handled knives sticking out of his belt. Sart was willing to bet her favorite necklace that he knew how to use them.

If it were just the one, she'd be willing to test that theory, but he was a rover, and his friends were all lurking behind him, close to him in support, each with their own knives and short sabers and sickle-swords, bows and spears. Even Sart didn't think she could dodge that many pointy objects. Her skin buzzed with the swelling crawl of anxiety.

The brand on her right cheek itched, and she resisted the urge to scratch it. Scratching it would muck up the magic she'd put on the carefully painted design of river mud. The rovers in front of her saw pink scar tissue in the shape of the halm rune, the symbol all halm-workers wore throughout the land. Halmers were rare enough that rovers wouldn't outright kill them, and most of the time rovers would even give halmers a wide berth. Those who were skilled at making weapons from the densest hardwood were often also skilled at using them.

Sart was the latter, but not the former. Using magic to mimic the halmer branding had been a gamble, and she'd just lost. She looked the rover in the eyes, straightening her shoulders and drawing herself up to full height. "There are plenty of halmers to be found in Crevasses. I'm busy."

"But you're so conveniently located."

"That isn't permanent." Sart kept her eyes trained on the man in front of her, but she used her peripheral vision to assess his band. They were all well-muscled, which wasn't remarkable. She saw three knifers like the leader, a man and woman both built like the squat mud-daub storecaches of the Bogger region waymakes. An archer, who picked hys teeth with a fletching feather, looking bored, and two women with curved sabers of bronze and stances that told Sart they were well-capable of wielding them. Another man held a sickle-sword at his side, partially loosed from its baszyt leather strap across his upper leg already.

That many working together with bronze weaponry—that was remarkable.

They stood near one another, their proximity showing that they trusted one another to be within killing distance. Usually in these bands one or two would be just farther from the others, just enough to tell Sart they were the crumbling link in the chain, but not these ones. They stood like a unit, moved like a unit, and—Sart noted with a mingling weave of respect and disgust—smelled like a unit.

"If you're in that much of a hurry to leave, maybe you're not a real halmer," the rover leader said. "Maybe you're one of them who get the brand so folk like me'll leave you be. Maybe you're just a liar, and I should have Tark back there slice you up until you prove you deserve that mark of yours."

Grim now, Sart set her lips. She deserved her brand well enough; the magic she used to create the illusion was almost pure will, and that had been earned, even if the title of halmer had not been.

"Very well," she said. "I'll prove myself to you and craft exactly two items for you. I'll only be three turns late to meet with Culy."

The man blanched a bit at the mention of Culy, but he recovered, nodding at Sart. Sart reminded herself to tell Culy hys reputation was getting tarnished. Most rovers wouldn't ignore that, no matter how big their band. Anxiety prickled through Sart's skin.

From his rucksack the rover produced a hunk of halm about the size of a peat brick the boggerfolk burned in the winter months, as long as her forearm and two hands wide. It gleamed in the afternoon light, pretty enough Sart wished she *could* bend it to her will.

While Sart could no more craft a blade or a flute from halm than she could convince a kazytya to carry her on its back, she had learned enough about the trade to do what was necessary—trick the rot-gut rover long enough to get her away from the band and on the road to Salters to see Culy.

Culy was Sart's oldest friend. Truth be told, since Sart had few friends in general, Culy was near enough her only friend and somewhat of a whispering legend throughout the lands. Whip-like with intellect and magic alike, slow to anger but quick to vengeance—sy also made sure to feed mouths that could find no food for themselves and thus was perhaps the one person alive someone might seek out for goodwill.

Sy would not be happy if Sart died at the hands of these mud-born rovers, but if that happened, there wasn't anything Culy could do about it from Salters. Sart tried to stem the panic again.

The road ran alongside a mucky creek, the runoff from the mountains blending with the clay-dense earth to turn it a sickly brown. Leeches liked to live in the creek shallows. Only five paces wide, even in the early summer the creek wasn't much to look at. Sart had heard tales—mostly from Culy—that, cycles past, the river had been a hundred paces wide and flowed clean enough to drink. If you were upstream from any wild ihstal herds, that is. As it stood, Sart wasn't sure she believed Culy. Hys tales seemed spun from the green glass of the salterfolk: pretty to look at but fragile and useless.

It was to the muddy bank of the creek that she strode, not looking at the band of rovers behind her. Pulling a spade from her rucksack, she dug a small hole near the bank, into the brown clay. As a child, she had liked to play there, gathering clay until it dried enough to sculpt into vessels and fire in Alys's kiln and give out to the folk who would pass through the Crevasses each season. But then Alys had died of the skin-rot, and her kiln had gone cold, and Sart realized as she dug her fingers into the slick muck that it was the first time since Alys's death that she'd felt the coolness of clay on her flesh. After packing just such clay over Alys's decaying, still-living body, soothing her self-devouring skin with the cool packed clay of the creek, Sart had lost her taste for clay-shaping.

Feeling sour and determined, Sart placed the brick of halm into the hole and covered it in the wet clay. She piled a cairn of jagged pebbles atop the spot, then sat back on her haunches to look at the rover, her hands smeared with clay. He stood over her, looking down as if expecting a halm sword to burst from the muck fully formed.

"Unless you feel like watching those pebbles settle into the mud all day, you might want to occupy yourself with something else."

He grunted at her, then pointed around her, where the rest of his band had spread out in a semicircle around the bit of creek bank Sart occupied. "You watch them. And don't try to run. Kahs can hit a hare at two hundred paces with hys bow, and sy'll have you leaking blood from a hundred holes before you even get that far away."

That was clear enough a threat.

Sart stood and walked to the creek, washing her hands in the water. While the rover leader sauntered over to the archer—Kahs, she supposed—Sart busied herself with building a small fire, feeding it until the flames licked the air at the height of her knees. From one side of her rucksack, she pulled a bronze tripod with a cooking hook, setting it up over the fire. She pretended to be occupied with pots of water from the creek, straining it through a densely tatted fyajir wool cloth to catch most of the silt and transferring the cleaner water into a pot to boil. But it wasn't the water potting she focused her mind upon. The voices of the rovers danced across the air, low murmurs meant to keep themselves from her ears.

Wariness was one of Sart's favorite traits in herself. Walking back to the creek, she dipped her hands in the sluggish waters, feeling the low flow of the current on her skin. As always, the feel of magic was a quiet hum, like the wind ruffling the highest branches of trees or the sound a plucked harp-string made just before fading into silence. She caught it from the water, letting the movement of the liquid over her palms spool within her like a spinner's work-gathered yarn. The breeze blew from the north, carrying with it that same scent of sand and arid dustiness, and Sart gathered that, too. The wind brought tales from afar, just as the creek carried its silt downstream, and Sart nursed that hum until it began to buzz her ears with an almost-unpleasant sensation.

As always when she did this, for a moment her heart seemed to suspend itself in her chest with nothing to anchor it. The creek's flow slowed against her skin, the breeze softened its touch on her short black hair, and in the murmurs of the rovers, their words became clear.

"If she's a halmer, I'm a baszyt," Kahs said.

"If she can't do it, we'll gut her clean and right," the leader replied. "You saw her pack. That's some fine stitching. She's even potting some water for us."

Kahs grunted a laugh. "Ripe enough. If she turns out to be a halmer right and proper, we'll have what we need for Wyt to supply her band. Should be able to turn out those mold-muck boggers from down Lahglys way, like you wanted."

Sart looked straight ahead at the far bank of the creek, grimness setting into her face like a cloud settling in to rain. Two items of halm wouldn't be nearly enough to oust a set-in band of rovers. There was no way—none—that these rovers planned to let her go.

A STRANGE FOG had covered Carin the moment she set foot on the north bank of the Bemin, leaving her lightheaded as she walked westward toward Bemin's Fan and a life she could no longer predict. Her feet stumbled on the path. As Lyah had left her home, dread had filled her that Dyava might follow, that he might break tradition in some small way to greet her before the naming ceremony. He had not. If he had, Carin didn't think she would have had the strength to leave. The sun shone from high in the sky, its rays failing to warm her in spite of the heat of the day. Though her skin glistened with perspiration, she felt cold within.

Nameless.

She was Nameless.

Carin ignored the burning weight of her rucksack's burden on her back and the bowstring that cut into her collarbone. The world of Haveranth would go on without her, erasing her slowly from memory until it would be as if she'd never existed. Dyava would forget her. The cycle that had seen their love grow would fade away.

She thought she should feel sick, but instead she felt a dizzy buzz, as if she'd had a bit too much iceberry wine. The villagers wouldn't come looking for her; that thought was the only certainty she had. When she didn't appear at the naming ceremony at the village hearth-home, they would declare her Nameless, and she would be gone.

Would they come after her? She didn't think so. She would vanish, first from the village, then from their histories, then from their minds.

Her feet found their footing at last, and their measured strides went on without her guiding them. She continued into the west as the sun crept its pace across the sky and Toil Moon rose with her sister at her side, just a day past full. Birds still flew overhead. The Bemin rushed on to the sea, its blue waters sure of themselves. The only thing out of place was Carin.

Nameless.

Her mind tried to grasp the word with slippery fingers as she walked, but she found that she could not, however she tried, tie that word she had so dreaded to herself. She was still Carin el Rina ve Haveranth, regardless of what her people murmured in the distance. A fierce obstinance grew in her chest, and she pulled her name to her like she might gather the folds of a fur coverlet to her chin on a cold winter night. She was still Carin. She had a self. She would hold to that self.

In her mind, the name she had heard in that cave in the Hidden Vale, far away from where she walked now, sounded like a sibilant whisper. *Caryan.*

She allowed it to take up residence in a small part of her for a moment, a brief wonder of who Caryan might have been winding through her thoughts like a snake. And then she sloughed it off, shunted it away, and made room only for Carin.

She thought of Ryd, pulling him out from underneath a pile of giggling children yet again. High Lights was the day they were supposed to take their first steps toward adulthood, joining Haveranth newly named. Instead, Ryd was leagues behind her, Lyah with him. Jenin was dead and Carin simply walked, each step fraying another thread of the life she had left.

Thinking of Jenin slowed her on the path. Carin would never know what happened to hyr now. Carin had always thought her village as a place without secrets—oh, for certain there had been the tiny falsehoods, the typical day-to-day deceptions. But not this. How many times had Dyava held her in his arms and not told her what he knew? How many moments had his smile hidden the truth of their home?

Carin's feet carried her westward through the afternoon and past sunset until the sky was almost dark. Toil's light lit the countryside enough for her to see, and when she finally made camp at the base of a sycamore, she could see well enough to find tinder and fallen branches to build a fire. It crackled merrily, and she sat by it sobbing, staring into the flames. The heat of the fire dried the tears on her cheeks and tightened her skin.

She sat that way for a long while, until her face burned and she had to look away.

She needed a plan; Bemin's Fan would no more welcome her in than would Haveranth or Cantoranth. By now Merin would have sent word to the other two villages of the Hearthland that there was a Nameless one wandering the land. The soothsayers would make sure Carin could find no harbor.

What had she done?

The pit of her stomach churned, seeing again the void of the cave and worse. How could only a few moments change comfort to caprice, home to horror?

She could go north, into the mountains. There, she knew there was enough food in the summer months for her to survive the winter if she started now and gathered quickly. She could build a shelter and live as long as she needed to there. A smaller part of her whispered that she had never been alone. Her village had always been there. Someone who knew how to fish, to mend a pair of leggings, to show her how to raise the poles for the roundhome she had built with her own hands. Even on the Journeying, she had had Lyah and Ryd. She had not been alone. The Carin that had left Haveranth on Planting Harmonix moons before would not have made it back had she set out alone.

She was not certain her new self could face exile the same way.

Carin set snares around her small camp, hoping to catch a small squirrel or a rabbit by morning. When she settled down into her bedroll, she bundled the cloak that had been her Journeying gift into a pillow under her head. The cloak had kept her warm in the moons she had spent walking to find her name with Ryd and Lyah. Who would they be when the sun touched Haveranth tomorrow? Sleep came slowly, and several times before she sank into its depths, she jerked wide awake again, her entire body shaking and her hand reaching out to find Lyah's, finding only air.

Hours later, she woke harshly in the dark of night, her muscles sore and her heart beating quickly. The buzzing, dizzy sensation she had felt all day still lingered, and she sat up on her bedroll, scanning the land around her for whatever it was that had woken her.

Nothing moved in the camp, and Carin made herself lie back down. The air had chilled, and she unbundled the cloak to pull over her body.

She decided it must have been an animal in her snares, or simply a vivid dream that then fled her memory.

"Carin." A voice sounded in the camp.

Carin sat straight up, head snapping toward the speaker. She knew that voice. The sick feeling she had missed earlier now arrived, sending her stomach roiling with fear and anxiety.

She met Ryd's eyes from across the embers of her carefully banked fire. "Ryd."

What she wanted to say was, *Not you, too.*

For a long while, neither of them spoke. Dawn began to color the sky, and Carin got up and rekindled the coals of the fire into dancing flame, feeding them with the wood she had set aside.

Ryd simply took his rucksack from his back and set it against the trunk of the sycamore, rummaging about until he pulled out a fishing line and hook. He walked the bank of the Bemin until he found an eddy, and Carin watched from the fireside as he cast the hook out into the swirling waters.

When he came back with two small fish, Carin cleaned them, and she marveled at how quickly they fell back into the routines of the Journeying. The fish roasted in a pan held by Ryd's steady hand, which he switched every so often to give his muscles a respite from holding it in one position.

"Why did you leave?" He flipped one of the fish with a wooden fork.

"Why did you?" Carin countered.

"I couldn't go back to the way things were," Ryd said. The smell of roasting fish made Carin's mouth begin to moisten, but she wasn't sure she could trust her stomach with food.

"Nor could I," she said.

He looked at her, his eyes as pale as the pre-dawn sky against the brown of his skin. "You had everything in Haveranth. You had a plan to join the village, a home you built, a place."

Carin frowned, looking closer at this boy she had known since swaddling clothes. "You had those things."

But she knew before the words had escaped her mouth that his saying he couldn't go back to the way things were did not mean the same as hers. Carin thought of the many times she had pried children off him, and how she had done it without thinking of just how that would feel, to be the one at the bottom of that pile. How disrespected he must have felt, and rightly so. Shame filled her at the realization that she hadn't bothered to see something so clear.

Ryd now gazed off into the distance, to the north where beyond the tree line the mountains would rise with their snow-capped peaks and jagged stones. "No one even saw me go."

"What?"

"I was at the hearth-home, in the very center of things, when Merin called for the first born to name herself and you did not speak. I saw everyone react to your loss. Lyah started murmuring—I could see her lips moving, and she wasn't saying *Nameless* like everyone else was. Dyava's shoulders started shaking, and I saw him looking around for you. Then I saw you, on the far side of the river and almost out of sight. So I left the pavilion, and no one noticed."

Carin felt as though her heart would collapse in her chest. Dyava. The entire village would have been there, waiting for the naming ceremony and the feast to move them past another High Lights into the harvest quarter of the cycle. Surely someone had seen him...

But looking into Ryd's face, she knew he had the right of it. No one had noticed him go. For the first time in the life they had spent together, Carin felt as though she truly knew him.

She spoke haltingly then, her words jumbling in her mouth until she was afraid they would come out with no order. "For me...I couldn't stay. Not when I know what I know, what we all know. High Lights is naught but a bandage tied on a broken leg," she said. She paused before going on. "Did you realize that our whole families know this thing? Everyone beyond their eighteenth harvest. They have always known, what our people did to build our home. Who they have hurt. I couldn't stay. I had to leave. I don't know if I can ever do anything that will make it right, but..."

A light blush of color appeared on Ryd's cheeks, but he nodded.

The dizziness Carin felt buzzed around her as if she were at the center of a beehive. She meant what she had said, or she wouldn't have been there, so far from home. But home, the home she had left behind. Her mother. Dyava. Lyah. She blinked at Ryd, her skin tingling and crawling. The sky seemed to grow darker in her field of vision. She tried to form Ryd's name with her lips, but no words would come.

His face swam in front of her eyes, and the last she saw before she fell was his arm reaching out to catch her.

He missed.

JUST BEFORE dusk, Sart returned to the small cairn of pebbles where she had buried the brick of halm. By now the dampness of the clay would have seeped into the wood, softening it. A proper halmer would then begin to shave away the first chunks of wood to reveal whatever item they desired to craft. Sart dug up the brick, keeping her eyes alert on her surroundings. None of the rovers paid her much attention; they seemed to know enough about a halmer's craft to know that nothing happened quickly and that it would be morning before anything started to truly take shape. The wood would have to be buried and shaped at least twice more. From a brick this size, a halmer could indeed make two belt knives.

Sart's spade struck the brick, and she carefully sat back on her heels, clearing a space around the brick. Kahs had taken to having a boring conversation with one of the knifers, and the rover leader stood off by himself then, peeling long strings from a chunk of dried smoked meat.

The brick of halm uncovered, Sart moved it to the side in the hole she had dug and surreptitiously began to chisel out a hole on one side. She worked quickly, displacing the clay and smearing it around the edges of the main hole. When it was large enough, she pushed the brick of halm into the wall of the hole and smeared clay over it, leaving a large empty divot in the ground, devoid of the wood the rover had given her.

Sart pushed the spade down into the bottom of the hole, burying it deep in the clay. There weren't many rocks there, but she hoped she wouldn't come across a layer of soil or sediment. She pulled the spade out and looked at the tip. Still clay. Pleased, she worked the spade around in a rectangle the same size of the brick she had just hidden away. No one paid her any heed as she worked, and after a few minutes, she had a clay brick. She filled in the gap at the bottom of the hole with stones and a thin layer of displaced clay.

Returning to her fire, she unrolled a cloth set of tools, their handles worn and shaped by hands that were not hers. This was the risky bit, she knew—because the moment they saw her working with tools, they would be curious enough to watch her. She re-rolled the tools and held them close to their body, returning to the hole and positioning herself with her back to the rovers. Sart took out a few of the large chisels and laid them out in front of her.

The magic she had spooled within her still filled her with a hum, and Sart allowed the voices of the rovers to dissipate, saving what magic she had for the task she planned. The first thing she did was draw the moisture from the brick of clay until she could pick it up at one end without the other sagging. Satisfied, Sart felt a small radius of humidity around the brick as it gave off the water, watching wisps of mist form in the cool sunset air.

Footsteps behind her made her freeze.

"Why is it that color?" The rover leader grunted.

Even from where she crouched, Sart smelled the smoked meat on his breath.

She filled her voice with as much disdain as she could muster. "It's been buried in clay all day. That's the clay you're seeing."

"What are you waiting for?" he asked. "Aren't you going to carve it?"

Sart's teeth ground together, and she tried to suppress the sound. She hadn't had the chance to get to the next bit of her illusion; if she cut into this block of clay with him looking on, she wasn't sure if she was good enough that he would see the whiteness of halm appearing under the chisel or only the thick brown clay. To buy herself time, she nodded and stared at the tools she'd laid out, her mind whirring through possibilities.

She made a show of choosing a tool, picking up one chisel after another and making an unhappy sniff with each until she found one and twirled it in her fingers.

"Get on with it," the man said.

"This is more complicated than whittling a child's bauble out of driftwood," Sart growled. "Unless you want something as useful, I suggest you find some patience."

Her irritation was unfeigned, and Sart looked back and forth between the chisel and the brick, ignoring the rover where he towered over her, his shadow stealing away her light.

Illusion was something best done outside the eyes of the one to be deceived; her mud-drawn brand had been with her for several days now, and she had completed it far from the seeing of anyone in the Crevasses. Not that most of the folk there paid Sart Lahivar any mind except to dip their heads out of respect when she crossed their paths—or thumb their bottom lips if she'd beaten them at bones recently.

Now she was going to have to attempt to alter the perception of an item in front of the person she was trying to fool, and Sart would have much rather sat back in front of her fire with a cup of pine ale and some of the rover leader's dried meat.

She had watched halmers work their craft before, and she brought those memories to mind now, thinking of the way they had slid the chisels across the bricks of halm, exposing white flesh like jicama from the clay-moistened wood. Sart took hold of the chisel in one hand and the brick in the other, her fingers finding the clay and comparing the feel of it to that of the halm she had tucked into the wall of the hole and hidden. She allowed the hum of magic to rise around her, filling her mind with the feel and picture of halm. Its density, its paleness that almost glowed, its smoothness in all forms. The soft give of the clay beneath her fingers seemed to harden, and Sart traced the corners of it while the rover looked on.

Sart felt a presence behind her, and she looked up to see Kahs and the knifer woman sy'd been speaking to. "Don't look over my shoulder like that," she said, pointing to the opposite side of the hole. "I can't concentrate with your breath on my neck."

"I'm not breathing on you," Kahs said, hys feet squelching in the clay behind her.

"It's an expression. Move."

"I'll give the orders here, halmer," the rover leader said, and she turned her head to look up at him.

"If you want me to work, make hyr give me some space."

"Kahs, move."

Kahs spat—the gob of saliva sailing by dangerously close to Sart's cheek—but sy moved as told.

"What's your name, rover?" Sart asked the leader. She had a rather decent list of those who'd wronged her, and she wouldn't be opposed to adding his name to it.

"Barit."

Sart was somewhat surprised that he answered, but then remembered that he planned to kill her if she didn't perform the task he wanted, so she figured she wasn't much of a risk.

Her fingers told her that the magic had worked all it was going to. The feel of the brick against her flesh was right, hard and smooth with sharp corners. A moment with the chisel would tell her if the illusion she had built would extend to its innards.

Sart licked her lips, then pinned her tongue between her teeth, frowning as she pushed the chisel into the enspelled clay brick. Her forehead felt clammy where perspiration had broken out, but she ignored it.

Clay rolled back under the chisel, curling away. Easy, quick, and... white. Sart breathed her relief as inconspicuously as she could. The curl of clay looked just as halm should, like sharp white cheese, but smoother and more pure.

Sart's mouth slowly began to lose its dryness, and she made sure to keep her breaths even and deep.

Out of the corner of her eye, she saw Barit's lips spread into a grin.

He had a bit of dried meat between his teeth.

RYD'S BREATH came sharp and shallow as he shook Carin. She'd fallen sideways, almost landing in the fire, and he'd been hard-pressed to move her before her hair caught flame. A few black strands had singed, curling in on themselves in kinked spirals.

She was breathing; that much was good. Her eyeballs seemed to flit back and forth beneath her lids, and the sight unnerved him as much as the mere fact that she had collapsed in front of him. The fish he'd caught still sizzled in their pan where he'd dropped it on the ground.

Carin's lips showed a white line around them, harsh against the brown of her skin. Ryd patted her cheek, panic rising within his chest like a flock of birds taking off from his parents' fields. One moment she had been talking to him, the next she had dropped like a stone into a pond. Ryd didn't know what to do.

"Carin!" He shouted her name at her, then choked on it as he remembered that it wasn't her true name, that he'd never heard her true name spoken. He felt for a moment as if the two of them had frozen in time somewhere, continued on a path they weren't meant for.

Her eyelids fluttered, then opened, exposing her irises, deep blue and unseeing.

Ryd reached out and patted her cheek again, and her hand snapped up, closing tight around his wrist. Her breath hissed out, and her chest went so still that for a moment Ryd wondered if she had died, and his entire body tightened like a snake in a striking coil.

But then she sucked a deep breath in, raising her free hand in front of her face, her fingers seeming to trace something there that Ryd could not see.

Her fingers dug deep into the flesh of his wrist. For several long moments they sat like that, until Ryd's arm began to ache and his fingers went numb from the pressure of hers restricting his blood.

Ryd carefully pried her hand open to release his wrist, and she let him, her arm falling to her side. She made no other move to change position, her right hand still moving in the air and her eyes fixed on something he couldn't guess at.

He tried to get her to move, but after several attempts he left her there, face up on the ground, soil and leaves clinging to her hair.

Ryd ate one of the fish and wandered the camp in a circuit, always keeping Carin in sight. He didn't know what to do. He'd never seen anyone in this type of state, and watching her watch nothing made his mind spin. Instead of sitting next to her, he walked the perimeter of her camp, finding her snares. One had a rabbit in it, and the animal had strangled itself on the snare.

Ryd hadn't cleaned a rabbit in cycles, but he found the memory of how to go about it returned quickly enough. He somewhat clumsily scraped the pelt—bits of flesh clung in some places and his knife blade cut through in others—but he succeeded as much as he hoped to. The rabbit meat he cut into strips and set up to smoke over the fire. As he watched it steam and then sizzle, he tried to keep the knot of panic from jostling his ribcage. His mind wove to and fro through worries. What if Carin never recovered? Where were they supposed to go even if she did? How was he supposed to know what to do?

For over an hour, Ryd sat, until the heat of the fire made perspiration bead on his upper lip and his eyelids stuck when he blinked, then began to water. He made a few circles through the camp, looking out at the bushes around them for any berries or edible plants he could gather. He didn't find much nearby; a few sparkleaf bushes yielded a double handful of citrusy foliage they could eat, but Ryd couldn't bring himself to venture farther out of the camp. When dried and boiled or smoked, the sparkleaf would also dull pain and cleanse wounds, but there wasn't enough to spare for the drying of it.

The sun continued its arc to the sky's zenith, then began its descent as Ryd tended the fire, turned the strips of rabbit, and kept a close eye on Carin. Three more times he attempted to rouse her, but she didn't respond to his shaking of her shoulder or his yells right beside her face.

When the grove went silent around him after one loud yell, Ryd stopped trying that way to wake her.

For the first time in his life he felt completely and totally alone. Vulnerability he had felt; his childhood of being smaller than everyone else had given him that. He had never been this physically alone, however, and the slow-returning sounds of chirping and buzzing reminded him that he had no concept in his mind of what to expect outside of the boundaries of the village he had voluntarily left behind.

Ryd thought of his parents, thought of the village that would be celebrating Lyah's entry into full villager status. Her name. He and Carin would never know what that name was. His own came unbidden to his mind. *Ryhad.*

In the Hidden Vale, with the return journey to Haveranth still ahead of them, his name had fallen into his core with the same resonance of two strings plucked in harmony. Now it felt jangled and wrong, as if he had no right to it. He had chosen to forever be Ryd. His clothes were loose upon his body, and yet everything felt too tight. He fought back the rising wind of panic.

A few feet away, Carin stirred, her right arm finally falling to her side, where her fingers still twitched slightly, pale from the lack of blood flow. Her eyes, so wide and unblinking for so long, closed for three breaths. Ryd hurried to her side, taking her right hand in his and rubbing it to return circulation.

Carin opened her eyes. Red blood vessels showed through the whites, making the blue of her pupils stand out vividly like the first ripe Early Bird apple on the tree.

"Carin?" Ryd said her name gently, still massaging the palm of her hand. He didn't expect a response.

He counted her breaths as time passed. Sixty. One hundred. Two hundred. She blinked occasionally now, tears leaking from the corners of her eyes and running down her cheeks to wet her hair. She closed her eyes again.

Another hundred breaths passed before anything changed. Finally, Carin's eyes opened and focused on Ryd's.

"Ryd?" She said his name almost as a whisper.

"What happened?" he asked. "Are you okay?"

Carin didn't answer, but she squeezed her eyes shut, her throat convulsing and her hand tightening against his. Perhaps it was shock, like the way they had all reacted after Jenin's death. How could someone change everything they ever knew so quickly?

After a moment, Carin dropped his hand and sat up, blinking to clear the tears from her eyes and looking around the campsite. Carin pushed herself to her knees, and though Ryd clearly saw the shaking of her right arm as she used it to brace herself against the ground to stand, she ignored the quivering limb as she rose to her feet. She straightened her shoulders, rolling each backward, one after the other. Her gaze scanned the campsite, then took in the river beyond, the position of the sun and shadows. She swallowed once and let her hands fall to her side.

Ryd watched her, a stone sinking into his stomach. She wasn't going to talk to him. He could almost see her body closing its shutters.

Sure enough, when she spoke, Ryd knew whatever happened was her experience alone.

Carin gave the air an experimental sniff. "Is there food?"

LYARI VE Haveranth sat by the banks of the Bemin, watching the sun slice clean lines across the late afternoon stillness. A climber fish jumped—she knew what it was from the silver-green scales that flashed in the light—and for a fleeting moment, Lyari wished she could be that fish. To have a simple existence. To spawn, swim downstream, grow, eat, mate, toil your way back upstream, up ladders of rocks and white-capped rapids, lay your eggs, continue, continue, continue, fearing only a fisher's spear or a tiger's paw.

She envied the fish she was so good at ending. Even from where she sat, she tracked the climber fish's movements under the water, a blur near the surface, vanishing as it dove deeper, then reappearing as a bend of light before jumping once more. Lyari allowed the fish to disappear from her sight, instead standing and turning back to the village. She let her feet carry her where they would, and they took her in the direction of Carin's roundhome.

Opening the door to enter felt strange, like putting someone else's shoes on your feet. Lyari thought of the hundreds of times she'd climbed through Carin's bedroom window, her feet covered in dust or water or snow depending on the season of the cycle. She thought of clambering into bed with Carin, their breath scented by the vanilla-tasting rilius resin that cleaned their teeth, giggling into their pillows so as not to wake Rina.

The hearth was cold; never had a fire been lit on its stone. The chimney above was clean and unmarred by soot. The beautiful carved maha table stood to one side, and the sight of it made Lyari want to sick up and cry at the same time.

This home had been meant for her fyahiul, for the woman Carin had been meant to become. But Carin was now dead, or as good as. Nameless. The adult who was meant to live in this roundhome had never come, leaving less than ghosts to haunt its spaces.

Lyari made her way into the bedroom, where the sick feeling strengthened. Here there was evidence of Carin's departure. A set of torn leggings from their Journeying, their knees saggy and stretched. A rumpled dent in the coverlet. Lyari kicked off her leather clogs and climbed into the bed. The room was hot in the summer afternoon, but she burrowed under the coverlet anyway, rolling onto her stomach and pulling one of Carin's pillows to her chest.

She expected tears to come, to fall down her cheeks in salty rivulets to mourn the loss of her oldest friend. Instead nothing came, only a cavernous hollowness in her chest that seemed wont to consume her.

Lyari lay there for some time, until sweat slicked her back and her face stuck to the pillow's bavel surface. Finally, she kicked back the heavy coverlet and stood, feeling lightheaded. If she'd thought curling up in Carin's bed would help, she'd been wrong. Instead, Lyari felt the gaping loss of her friend all the more acutely. She straightened the coverlet and replaced the pillow, fluffing it between her palms as if perhaps Carin would return to lay her head upon it.

When she bent to fluff the second pillow, something rough touched her hand.

Pulling the pillow to the side, she saw it. A folded piece of parchment. *Lyah,* it read.

With a shock, Lyari realized that Carin wouldn't have known, couldn't have had any way of knowing her new name.

> *You won't understand why I've had to go. I couldn't return and ignore what we learned. Maybe this is what Jenin meant, when sy said the Journeying was just as much choice as a quest for identity. I know who I am, and I cannot be what I must to continue on in our home.*
>
> *I will miss you, and Ryd, and Dyava.*

That was all. The pen's nib had scratched into the parchment on some words, and on *what we learned* it seemed to have shaken, the runes forming the words uneven and jagged. Lyari stared at those lines, willed herself to look deeper within them, to connect with Carin and see what was in her friend's mind.

But simple will could not bridge that distance.

"She wrote to you."

Lyari started, then turned to see Jenin leaning against the wardrobe, hys eyes somber. The sight of hyr made Lyari's heart jangle, and she swallowed, nodding. Lyari read the note aloud, watching Jenin's face as the words tumbled from her lips. On the Night of Reflection, children were given the chance to pick tokens out of a bag. Each would correspond to a gift, and each gift was handmade by one of the adult villagers. As Lyari read the note to Jenin, she felt the childish apprehension of reaching into that bag, as if within her was a pile of emotions and she wasn't sure which would come out in her hand.

Jenin cleared hys throat when she finished, and fleetingly, Lyari allowed herself to look at the jagged slice across hys neck. The sight gave her a start.

"You see me as you expect to," Jenin said, raising hys fingers to hys neck. "My body is only as mutilated as you think it is."

Lyari didn't know what sy meant by that. Her gaze flicked upward to Jenin's eyes, standing straight, her fingers holding the note with a light touch that kept the parchment from falling only barely.

"What do you think she meant, that she couldn't stay here?" Jenin changed the subject back to Carin, eyes boring into Lyari, seeking an answer at which Lyari could not guess.

"She meant that she could not live with this sacrifice." The word came easily from Lyari's tongue. Sacrifice. What was this life in Haveranth if not that?

"Is that all she meant?"

Lyari thought about that, about what that meant. She looked again at the shaky runes that spelled out Carin's reason for leaving. What did it mean if Lyari could live with something Carin could not?

Weakness, a voice in Lyari's mind whispered. She shook the word away, met Jenin's eyes, and shrugged.

Jenin seemed not to care that Lyari hadn't answered hys question. Instead, sy looked around at the bedroom and gestured widely. "It is a shame such elegant work will be turned to ash."

Lyari nodded, wistfully gazing around the roundhome. She finished making the bed, placing the pillows atop the coverlet and smoothing out the wrinkles. She tucked the note into her belt pouch, feeling Jenin's gaze upon her.

This home was a reminder of so many things. Of a past now washed away by a village's whispers. Of a friend lost to the wilderness. Of how easily change could engulf a life.

Lyari met Jenin's eyes once more, and she made a decision. She would move into Carin's home, and though the village would erase Carin from memory, Lyari would not. As apprentice soothsayer, she would remember.

It took only a few hours to carry her necessities into the roundhome, to arrange the bedroom and the kitchen to her liking. Someone had stocked several items on the worktop. Bundles of hanging herbs, a few scattered carafes of conu juice and icemint tea and goat milk. The milk was warm, but did not smell curdled. She placed it in the shallow, stone-lined cellar off the kitchen and found bundles of brined meat. These things would have gone to waste before anyone else thought to look for them. For Rina, Lyari supposed, coming here would be too much to bear, at least until time washed her daughter away. Jenin came and went as she worked, hys face curious or neutral, never speaking again for the remainder of the day.

Lyari once saw Rina, her shoulders bowed, carrying a sheath of bronze ingots from her shed to her forge.

Time would erase her daughter from the village consciousness, this Lyari knew. No one spoke of the Nameless. For anyone else, moving into the home built by one would be taboo, but Lyari was the soothsayer's apprentice.

Still, she would have to tell Merin, if no one had yet done so themselves.

Lyari made her way to the soothsayer's home outside Haveranth. As always, she did not knock, only pushed open the door. Merin was not in the central room by the hearth, though Lyari heard her voice from the far room and followed it. The door was closed, and she waited outside.

"Harag, it is already done." Merin's voice sounded as though it had been stretched out like gut twine to dry in the sun. "Sahnat hunts, and he never fails."

"This is not a thing we were prepared for." The voice that responded to Merin's statement was thinner still than Merin's, as if heard from the opposite side of a cavern, and it was unfamiliar to Lyari, though the name was not. Harag, soothsayer of Bemin's Fan.

"I know that as well as you. I received your message. Not long remains."

Lyari listened, intrigued by the words she heard. Merin had spoken before of an event coming, one she said she would explain to Lyari after her Journeying. Now it seemed that time would come sooner than Lyari had expected.

"We will prepare as best we can," Merin said. In her tone was resolve, but also worry.

A thin tendril of the same worked its way into Lyari's breast. After Merin's words faded, no more came.

She started when the door opened in front of her, though Merin looked unsurprised to see her.

"Lyari." Merin reached out and clasped her shoulder, her eyes assessing as if she could see into Lyari's very thoughts. "Come, child. It is good you heard that. There are things it's time I told you."

S ART WORKED into the night, the flickering light of the fire dancing across the white wood illusion she had built. Every once in a while, one of Barit's rovers would come up behind her on her watch, pausing to ask her a question about halmwork—she answered with responses cut of whole cloth and about as true as a child's answer to who had first hit whom—but for the most part she worked in peace. When dawn broke to the east, she had two sharp knives upon her lap. Toil waned above, its sliver of a crescent working toward the tree line to vanish shortly from sight.

When Barit stirred from his blankets with a yawn and a loud fart, he immediately came to her side and let out a whoop at the sight of the two knives on her lap.

He reached for one, and Sart slapped his hand away. "You have not yet guaranteed my safety. I have made you what you asked for. You will get it when I say you may have it."

The back of his hand smashed into her cheek, sending her sprawling on the muddy creek bank. "I didn't ask for nothing, halmer." He spat. "You're here because I told you to be here."

Sart's chest tightened with a hot ball of rage. Her cheek smarted where he'd hit her, and the two knives had landed in the dirt. Barit walked toward her, one foot on either side of her legs. He bent to pick up one of the knives, and Sart froze. His proximity would work to her advantage; the other knife was well within her reach, and even without it she could land a punch to his eggsack or drive a pair of fingers up under his kneecap. Two knives wouldn't be enough. Sart already knew that from what she'd overheard from Barit and Kahs that first day. She concentrated on the hum of magic in her skull, felt the buzz of it through her bones as if it were waiting, hoping for the chance to lash out. Or maybe that was just her.

Barit tested the edge of the blade on his thumb and grunted his pleasure at the sharpness of it. Sart carefully schooled her face in nonchalance with a touch of the fear she knew he would expect. She allowed her chest to rise more quickly, to show her anxiety at his closeness. She let her gaze settle upon the knife she had made from clay, the one that even now fooled his eyes and hands. She gave him reason to think she feared its blade against her skin.

The rover leader caught her by the hair, his fingers barely finding purchase at the back of her head in its short black length. He nodded to Kahs and one of the knifers. Tark, Barit had called the knifer. "Seems we've caught ourselves a halmer proper." Barit said, sneering. He jerked Sart out from where she still lay sprawled, pulling her to her knees. "Let me tell you how things are going to be, halmer."

Sart hated the feeling of his fingers in her hair. She could smell his breath even at arm's length, and it smelled of morning dryness and rotten meat. But she forced her head to bob in a sharp nod.

"You're going to make Kahs here a new bow," he said. "Sy's in dire need of a nice halm bow. Isn't that right, Kahs?"

Kahs gave a laugh, reaching out to punch Tark lightly in the shoulder. "A new bow'd be welcome, sure as spring," Kahs agreed.

"And when you're done with that," Barit went on, "You're going to make me a sickle-sword. These here knives are for Targ and Owit. You can make a couple spares after that."

"And where exactly am I supposed to find enough halm to work all that?" Sart spat. Her cheek still throbbed where his hand had smashed into it. She'd have a bruise, to be sure. Culy'd be thrilled to see that, assuming Sart ever made it to hyr.

"We've got your halm," said Tark. "You've got work to do."

Sart decided she'd had quite enough. The balance of risk had tipped away from her benefit. She had to get away, and she had to do it now.

She bowed her head contritely and lifted two fingers to her lips to indicate thanks, her mind rushing through possibilities.

"Good little halmer," Barit crooned. "Get up."

Sart rose to her feet. She couldn't quite tell if Barit and his band were very stupid or very smart. They'd caught her, to be sure, but they hadn't thought to check her for weapons, only taken her shortsword and belt knife that had been in plain sight. They'd left her pack unopened—not that she had anything of value they could find in it—and they hadn't posted a guard for her. As she stood, waiting for Barit's next command, she raised her hand to her swelling cheek. Her eye felt puffy and hot, and the lids were starting to tighten. If she didn't move soon, the wound would obscure her vision.

She was glad he'd missed her nose. She liked her nose.

The wind blew again from the north today, bringing with it that same scent of dust from Sands, that summer dry heat that took over so much of the land beyond Crevasses. Sart felt the wind pool around her, gathered it to her, took it into herself. Her pack sat behind Tark a short distance, and her shortsword's hilt protruded from its scabbard on a pile of supplies a bit beyond that. She followed Tark toward that pile, keeping her eyes watchful to see if she could spot her belt knife. She liked that knife.

Tark led her past the mound of packs to a lashed bundle about the length of a child who had seen ten harvests, though half as wide. The bundle was wrapped in waxed canvas and secured with leather straps. Sart let the feel of the wind wash away the memory of Barit's fingers tangled in her hair and thought out her options. She couldn't fight ten rovers, not alone. Even five at a time would be too much, with Sart exhausted from a night without sleep and maintaining the illusion on the false halm knives. Too risky. She had to thin them out.

Sart hung back from the bundle, staying near the pile of supplies where her shortsword sat like pillaged loot. She supposed it was.

There wasn't much within reach that she could use. Her sword alone would only provoke the type of fight she didn't want. She had to do something to tip the balance of risk back in her favor. Surly, she wished she had real skill at the halmer's craft. A halm knife or two wouldn't go amiss.

A glint of bronze stood out from the supply pile, a curve of smooth metal. A horn.

Tark busied himself with the long bundle, undoing the straps of leather and peeling back layers of waxed canvas to reveal lengths of halm. Enough for all the weapons Barit had listed and more—they had planned this. Sart thought of the rover leader Barit had mentioned to Kahs—Wyt?—and made a note to pass that information on to Culy if she ever made it to hyr. Glancing over her shoulder, Sart saw Barit and the others examining the false halm knives with triumphant faces. Mind whirring like a spinner's wheel, she bent, kneeling in the damp ground. She tugged the brass horn from the pile and pulled on the wind that ruffled her hair. She imagined the wind's source, far to the north. Picturing its path across the leagues, she closed her eyes and saw the land just to the north, over a rise in the trail. Sart brought the horn to her lips, bending so the pile of supplies hid her from all view but Tark's, and he busied himself only with the parcel of halm.

Sart blew on the horn, the wind humming around her. The sound rose, clear and strong and...distant.

No sound rang through the land around her, only blared overland from the north, like the wind, carrying with it a threat.

Tark dropped a chunk of halm with a clatter, and Barit let out a yell from the campfire. Two of the knifers and one of the swords went running northward on swift legs. That left seven rovers for her to dispense with. Tark's eyes were on the north, and with one smooth motion, Sart unsheathed her sword from the supply pile and, with two long strides, buried it between Tark's shoulder blades. Yanking it back out, she drew it across his neck, and he died with a gurgle. Bright red blood splashed across the newly uncovered whiteness of the halm. He had a dagger at his belt, and Sart bent, unbuckling his belt with one hand, edging herself behind a tree trunk. The tree's limbs were covered in bark-rot, but one half of the tree bore bright green leaves. Life and death sharing one trunk.

Sart buckled Tark's belt around her middle and then moved out from behind the tree, keeping in a low waddle, listening for any sounds of approach. She unsheathed the dagger and wielded it in her right hand, point low along with the shortsword in her left. Wishing she had time to rummage through the supply pile, Sart skirted it. Her heart pounded in her chest with a steady thumping. She drew again on the wind and clashed her sword and dagger together. Again the sound seemed to echo far away, like a distant battle. Her mind still full of the buzzing of magic, Sart sucked in a deep breath. Her blood danced in her veins in spite of the fatigue she felt.

Kahs and Barit stood near the fire, both looking into the north. No one had yet noticed Tark, and Sart felt a swell of relief.

A shout made her spin to her right, where one of the saber-wielding women stalked toward her, eyes blazing. The woman had a deep scar down one cheek, and Sart felt a grin spread across her face. "Want one to match?"

The woman yelled, charging at Sart. Sart flitted to the side and parried the first slash of the woman's saber with her shortsword, driving her dagger into the side of the woman's neck. Barit saw her then, and his snarl of rage bellowed through the camp.

Sart looked behind her. Seeing no one, she skipped backward in a zig-zag pattern, angling herself toward her pack. Two of Barit's people gone and two dead. That left five for her to deal with. She saw Barit and Kahs, the other saber-holder, and one densely muscled knifer visible a bit ahead of her through the trees. Only a crack of a twig behind her made her turn to see the man with the sickle-sword coming toward her. He moved quickly, and Barit and Kahs closed in on her. Sart searched for Kahs's bow and didn't see it; either sy had left it unstrung and useless, or sy had set it down not expecting trouble. Either way, Sart was thankful for that reprieve.

Barit spat something at her, and Sart darted out of the middle of the three incoming attackers. Barit still held one of her false blades in one hand, and she tried her best not to look at it. He didn't know. The man with the sickle-sword moved like fluid over the land, cutting off Sart's retreat.

The two who had run off to investigate the horn call could return at any moment, Sart knew. She felt a grim smile spread across her face. She hoped Culy would forgive her if she died.

She had to stay out of Barit's way. That knife would be his choice weapon; that she knew. Sart dropped into a roll just as the sickle-sword whistled through the air toward her, swung in a wide arc by its wielder. She tumbled across the ground and leaped to her feet, darting toward Kahs. Sy hadn't gotten hys bow, and Sart came up mere feet from hyr, spinning and landing a kick in the middle of Kahs's stomach. The impact sent the archer flying backward, and even before sy hit the ground, Sart was on hyr, stabbing her dagger into hys draw arm just below the wrist. Kahs screamed.

Sart sprang away, but Barit caught her sword arm. The false halm knife punched into her ribcage like a fist.

It crumbled to dust.

Barit's surprise loosened his grip on her arm, and she pounded her knee into his groin. Snapping her leg back, she kicked him in the kneecap. He crumpled to the ground, swearing. Breath leaping in Sart's throat, she whirled to face the sickle-sword owner. Whispering a string of words, Sart pulled again on the wind, swirling it around the man's head so the sound of her whispers would wrap around his ears. He shook his head, eyes darting to and fro as if he could shake them off. He advanced on her, and in his eyes Sart saw the certainty that she was to blame for the words in his ears. She smiled at him, showing her teeth, her whispers still hissing from her mouth in a string of nonsense words.

His sickle-sword flashed out, and she parried it, striking out with her dagger. It sliced into his shoulder, and he drew back and slashed at her again with his sword. Sart ducked below the sword and swung her leg around, cutting his leg out from under him. He stumbled to the side, but righted himself quickly. Sart reassessed the man, warily hanging back. She didn't want to end up hooked on that sickle of his. Barit clawed at the dirt, still cursing. Kahs had torn a strip from hys shirt and tied it off around hys bleeding arm.

A wave of dizziness crashed over Sart, and she stopped the whispers. She used the moment of disorientation in the sickle-sword's owner to dart forward and stab at his unprotected middle. He spun out of the way, clumsily swinging his sword at her. Sart parried with her dagger and struck, not at his middle, but at his leg. Her short sword, wielded in her left hand, swung out around his right knee. She felt it make contact with the back of his leg, and she pulled it toward her with a sharp motion that left the blade bloody and sent him falling to the ground. Sart kicked his sickle-sword out of his hand, stomping on his wrist and landing a kick on the side of his head. His eyes glazed and rolled backward. She leaped toward Kahs and did the same, her foot finding a target just above Kahs's ear.

Striding toward Barit, she stepped over his crumpled form until she fully mimicked his posture with her earlier. She leveled her sword point at his throat.

"The day I see you again is the day you die," Sart said.

The ball of her foot slammed into his chin.

She relieved the rovers of as many weapons as she could carry, as well as two waterskins and a large bundle of dried meat. Finding Kahs's bow behind a tree, Sart stooped to slash the string with a twang. She worked as quickly as she could, knowing it wouldn't be long before the rovers who had hurried to investigate the horn blow to the north returned. The final rover who had stayed at the camp saw her, but made no move to engage her. She gave him a look that said she commended his intelligence. He thumbed his bottom lip, face grim, but said nothing.

Her pack was heavy as she left, walking in the creek bed to disguise her footprints. Sart was sure she hadn't seen the last of these rovers, but with several of them dead and others injured, they wouldn't be able to catch her, even as tired as she was.

She scratched the halmer brand from her cheek as she walked, flakes of days-dried mud dropping into the murky creek.

Sart considered that lesson learned. Her nails felt good on her face.

CARIN HAD managed to keep conversation to a minimum for nearly an entire moon. She saw the questions in Ryd's eyes often, and sometimes he would open his mouth as if to speak, but he never voiced them. For that, she was thankful. She had no need of discussing something even she did not understand. Her body hummed like a struck dulcimer string, and when she sat still enough, she felt as though she might gather that hum until even Ryd could hear it. He seemed unaware of her state, though he still treated her with wariness as though she might collapse again. Carin wasn't entirely sure he was wrong.

They had finished the last of the food she had packed turns before, and Carin thought she would have gladly traded one of her hands for a single pocket of Dyava's making. With each league she and Ryd covered, her life in Haveranth seemed to recede like a dream more than simple distance.

In the bloom turn of Gather, the moon's fullness floating through the azure summer sky with her sister trailing beside her, Carin realized they were not alone.

The feeling came first as a hunch, the woods around them growing sometimes too quiet with even the buzzing of insects fading before resuming as if the animals had been startled into silence. The next day, Carin heard the death-scream of a saiga and felt sure it had not died at the teeth of a hunting tiger. She motioned to Ryd to walk beside her.

"I think we are being followed," she said. The very notion of it felt ludicrous, but then, had anyone told her in the summer before last harvest that she would be walking westward with Ryd, Nameless and exiled, she would have thought the person had gotten into the sparkleaf and mixed it with fermented goat's milk to cause hallucinations.

Ryd's face told her he didn't believe her, and Carin shrugged.

The next night clouds rolled in and it rained. Carin sat beneath a maha tree, attempting to start a fire with flint and tinder that would not catch. Carin sat cross-legged on wet ground, half on a tree root and half on dirt. Frustration made her want to throw her flint into the Bemin. She guarded the small pile of tinder, dried sycamore leaves she had plucked and left beside the fire in the days before, and grasses she had done the same with and brushed them with fish oil. The sparks from the flint fell on the tinder and smoldered into nothingness. Ryd left the camp to search for dry wood to use and had not returned, and Carin felt dampness seep through her trousers, wetting her skin.

Surly, she struck her flint again. Three sparks landed on the tinder, and she exhaled slowly, watching them brighten into a deep orange before fading once more. She struck the flint again. Then again. Each time sparks landed, but they did not catch. At the birth of the new moons, they had run out of the last of the food from her roundhome in Haveranth. They had with them two snared rabbits and a string of fish, but without a fire, they would either have to eat them raw or watch them rot. The clouds above were heavy and grey, pregnant and bloated with rain waiting to fall. Carin knew these summer slogs; there were at least another two to three days in this one before the sun would again pierce through the cloud cover to dry the countryside. Until then, if they wanted to eat, they would have to find some way to start a fire.

Carin bundled the tinder beneath her cloak for a moment, cradling it in her hand. All through the previous season-cycle, she had tended the village hearth-home with Ryd and Lyah and Jenin, ensuring that the fire always burned and never went out. It was ritual that those preparing for their Journeying kept that vigil, making certain that the village had fire for cooking and light to work by. But now, far from the hearths of any village, Carin realized how easy her job had been. The village hearth was sheltered by a wide pavilion, kept covered where rain could not wet the embers and blocked from winds that could disrupt the flames. There was dry fuel in abundance, much like everything else in the village. Oils to quick start banked embers into roaring flames. Dry tinder that would quickly yield bursts of fire. Logs and dried dung and peat that burned hot and bright. So many options to keep a single fire going, and here in the wilderness, Carin could not get a ball of fluff to spark to flame with her flint.

She closed her eyes, fighting back frustration. *If only rain could be useful in starting fires,* she thought bitterly.

The hum she had felt since collapsing seemed to rise up around her with a murmur. She took several deep breaths. She would try again in a moment.

The tinder in her hand grew warm, then hot.

Carin's eyes snapped open, and she dropped the tinder on the ground. A tiny flame licked from it.

Heart pounding, she quickly fed it small twigs she kept bundled in her rucksack. The flame rose and grew until she could stack larger kindling on top of it. When Ryd returned with a small armful of mostly dry branches, she had the fire crackling. Carin stared into it, her left hand turned palm up on her knee. A bright red spot covered the center of her hand, and it stung like she had placed her bare skin on a hot pan.

"You got it started," Ryd said. "Well done."

Carin nodded, then closed her fist to cover the red mark.

They cooked all the meat that night and feasted, each eating half a rabbit and some wrinkled Early Bird apples they had found on a tree. The apples had been mushy and too sweet, but Carin made herself choke hers down anyway. The autumn apples would be starting to go to fruit soon, but Carin didn't think they would come across many apple trees on their path westward. As they bedded down to sleep that night, Carin traced the red patch on her palm with one finger. No sparks had caught on that tinder; she knew that as well as she knew the path of the sun across the sky. That flame had come from her. How, she didn't know. She didn't know magic.

For the first time in several turns, she remembered the scroll Lyah had given her. When Ryd shook her to take over his watch—she hadn't managed to sleep—she waited until his chest rose and fell with even rhythm and dug the scroll out from her rucksack, using the dim light of the small fire to read.

Much of the scroll said things she already knew, about the origins of Haveranth and the branches of magic Lyah had described. But something caught her eye. Lyah had mentioned that magic needed a catalyst to work, but she had never mentioned what that might be. In the scroll, she had written that the catalyst was different for everyone. A death in the family, or an immense trauma. Murder. Carin shuddered at that thought, of a murderer in possession of magic. It made her think of Jenin and hys killer and whether or not the hand that had wielded the knife against hyr now had unlocked some ability to twist reality with magic power. She tried to come up with a common thread between the examples Lyah had listed. Death seemed to be one, though trauma did not necessitate the death of anyone to be traumatic. Perhaps it was simply change, an immense personal change. For some, murder would be a simple thing—again Carin shuddered to consider the type of person for whom taking another's life would be a simple thing—but for others it would alter their entire being.

The more she thought about it, the less she understood. As the rain around her grew hazy with the light of the coming dawn, Carin thought of her collapse again. What was becoming Nameless if not an immense personal change? Everyone was different; Ryd's choice to leave Haveranth was not motivated by the same thoughts as Carin's. They had both chosen, but chosen differently. It had yet led them to a similar path.

She thought of *dyupahsy,* potential. The possibility in each seed to become whatever it would. Had this potential been in her all along? Carin wondered if potential could wither and die or simply shift. Her love for Dyava, for Lyah, for her mother. For the home she had crafted with her own hands. When a villager died in Haveranth, their dwelling was burned to return them to the earth. Was that what would happen to hers?

She read and reread Lyah's scroll, but found little of use for her present situation. Carin ignored the fear that spread through her with the twinges of heat in her palm. She hadn't meant to do what she did to the tinder, whatever it was. She had no control over it, yet it had happened, and Carin felt sure she could do it again.

Carin began breaking down camp before dawn had fully arrived. By the time Ryd woke, she had caught and cooked three fish. Her eyes felt sandy from lack of sleep, but she doubted even then that she would be able to rest if she were to close her eyes and lay down.

The hum in her body did not abate.

The next moon took them into the foothills of the Mad Mountains, leaving the Bemin behind to follow one of its tributaries northward away from the river and away from any possibility that they might encounter villagers from Bemin's Fan venturing upriver to fish. Each night when it rained, Carin lit a fire with her newfound ability. When the ground was dry and no rain fell, she let Ryd do it, and each time they stopped on those nights, she made sure to replenish their stash of tinder. She didn't think he ever noticed that on those rainy evenings, she managed to light their fire with little effort. If he did, he gave her no indication. The sense of being followed at a distance never waned, and when Gather Moon became Cultivate and then Sustain, they found themselves in the cooler air of early autumn, the trees in the distance beginning to turn yellow and orange and white.

For those long turns and the waxing and waning of the moons, neither Ryd nor Carin spoke of where they would winter. Neither had ever spent the cold months in the mountains, nor had they spent them without solid walls and hearth to warm them. They would need some form of shelter, and they would need it soon.

They passed an Early Bird apple tree covered in buds one day in the late days of Sustain, and both stopped beneath its branches, looking up. *Dyupahsy,* Carin thought, wondering which of the buds would bear fruit and which would be blown off by the wind to die.

"First frost is coming," Ryd said. The buds would open on that first frost. The Early Bird trees were the best indication of when the day of first frost would arrive; their buds quickened over the turns before, finally flowering with snow-bright petals that glistened and sparkled with frost crystals. If Carin had to guess, she'd say these buds had maybe one turn, maybe two, before they opened to the sun.

For the past two moons, they had set aside a third of what they caught, be it fish or small game, tuber roots or berries. They had dried things when possible and stored it in their packs. Carin guessed that they had enough food to last them for one moon, which she knew wasn't enough. Their rucksacks could hold more, but as they moved into the mountains, Carin wasn't sure how much weight they could bear. The saiga would dissipate the higher they climbed into the mountains, and even if Carin were to shoot one of them per turn, there was no way they would be able to carry whole sides of saiga up the mountains.

"We will need to find a shelter for the winter," she said softly. "Soon, before the snows, so we can hunt during the animals' fall forage."

Or we will starve.

The words hung in the air unsaid, but Carin knew Ryd knew them just as she did.

"I don't know what lies ahead," Carin said. She pointed north. "We could find a glen like Haver's, though I have never seen one like it on a map. We could also find nothing and have to build a hut ourselves. There will be heavy snowfall here."

When she said the words, she felt their weight like the feet upon feet of snow that would soon bury these mountains.

Ryd was quiet for a long moment. "Are we going to survive?"

"I don't know." Perhaps that was why there was never any tell of Nameless returning to villages. They couldn't survive their first winter in the mountains. Mountains to the north or mountains to the south—it would make little difference.

A man stepped out from behind a maha tree, an arrow drawn in his longbow. "I don't think you have to worry about surviving the winter."

High above their heads, a hawk screamed and winged its way southeast.

L YARI FELT cold. Beyond the chill of the autumn air, deeper than the numbness in her bare toes on the wooden floor of Merin's round-home, she felt a seed of ice take up residence in her chest. Merin spoke, her words calm and measured, but Lyari wasn't listening.

For the first time since accepting Merin's invitation to become her apprentice, Lyari thought she had made the wrong choice.

The older woman had spread out scrolls all over the trestle table, weighted down by geodes that sparkled in the firelight from the hearth. The scrolls told a story Lyari had already heard, and she couldn't bring herself to look at them. Beyond the old soothsayer at the table, Jenin sat in a rocking chair, hys eyes closed, body still.

Hys presence had become a constant for Lyari, something she could count on. She knew her lover was dead, and yet seeing hyr was welcome, wanted. A reminder.

Merin was telling her about the spell, the Hearthland spell that had given their land such bounty. It wasn't new information, but Lyari knew she ought to be listening. The spell was meant to last five hundred cycles, and if Merin's calculations were correct, it would only last perhaps three more now. It would be their job to reinvoke the spell, to find the sacrifices necessary to ensure the bounty of the Hearthland for five hundred more.

When Lyari had told Merin that she could do no magic, Merin had waved her hand and said she needn't fret about it. That if Lyari could not find her catalyst in time for the reinvocation of the spell, the sacrifices would serve as the necessary catalyst. Because of that, Lyari had spent the past two moons studying all the magical theory Merin could teach her. Like now, where Merin sat droning on about the balance of forces and the drawing of will from within oneself.

Lyari traced a design on parchment with her charcoal stick. The rune for the Sustain Moon, a single vertical line with two horizontal crosspieces, the upper crossbar less wide than the lower. Even. Steady. Sustain. She traced over it again, then once again until the black line seemed to devour all light from the fire like a hole.

"You should be listening, Lyari."

Lyari started from her introspection, sheepishly meeting Merin's gaze. "I'm sorry, Merin."

The older woman harrumphed and rapped her knuckles on a scroll on the table. "Magic is useful even if you cannot apply it just yet," she said. "Even being able to recognize it for what it is can be the difference between life and death."

Any mention of death brought Jenin to Lyari's mind, and she looked past Merin at Jenin where sy still sat in the chair, hys eyes fluttering open to meet hers. Sy raised hys finger to hys lips, as if to say, "*Ahsh.*"

Whatever magic brought hyr back to Lyari, Merin clearly could not see.

"Do you know who killed Jenin?" Lyari asked suddenly.

Merin's gaze turned cloudy, and she looked at the hearth, where the dancing flames reflected off a row of glass bottles on the stone. Cordials, Lyari knew, of hibiscus and iceberry and sweet honey mead. "We would all like to know who killed Jenin," Merin said.

Lyari took that answer for what it was—not an answer at all. She knew, somewhere deep inside her, that Merin knew who had killed her lover, but she knew just as deeply that Merin would only tell her once she thought Lyari was ready.

Which was why Lyari would have to find out for herself.

She turned back to Merin to ask a question, but the old woman's eyes had gone distant, her pupils contracting to black points. A moment later, they resumed their normal size, and she started, a look of satisfaction creeping across her face.

"What is it?" Lyari knew soothsayers had ways of getting information; she had, after all, overheard Merin's conversation with Harag, who had been in Bemin's Fan at the time. But these were not secrets Merin had yet shared with her.

"Just a bit of good news," Merin said. "Now. Concentrate. I'd like you to tell me the necessary steps for restoring the hearthstone spell."

Two hours later, Lyari entered her—formerly Carin's—round-home with an aching head and a sore back from sitting up on Merin's bench all evening. Jenin walked at her side, as usual, but did not touch her. As Lyari readied herself for bed, Jenin sat on the edge of the mattress to watch her.

"Why did you ask who killed me?" sy asked, curiosity lighting hys face in the flickering lamplight.

"I want to know."

"Did you ever think to ask me?"

Lyari looked at hyr, frowning. "I have asked you."

"I didn't say I'd tell you."

Jenin's smirk was infuriating, but Lyari couldn't help the futile chuckle that escaped her throat. "I need to know who it was," Lyari said.

"You'll find out."

"Will you help me?"

Jenin was silent for a long moment, then sy patted the mattress beside hyr. Lyari went to hyr and sat, meeting hys gaze with eyes that filled with tears unbidden.

"Merin is teaching me magic," Lyari said.

"I know. I see your lessons."

"I will use it to find your killer."

"Magic has many more uses than simply that."

"It's not simply anything," Lyari told hyr. "I need to know."

"You have hardly even spoken to my brother," Jenin said.

"Dyava?" Lyari's eyes widened. "Did he—"

"Of course not," Jenin said, hys face an ever-changing sky.

Jenin's fingers brushed Lyari's chin, a flicker of consternation in hys eyes. Lyari knew that look. Jenin had often looked that way when Lyari had missed the point of something sy was saying. Just then, though, Lyari didn't care. She felt only that touch.

Simple, tiny touches were all she ever got from hyr now, like the kiss of a ghost. Lyari remembered the long afternoons they had spent on the Bemin's banks fishing or simply lounging about talking about the future. Their future. It had been too much to ask to get that future, it turned out. She missed those days, back when Jenin's chest was solid beneath her head, when hys arms were solid around her shoulders, when hys lips were solid against hers. Lyari wanted to cry, wanted to bury her face in Jenin's shoulder, but she had tried that before to no avail. She had found only empty air, and she needed so much more than that. Looking into Jenin's eyes, she could not bear the thought of speaking to Dyava and seeing his, much the same, alive.

"I will find your killer," she said aloud again.

But Jenin was already gone.

RYD FROZE at the sound of the man's voice cutting through the stillness of the foothills. The hawk's loud cry still echoed in his mind, and for some reason, that sound had given him even more terror than the sight of an armed man with an arrow pointed directly at his heart. Four more people stepped out from behind trees, and suddenly Ryd wanted to apologize to Carin for not believing her when she said they were being watched.

She reacted before he did, nocking and drawing an arrow and loosing it toward a woman to her left. Ryd dived to the ground at the dual twang of bowstrings, and he felt an arrow whistle by his face even as he heard a scream. Another one of Carin's arrows sprouted from a man's throat, blood spurting. A woman came running at Carin, and she loosed another arrow into the woman's chest, then a third arrow that sank into the woman's stomach. The attacker fell to her knees, and Carin kicked her in the face.

The first archer had another arrow nocked and aimed at Ryd, but seeing two of his people down, he turned it toward Carin. Ryd rushed him, darting back and forth the way he'd seen rabbits try to avoid a predator. The man's bowstring twanged again, and Ryd threw himself to the side. The arrow caught his tunic, and a flash of hot pain traced the outside of his arm. One step to the left and the arrow would have punctured his heart.

Carin got to the bowman before Ryd could, knocking him backward with her hands about his throat. Ryd unsheathed his belt knife and hurried to her side, not sure what to do. His tongue tasted of bile, and his vision swam. The cut on his arm burned, and he looked wildly around. Someone grabbed him from behind. His knife skittered from his grasp, landing with a thud on the ground.

"Carin!" He gasped her name as his attacker dragged him backward. Spots swam in front of his eyes, and even though he knew he ought to be feeling fear, fear for his life and fear for Carin, what he felt was shame. He couldn't fight off a swarm of sweaty children; what made him think he would ever be able to fight grown adults?

Carin released the throat of the first archer and stalked toward him. Ryd's feet dragged in the dirt, and the blade pressed up against his throat.

"Don't move," said a voice behind him, breath hot against his ear.

The blade dented the sensitive skin of Ryd's neck. Panic filled him. Was this what Jenin felt just before sy died?

When I say move, move.

It sounded like Carin's voice, but her lips weren't moving. She suddenly dropped to the ground, her hand closing around something. Ryd's knife.

Move!

Her voice bellowed through Ryd's mind, and he threw his weight backward into the body of his attacker. A loud thump sounded by his head, somehow wet. When the pressure at his neck fell away, Ryd fell backward onto the ground, breathing hard. His knife protruded from the forehead of a woman, a trickle of blood falling sideways over her eyebrow.

Something wet dribbled down his neck. He raised his hand to the skin, and it came away red.

Carin's face drained of color, and she launched herself past the dead body to his right, slamming into someone. Ryd scrambled to the side, gasping as Carin rained down blows on a man half again her size. The air seemed to grow colder.

A flurry of motion caught his eyes, and Ryd tried to snatch his knife from the woman's forehead beside him as Carin grappled with the larger man. The knife was stuck fast, and whoever it was wasn't running toward them; he was running away.

The final man Carin was hitting didn't hit back, but he put his hands up to cover his face. "I yield!" he yelled.

Just like that, and as quickly as it had begun, it was over.

Four bodies littered the ground around them. The two Carin had downed with her bow—one of them took his last breath as Ryd watched—and the third lay still by the maha tree, his neck the wrong color, almost blue-black like an old bruise. His hand was curled in a tight claw, a densely woven leather cuff on his wrist, intricate and well-formed. Ryd stared at that detail, then looked to Carin.

"How did you do that?" Ryd asked Carin.

Her chest heaving from the exertion, she scrambled to her feet, placing one foot on the mouth of the woman she'd killed with Ryd's knife and jerking the hilt. It popped free with a sickening squelch, and she fell to her knees beside the final attacker, pressing the blade against his throat.

"Who are you?" she demanded. "Why are you trying to kill us? We're not anyone."

"You're Nameless," he said.

Ryd felt as though he had wandered into a conversation he didn't understand. "How did you know that?"

The man's gaze flickered toward Ryd, contempt showing as clearly as the sun on water.

"Who are you?" Carin said again. She gave the blade a push, leaving a smear of the dead woman's blood on the brown skin of the man's throat.

"I am Ras va Cantoranth," he said. His eyes looked beyond Carin, in the direction the final attacker had fled. "Or I was."

"What do you mean, you were?" Ryd felt as though the world had begun spinning around him, and he couldn't stay upright. He pulled himself over to a doubloon tree and leaned against its silvery bark.

The man didn't answer for a long moment, but then Ryd saw him swallow, making the knife blade bob at his throat. "I was Ras va Cantoranth, but with my companion's speedy...exit...I have just become Nameless, just as you are Nameless."

"What are you talking about?" Carin still held the knife to Ras's throat, but her hand shook on its hilt.

"If you take that blade away from my neck, I will tell you. Unless you would rather kill me; it may be a mercy."

Carin blinked, and Ryd sucked in a breath. The dribble of wetness still flowed down the side of his neck, and this time he raised his hand to it again, tracing it upward. His fingers touched his ear and something stung. Something there...dangled. When he brushed at it, he felt a plucking sensation and something fell onto the ground.

"Ryd?" Carin looked at him, alarmed.

Ryd pointed at the hunk of flesh, then held out his hand, his fingers covered in blood. He felt sick.

Carin's eyes widened, and she turned back to Ras va Cantoranth. "If I remove this knife from your throat to tend to my friend, will you guarantee our safety?"

"Killing you now would accomplish nothing," he said. "Jahd will return to Bemin's Fan before I could catch him, and he will get news to the soothsayers. I am already Nameless. I can either choose to die now, or live a little longer and die later. We are on equal footing, you and me."

Carin laughed, a quiet, empty sound.

Ryd got the impression that Ras va Cantoranth was speaking only to Carin, but he couldn't bring himself to think that smarted any more than the ear that had been partially lobbed off.

Carin removed the blade, wiping it on the tunic of the woman she had killed with it. She then knelt in front of Ryd, pushing his hair back from his face with rough fingers.

"Your ear," she said.

"It's on the ground," Ryd said stupidly, pointing.

She looked at the lump of flesh, now coated in dirt and blood, then she pushed his chin to turn his head sideways. "The bleeding is already slowing. It was just the lobe and a bit of cartilage," she said.

"Just the lobe."

"Are you expecting to walk in circles now?" Ras asked, tone snide.

"Shut your mouth, or I will sew your lips closed," Carin said absently. Ryd trembled. She couldn't actually mean that. Over her shoulder, Ryd saw Ras blanch, and Carin met Ryd's gaze. A small smirk appeared on her face, and he let out a breath he hadn't realized he'd been holding. She joked.

She looked at Ryd then, and he was surprised to see tears forming in her eyes. Carin took his cheeks between her hands and kissed each soundly, then squeezed his shoulders once.

After a moment, she turned back to Ras va Cantoranth. "You will tell us everything. Now."

THE TANG of salt air stung Sart's nostrils as she reined in her ihstal mount on the sandy beach at Silirtahn. Waves crashed against the shore, leaving squiggles of foam against the pale brown sand. The ihstal whistled, and Sart leaned forward to stroke its neck. The ihstal either hated beaches or liked them too much, and from the eager whistles that had become more frequent the closer they drew to the sea, Sart guessed that, for this particular beast, it was the latter. If she'd had the time, she would have happily allowed her mount to gallop up and down the beach, to feel its lithe muscles bunching and stretching beneath her and the wind in her face.

As it was, she was two turns late to meet Culy, and she wasn't sure if the message she'd sent ahead of her with a rider before she acquired her own transportation had arrived or not. The waymake of Silirtahn was finally visible in the distance, and she walked the ihstal toward it. A Salter stave-holder met her halfway, hys driftwood staff inset with murderously sharp oyster shells that covered the top foot of it. Sart couldn't tell hys gender.

"Sart Lahivar," sy said, tossing hys hair back from hys face and lowering the staff in acknowledgement.

"Have we met?" Sart eyed the stave-holder, trying to place hys face.

"I'm Valon ve Avarsahla, and no, we haven't met. Culy, however, has spoken of you very highly."

"Ah." Sart dismounted her ihstal, keeping one hand tight on the animal's reins. Its long neck stretched out, nostrils twitching at the breeze. The stave-holder hefted hys—her, Sart amended, having heard her appellation—staff and motioned toward Silirtahn. "Culy's been expecting me. I ran into some trouble."

"So your message said," Valon said. A small smile spread across her face, which would have irritated Sart had she not found Valon's dimples endearing.

"Culy got my message, then."

"I'm afraid not."

"What do you mean, you're afraid not? Where's Culy?"

"Sy had to move on. I'll tell you about it in hys hut. You'll have a place to stay as long as you're here."

"That was thoughtful of hyr." Now irritation did spread through Sart, tickling at her like a feather between her shoulder blades. "By how long did my message miss hyr?"

"Two days."

"Rot."

Valon motioned to a line of posts with her staff, and Sart carefully tied the ihstal to the first one in the line. So Culy had had to move on, and Sart had bought an ihstal for nothing. At least the Salters folk in Silirtahn were an easy enough lot to get on with. They liked Sart's tricks and turns, and she never had to want for opponents at the shells board, no matter how much she'd lifted off them with her winnings in her last visit. If she remembered correctly, last time she'd paid a visit to Silirtahn, she'd left with a sack of dried oysters, a new spade, and a conu fruit that must have washed up on shore somewhere. Veritable treasure.

She'd learned that you could tell a lot about a person by where sy spent the most time, and Salters folk may have been born in Crevasses or Sands or even Taigers, but once they came to Salters, they didn't stray far from those waymakes even though they, like everyone else, moved with the turning of the cycles.

Sart followed Valon into the waymake, raising her two forefingers to her lips in greeting to a few familiar faces who exclaimed her name as she walked past. Apart from Crevasses, Sart liked to visit Silirtahn the most out of all the region's waymakes. Friendly folk. For stories and a few tricks you'd have their friendship, as long as you didn't steal from them or bring rovers their way.

About the rovers. Sart winced. "Valon," she said. "Have you heard of a rover leader called Wyt?"

Valon looked startled, nodding. "Up near north Sands, somewhere around the edge of Boggers. She's got a big encampment there, some twenty rovers who listen to her and do what she says. I heard tell they were looking for weapons."

"I'll be an ihstal's turd," Sart muttered. "You heard right on that tell. I got picked up by a band of rovers. Was passing myself as a halmer."

Valon frowned at Sart. They passed by a sandsmith, the heat from the forge reaching out to the path as the smith pulled a ball of glowing glass from inside. Shelves stood beyond the smith, rows of glass trinkets littering them and glinting in the dim sunlight that cut through the thin layer of clouds. Green and blue, clear like the seawater, shone bright. Red and purple items, mostly broken, glowed but did not shine, their glossy sheen dulled by the sea's tossing them against the sand. Where they came from, no one knew, but occasionally salters would find the red and purple glass items along the beaches. Pretty, if one liked baubles. Sart didn't care for them herself.

Sart's feet sank into the sand as they walked. Eventually, they came to a low hut of waxed canvas, its bottom edges buried deep into the sand. Valon pulled back the hut's door flap, motioning Sart to follow her in. Sart ducked to enter the hut. Inside, lamps of burning seadog oil were spread on a central table with a brazier at the center, burning coals. A bed mat of driftwood raised a pallet off the sand, and there was a tightly wound scroll in the center of it.

"From Culy?" Sart guessed, her heart sinking.

Valon nodded. "If you need me, I'll be right outside."

"You don't have to guard me, you know."

"Culy doesn't want you left alone here."

"Sy didn't leave anything in here for me to steal." Sart grumped, flopping down on the pallet.

"I think sy meant for your own safety."

"I don't know what sy's talking about. I'm not a *child*. Everyone here likes me just fine."

"Perhaps not a child, but I'm not sure you want to grow up quite yet."

Valon smirked and exited the hut, leaving Sart to sit and stare into the brazier. After a minute, she unwound the scroll. Each line of Culy's neat hand made Sart's stomach sink just a bit deeper into her core. Not only had she missed Culy by less than a turn, but Culy had gone in the exact direction Sart had come from—by way of Sands, but still. Sart reread the note, which asked her to meet Culy in Crevasses at the height of Foresight Moon.

Sart spent about an hour swearing and strategizing, then left the hut to tend to her ihstal. She gave the beast free reign to run up and down the beach near Silirtahn, and the ihstal, seeming to sense Sart's frustration, opened up its speed, kicking up sand in a glorious cloud of grit for the better part of an hour. When the sky began to darken, Sart made her way back into Silirtahn, tethering the ihstal just outside the waymake again. She'd have to give the beast a name one of these days.

She traded one of the more worn knives she'd lifted off the rovers for five smoked fish and a pouch of salt. They'd make her rucksack smell awful, but she wouldn't have to worry about food for a few days. The salt she'd be able to trade to someone on the road back to Crevasses if she needed to. After eating half of one of the fish—the rest she wrapped in waxed canvas and tied with gut string—she sat down on the mattress to figure out what to do next. She knew she ought to turn about and head right back to Crevasses; the journey backward would take the better part of the moon's wane, and she'd have to avoid the Lahi'alar, the roadways that connected the regions like a vast web. Rovers mainly kept to the Lahi'alar, as there they would find most other travelers to rob, and Sart had had quite enough of rovers for a time.

Briefly, Valon's comment intruded. Sart had seen nineteen cycles pass. Plenty of folk got half as many. She might as well be half a hundred cycles into life for all she'd seen.

Sart took time the next day to rest and wander through Silirtahn, playing a few games of shells with local folk and carefully chatting to passers-through about rover activity. She didn't learn many new things, but three separate people confirmed what Valon had said about Wyt up in north Sands, and that alone was disturbing enough for Sart. Culy would want to know about this, if sy didn't already. Sart was beginning to feel like a child's ball batted back and forth.

A small family caravan entered Silirtahn from the north, and Sart listened to the mother barter urgently with the local sea-speaker for medicine, trading nearly a moon's worth of dried lizard meat—an exorbitant price—for a small vial of spike-fish extract to treat a dying child. Sart could hear the child coughing in the family's wagon over the mother's firm voice. The mother's tone didn't convey her panic, but her willingness to part with that much food did. What use was it to save the child's life today if sy would simply starve next turn? And a starved parent could save no children.

Sart didn't stick around to find out. By the end of the day, Sart was ready to move on, even if it meant going back in the direction she'd just come from.

She packed up and left in the dark hour before dawn, bidding Valon a plentiful day. Sart wasn't sure, but she thought Valon's eyes lingered a bit longer on her than simply being a guard would account for. Sart considered for a moment staying to explore that possibility, then quickly decided against it. Whatever would be would be.

Her ihstal danced on the sand when Sart mounted, whistling excitedly. *"Tahin,"* Sart said to the mount. "Dancer. I think I've found your name."

RAS VA Cantoranth felt like he had strode into a corral knee deep in shit.

He fought the panic that continually clawed its way up his ribcage every time he looked at the Nameless. They still called themselves by their child-names, of course, but that didn't change the fact that they were Nameless. And he with them. Jahd would return to Bemin's Fan and pass on the news, if Merin and Harag didn't already know, along with Reynah in Cantoranth. The three soothsayers of the Hearthland had their own ways of keeping eyes on things.

Sahnat was dead. Ras could have drawn up fury about that, but he couldn't blame the Nameless woman for protecting herself. Though how she'd managed to strangle Sahnat, who Ras had once seen take down a tiger barehanded, escaped him.

The air felt as crisp as an Early Bird apple, and he woke each morning waiting for the frost. Four days had passed since the fight in the pass, and Ras had simply followed the Nameless north, farther into the Mad Mountains. He heard them discussing shelter for the winter, and eventually he would have to say something to them. Their naïveté was unsurprising; they had no way of understanding the situation in which they found themselves. Still, Ras grappled with the dawning realization that their situation was, in truth now, his situation.

They stopped for the night on the leeward side of a sharp rise. Wind blew from the mountains, smelling of dry snow and cold coming in its wake. The man and woman discussed in low tones what they would do for food, and as he watched, they laid out their stores. Much of it they had already had with them, but some they had taken from the bodies of his friends.

So far, Ras had avoided telling them much, for all the woman had demanded that first day. That he had been sent to kill them was obvious enough. Though he offered to take up watch at night, neither would let him, and he didn't blame them. Apparently their naïveté did not make them entirely stupid.

But with that wind blowing in from the north and the knowledge that snow and winter were imminent both, Ras sat down next to the woman and their food. She looked up at him, her eyes as dark blue as the Jewel in the mountains to the east. Her skin was as golden as the afternoon sun, and her hair, though unwashed and untidy, was as lustrous black as anyone's. He made himself think her child-name. Carin. And her companion was Ryd.

Even now, their village would be forgetting them. He was staring at ghosts.

You're a ghost, his mind reminded him.

"What do you want?" Carin asked. She returned to looking over the stores. With two people, it might have kept them fed until the Night of Reflection. With three, they'd be lucky to get one moon past Harvest Harmonix. The High Harvest. What should have been a feast would now be nothing but a famished day under the moons and sun as they shared the sky like old friends, meeting once every five cycles at midday.

"I haven't told you everything," Ras made himself say. The words felt thick and gummy, like cold syrup on a winter morning. The man, Ryd, snorted.

"We know that," Carin said softly. "You're only alive because I don't feel like killing another person. For now."

"If you kill me, you'll never get through the mountains," said Ras. More confident now—a good bargaining piece was always useful, and he had that—he drew his shoulders back.

"We probably won't get through the mountains anyway." Ryd looked northward, his eyes as pale green as jade and twice as stony. If a look could level a mountain range, that would have done it. For a slight man, Ryd seemed to vary between quiet observation and bitterness. Ras made note of that.

"Probably not," Ras agreed. "They'll send more hunters to kill you, you know."

Carin's head snapped back to look at him. "What?"

"You really thought six people would be all? They'll send more."

"Why? We're no one anymore."

To Ras's eyes, Carin seemed to avoid looking at Ryd. Maybe making eye contact with someone she'd grown up with would make the threat of death more real, or maybe she was simply imagining who back home would be orchestrating her murder.

"You're Nameless. You're a threat to everything the Hearthland is," Ras said, then spat. "You know about the spell the founders cast. You know about the Northlands and what they did to us, how they pay for it now."

Ryd made a bundle of dried meat, his hands steady and silent on the waxed canvas. "We're not much of a threat to anyone right now."

"No Nameless may live."

Carin stared at a small bowl of dried roundberries, their deep blue darkened to black. Ras couldn't tell what she was thinking. Whatever he saw on her face—acceptance, maybe, or resignation—was quickly schooled away.

"Who sent you? Merin?" Her guess came suddenly, and Ras blinked. "Yes."

Ryd's eyes widened. "Merin stood birth-vigil for me."

"She stood birth-vigil for everyone in Haveranth," Carin muttered. Her eyes went distant for a moment, and something seemed to pass between her and Ryd that Ras couldn't quite comprehend. Then she turned her gaze on Ras. "So Merin wants us dead. You said if I kill you, we'll never make it through the mountains. The implication in that is that I leave you alive, we will. Or at least we'll have a chance. What is it you know that we do not?"

Ras rummaged in the folds of his cloak and pulled out a large piece of folded parchment. "Hunters have to know the land better than anyone else. Much of the cycle, we bring back food for our villages, but when there are Nameless, we are responsible for making sure they do not live." He unfolded the parchment, spreading it out over the hard, dry ground. It showed the expanse of the Mad Mountains, spanning from Bemin's Fan to the far east of Cantoranth, where they curved southward to sneak back around to the sea. On the map were the three villages of the Hearthland, with each of the few solitary homes that dotted the area marked. And into the mountains were deep red lines, the ink pressed from the bloodleaf plant that grew in the southern fields. There weren't many lines; the mountains to north and south were nearly impassable. But there were lines. Some few. One led north from the Hidden Vale—none of the Journeyers who would later become Nameless would know that a pass northward to freedom was then within their grasp, if they simply never returned to their villages and pressed on into the Mad Mountains. Another two led south, one far to the southeast past Cantoranth, Ras's birthplace. Another skirted the coast south of Bemin's Fan.

And another...Ras traced the last one with his fingertip, stopping in the foothills where they currently sat.

"If we follow this line, we will find the path our ancestors took to the Hearthland. We can go north, into the lands beyond. Find a new life."

He kept his voice steady, or at least he thought he did. To his own ears his terror seeped between the cracks in his words. Into the Northlands, where disease and starvation were rampant. Where there would be wars for clean water. A harsh land. A broken land. Or possibly none at all. No one really knew. It had been hundreds of cycles since their ancestors left, maybe more.

Still, the risk was better than simply having his body returned to the land.

Ras knew the path ahead was not an easy one, but he wanted to live. He folded up the map and placed it back into the folds of his cloak. There were many things Carin and Ryd did not know, and Ras would keep those things close until forced to share.

He scanned the sky above their heads, but saw nothing. No hint of snow, no clouds rolling in.

They would race the winter into the mountains.

SITTING ACROSS from Merin at her table, Lyari tapped her fingers on the wooden edge. A jingling sound came from Merin's room.

"Excuse me, Lyari," Merin said. "I won't be gone long."

She left Lyari at her place, and Lyari looked after her, knowing the old woman was satisfied with her work. Lyari felt a tingle in her skin, the hairs prickling.

Merin shut the door to her room, smiling at Lyari.

Lyari smiled back and turned back to the scroll.

A hand passed over the scroll. She jumped.

"Jenin," Lyari said. "You gave me a fright."

"Look at Merin's door," Jenin said.

"Jenin—"

"Look at it."

Lyari obeyed, mystified. Merin's door was closed. There was nothing to see.

"Look closer."

Lyari squinted. "I don't know what you want me to s—"

Jenin's palm landed on the back of Lyari's hand. The door blurred, and then vanished.

Merin sat on the edge of her bed, fingers touching the edge of a scrying glass she kept on the bedside table. Lyari had seen that glass before. The jingling stopped, and Lyari felt a tingle of something spread through the room.

"Watch," Jenin said softly. "And be silent."

"Merin," a voice said. The soothsayer of Bemin's Fan looked out from the glass, her eyes a deep gold the color of melted brown sugar. Harag, she was called. "Jahd returned."

Merin grasped the glass a bit tighter in her hands. "Jahd returned. But not Sahnat? Where are the others?"

"Only Jahd returned." Harag turned her glass, her face leaving the frame in place of the person who must be Jahd, whose angular features filled the scrying surface.

Lyari opened her mouth to ask what was happening, but Jenin pressed hys hand tighter over hers with a sharp shake of hys head.

Jahd waited several moments to speak, as if unsure how speaking into an oval of glass in Bemin's Fan would convey his words and likeness to Merin in Haveranth, leagues away. Lyari had never seen the glass work herself. What a wonder it would be, to use such a thing. Sahnat was a hunter, Lyari knew. Was he in danger?

"We were successful," Jahd said, swallowing. "But at the cost of lives. I was the only survivor."

Merin went still. Her breath came fast in Lyari's chest. Sahnat, dead? "Sahnat is dead?"

"The Nameless woman killed him with her bare hands. I put an arrow in her chest."

Lyari froze. Carin. Carin had killed someone? Bare-handed? Lyari's breath stopped, stuck in her throat.

It couldn't be true. Why would Carin do such a thing?

"But the Nameless are dead." Merin's knuckles showed white where they grasped the glass.

A small sound escaped Lyari's mouth, and Jenin's free hand quickly covered it. Solid flesh, or so it felt. Lyari felt as if the bench beneath her had crumbled to ash.

"Look at the parchment," Jenin said urgently. "*Now*. Look down."

Lyari did, tilting her head downward just as a flicker of movement in her periphery told her Merin had turned to look at the door.

"The Nameless are dead," said Jahd's voice. Lyari no longer saw his face in the scrying glass. The runes on the scroll swam in front of her eyes.

Merin went on as if she were discussing the climber fish run.

"And Sahnat's body? The bodies of the others?"

"Burned in the pass."

Merin nodded. "Thank you, Jahd. I wish you a bountiful High Harvest."

"And you, soothsayer."

Lyari looked up involuntarily, the terror of perhaps looking up to see Merin's eyes on hers eclipsed by the need to see what was happening. Merin's back was to the door once more, the glass visible like a waning moon behind the curve of Merin's head.

Harag's face reappeared in the glass, and Lyari heard the sound of a door closing far away in Bemin's Fan. "Do you want me to check?"

"I'll do it, Harag." Merin went silent for a moment.

"You're sure your apprentice will be ready to do what needs to be done?" Harag's young face was yet unlined, though she had seen twice as many harvests as most of the villagers in Bemin's Fan. "Markat lost hys pregnancy yesterday."

The news seemed to hit Merin like a blow. Markat's pregnancy was the first Bemin's Fan had seen all this cycle, and if sy had lost the baby...

"Lyari will be ready."

"She doesn't yet know of the fate of the Nameless?"

"She still needs more time, especially after Jenin. Once the memories have yet faded a little in the minds of the villagers here, then I will be able to tell her. She will need to be prepared to do what is necessary."

Lyari's fingers clawed against the tabletop. Her throat felt dry and gummy in spite of the tea she'd been drinking all day.

"There is not much time." Harag's brow creased between her eyes. "If there are yet three harvests between now and the reinvocation, we may take the entirety of the next five hundred cycles simply recovering our population."

Merin put the scrying glass aside, and Lyari dropped her gaze to the scrolls again.

Jenin's hand left Lyari's.

"Please don't leave," Lyari whispered hoarsely. "How am I supposed to face her?"

"You have to," Jenin said. "You have to learn everything you can from her."

When Merin returned to the central hearth, a cup of goat's milk cut with bitterberry extract in hand, Lyari forced herself to look up from the scrolls on the table.

"These spells. How did you learn them?" Lyari asked. Her voice sounded far away to her own ears, but Merin didn't seem to notice.

"The soothsayers before me passed them down, perfected them." Merin sat across from Lyari at the table and selected one of the scrolls.

Lyari reached out to touch it. The scroll was the one that governed the Nameless, leeched away the memory of them from the village. She couldn't fully grasp the scroll's contents, even if she could understand the runes on the parchment. That was only half the knowledge required to understand the composition of a spell. The words were more than an explanation but less than a focal point; they were far more than incidental to the construction of wide-ranging magic, but magic was not contingent upon their existence. Merin, in her many, many cycles of study, had told Lyari that the runes and words used to formulate magic for human use were only a very human way of making something very large seem somehow manageable.

The reality of magic was that you could only point it in a direction and make educated guesses of what would happen. Lyari would have to learn this in the time that came before the reinvocation. From this woman who had murdered her oldest friend and now handed her a spell to erase that friend from the village's consciousness.

"Tell me the branches of magic again," Merin said, replacing the scroll on the table as if it were a stray leaf, that parchment that would erase Carin and Ryd from existence.

When darkness fell over Haveranth hours later, Lyari left Merin's roundhome, the whole of her body numb instead of stiff from the day of study. She left, but did not go home, unable to make her feet move. Shadows shrouded her where she stood amid a small grove of trees. When Merin left the roundhome some time later, Lyari followed, strafing sideways in the shadows to avoid notice as Merin went to her clucker coop and touched her hand to a withered claw that hung from a rafter. The dim lamplight cast more shadows across the walls. Lyari had seen the claw before, but until that moment, she didn't realize what it was for.

A flap of wings came moments later, followed by a clicking sound. The hawk descended through a hole in the coop's roof and landed on a perch in front of Merin. Merin stroked the claw, and the hunting bird ducked its head at her, beady eyes flashing in the lamplight. From where Lyari stood, she could see a glint of green in the hawk's eye, green like moss.

"Seek," Merin said. The hawk's tail was banded in black, and the bird fanned it out, clawed feet clinging to the perch. Merin reached out for a small bucket of offal she kept and fed the hawk from her fingers. It gulped down a chunk of liver and worried its beak.

After another moment, the hawk flapped its wings and soared upward, out the hole in the eaves and into the night.

Lyari turned, cold as a winter wind, and walked home.

ON THE sixth day after Carin's first murder, frost covered the ground.

She knew that, to the south, the Early Bird trees would be covered in rich blooms for only the day, flowers that would sparkle in the sunlight and then drop their petals to the ground. Here, in the southern reaches of the mountains, there were no apple trees to be found now.

With one more mouth to feed, Carin found herself obsessing about food. Each day she kept her strung bow across her back, ready to catch any animal that might stray across their path. As long as they were able, she would feed their party with animals she caught each day rather than digging into their food stores.

She hadn't wanted to say it aloud to Ras, but Carin knew Ryd was thinking the same things as she was. This was the world Dyava and Lyah had willingly affirmed. Could Merin be the reason Jenin had died on the morning of their Journeying? That the very woman who had brought her into the world from her mother's womb could be responsible for trying to return her to the earth felt like a deep and unbreachable wrongness. Still, Ras insisted that more hunters would be coming, and if his map were any indication, they would know exactly where to start searching.

Her instinct told her they ought to veer from the red line on the map, away from the known passes through the mountains. Find a valley in which they could winter, build a shelter away from the paths Merin or any of the other soothsayers or hunters would expect to find them struggling along. But instead she pressed on with Ryd and Ras, wishing she could have a moment to discuss things privately with Ryd and still ever-distrustful of Ras, for all his maps and knowledge.

When Ryd stopped under a doubloon tree late in the afternoon one day, Carin walked up to him, where he stood staring upward at its silvery branches. Still some bright buttery gold leaves clung to them, others falling in fluttery circles here and there around them. The beauty was not lost on Carin, but she did not think that was why Ryd stopped.

"It's going to snow soon," he said.

Carin nodded. Ras had ranged a bit ahead, looking pointedly at the sun that sank toward the mountain ridge. She knew he was trying to indicate that they ought not waste what little light remained, but she ignored him.

"What are you thinking, Ryd?" Carin asked.

"The snows in the mountains aren't like what we get in Haveranth. Not a few inches here and there. Feet. We'll be buried."

Grim, Carin nodded. "It will slow our progress, to be sure."

"We can go leagues each day right now. When the snows come, we won't be able to do that anymore. I was thinking I could make us shoes like the hunters use when they go into the mountains in winter. You've been making twine from gut; I've seen you."

"It's not the best. I'm not sure it would support the weight of a person."

"It's worth a try. I can ply it together if I need to." Ryd's face was set in a determined mask. When he turned his head, she saw the rough edge of his ear where the hunter had taken off the lobe.

Carin remembered how he had frozen in the fight. Maybe this was his way of wanting to contribute. Ras had come to look at her with grudging respect, but he treated Ryd like an enigma, and sometimes Carin caught Ras looking at him as if he wondered how Ryd had survived this long.

She nodded. "We can stay here for a couple of days. Hunt while you do that. Try to build up as many stores as we can for winter."

It went unsaid that they all knew the futility of any preparation. The chances of them surviving the winter with hunters after them and the cold and the scarcity of food ahead—too small. Yet it also went unsaid that they would continue to try. It wasn't worth it to stop and give up. Carin didn't want to die, but if she had to look death in the face, she would do it with fire in her eyes.

They spent three days there in the doubloon tree grove while Ryd collected springy boughs from the trees and bent them into teardrop shapes. He unrolled a set of carving tools and dug notches into the boughs at intervals, and while he worked, Carin and Ras hunted and fished. Carin set up a smoker with tree branches and pine boughs and hung fish to cure, laying out grids of rabbit, saiga, and a few pika they found gathering food. She took as much time as she could to scrape the pelts of the animals they killed, pulling the intestines for twine. Three days was far from long enough to do anything well, but the furs they collected would do well to warm them in the winter months.

Ryd worked by himself on the far side of the camp, plying and tying gut twine, then looping it over the doubloon boughs, building a mesh of webbing that would both hold their feet to the snowshoes and help the structure maintain its shape. On the third day, a light rain began, and as darkness sank over the mountains, the rain turned to chunks of ice and then to thick, wet globs of snow.

Carin watched the large flakes fall to the ground, where they melted almost immediately. For some reason, the sight exhausted her. For the past nearly seven moons, she had been racing the turning of the cycle. First fleeing Haveranth at Planting Harmonix and running against the coming of High Lights. Now she ran into the mountains to face starvation, freezing, and a homeland that wanted her dead.

The snowshoes were finished that night, with Ryd using straps of braided leather to secure them to his feet. He looked silly waddling around the campsite on the wide contraptions, but the look of satisfaction on his face made Carin feel hope for the first time in several turns. Harvest Moon waned above them. Harvest Harmonix had passed unnoticed by Ryd and Ras. What would have been a feast day in Haveranth had become simply another day here. High Harvest, at that.

Carin had marked it. The sky had cleared enough to show the sun and moons together at their zenith, full and round, three globes of light. In Haveranth that day, people would be sharing gifts, feasting, declaring bonds and news of blood and kin. Someone might have declared a new appellation to the village. That someone might have been Carin. She looked up at the waning moon, a lifetime away from the ceremony that might have brought her closer to herself, and when Ras met her eyes questioningly, Carin could only look away.

Caryan vy Haveranth she might have been that day. But even that did not feel right.

That night, as they sat around the campfire eating a rabbit stew with tuber roots and reconstituted pricklebush leaves, Ras told them of snow dwellings, small, rounded huts they could make from snow once the depths were high enough.

"Wouldn't that be too cold?" Ryd asked, wiping a bit of stew from his lips.

Ras shook his head. "The snow keeps itself at a certain temperature. It won't get colder than that, and it will shelter you from the wind. If we need to live in snow dwellings for the worst of the storms, we can."

"Tomorrow we will move on," Carin said. She looked southward, almost involuntarily. "We have seen no more hunters, Ras. Why do you think that is?"

For a brief moment, the man's confidence faltered, and he followed her gaze to the south. "I don't know," he said. "I expected someone to come before now."

"Could we have outpaced them?" Carin didn't think that could be the case; they moved too slowly, and they were the hunted, not the hunters. Not for the first time, she wondered if they were escaping death or simply postponing it. What could await them on the north side of the mountains? What she knew from the Journeying's visions in the Hidden Vale was not encouraging, and still they ran toward it. Any life, even a difficult life, was better than no life at all.

Ras shook his head. "We know these paths too well and are not overburdened with supplies."

Carin didn't like that he used the word *we,* and he seemed to catch his slip.

"They will find us," he said after a pause.

The next morning, a few inches of new snow covered the ground.

LYARI WATCHED as Rina hammered a blade of bronze, the hammer ringing out through the smithery. The woman's corded muscles bulged in the light of the forge, her sleeveless hardened leather smock baring her arms to the shoulders.

Not for the first time, Lyari noticed the pale marks up and down Rina's arms where sparks had flown and burnt her brown skin. Some were pale pink and still healing; others had long since scarred silver.

Lyari had her own silver webs across the arm the mist had grabbed.

"Tell Merin I'll have the sheets ready for her by Second Seed of Foresight." Rina didn't look up from what she was doing, and her voice didn't portray the strain of the physical effort she expended to shape metal to her will.

Lyari wondered what it would be like to build with her hands the way Rina did. Though Carin had learned more trades than simply metalworking, Lyari had focused more on study, learning a little of a lot of paths, broad knowledge instead of specific.

When Lyari didn't answer, Rina's eyes glanced upward to meet hers, waiting for acknowledgement of what she'd said.

"Yes, Rina, I'll tell Merin," Lyari said belatedly. Though she knew she was being dismissed, she lingered, watching Rina work. When she'd been a small child, she and Carin had come in here and watched under the strict orders to stay still and out of the way. The marvel of seeing molten metal molded into new creations had always been full of awe for Lyari, and even now after so much had happened, that awe had not abated. They all made new things out of old. It was the entire reason their village existed. Life from death. *Suo vo dyu, dyu vo suo.* Light from darkness, darkness from light.

Thinking of the proverb reminded Lyari of that day by the Bemin with Jenin, and as if thinking hys name summoned hyr to Lyari's side, Jenin appeared beyond Rina's shoulder, light from the forge glinting in hys eyes.

"You've not stayed this long to watch me in at least five harvests," Rina said, her attention still focused on the blade she hammered against the anvil. "Is something bothering you?"

"Yes," Lyari said without thinking. "Many things."

"I imagine you're feeling alone," Rina said. "The only Journeyer we had this cycle. You spent three moons by yourself. Came back scarred."

Lyari's hand went to her arm, where the tendrils of mist had grasped her, leaving a spiral of web-like white scars across her skin, but that wasn't what made her skin erupt into gooseflesh. "Alone," she said aloud. Her heart began to accelerate in her chest, thumping against her ribs in a stuttering rhythm.

Wrong, wrong, wrong. Lyari met Jenin's eyes over Rina's shoulder, and sy nodded. Lyari opened her mouth, wanting to say that she *hadn't* been alone. She had had Carin and Ryd with her. Together they had braved that mist, gone hungry and had their bodies whittled down to so much muscle and tendon, their bellies concave. In the moons since Lyari had returned to Haveranth, her flesh had remained tight against her bones even when she ate her fill at every meal. Carin might have been starving now, with winter breathing its icy wind upon the land. And her own mother did not remember her. Worse, she should. Rina was an elder of the village. She should have remembered Carin.

Rina put down the hammer she held. "Lyari, are you all right?"

"I'm fine, Rina," Lyari lied, then backed out of the smithery, shooting a glance over her shoulder, not for the metalworker but for Jenin behind her. Hys eyes took on a pitying cast, and he followed a short distance behind Lyari as she walked out into the streets of Haveranth.

As the bloom of luck would have it, the first face she saw on the street belonged to Clar, Jenin's cousin, her arms full of wood for the village hearth-home's fire, as was her duty for the cycle leading up to her own Journeying.

Jenin's face became sadder still at the sight of Clar, and sy let out a sigh loudly enough that Lyari watched Clar walking for any sign that the girl had heard.

Lyari followed Clar to the hearth-home and took a cup of spiced iceberry wine from Tamat, who tended a spit of mutton as always, ready to give some to anyone who might ask. Sitting on a wide bench by the fire, Lyari motioned to Clar to join her. The girl's face had grown thinner, Lyari thought. She signaled to Tamat to slice some mutton onto a plate and handed the plate to Clar as the younger girl sat. Clar took it, but after only three bites set it aside.

"How are your studies, apprentice?" Clar asked politely. The fire roared in the hearth, its heat welcome in the autumn chill.

"Just fine, Clar. You can call me Lyari, you know."

The girl flushed, looking at her knees. "I know." She didn't speak more.

Lyari sat in silence for a moment, considering getting up to leave.

"I know you and Jenin were close," Clar blurted out.

Tamat turned the spit more quickly for just a moment, then slowed it back to normal. Sy didn't meet Lyari's eyes.

"We were," Lyari said slowly, wanting to instead say *we are* and stopping herself. Even now, just to her left, Jenin sat on the bench next to her. Amusement lit hys features, and Lyari felt a flash of annoyance. Sy may have come to terms with hys being dead, but that didn't mean Lyari or Clar had.

"I still think about it," Clar said. She wrung her hands in her lap as if washing them, and Lyari pitied the girl, several emotions warring in her chest. "Dyava said I can talk to him about it, but I can't. I can't make him listen to me talk about Jenin's death."

How could it be that Jenin was remembered where Carin and Ryd were not? The easy answer was that Jenin had died before hys Journeying, before having any chance to become Nameless. Lyari understood why she remembered her former friends—soothsayers had to know the names of all, remember the Nameless—but having just come from Rina's smithery and hearing the woman speak so casually over the chasm where her daughter had fallen made Lyari itch all over. Perhaps this was yet another reason why Lyari could not bring herself to speak to Dyava. The village was not vast. Lyari would not be able to avoid him forever, but she would postpone it as long as she could. To see Dyava's face, to see Jenin's eyes looking out from it, to know no memory of Carin dwelled behind them would be too much. Forgotten by mother and lover alike—Carin deserved better.

Shaking herself back to the moment, Lyari reached out and patted Clar's shoulder. "I understand. You found Jenin that day, did you not?"

Surprised her tone was so even, Lyari gave Clar's shoulder a squeeze.

Clar picked up a chunk of mutton between two fingers and pushed it into her mouth as if eating were more of a chore than constantly tending the village's central fire for the entirety of a season cycle. "I found hyr. Sy was like sahthren to me, Lyari. We were raised together. I thought sy would be there to welcome me back from my Journeying. But I had to wash hys blood from my hands. I can still feel it."

Pity filled Lyari, and she found herself blinking away tears. A slight pressure on her back told her Jenin had reached out a hand, and that light touch gave her some comfort. If only she could tell Clar that Jenin was still here—though Lyari knew that just because she saw hyr, it didn't mean that Jenin was really there. She could accept that and go about her life.

Still, there was little comfort she could give this young girl.

"I want to know who killed hyr," Clar said, the ferocity in her voice surprising Lyari.

Tamat still turned the spit slowly, though sy must have heard what Clar said. Lyari frowned, wishing they were in a less public place for this conversation. Leaving now would only cause talk, though.

"Know that Merin will ensure that Jenin gets justice," Lyari said stoutly. "Do not doubt it."

"If I knew who it was, I would serve justice myself." Clar's eyes burned in the firelight, and she licked grease from her fingers.

Lyari wasn't sure she knew what justice was.

DEEP IN the mountains, Carin paused at the crest of a rise. The snowshoes Ryd had crafted from doubloon boughs and gut twine were caked with snow, but they kept her from sinking into the three feet that had fallen over the past turn. Ryd came up beside her. Even in the cold of the snow falling, he smelled of perspiration and half-cured leather. She didn't want to know what she smelled like.

The days shortened with each passing turn. Carin didn't care to admit it, but fear had taken deep root within her. On top of their boots, they had lashed rabbit furs around their ankles to better insulate their feet from the cold. Carin was deeply grateful for the cloak her mother had given her; its warmth had been a boon beyond measure as they trekked deeper into the mountains.

Ryd's cloak was not so useful. Many of the pelts Carin had scraped during their journey westward were given to Ryd to sew onto the cloak around his shoulders and arms, but still in the cold of night he shivered. Many nights in their shelter, Carin would pull Ryd to her under her own cloak, warming them both. For now, their food stores held, and Carin had been able to continue to hunt until the snows got so deep that they needed the snowshoes.

The hum she had felt since collapsing on the banks of the Bemin continued to haunt her. She had become the fire handler of the party, always managing to kindle flames from sparks where Ras and Ryd could not. Ras proved himself useful in picking out the trail and navigating them northward, though the longer they continued into the mountains without any sign of more hunters, the more apprehensive Carin felt about the explanations Ras had given them. She slept with her belt knife close at hand.

And throughout the peaks that rose around them, Carin sometimes heard the sound of flapping she and Ryd had heard on their Journeying. Never did anything appear; indeed, even owls were scarce this high into the mountain range. She knew that the flapping she heard could be no owl. Whatever it was had to be large, the size of a tent or bigger.

When she asked Ras, he only shrugged. "There are many creatures in these mountains. Most will leave us be. Some will hunt us. If they do, we shall kill them first."

Carin wasn't sure about Ryd, but she found that answer less than helpful.

Three days later, Ras pulled her aside as Ryd dug into the snow to build a fire. "I need to speak to you about something," he said. He motioned at the peaks ahead, which were partially obscured by clouds. The day was mostly clear, but Carin could see more snow coming their way, like a sheet of white waving in the wind.

Carin stood a pace away from Ras, turning to frown at him. "Is it something you have decided Ryd cannot hear?"

"I want to tell you first, so as not to alarm him."

Unsure whether she accepted that, Carin nodded acquiescence anyway. "Just tell me."

She had a feeling she wasn't going to like whatever he had to say. In the course of the last moons spent walking into the mountains with him, Carin and Ryd had learned little about the man. He was older than them both, to be sure. Past his twentieth harvest and thus a full member of Cantoranth. He had spoken of his job, meant both to supply food for his village and to patrol for Nameless when there were any. It chilled Carin more than the icy wind to think that, her whole life, there had been hunters in the foothills of the mountains, prepared to hunt down people for simply daring to balk in the face of their land's deception. It chilled her all the more to think that likely she herself had been considered for the job, with her bow skills and her mother's training. She wondered how the last Nameless from Haveranth had died. An arrow in the chest? A knife across the throat? Not for the first time, she wondered if these hunters had been responsible for Jenin's death, but she didn't trust she'd get a truthful answer from Ras if she asked.

His next sentence chased all other thoughts from her mind.

"My map does not reach all the way to the Northlands."

"What?" Carin's gaze flicked to Ryd, who was still shoveling snow aside with his hands, clumsily covered in rabbit furs that kept them warm, though they destroyed his dexterity. He looked like a fish trying to swim through the snow. She turned back to Ras and advanced a step, coming face to face with the man. He wasn't much taller than she, and she looked him in the eyes over the long scarf of wool he had wound around his face. "You said you knew how to get us to the Northlands."

"I thought I did." He pulled the mitts from his own hands and held them between his knees, reaching into his cloak to pull out the map. Tiny, icy snowflakes landed on the rough parchment, beginning to fall from a rapidly greying sky. He pointed to the red line where it snaked into the mountains between jagged peaks. Then he pointed past the edge of the parchment itself, to blank air. "We're here."

Carin felt as though her heart were about to freeze solid in her chest. "That can't be." she said, exhaling. "Why does it not show farther?"

Ras gestured to the edge of the map, which cut off in the middle of the mountain range. "I don't know. At my best guess, we are about two thirds of the way through the mountains. This is the best pass to travel north by, that much I know. But I did not expect the map to cut out."

His eyes crinkled around the edges, and not from smiling. The strip of his face that showed between folds of wool was dark and troubled.

"Ryd needs to hear this," Carin said. She called him over, and he came, brushing snow from his mitts.

Together she and Ras pointed out the map and where they stood, in the uncharted mountains with winter all around them.

"What do you think this means?" Carin asked. "The hunters are supposed to know about all possible routes out of the Hearthland, are they not? Haven't you been this far into the mountains before?"

Ras shook his head. "No. None of us ever have."

Ryd went still. "So you were only told you knew the routes."

"We did know the routes."

"Not all of them, clearly." Ryd gave Ras's shoulder a sharp push. "Don't you understand? They didn't even trust you lot with the ways out of the Hearthland. They gave you just enough to make you think you had the secrets, but you only saw a few feet farther than any of the rest of us."

Carin knew Ryd spoke the truth. She looked north, where a wall of white was coming their way behind the flurries that already swirled around them. "You truly don't know what lies beyond."

"Sahnat said once that if we lost our maps to keep the largest mountains on our left side if we were going south. To bring us safely home." He motioned ahead, where the snow had obscured the face of the mountains beyond them. "That's how I've guided us the past three days, keeping them on our right instead since we are going north and not south."

"Then we will continue on," said Carin.

"Do we have any other choice?" Ryd's voice cracked on the question, and he stumbled back through the snow toward the burrow he'd been digging.

Carin looked at Ras, and after a moment she couldn't help the helpless laugh that escaped her.

"What?" Ras demanded.

"What you told us that first day is true after all. You are indeed in this as much as we are." Carin heard the bitter edge in her own voice.

"I have lost as much as either of you," he said after a moment of indignation.

Carin sobered. "I truly do not think you understand what we two have lost." The image of Dyava's face in sunlight filled her mind, then vanished.

Ras opened his mouth, but it seemed he had no answer to that.

They used the remainder of the daylight to build a snow dwelling around the dugout Ryd had created, shaping blocks of snow and packing it between the cracks. By the time they finished, the wind howled around them, and snow fell in sheets, blowing almost sideways in the force of the gale.

The three crawled through the tunnel entrance into the snow dwelling. Big enough to crouch, if not to stand, they huddled together as the storm raged outside. The next morning, the snow had subsided to a slow shower, and they ate a quick breakfast of two strips of dried meat each before crawling out of the dwelling.

The brightness of the sun on the snow made Carin blink back tears.

Something exploded out of the snow in front of her.

Carin stumbled backward, falling into Ras as he exited the snow dwelling. The sound of flapping filled the air, and something white rose up from the snow, great wings reaching up toward the blue of the sky and...vanishing.

"What is that?" Carin shouted. The creature's wings clawed at the air, fanning wind toward Carin's face. It carried with it the scent of damp fur. She could still see it, like a traveling ripple against the snow and sky. "There!"

The sound of the creature's wings was like the wind catching a sheet of canvas, and Carin stared in the direction it traveled, away from them, to the north. She followed the ripple of movement as far as she could, wondering how so massive an animal could simply disappear. She could not make out its shape, nor that of its wings, but whatever had erupted from the ground in front of her had been at least the size of a person. Larger. The wings alone would have spanned the village hearth-home in Haveranth, judging by the sound they made when moved.

Slowly the sound faded, and with it, Carin's heart returned to a normal rhythm.

Ras stood, just as dumbfounded as Carin.

Ryd, who had still been within the snow dwelling, had not seen anything, only heard the flapping and Carin's yell. He came crawling out of the leeward tunnel, face red and hair disheveled. "What was it?"

Carin still stared in the direction the animal had fled. "I don't know."

First the Journeying, now here. She felt sure the creature—or creatures—had seen them on their Journeying. Now it tracked their movement north.

"Did you see it?" Ras asked. "You almost fell on me. I couldn't see anything."

Carin shook her head. "Whatever it is, it's hard to see. It seems to blend in with everything around it." She thought of what she could tell about the creature. As large as a wall, winged, capable of disguising itself. Intelligence was almost a certainty. It also didn't seem hostile, but...curious.

She pointed north and just a bit west. "It went that way."

RYD WASN'T sure about Carin's idea to follow a mysterious invisible beast northward, but as the creature's path seemed to be one and the same as Ras's assertion that they keep the larger mountains on their right, he went along with it. They were likely going to die in the mountains anyway, so why not chase a giant flying thing to their doom?

The weather held for the entirety of the next turn, and with his snowshoes, they made good time through the snow. Ryd thought if he were ever able to curl up by a fire in a warm home again, he would die happy. Out here in the cold, he was either sweating or freezing. His perspiration had soaked into his clothing, the leathers he piled onto his person, his boots. All his life he had taken for granted the simple privilege of donning a clean pair of clothing in the morning, of washing when he was dirty, of being warm when outside it was cold.

Now he wished he could go back to any moment where he was fed, warm, and clean.

He walked beside Ras, each of their footsteps in time with the solid thump-thump-thump of snowshoes in the powder. The snow was dusty here, not easily packable as it had been even the day before when they had built a snow dwelling. They would have to find a different form of shelter when it got dark—without the right kind of snow, they wouldn't be able to make a single block, let alone an entire building. Again, Ryd realized the difference in his thoughts now. Never before had he worried—truly worried—over the right kind of snow.

Carin led them on an upward climb, skirting the base of a massive peak that rose stark and bright into the ice-blue sky. Slowly they made the trek. The mountains here were silent but for the whooshing of the wind. There were no pikas to hear chittering on the rocks—no rocks for pikas to sit upon, even. Above the tree line, there was nothing but snow.

Without discussion, they cut down the amount of food they ate each day. They came to the end of the dried roundberries. They came to the end of the smoked fish. And soon, Ryd knew, they would come to the end of the rabbit and saiga and tubers. He only hoped they would first come to the end of the mountains, but he did not trust that would be the case.

"Why did you become a hunter?" Ryd asked Ras suddenly. His words were muffled under the woolens he had packed around his head, leaving only a slit for his eyes. His breath steamed even through the weave of the wool.

Ras didn't answer for a long moment, but then grunted. "Seemed like a good thing to do. Protect the homeland. Keep my family safe."

"Where is your family?"

"My parents still live in Cantoranth, though they are getting old. My father is a cooper, and my mother works the quarry. Her stonework is some of the best in Cantoranth."

"Do you have a bond-mate? Children?" It bothered Ryd not knowing about this person who they had found thrown in with their journey. He didn't know that he could trust Ras—Ryd was sure Carin felt the same way, that trusting him would be foolhardy at best. But still, getting to know the man would possibly make him feel more at ease. He would have felt somehow better if more hunters had appeared in the passes, but indeed there had been no sign of any people. No habitation, no tracks, no indication of any other life aside from the occasional animals and the giant winged creatures who seemed intent on observing their progress.

"No," Ras said. He shifted his shoulders, causing his pack to clank. "I like being on my own. Hunting suits me. I can go out into the mountains and find prey that will provide for my village. I can become better at my skills, survive. Ensure the survival of my people."

"So killing Carin and me would ensure the survival of your people?" Ryd surprised himself with the venom that injected itself into his words. *Who are your* people, *Ras?* "You had planned to hunt us down like animals."

Ras stopped in the middle of the path, and ahead Ryd saw Carin's shoulders tense. "Well, I'm not trying to kill you now, am I?"

Ryd was sure that was no answer at all. "Maybe you're the hunter we should be expecting. Maybe no one else is coming at all. Maybe you're just waiting to kill us both."

Carin stopped. "Ryd."

"Don't say my name like that, Carin," Ryd said. "You know as well as I do that he could just be waiting to kill us."

"Ryd!" Carin pointed up ahead, where the air seemed to ripple in front of a snowbank.

Ras snarled something unintelligible, until his eyes fell upon the ripple in the snow.

Carin froze, and Ryd came up to stand beside her. He followed her finger where she gestured in front of them. There wasn't just one ripple in the snow. She moved her arm across her body.

"Seven." She said, taking a breath. Her bow was slung across her back, but she didn't reach for it. Instead she held out her hands, her face pensive. "They're watching us."

"What is watching us?" Ras moved up, standing at Ryd's shoulder, his snarls forgotten. His hand went to his belt knife, mitt loosened from his grip.

"They are." As Carin pointed, the ripple of strange movement became more pronounced. Shapes began to form against the snow.

Ryd's mouth fell open inside the bundled woolens around his head. The creatures were as tall as a person, though they leaned forward on long forearms. One stretched, and Ryd saw that their forearms were not forearms at all, but folded wings.

They were not far away—only about the distance from one wall of Ryd's childhood roundhome to the other. As the ripple of movement shifted into fully formed shapes, he heard Ras hiss in a breath.

"Bats," Carin whispered. "They're bats."

SART WAS half-covered in mud and very unhappy about it. Winter had brought with it a deluge of slushy snow that turned the ground to mush and didn't stick this close to the coast. Avoiding the main roads meant Sart had to ride Tahin overland and leagues to the west of the main route into Crevasses, and both ihstal and rider were spattered with sour-smelling mud from feet to midthigh. The ihstal's pale beige coat was speckled with spots from its churning padded feet, and it seemed far more delighted with the sensation of getting sprayed with murky mud than any living creature ought to.

They had journeyed close enough to Crevasses for the tree cover to begin, and Sart made sure to keep away from any known encampments and waymakes off the main road. Doing so had stretched out the time of her route, but it had kept her away from any bands of rovers. She certainly didn't want to chance meeting Barit or Kahs again. She found herself thinking a bit of Valon and her dimples. Pity Culy had moved on so quickly, or Sart would have been happy to stick around and get to know Valon Avarsahla a bit more.

Sart drew from her waterskin, squeezing out the last drops. She had one more in her pack, but she would need to find water—and soon. The snow that fell from the sky didn't stick, and even if it did, it would be too mixed with mud to melt into drinking water.

She nudged Tahin toward a stand of trees in the distance, west of the route she wanted to take, but the trees were the best indicator of drinking water she had seen in days.

Riding for the better part of the afternoon, she followed the trees toward the mountains, which, even through the stubby tree cover, were visible as a dark smudge in the distance. Sart paused for a small meal, tethering Tahin to a dead sycamore sapling that seemed to have picked a terrible place to grow. How it had taken root at all was a mystery. She spotted another dead snag not far away and left Tahin to graze on the sparse winter grasses. The tree was an easy climber. Sart's fingers found a nice indent in the bark just above her head and easily pulled herself up enough to catch hold of the first branch. Swinging her legs up over it, she scrambled up the tree farther, looking out to the north.

A hill rose to the east, several leagues away, over which Sart knew was the main caravan route from Salters to Crevasses. The mountains to the south were unremarkable, shrouded by fog where they met the sea and clear ragged peaks farther east. To the southwest though, she saw something strange. Where most of the trees around her were dead from lack of water, a grove grew to the southwest. Evergreens with thick blue-green needles untouched by rot or beetles. What looked like a sugar-tree, a few splashes of red-orange dotting its branches where early winter had yet to tear down its remaining leaves.

Sart slid down between the branches of the snag and caught the lowest with her hands, lowering herself with her arms to drop back onto the ground. She gave Tahin a sip of water from her skin—ihstal were hearty beasts that required little in the way of hydration—and remounted the animal, giving its reins a tug to ease it in the direction she had seen the trees. It took about an hour to make the ride. As the trees grew larger in her field of vision, Sart noticed changes beneath Tahin's feet. The grasses, sickly green-brown in winter, as they tended to be in every other season, started to shift. Green-brown gave way to simply dark blue, and as Tahin trotted southward, took on a brighter tinge. Culy had told her stories of grasses so healthy they were deep blue, but she never thought she would see such a thing with her own eyes. When she reached the trees, the grasses were decidedly blue. The fir trees around her wore needles almost the same color, and the pines were as deep a green as she had ever seen. What she had thought was a sugar-tree was indeed, and against the greens and blues around her flamed spots of fiery red-orange.

Riding deeper into the grove, Sart nearly held her breath. Could there exist such a magic, to bring the land to life this way? No one could sustain such a thing.

Then she heard it.

It started with a burble. Sart turned Tahin toward it, nudging the ihstal to follow the sound. Tahin, exuberant as usual, whistled approval and danced toward the noise. It grew louder, and Sart pressed her knees into Tahin's flanks, driving her to move faster, faster, faster in the direction of the burbling sound.

Around her, the trees seemed healthy, though young. Most were likely new growth, only having seen one or two cycles pass. Tahin pranced, padded cloven feet on the deep blue grasses. The ground descended a bit, taking them downhill. All the signs pointed to the one thing in these lands more powerful than any magic of Sart's: water.

The decline of the ground leveled out, and there, before Sart's eyes, was a stream.

Far from the muddy murk of the creeks in the Crevasses, this stream ran *clear*.

No silt. No muck. Clear water, burbling over rocks.

How had no one found this?

Sart urged Tahin along the banks of the stream, following it southward where it curved toward the west. The burble leveled out into a clean rushing sound. At the cleft of two hillocks was a pool. Clean water bubbled up from the ground, spilling out to flow downhill. The stream's source.

A spring.

A clean spring.

Flowing in early winter when the groundwater would be nearly depleted from summer's lack of rain and runoff.

With an inhuman noise that tore itself from her throat, Sart almost fell from Tahin's back. She tied the ihstal's reins to a low branch of pine with as much haste as she could. The water flowed, its movement constant and steady, but Sart ran to it as if she were racing its end. She dropped to her muddy knees in the blue-green grass of the stream's bank and sank her hands in the cold spring water to her wrists, lowering her face directly to the surface. Her body shook as her lips touched the water.

Sart sucked in the clear, clean liquid, sweet and icy cold.

She had never tasted anything like it.

It tasted alive, unlike the flat, overboiled dullness of the water she usually drank. Better than the rainwater she'd tasted only rarely in her life.

Sart tasted salt and realized that tears were flowing down her face, mingling with the spring water.

She drank until her belly grew tight and sloshy beneath her tunic and belted coat. Scrambling to her feet, she opened her pack on Tahin's back and pulled out her three empty waterskins and the one remaining full one. Sart looked at the spring and at the single still-bulging waterskin she held in one hand, squeezing the oiled leather to hear the water inside swish.

She pulled out the stopper, face burning with guilt and fierce lawlessness for what she was about to do. It took every ounce of will she had to upend the full waterskin on the ground. It splashed into the grass, not even clear when poured. Sart dropped the empty skins from her free hand and let some of the wasting water pool in the palm of her cupped hand. Murky, always murky. That was what water looked like, or at least the water they drank.

The sea was clear and green-blue, but no one could drink it except the ihstal.

This spring was sweet and clear like the glass the Salters made from sand and whatever black powder gave rise to their greens and blues to mimic the sea.

The final drops of murky water fell to the grass, and Sart gathered up the empty skins, falling to her knees again beside the pool. She dipped each of the skins in the water, filling them and rinsing their insides as if she could wash away all memory of every sip of water she had tasted up until that moment.

A part of her mind said that she could not stay at this spring forever, that she would have to pot her own water from the muddy creeks of Crevasses or the silty wells of Sands or gather it from the fragile glass contraptions of Salters again. But for now she bent and drank again, drank deeply although her stomach ached with fullness.

She filled each of her waterskins, five in all, and then led Tahin over to drink. The ihstal pranced at the taste of the water, whistling keenly.

"I know," Sart said, running her hand up the beast's long neck and scratching behind one pointed ear.

She tethered the ihstal again and sat on the soft grass, kneading it with her fingers, looking around as if she had stumbled into a dream.

Clean water.

Such a thing was worth more than food or medicine or a halmer's craft.

A slow sickness crept up upon her, and it had nothing to do with the amount she had drunk.

Once this place was discovered, it would be contested.

Culy had to know, and quickly.

WHEN LYARI shook the snow from her boots on Merin's doorstep, stepping into the warmth of the soothsayer's central hearth, she knew something was different.

There were no scrolls or parchments to litter Merin's trestle table, and the older woman sat hunched over on a bench, staring into the fire.

"Merin?"

Lyari entered the roundhome, closing the door and latching it behind her. She removed her cloak and hung it beside the door, pulling off her boots to set them to the side. She went to sit beside Merin on the bench, reaching out to touch her shoulder.

"Merin?" She said the old woman's name again, her tentative touch on her shoulder growing more urgent. Did the old woman know Lyari knew her secret? Alarm stilled Lyari's fingers against Merin's shoulder.

"I heard you the first time." Merin shrugged off Lyari's hand and raised her own fingers to her forehead.

"Then why didn't you answer?" Lyari made her tone teasing, but the woman's slumped posture concerned her. The fire had burned down to embers with only a few flames licking upward.

Lyari moved to the woodpile against the far wall, pulling two slender logs to stack atop the embers. After a few moments, the flames caught the dry bark of the new logs, sparking to life.

"Would you like to tell me what has you staring into nothing?"

"I'm not staring into nothing. I'm watching the fire."

"Very well. What has you so intrigued by the same fire you see every day?" Lyari returned to sit next to Merin on the bench. That her voice remained even was a feat.

Merin seemed to consider something, pressing her lips together and frowning into the now-crackling flames on her hearth. "It's not the fire," she said finally.

She seemed to be at war with herself. Lyari watched as Merin opened her mouth, then closed it, then opened it again. Was she planning to tell Lyari? Lyari wondered how Merin could possibly plan to tell her about the conversation with Harag. But she would have to eventually, if Lyari was to succeed her as soothsayer.

In the doorway to Merin's bedroom, Jenin stood, framed by the maha wood that formed so many of the fixtures in Merin's roundhome. Sy watched, looking almost bored.

"What is it, Merin?" Lyari asked carefully. "Do you want me to get the scrolls?"

Merin shook her head irritably. "No rotted scrolls tonight."

"Do you want me to leave? I can return tomorrow."

At that, Merin looked directly at Lyari for the first time since she'd entered her home. "Don't be absurd."

"Then teach me. Speak to me. Give me something to do besides sitting here and watching you sulk."

Merin's grey eyes flashed in the firelight. "You might regret you said that, apprentice."

Then she looked at the hook dangling over the fire.

"Start some tea."

Lyari obeyed, filling the kettle with water from the pump and hanging it on the hook to boil.

"Do you know why I needed an apprentice?" Merin asked the question to Lyari's back.

The question took Lyari by surprise, and she stared at the bronze kettle, at her wobbly reflection that stared back at her. "Because you don't live forever. I don't think."

Merin chuckled. "No, I don't live forever." Her face grew sober again, and she looked over her shoulder as Lyari turned back to face her, out the window where the humid air inside the roundhome had frosted over the glass. "I've told you a bit about the reinvocation, yes?"

Lyari nodded, moving back to sit beside Merin on the bench. "You said that every five hundred cycles, we have to cast the spell to protect the Hearthland again."

"Three cycles," Merin said. "That is all that remains between us and the next reinvocation."

"Were you at the last one?" The question sounded silly as soon as it left Lyari's lips, and Merin coughed a laugh.

"I'm not quite that old."

There was silence for a moment, but for the cracking of a log on the fire.

"Do you remember from your Journeying how this spell was first cast?"

Lyari nodded again, wishing Merin would get on with her explanation.

"Our founding families cast this spell to protect us."

"I know that, Merin." Lyari began to wonder if the older woman had been drinking her fermented hibiscus cordial from the way she continued to blink into the fire. But as she looked, she saw a gathering tear at the corner of Merin's eyes. For a bare instant, Lyari felt a moment of pity, quickly snuffed out like an errant spark.

"I needed an apprentice because the reinvocation will need many strong folk to succeed. Do you understand fully what we will lose if we fail?"

"Those to the north live without food and water," Lyari said automatically. "They have coughs."

"Disease," Merin corrected. "Disease."

"What is that?"

"It is something that happens to a body. It makes people cough or vomit or grow abnormally warm."

Lyari frowned, not understanding. "Does the food they eat make them vomit?"

"It doesn't come from food, not always. Disease comes from many things." Merin paused, then went on. "Where it comes from doesn't matter so much to this discussion. The point is that if we fail, all those things will come to the Hearthland. Starvation. Thirst. Illness. It is vital that you succeed."

"Succeed at what?" Lyari asked. For the first time in her memory, Merin sounded to Lyari like an old person who wasn't quite in control of her wits.

"A spell this large requires a great deal of focusing power. Come with me." Merin stood and took Lyari by the hand. In her kitchen, she led Lyari to the door to her cellar, pulling open the carved slat of maha to reveal the stairs downward.

Taking a stone lamp from the worktop, Merin stepped down into the cellar, and Lyari followed. She had never been into Merin's cellar before. Unsure what to expect, she followed the dim, flickering light from the lamp. Merin lit a second and third lamp from the flame of the first, lighting the cellar. Lyari looked around. Whatever she expected, something magical or unusual perhaps, didn't appear. Instead there were shelves of foods, cheeses dipped in wax and bundles of dried herbs. A barrel of apples sat in the corner. A worktop covered with a series of mortars and pestles where the scent of ground spices lingered, of yellow turmeric root and ginger, green coriander and violet cave chilies. A set of shelves containing glass bottles of cordials and the syrups Merin was known for across the Hearthland. On the far side of the cellar, Merin led Lyari to a large stone slab.

The stone was unremarkable to Lyari's eyes. The top bore five deep indentations, like cup marks. Next to it was a chest, and Merin set the stone lamp on top of the slab to open the chest. From the chest she pulled a large scroll and unrolled it, revealing a map of the Hearthland.

At its very center was a rune, a sharp V with a spoke up the middle, like a stylized person with raised arms. Renewal, Lyari knew.

Merin rapped the rune with her knuckles. "Three cycles from now at High Lights, villagers will take this slab to that spot, and you will cast the reinvocation."

"Me?" Lyari's voice came out and cracked in the air. Whatever she had been expecting, it wasn't this. "Not you?"

Merin snorted. "If I could do it myself, I wouldn't need you."

"Why me?"

"Don't ask stupid questions, Lyari. This is your job. I'll tell you what you're to do." Merin plopped down on the edge of the stone slab. "Three cycles from now, it will be your job to ensure the sacrifices necessary to reinvoke the spell are present and ready. You have, very truly, the most important duty in all the Hearthland. Your work for the next three cycles will secure the safety and the bounty of our people. If you find a bondmate, you will allow hyr and your future offspring to flourish. If you value the lives of your family, you will protect them. Can I trust you to do this thing?"

"You can." After a moment, Lyari said, "Merin?"

"Yes?"

"Why doesn't Rina remember Carin? She's an elder. She should."

Merin looked at Lyari sharply, and Lyari was not sure if it was for speaking the name of a Nameless or something else.

"I wasn't prying." Lyari rotated her wrist where her apprentice cuff had stuck to her skin. "She said my Journeying must have been harder for my being alone."

"When a Nameless is the child of an elder, I consider it a mercy to ensure they forget, along with the rest of the village."

"Did Rina have a choice?"

Merin's face flattened into a stony expression, and that was enough answer for Lyari. "Enough talk of the Nameless, Lyari." She motioned at the room around her. "Repeat it back to me again."

Three hours later, Lyari returned to her home, Jenin walking silently beside her.

"You can't do this thing," Jenin said.

"I have to." Lyari opened the door to her roundhome, brushing the snow from her hair with her fingers.

"Lyari, do you understand what was asked of you? What you will have to do to reinvoke this spell? Do you understand what the Hearthland's soothsayers have done?"

These were the most words Jenin had said to her since she had returned from the Journeying, and she turned to face hyr. "This is for our homeland, Jenin," Lyari said softly. "It's for the safety and the well-being of our people. Without it, everything you and I ever knew will die."

"It's wrong."

"You didn't go on the Journeying. You didn't see what we saw."

"You mean what made Carin and Ryd choose exile and death over their homes?" Jenin raised hys hand to scratch at a flake of dried blood on hys neck. "I did see what you saw, Lyari. I knew before any blade touched my skin what you would find on the Journeying. I tried to tell you. I wanted to tell you."

Lyari went silent, the wind howling through the still-open door. She closed it, changing her boots for leather clogs and moving to the hearth to stir the banked embers into flame. "You're wrong, my love. This is what has to be done. It is for our people."

Thinking of Rina and the gap in her life where her daughter had been, Lyari considered the word *choice*.

She reached down to pick up a log, setting it atop the still-glowing embers in the hearth. She blew on them, watching them glow deep orange before the wood caught flame.

"Who are our people?" Jenin asked from behind her.

When she turned to answer hyr, Jenin was already gone. Again.

CARIN STOOD face to face with one of the creatures, her snow-shoes sinking into the soft powder of the pass. Intelligent eyes assessed her, round and black and shining. Before, she had smelled damp fur when the creature had taken off from the snow in front of her, and now she could see why. The bats—enormous bats!—were covered in thick white fur. Their noses, flat and upturned like the snout of a wild hog, were the bright yellow of spring horn flowers, as was the fur that ringed their large ears. The bat leaned forward in the snow on massive wings, and it gave off waves of warmth from its body.

Ryd and Ras had hung back from her when she advanced, but Carin feared nothing from these creatures. She couldn't explain why she trusted them; perhaps it was the constant hum that had faded into the background of her notice like heartbeat or breath. Perhaps it was the knowledge that, with their abilities to remain unseen, they could have swooped down and killed all three of the earth-bound travelers without a second thought. Carin could have heard only the flapping of wings before being caught up by clawed hands and dropped from the air to die, broken on the rocks of the Mad Mountains.

But now, looking into the eyes of the creature, Carin believed that they had wanted to be seen—or they wouldn't have been.

Hearing them back in the Mistaken Pass, the flapping of wings as they climbed now, the creature in front of their snow dwelling...it all meant to show themselves, to be less surprising.

As if an enormous white bat could be anything but surprising.

"Who are you?" Carin asked. She pulled the wool down from her mouth and asked the question again, the cold wind chilling her face where her breath had moistened it under cover of her scarf. *Who* indeed seemed the correct word to use with these creatures.

The bat in front of her leaned forward, and she felt its breath on her cheek. It smelled of snow and fur and fruit.

Its cheek touched hers, and the humming in her body grew loud like the wind.

Images appeared.

She saw a cave, high in the mountains, above a lush vale. The Hidden Vale? The cave was full of these creatures. Her ears hummed with sounds, and the longer the bat's cheek pressed to hers, the more the sounds solidified into something recognizable. *Ialtag.*

"Ialtag," Carin said aloud.

A rustle of wings around her seemed to convey pleasure.

The ialtag showed her more images then, of herself and Ryd and Lyah climbing through the Mistaken Pass, entering the cave in the Hidden Vale, and later leaving. It showed her the path beyond the Hidden Vale, the true pass that led northward, as if gently correcting the trail she had taken, believing the north as her true destination all along.

And then it showed her the path ahead, blocked almost entirely by snow. She saw a series of pictures, of the pass cleared, but of giant sheets of snow breaking away to cascade down the mountainside. The ialtag's images seemed to bring with them a warning, a sad caution.

"The path ahead is blocked," Carin said. She heard the noises of surprise from Ryd and Ras behind her, but ignored them.

The next image the ialtag sent her was herself, held aloft by one of them, soaring over the mountains.

The ialtag wanted to *help* them.

Carin almost fell backward with shock.

She wasn't sure how to communicate her own thoughts to the creature, but she did the best she could, forming an image in her mind of seeing them before, of watching the ripples of their near-invisible movement, her sense of knowing she was watched. Again she felt a wave of affirmation from the ialtag, and pleasure to be understood.

Although she knew herself to be safe, Carin's breathing became quicker. Never had she considered the possibility of finding another intelligent being, and now she stood cheek to cheek with a creature she had never even heard of.

The ialtag seemed to sense her thoughts, showing her images of ialtag vanishing from view of other people, of their colony deep in the moun-

tains where no people ventured. They were curious, yes, but shy. If the ialtag communicated by touch—at least with other species—Carin wasn't
sure any people faced with a giant bat wouldn't shoot it full of arrows.

At that, she felt a rumble of unease and confirmation in the ialtag
gathered around her.

Carin felt tears well up in her eyes. She pictured her hand touching the ialtag's face and received a positive image back of the same. She
removed the mitt from her right hand and raised her palm to the ialtag's
furry cheek. Its fur was coarse, but smooth and thick and warm. While
she seemed to be able to hear only what the ialtag in front of her wanted
to say, all of them behind it seemed to hear her. Could they have a com-
munal mind, like bees seemed to?

"Carin?" Ryd's voice sounded behind her, uncertain.

"They want to help us," Carin said, letting her hand drop from the
ialtag's face. "The pass was blocked by an avalanche. We'll never be able to
go through without them."

"How exactly do they plan to help us?" Ras asked. His voice was
incredulous, and not entirely trustful.

"They're going to carry us."

RYD THOUGHT Carin had gone mad—utterly and completely
mad—up until the moment a rush of wind from giant wings beat
around him and a hand larger than his head closed around each of his
upper arms and lifted him from the snow. His feet dangled beneath him
in the air, and he resisted the urge to scream.

In his mind came an image, of the bat—ialtag, Carin had called
them—carrying him over snow-covered mountains to a cave. It felt very
reassuring until the ialtag showed him a picture of him falling through the

air. Ryd almost cried out for help, but was immediately flooded with hurried images of the giant bat catching him.

Had it made a *joke?*

The ialtag sent forth a wave of self-assuredness, as if it were pleased with itself. "Sure," Ryd called out into the wind rushing past his face. "It's funny if you can fly!"

He wasn't sure bats could laugh, but the sense of mirth he got from the ialtag that grasped him tightly was unmistakable.

They soared above the trail, higher and higher, until the blocked pass came into view and the wave of feeling from the ialtag turned somber. Without them, Ryd knew they would never have made it through the pass. They would have had to turn back southward, toward the hunters of the Hearthland who wanted their blood spilled on the snow, or they would have frozen or starved to death.

The ialtag seemed to agree.

Ryd wondered why they had chosen now to show themselves to people—and why they had chosen his group to be those people. In response, he got a series of images almost too quickly to bear. A series of large stones that seemed vaguely familiar. Murky rivers. A child wiping a gob of green slime on the back of hys hand. Blood running over stones. A group of people migrating together, faces steely and determined as they trekked southward with destruction in their wake.

He hadn't been expecting an answer, yet he had gotten one. Somewhere in the memories of these ialtag were the watchful chronicles of his own people. They had helped him and Carin and Ras because they were leaving that life behind. What did they think could be done to fix it? Was it simply the moral choice of choosing a life of deprivation over bounty built on the backs of others? Ryd felt shame then, as his decision to leave Haveranth was based more on his own unhappiness than that of those north of the mountains.

The ialtag showed him his fall again, then, just as quickly, showed him being caught as if to remind him that it was a joke.

By the time the ialtag flew north, skirting down the slope of a mountain close enough that Ryd's toes could almost brush the snow, he thought his arms might fall off. The ialtag carrying him, in turn, showed him the image of him with both arms fully attached, as if offended he would think such a thing.

Ryd had never communicated so clearly without words. Sure, his people could manage a nod or a headshake to portray answers, and he could tell the difference between a smile and a frown without someone stating joy or sadness, but he had never before imagined such a thing was possible.

Then again, he had never considered giant intelligent bats existing, either.

The ialtag seemed pleased, and at the base of the mountain, it swooped around an outcropping and deposited Ryd on the ground. Arms, Ryd had to note, fully intact. A twinge in his ear reminded him that he wasn't fully intact all over, but he decided losing a chunk of ear was much preferable to losing an arm.

His feet didn't want to hold him up when he took a step, and he stumbled, pitching forward onto his knees. A moment later, Carin and Ras landed behind him, both struggling to remain upright as much as he had. Carin reached out and grabbed his hand, and for a moment Ryd felt bereft of the ialtag's way of direct communication, expecting her touch to come with feelings, images, thoughts. Instead it was just Carin, her hand damp from being stuffed inside her fur mitts.

Her eyes, though—those conveyed the wonder he expected to feel. For the first time in moons he saw something of awe in her, and marvelous glee.

Inside the ialtag's cavern, there was little light. What existed came from the entrance, reflected from the brightness of the snow outside. It was enough to see around them but not much else. A rustling scratching sound drew Ryd's attention, and he found himself surrounded by ialtag of all sizes. Some, like the ones that had carried them through the pass, were half again as large as a person. Others were smaller, and those came up close beside them.

Ryd found himself suddenly full of dismay at the idea of being sat on by ialtag children.

Close as they came, however, they didn't sit on him. Instead, they clustered around the three Hearthlanders, their warmth welcome after the frigid wind of the mountains. Ryd looked up—and regretted it almost immediately. Above his head, ialtag hung from stone outcroppings, upside down like every small bat he had encountered in his life in Haveranth. Their eyes reflected the light from the cave's entrance, and all were turned to the newcomers.

A moment later, the gaggle of ialtag around Ryd parted to admit a full-grown creature, nudging before it a large piece of bark covered in fruit. Fruit, in the middle of winter.

Most of it was just past ripeness, but Ryd fell upon it like it was his first meal since High Lights. A child—he could not help but think of the small ialtag as children, their curiosity and gentle warmth somehow comforting to Ryd as he ate—came up beside him and pressed its cheek to his free hand. The images from the small ialtag were more disjointed. A picture of a sandy beach with a palm tree growing. The face of a grown ialtag. A particularly round stone. They were the things that would matter to a child, and Ryd felt as warmed by that show of excitement as he did by the community of furry bodies that insulated them from the cold.

The adult in their midst nudged the children away with its nose, leaning down to touch its cheek to Carin's.

After a moment of quiet, Carin spoke. "Take my hands."

She reached out her hands, and Ryd and Ras each took hold of one.

From the ialtag, he saw where the fruit had come from. Some from the Hidden Vale, as he had guessed, where some phenomena of magic or weather kept the land full of abundant fruit even in winter. Some from islands off the coast of the mainland, and Ryd let out a small gasp of surprise at that. His world expanded as the ialtag showed them the territory they spanned, from coast to another coast across the breadth of the mountains and over even the sea. Their wings allowed them to cross immense distances, and Ryd found himself reeling at the thought of how far they could travel—and at how much land existed outside that which Ryd had known.

But there was a point to the ialtag's communication, as there had been before. They had seen the land and how it suffered to the north. The memory of their kind stretched back and back and back, unburdened by finite lifespans or parchments of history that could crumble to dust or burn in a fire, never to be seen again. Their memories remained, because they were kept by all.

Their memories were what the ialtag showed the trio of humans in that cave in the Mad Mountains. Memories of a time where the Northlands had been on the brink of widespread settlement, of cultivated crops and enormous villages made of stone. And memories of what came next.

The ialtag hadn't seen the spell itself; they hadn't borne witness to whatever magic the original Hearthlanders had spun to siphon off the energies of the Northlands to feed their new home to the south. But they had felt it, seen its immediate aftermath, and in his connection to these creatures through the touch of Carin's hand, he felt the fear and panic the ialtag had felt, the reverberating shock that had shaken the very earth and raised mountains from hills.

With that memory came mourning so deep that Ryd's very bones seemed to tremble. He couldn't have put voice to the images and senses he got, of ialtag lost in that cataclysmic moment, but he was sure he was being shown a list of their dead.

It came to him on that wave of grief, the knowledge of what the ialtag wanted from them.

They wanted an end to the imbalance of power in their lands. It manifested in Ryd's mind like thousands of bushes bursting into bloom, like clear water springing from the earth, like heavy fruit hanging ripe from dipping branches.

"How?"

It was Carin who voiced the question, and Ryd echoed it silently.

He saw again the images of great stones, five of them, scattered over the Northlands.

In his mind, he saw the image of a nut being cracked, a branch snapped, a bone smashed.

And words, pushed forward with the weight of eternity behind them. *Break them.*

L YARI WAS sipping sweet icemint tea from a steaming mug when Old Wend knocked on her door.

"Come in," she said loudly.

A moment later, he entered her roundhome, stomping his feet on the landing outside to knock snow from his boots. "I can't stay," he said, "but there's a hunter here looking for Merin, and she's nowhere to be found."

"A hunter?" Lyari put her mug down on the polished maha table next to the rune for family. Jenin sat across from her without saying a word, just watching Old Wend with expectation in hys eyes.

"Name of Jahd va Beminohna. Just come in from Bemin's Fan and wanted to give something to Merin."

Jahd.

"I'll go meet him. Thank you, Wend."

Old Wend shook his head. "He's right behind me. I brought him to you."

"I see. Well, send him on in." Lyari stood, straightening her long woolen tunic and adjusting the wide leather belt that circled her hips twice. Her heart gave a thump. Jahd, here in Haveranth. Lyari could get answers from the man himself. On her wrist she wore her bronze cuff, tooled in runes that showed her new station. It moved too much when she shifted her arm's position, but Lyari thought she would get used to it. Eventually.

The man who entered her home was taller than she by a head, and he nodded at Old Wend before kicking the snow from his boots and stepping inside. Wend closed the door as he left, raising two fingers to his lips and making eye contact with Lyari briefly before the door shut, and she heard him stumping away down the path.

"Jahd," Lyari said. "Come in. Sit at my hearth. Would you care for tea?"

The man nodded and came into the roundhome, perching on the stone lip that surrounded the hearth. He had a rucksack with traveling things belted to it. Snowflakes clung to the outside of his pack, and to his hair, melting into pinpricks of water. He looked around. "Beautiful home you have."

Lyari thought of the hands that had built it, the hands he had stilled forever, and picked up her mug from where she had set it on the table, taking a drink of her tea before moving into the kitchen to prepare a mug for her visitor. "Thank you," was all she said in answer.

She filled a mesh sack with new tea leaves and set it in an earthenware mug with two spoonfuls of brown sugar, pouring still-hot water from the kettle over the top of it and handing it to Jahd with a spoon. "You said you had something for Merin?"

Jahd stirred his tea and nodded, setting the mug down on the stone beside him and reaching into his pocket. He pulled out a woven leather cuff, the craftership intricate and beautiful. The hatch pattern was tight and well-made. Jahd tossed it to her, and Lyari caught it.

"That was Sahnat's," he said. "I reckoned she'd want to have it since I was on my way up to Cantoranth to speak with Ras's family there about what happened."

Lyari frowned, looking at the cuff. She'd heard the name Sahnat even before Jenin had helped her listen in on Merin's conversation with Harag. She recognized it as that of a leatherworker who brought his wares to the village to trade. "What exactly happened to Sahnat?"

Jahd took a drink of his tea, holding the spoon to the far side of his mug as he drank. He licked his lips before putting the mug back down. "Merin didn't tell you? You're her apprentice, aren't you?"

Late that night in Merin's cellar, with the feeling of something floating just outside her grasp, Merin had stripped the word *apprentice* from her title. "I am now soothsayer, Jahd. I have not seen Merin in three days; perhaps she planned to tell me when she returned."

Jahd seemed to accept that, and he nodded. "Sahnat was killed by one of the Nameless as they fled into the mountains. He along with the rest of my hunters. They thought to catch the Nameless unaware, but that rotted woman stuck two of them with her arrows before I got her back with mine."

The air seemed to suck itself out of the room through the chimney, even though Lyari had already known. She tried to breathe and found her lungs stuck, her ears ringing with the sound of wind over a pipe.

"You...killed her." Somehow she spoke.

Jahd nodded vigorously then, mistaking Lyari's shock for something she couldn't comprehend. He seemed oblivious to the fact that Lyari would have undoubtedly grown up with the Nameless he killed. Was this how it always was? Jahd was still talking. "—Stuck her good between the shoulder blades from fifty paces. The scrawny one, too. Saw Riah cut his throat with her dying breath. I was the only one who lived."

The bench where Lyari sat at the maha table—Carin's beloved maha table where they had shared meals, kicked their feet above the floor, laughed, spilled conu juice, cried over disappointments, lived, lived, lived—seemed to tilt beneath her, and Lyari grasped the edge with both hands as if she could secure herself to it.

Carin, dead. Ryd, dead. Truly dead. What magic Jenin had shared with Lyari had been truth. Until that moment, some tiny part of Lyari had hoped it was a ruse.

The leather of Sahnat's cuff in her hand dug into her palm between her skin and the edge of the wooden bench.

Merin did this.

She may not have thrown the knife or felt Ryd's blood cover her hand when she slit his throat—the way *Jenin* had died, the exact way—but Merin had done this.

Jahd went on, and Lyari forced herself to listen.

"...Never had this happen before. Not thirty cycles back when we had Nameless two Journeyings in a row. Never been this way before. Never saw anybody move as quick as she did with a bow. I burned the bodies myself." Jahd hefted a sack that was belted to the side of his travel pack. "Nameless ashes went to the sea. These here belong to Ras. They'll go to his parents in Cantoranth."

Lyari found herself nodding, then something stopped her. "Ca— one of the Nameless had a halm bow. What did you do with it?"

"Burned it." Jahd's face said he was more upset about the burning of a legendary weapon like that than he was of its wielder. "All things of the dead go back to the earth."

"Thank you," Lyari said. She stood, knowing that Jahd's tea was only half drunk and that her standing to dismiss him was a slight, an improprietous gesture to someone she'd invited to her hearth, but she didn't care.

Jahd looked startled, if not affronted, and he gulped down the last of his tea, standing and taking up his rucksack again. "Is there anything you would like me to pass on to the soothsayer of Cantoranth?"

"Only what you told me," said Lyari.

When her door closed and latched behind Jahd, Lyari went to her room. Bundling herself in warm furs and thick, pimia-oiled boots, she stalked back into her roundhome's central room. Jenin still sat at the table, seemingly unmoved by Lyari's barely tamped fury.

"Merin did this," Lyari said.

"Of course she did."

Jenin said it so matter-of-factly that Lyari almost threw her empty mug across the room, instead clasping her fingers around it until she thought it might meld to her skin. Her vision seemed obscured by sparks, sparks that drifted in front of her eyes and burned them, sparks that kindled something within her.

"Don't you understand?" Jenin said then, not meeting Lyari's wrathful gaze. "Merin knows everything that happens in the Hearthland. The other soothsayers, they do their jobs. Keep the chronicles of their people. Keep people calm and placid. But Merin is the real soothsayer of the Hearthland. As you will be."

Lyari went very still. The heat of the fire burning in her hearth cast a sheen of sweat over her forehead. Bundled from head to toe in winter vestments, Lyari was warm. Too warm. But it was nothing in comparison to the fire that took hold inside her core.

She didn't look at Jenin. Instead, she tucked Sahnat's wrist cuff into her belt pouch and set off to Merin's.

The snow outside was deep, up to her thighs. It was a large amount of snow for Haveranth, far more than the few inches they normally saw dusting the ground in the turns leading up to the darkest day and the Night of

Reflection. Harvest Moon still shone above her head, though only a sliver before Foresight would be born. So much snow for so early. Lyari struggled through it, made herself follow the road to Merin's home. It took nearly three times the usual to reach the soothsayer's roundhome.

The chimney gave no smoke, but a lamp was lit on the trestle table, and when Lyari peered around the wall of Merin's roundhome at the clucker coop, she saw light and a path of footsteps breaking through the deep snow.

Lyari pushed through the snow, following the path around to the coop. When she nudged the door open, Merin stood with a hawk on her arm, murmuring something into the bird's ear.

Merin knows everything that happens in the Hearthland.

Everything, including the path of three Journeyers to the Hidden Vale.

Everything, including the deaths of Lyari's oldest friends at the hands of hunters in the mountains.

Everything, including the identity of the person who murdered her lover.

Likely she was the person who had murdered Jenin, or as good as done it. Jenin said sy had known the secrets of the Hearthland before the Journeying; likely that would be enough to merit hys death.

Lyari knocked lightly on the doorjamb to the coop, and Merin looked up.

"Ah, there you are. I was going to send for you. This is Lin," Merin said, feeding the bird what looked like a clucker heart.

"I think we've met before," Lyari said, her voice steady.

Merin smiled. "So you've found me out."

Lyari didn't trust herself to speak, so she nodded instead.

The old woman jumped then, jerking her hand back. Lin's beak had caught the soft flesh between her forefinger and thumb, and a large drop of blood welled up.

"Come," Lyari said. "I'll help you bandage that."

Some minutes later, Lyari had a stout fire roaring in Merin's hearth. She prepared a simmering tea of sparkleaf mush and boiled a strip of bavel in the mixture until the bavel turned pale green from the leaves. Setting the kettle on the hook to boil, Lyari set the corked pot of icemint out to brew after bandaging Merin's hand. Pulling the bavel strip from the mixture with a fork, Lyari blew on it slightly to cool it, then packed the steaming strip of fabric over the hawk's bite on Merin's hand. They both sat on the stone ledge that surrounded the hearth, and Lyari's back grew hot with the heat of the flames as she worked.

"Lin sees for you," Lyari said after tying the bandage tightly around the old soothsayer's skin.

Merin nodded. "She is very useful."

"Will you teach me to do this thing?"

Merin waved her hand dismissively. "There are more useful things you could learn, but if you are set upon it, there are scrolls to be found that will show you what you need to know. You will need magic to do it."

Magic Lyari did not yet have, though Merin had insisted in the cellar that performing the reinvocation would be enough to be her catalyst. Three cycles hence, Lyari would have her magic. She would be the true soothsayer of the Hearthland.

Lyari sat in silence for a moment. Jenin appeared, sitting at the trestle table with knees spread, leaning forward to look Lyari in the eyes.

"Do not do this thing."

Lyari felt the heat on her back and the sparks in front of her eyes. She did not answer her dead lover, but turned to face Merin next to her on the ledge.

"Do not do this thing, Lyari!" Jenin cried out.

Lyari took the older woman by the shoulders and shoved. Merin's head hit the heavy kettle on its hook with a clang, and she yelled as she fell backward into the roaring fire. Her hair caught first, flaming up in red and black and silver. Acrid smoke filled the roundhome, and it stung Lyari's eyes. Struggling, Merin tried to sit up, clawed fingers grasping at the stone wall that surrounded the deep hearth. Lyari grabbed the soothsayer's knees and yanked them upward, sending Merin back into the flames. Merin screamed, the fire licking at her shirt now. The tang of burning hair and cloth filled Lyari's nose, then sucked up into the chimney where it would bellow out into the winter cold.

"You killed them all," Lyari said quietly over Merin's shrieks of pain.

Outside, the howling of the winter wind was the only sound, though one villager would later say he heard a hawk screaming defiance into the raging storm.

It took Merin a long time to die.

CARIN FELT as though her world had grown and burst open like nuts roasted on hot coals.

Her whole life, all that had existed was Haveranth and the Hearthland, with even Bemin's Fan and Cantoranth feeling distant and remote. Now in the cave of the ialtag, every passing moment seemed to grow the world around her and in turn make her dwindle in size, shrinking even as she kept her shape. If she could sit at the feet of the ialtag and watch the cycles pass, connected to their mind and hearing their stories, she would. The cave where they dwelled was damp but much warmer than the outside pass. The fruit they brought the Hearthlanders was just overripe, but sweet and filling, and they had even taken to bringing back fish to add to the offerings. However different the ialtag were from her, she felt at home.

The feeling was at once welcome and incongruent, like rain falling when you were hot from working in the fields but still had work to do.

So much from before now felt like lies.

She couldn't help but remember the way the ialtag had gently shown them their error—that they could have continued on through the Hidden Vale to find a pass to the Northlands. All her life that pass had been named Mistaken, and Carin had believed that as surely as she believed following it to the vale would bring her to her name. Now she understood, as she never had before, the deception that wove itself through each of her memories. How clever were the soothsayers and elders to call it the Mistaken Pass, implying so quietly, so subtly, that it was no pass at all. So no one would look, content that those who came before them had found it futile.

Hidden in plain sight.

Carin didn't know why they tried with such vigor to make sure the Nameless never made it north through the mountains, but she felt certain that in all the cycles since the spell was first cast, hers and Ryd's and Ras's were the first Hearthlander feet to touch ground this far north.

She had watched Ras with some suspicion ever since he joined them. It was his interactions with the ialtag that soothed away those spiky edges. He met them with such wonder, such awe, that Carin trusted him a little more with each child that came to sit near him, each grown ialtag who drew him aside to show him something. Had he reacted to them with fear or disgust, it would have grown the distrust she felt instead of slaking it.

It did her good to feel, as the time came when they would have to leave this place and venture still further north into the lands beyond the mountains, that she was going with people who she could trust. Ryd she had no doubt of—his ear had healed, and he had taken to carving small trinkets with his tools for the children among the ialtag. He seemed to unfurl himself here, as if his whole life he had been curled into a lumpy mass and only now could stretch out. The ialtag adored him, and around the cave when she ventured further inward, Carin now found small caches of his whittled creatures. A kazytya with its tufted ears and enormous paws. A saiga, spiraled horns exquisitely detailed. A climber fish, tail ready to splash you.

Carin had never even really known Ryd could carve.

The days passed in easy camaraderie and fellowship...until they didn't.

The snows outside grew heavier, and at night the Hearthlanders retreated farther into the cave to escape the whipping wind and the flurries of flakes that spat in from the outside valley. They couldn't afford to winter with the ialtag, and the days grew shorter and shorter.

One of the ialtag—or all of them, really—had shown Carin somewhat of a marvel. North of the mountains, the snows had only just begun, and those only seldom. Even farther north, there would be no snows at all, even in the darkest night. It was through those long conversations with the ialtag that Carin slowly learned of the world to the north, of the vastness of sands that blanketed the land in that hot band of earth, of the way the weather would again grow cooler farther north than that until a place of near-perpetual winter spread over the land until it became nothing but ice.

Carin had never imagined a world so large, so varied, so open.

The ialtag had seen it on their flights, the coupling of a need for food with their natural curiosity taking them to explore. And yet, even as she learned from them, Carin sensed that they kept some things locked away as if exposing all their secrets at once might melt her into a puddle. She felt flickers of unease in those moments, wondering what they didn't share.

The turns passed until Foresight shone heavy and bright above their heads, and the Hearthlanders knew it was time to go. Two moons hence, the Night of Reflection, the longest night, would be upon them, and they didn't need the ialtag to tell them that staying that long would mean staying until spring.

The ialtag gave them one more piece of advice before showing them the path they would take down the mountains: *Fill your waterskins.*

She tried not to think too long on what that might mean.

Carin woke early that morning and pawed through her rucksack to make sure she had everything. The ialtag had brought more fruit than usual, and Carin had dried it over the fire to give them something to eat as they descended, along with fish. In her bag, tucked between now-filthy leggings and hastily washed stockings, was the scroll from Lyah. It had been moons since she pulled it out to look at it, and it had been flattened and crumpled by the many other items in her rucksack. She pulled it out, smoothing it against her knee.

She didn't expect its contents to have changed, and indeed they hadn't, but Carin reread the scroll anyway, stopping when she got to the bit about the original spell. Sometimes the words didn't have to be new; only what surrounded them. And now, what surrounded the words on the scroll was Carin's knowledge from the ialtag, their adjuration for her to break the stones. One word caught her eye: *inviolate.*

The inviolate hearthstones. Carin thought about that word and what it meant. It was an imposed word, an accepted word. In order for it to work, something had to protect the object, whether it was belief or a barrier or just banded together folk bent on keeping something sacred. The village hearth-home in Haveranth, its fire was inviolate. Maintained at all costs, and for all Carin knew, it had burned for hundreds of cycles without going out. The hearthstones then, were they protected by something or were they merely inviolate because the founding families needed them to be? A warning not to touch them? The spell would only last as long as the stones remained safe?

It fit, and the knowledge struck Carin keenly.

She called Ryd over and showed him—Ras was out filling water-skins—and Ryd immediately met her with excitement.

"It's like the ialtag told us," he said. "Break the stones, break the spell."

"I can't believe it's that simple."

"Probably not," Ryd said gaily, rolling a round stone between two fingers. "But it's a start."

Carin murmured her agreement, but her mind didn't stop rolling thoughts around like Ryd with his stone.

Not long after, when they were again bundled into their furs and cloaks and snowshoes, the ialtag saw them to the edge of the path that led northward into the foothills of the Mad Mountains. Carin felt the strangeness of it, to live her whole life so far on one side of the mountains and now be going to live the rest on the other. One of the ialtag, whose name she wish she could voice—it was something like a spring breeze or the first growth of grass that had no word—laid his cheek against Carin's, and all that came forth from his mind was a sense of pride and relief.

"How did you know we would come along?" Carin asked. She wanted to ask why the ialtag didn't just break the stones themselves if they knew that's what had to be done, but she didn't think she'd get an answer.

The answer that came to her voiced question came on a quiet wave of whispers. A blank expanse, of cycles passing with no one venturing into the mountains, empty foothills, dead Nameless.

We didn't.

So they set off, and Carin kept that answer to herself.

They spoke in low voices for the first part of the descent, of seeking out a village soothsayer, of sharing what the ialtag had told them, of searching for help. Ras and Ryd both agreed it was for the best.

But still, Carin held tight the advice from the ialtag—*fill your waterskins.*

She couldn't shake the feeling that they had no idea of what they would find at the foot of the hills. She looked in the direction the ialtag had shown her, their shared memories laying out the map better than any drawn parchment could. There was a village there, two or three turns' walk away, folded into the ripples of the hills.

People.

Their new people, at least she hoped.

She turned back once, not back to look over the path they had just walked, but southeast, toward Haveranth and the life she had left behind. For the barest moment, Carin let herself picture Dyava's face bathed in the sun of early spring. Winter would soon grip Haveranth even as it laid claim to the mountains here in the Northlands. She turned away and quickened her steps to catch up with the others. The clouds hung low, obscuring the sun. One day the light would reveal all for good or ill.

SART WAS fairly certain she would never see Culy again until her hair was silver and her teeth had decayed right out of her mouth.

This certainty had crept up upon her as she navigated into Crevasses from the spring—oh, that spring!—mostly because she couldn't seem to go half a league without running into a person, even off the Lahi'alar and far away from any known waymakes or junctions.

She had just passed into the heart of Crevasses when she ran into the first travelers. They weren't rovers, though at first Sart was afraid they were and that she'd have to kill them. It was two men, walking through the muck from the previous night's slushy snowfall, and when they waved her down, she very nearly had Tahin trample them just to be safe.

Sart settled for keeping her distance and using some of her carefully spooled magic to snap the left man's bowstring. She didn't want to chance him loosing an arrow at her back if she tried to flee, especially since she was riding precious currency. Ihstal weren't usually worth killing for, but Sart's luck seemed rotted through lately.

Keeping Tahin a few spans away from the men, she watched them even as she called out. "What is it you need? I'm in a hurry."

The man on the left had cried out in dismay at the snap of his bow-string, and even then had unslung it from his shoulder and was inspecting it. The other stepped toward Sart, one hand reaching out to touch his companion on the shoulder as he passed.

"Please," he said. "Do you have any water?"

Water. The only water Sart had was the water from the spring, three days' ride in the other direction. Giving them that was bound to raise questions. She looked them over, top to bottom. Boggers, from the looks of them, or at least they were coming from that direction. Both wore the above knee boots oiled to some semblance of watertightness, both had a small pouch hanging from their belts that Sart knew held flint, greased twine, and a handful of blacknut shells. Bogs were fickle places, but those who'd grown up in and around the Boggers region knew that the currents were the only real way to tell the direction when the sun was shrouded behind petulant clouds. Light a tiny lamp, set it on the water, and watch where it went. Follow the current. If you were lucky, you might find a good fishing hole if something tried to eat your navigation tool.

Just now, they were coming from the direction of Crevasses, where water was, if not plentiful, at least available.

"Why don't you have your own? I've got only a little and a long way to go with it. And a mount to keep." Sart kept her hand on Tahin's neck, ready to ease the ihstal into a run if she needed to.

"Rovers," the man on the left said, tucking his bow into his belt. When he went on, it was with a panicked sob that strained to break through even as he tried to swallow it. "Took all the water. Bunch of them were injured, but two got the jump on us. Amat managed to club one of them over the head and stab the other, and we tried to run, but—"

The man on the right, Amat, nodded and interrupted. "One of the injured ones started shooting at us."

Sart wanted to scream. This had to be Barit and his rovers. If Kahs had managed to shoot at them, hys skills were better than Sart had thought.

She should have cut off Kahs's drawing arm. Or destroyed the bow and not just the string. Or killed hyr.

She gave them an entire waterskin, dropping it on the ground, and rode off before they could drink from it and discover what was inside.

That was the first interruption.

The second came four days later, and it was a woman this time. She had a wild-eyed look about her, and for a moment, Sart thought she might try to take her down just to get Tahin away from her. In the end, the woman must have decided against it, because she gave Sart a wide berth but kept looking over her shoulder until Sart was out of sight. Sart kept her eyes open and her mind alert after that.

The third came deep into Crevasses, two turns out from where she was supposed to meet Culy.

She wouldn't have stopped—but it was someone she knew.

She saw him when she crested a hill, and he was headed north. Their paths wouldn't have crossed, but Sart saw him and knew him and nudged Tahin into a run. "Geral!" She called his name when he turned toward the sound of churning ihstal feet.

He turned to face her, and his face was slack with relief. He looked back over his shoulder once before meeting her gaze again. If it had been anyone else, Sart would have expected someone to be chasing him, but with Geral, it was just him. She hadn't seen him this far north in five cycles.

Sart slid off Tahin's back and closed the distance between them, catching Geral in a tight embrace, which he returned with every ounce of matching strength, pulling her in close and tightening his arms around her shoulders. He smelled of sweat and smoke and pine, and his usually close-cropped black hair was longer. Where it had grown out from his scalp, the rest of him seemed to have shrunk.

"Geral, are you eating?" Sart pulled away from the embrace and went to her pack, rummaging in it for some strips of dried squirrel she'd been eating for the past two days.

"I needed to find someone. There was an avalanche." He didn't answer her question, but he did take the meat, his teeth taking half of it in one bite. His dark eyes glinted, always busy. His lips were dry and cracking, and just then they were tight with worry.

"Avalanches happen all the time in the mountains."

"Not like this one." He pointed up the valley out of which he'd just emerged. "Up there about fifteen leagues, maybe thirty. Lots of snow this cycle so far."

Geral said that last with a wryness that Sart knew all too well. What he wasn't saying was that the snow never came far enough north to help anyone in Crevasses. No, that was the perpetual joke. Plenty of snow. Good, clean water for the melting. If you could figure out a way to get it down the mountains. Usually families went up there to bring down snow from the first falls in winter, and if there were more snows sooner this cycle, it only stood to reason that more families would make the climb up into the foothills and beyond to see what they could gather. Couple ihstal, a sturdy sleigh or cart, a couple well-made barrels—might be worth the effort. If you could get back down into the world with it. No rover in the world would let a cart full of water go by untouched.

No one tried to simply live in the mountains. The weather was too unpredictable, the food too scarce. You needed water more frequently, but eventually you'd die without food too. Not that food was plentiful anywhere.

"What's so different about this avalanche?"

Geral hesitated. Sart raised her eyebrows, wondering what it was he didn't want to say. She'd known Geral since he tried stealing a water pot from Alys when Sart used to help tend her kiln. His punishment had been to cut clay by the banks of the creek, which had hacked off Sart because his punishment was her normal duty at the time. But then Geral had been the only one to stick around when Alys got the skin-rot and the rest of the waymake cleared out. He never was much for people. Sart reached out and took his hand. Even after all this time, she knew those hands.

"You can tell me," she said.

"I'd rather just show you."

· · · · ·

It took the better part of a turn to make it up into the mountains, even though Tahin was strong enough to carry both Sart and Geral. Sart told him about the spring she'd found, about the rovers, and that Culy was waiting for her. Foresight Moon rose high and fat in the sky when they finally reached the high valley. Sart apologized to Culy in her head, knowing sy couldn't hear her. *I'm going to be later still, old friend. Forgive me.*

When they reached the snow level, the wind brought a different scent down the mountain. Not the smell of wet rock or pine or snow, but something acrid and pungent. They found the reason not far behind the smell.

A family had camped by the trail, a barrel full of water sitting on a small wooden cart, wheels blocked. No ihstal were to be found. A man and two children, huddled next to a fire. They'd built a snow-dwelling not far away, though already it was melting. It wasn't late enough in the cycle for such a thing to stay with any permanence.

Geral ignored them, leading Sart past the family and uphill until her lungs tightened with cold and exertion.

The path, as he'd said, was fully blocked by snow. Geral pointed to a tree on the side of the path and held out a pair of bronze spikes on leather thongs.

Without questioning, Sart laced them onto her feet and took hold of the lowest branch, jumping and throwing her weight against the spikes. They sank into the bark, and she pulled herself up. She scrambled upward, sometimes hugging the tree with one arm, other times managing to catch a branch, until she was about halfway up the trunk. It wasn't a hugely tall tree, but she could still see over the blockage of snow.

And she saw exactly what was different about this avalanche.

It wasn't a lumping cavalcade of sliding snow.

It formed a firm line from the south as if someone had shaped it that way, or as if it had been funneled along an invisible wall. The strangest part was that in the center, right where the path would cut through, the wall of snow broke. From her vantage point, Sart could see that the path was only blocked fully because the snow on either side had since collapsed further and fallen in on itself.

The constant hum that lived in the back of her mind got louder, and when Sart looked at the unexplainable avalanche, she could almost feel the echo of something just out of reach.

Sart wriggled her way back down the trunk of the tree and, not bothering to untie the spikes from her feet, ran to the place where the path should be. The hum was stronger there, and it felt like free magic floating around. She let the hum surround her, listening to it, hoping it would give some sort of explanation. Who could be powerful enough to do such a thing, and to what end?

When the first tendrils of magic began to wind within her, they tasted old, like digging up a pot that had been buried long ago by someone who always meant to come back for it. It swirled deep inside her core until she swayed on her feet, pendulous. It felt...something seemed to tug her to the south.

A hand caught her shoulder. Geral.

"You see what I mean."

Geral knew some little bit of magic, Sart knew, but it was something they seldom spoke of.

This time Culy could wait no longer.

Sart led Tahin down the path, and she saw the hungry look in the father's eyes when he saw the ihstal next to his motionless cart. Sart still had two full skins of water from the spring and two empty ones. She looked at the barrel, full of fresh meltwater. It wasn't spring water, but it was better than the muck from the creeks of Crevasses.

"Who'd you lose?" Sart asked.

"Their mother and oldest sahthren," the man said.

Sart nodded and motioned toward the northwest, in the direction of the spring. "Three turns from here by foot, there's a spring. A clean one. If you leave your barrel I'll draw you a map."

The man scoffed an I'll-believe-that-when-your-ihstal-sings laugh. "Better you sell me your ihstal."

Sart pulled one of her full skins out of her pack and handed it to the man. "It's true."

He took a drink, then another. Even though it'd been in a waterskin for almost a moon, Sart knew it still tasted fresher and cleaner than any other water they could have. When he took another, Sart clucked and motioned for him to give the skin back.

The man obliged, and his gaze went to his children. Two children. Three, as had been. Sart couldn't remember the last time she'd seen a family of three. It felt right that they would be the ones to go to this spring, with its blue grass and its sugar-tree.

"People will want it once they find it," she said, her voice soft with the danger of what she was giving them.

"Why'd you leave it?"

"I don't have time to sit by the water."

She drew him a map, and they left even though the light was fading for the day, filling their waterskins from their barrel and giving Sart a look that said a lie would eventually cost her her life.

Geral watched the whole thing from a safe observation point, but came closer to Sart again once the father and children were gone.

He didn't say anything, but when Sart started gathering stones from their fire to build a warning cairn, he helped her.

She had a handful of white stones she kept in a pouch in her pack for such occasions, adding new ones when she found them to make sure she had them in hand. When they finished the cairn, she dug one out and placed it on top.

White for death. Go no farther.

L YARI SCREAMED. Screamed moons of frustration and anger and grief. Screamed justice for Carin and Ryd and Jenin. Screamed until her voice cracked like rocks at the quarry.

The scent of Merin's burning flesh and clothing burned her eyes and pulled tears from them, but they were not tears of grief. Not then. Not yet.

The winter screamed with her, and the wind carried the sound of her scream to the village.

It didn't take long for someone to come.

Rina, her hands red and chapped from the cold—she never wore mitts, said it hampered her movement—appeared at the door to Merin's hut and froze like ice to the floor.

Lyari's cloak dripped melting water, where it fell in ash and blood onto the charred hem of Merin's tunic.

Snow still clung to Lyari's cloak.

She had thought it all out.

She had, immediately in the moments after Merin finally died and settled onto the roaring fire to sizzle, walked back to her home, retrieved a scroll she had left, named all the moons of the cycle and all the runes, and returned to Merin's.

And screamed.

Now Rina stood, framed by the swirling snow and the darkness and the hand-hewn doorframe, and Lyari sat on her knees, which grew numb and spiny against the hard floor, rough sounds pushing her tongue aside to meet the air.

When Rina asked what happened, Lyari pushed out sounds and held back words that wanted to tear up her throat more than the scream had. She held them back, held them tight, and buried them deep within herself.

"What happened?" Rina's voice sounded thick in the air. Thicker than the smoke that filled the roundhome.

Merin killed Carin. Merin killed Ryd. Merin killed Jenin.

If Merin had not killed Jenin, she knew what happened. As for the others, she more than knew.

"What happened?" Rina asked again.

Lyari fell backward, landing on her backside on the maha floor. She had to speak now, had to let some words eke past those she held back from escaping. "I went to...get a scroll." Her own voice sounded shredded, raw, like the clucker hearts Merin had fed to Lin just before she died.

"You killed her."

Lyari's head snapped up, but it wasn't Rina's voice damning her. Jenin's. Of course Jenin's.

She ignored hyr.

Rina dropped to her knees at the sudden movement, clasping the back of Lyari's neck and pulling her tight against her breast. "It's all right, child. It's all right."

No one should have called Lyari a child, not after the Journeying and especially not after being named soothsayer. Eighteen or not, she was no longer a child. The bronze soothsayer's cuff on her wrist felt cold, cold.

"She got bit," Lyari said, the words dragging themselves from her throat. "Her hawk. I started the sparkleaf mush to bind her hand, started her tea. I went to get the scroll while it steeped..."

The scroll in question sat in a pool of melted snow.

"Sparkleaf mush," Rina said matter-of-factly. She gave Lyari one last squeeze like the bellows of her forge and pushed herself to stand. At the hearth, she peered into the fire, which had burned low to its embers.

Reaching in barehanded, Rina pulled out an earthenware mug and sniffed it.

The spilled icemint tea to the left of the hearth drew her next, like a honeybee to the redberry flowers in spring.

Lyari waited, curled on the floor, her fingers tight around a snippet of fabric from Merin's tunic. To Rina, she knew, it would look as if she were clinging to the memory of what was, of what had been. And perhaps she was, in a way. Lyari clung to that fabric, waiting for Rina to be the first to state the lie of what had happened here, because if Rina said it first, the others would believe it for truth.

"The tea. She must have mixed up her teas." There it was. Rina sniffed the earthenware mug again. "This was some strong sparkleaf mush. Must have been." She knelt by Merin's side and unbandaged the hand Lin had bitten.

A deep gouge, the hawk had left, necessitating a strong dose of sparkleaf. So densely steeped, a drink would disorient. And sparkleaf, when strongly brewed, tasted of mint. If one were expecting icemint tea, it might take two drinks to notice the difference. Rina knew that as well as Lyari; it had happened before in the village, but not to the effect of tragedy, only humor.

Rina touched one hand to Merin's hand where she had unbandaged Lin's bite.

"I will alert the elders," Rina said. "They will want to hold the funeral soon. You must take the things from here that you will need for your duties."

Lyari nodded, and her insides felt as though they were being pulled apart. The place she had stored tears for Carin each night she spent in the bed that ought to have belonged to her lifelong friend burst forth, trickling down her cheeks even as Lyari stood and straightened. She let them come, grief-tears. For Carin. For Ryd. For Jenin.

Rina bustled from the roundhome, her face set but lips quivering only just, leaving Lyari alone to truly face the scene of the murder she had made with her hands.

She should feel shame. Some of that grief ought to be for Merin, for losing this mentor. She did feel that, but she had lost that mentorship when she had discovered Merin's culpability in the deaths of her loved ones, not when the fire's flames licked her away with their burning tongues.

She should feel many things, and she did all at once with the warring upheaval within her breast and Jenin's accusatory words ricocheting throughout her mind and body.

But in some tiny part of Lyari, a voice that was not Jenin's sobbed.

• • • • •

The elders came quickly, as Lyari knew they would.

None of them wore white bands of mourning, but she saw them dangling from the belts of the elders as if they had to see Merin's body before they would believe in her death.

Old Wend, Rina, Varsu, Ohlry—one by one Lyari watched them tie the white bands around their upper arms. No tears from them. Theirs would come later.

Lyari stood apart from them, swaying on her feet. Her mind swirled like the seeds from the sugar trees as they spun from branch to ground. It occurred to her, as she watched the elders lay out Merin's body on her trestle table with careful hands, that these people could be just as culpable, just as complicit in Carin and Ryd's deaths—and Jenin's—as Merin. Were, likely.

She looked around the room for Jenin, but sy was nowhere to be found, and Lyari felt the coldness in herself sound deep as if in a well, for she was very, very alone.

She tucked away some of that coldness. For Carin. For Ryd. For Jenin. A tiny piece she tucked away for herself, to remember that it had always existed even when she had thought she was warm.

By sunup, the snow still spattering in hard, shard-like flakes against the glass panes of Merin's windows, Lyari and Rina had removed all of the scrolls and items Lyari thought would be useful to a soothsayer. Herbs and stones, the bottles of syrups and cordials from the cellar, a small stone box of pearls from Merin's bedside, and stacks upon stacks of pressed parchments all made their new home in Lyari's spare bedchamber. Finally, Rina and several of the more stout villagers fashioned a sleigh to pull the giant hearthstone the distance to Lyari's home. Lacking a deep cellar like Merin's, Lyari had it placed on the north side of her hearth, snug against the stonework Carin had carved with her hands.

When the other villagers finally left Lyari alone, she shuttered all her windows and sat at the trestle table, leaning her back against the table itself and propping her feet up on the hearthstone. Her heel wedged into the cup marks on its top.

Quiet consumed her roundhome. She knew before long she would be expected at Merin's funeral, when her home and body would be burnt and returned to nourish the earth as ashes spread across the fields of Haveranth.

When Lyari thought of it that way, she felt Merin's death bleed into her funeral like the sea bled into the sand at the shore.

Until sundown, she would sit. She watched the flames in her own hearth in silence. Her chest felt hollow and empty as a blown out clucker egg.

Soothsayer.

Lyari thought on what Merin had imparted to her before her death. The coming reinvocation of the Hearthland spell that would ensure her people's survival in the cycles to come. Three turnings of harvest. Jenin had seemed just as fraught about Lyari's participation in that as sy had about the murder of Merin.

Murder.

Lyari turned the word over, raking the backs of her nails down her legs to the dent of her knees beneath her thick breeches.

Not murder. Justice.

Soon she would take Merin's place with the elders. The protection of Haveranth was now in her hands, and there was no blood upon them. Only ash.

• • • • •

As the sun set over Haveranth, peering through the clouds as if wondering if it were safe to show its face, Lyari held a torch to the pimia-oiled lintel of Merin's roundhome and watched the flames race downward, following the dripping oil to the ground.

The other elders did the same at windows and the rear door, and within moments the home and everything in it was engulfed in flame.

THE SNOW formed a wall with a hole punched through it.

The sight reminded Ryd of Haver's Glen, and the familiarity left him with a sharp pang in his chest that echoed in his partly missing ear.

Carin walked up to the wall and poked it with her mitt. Snow crumbled away and fell, and she looked up dubiously at the rise of white that towered above their heads. The way through was carved but had collapsed partway down. With the snowshoes, they could amble up it, but Ryd wasn't sure he wanted to risk walking between those walls of white to get that far. It looked like the tempting smile of death.

Ras grunted and pushed past them. "I didn't lose my name and dangle from the claws of giant bats to let some pile of mush stop me."

Gingerly, Ryd and Carin followed behind him as he mounted the ramp of snow with a fwop-fwop, fwop-fwop of snowshoes. By now the sound had grown familiar, like the beating of a heart or the sound of breath. The passageway was barely wide enough for two of them to walk side by side, and Ryd looked at the wall as he walked, willing it to stay upright and not bury them.

"What caused this?" Carin murmured.

"Whatever causes a turd to fall into a latrine," Ras said, looking over his shoulder. "Water flows downhill, pinecones drop off trees, and snow tumbles down the sides of mountains sometimes."

"Thank you, wise leader," Carin said, and Ryd knew her well enough to know that the way she was eyeing Ras's snowshoes and fingering her belt knife at once meant she was considering whether slicing the gut on the back of his shoes would send him sprawling.

Ryd hoped she'd give in to the impulse.

Instead, she said nothing else as they reached the top of the mound, and Ras clomped forward.

The snow crumbled away beneath Ras's feet, sending him skittering down several spans until he came up sputtering and swearing.

Carin stumbled, but didn't fall, and she and Ryd managed a more graceful descent, coming to a halt at Ras's tangled legs.

Ryd's eyes were focused straight ahead.

A path.

A worn path.

A pile of grey rocks topped with a white, flat stone stood a small distance from them, but that wasn't what froze Ryd to the snow.

They had crossed the mountains.

The worn path in front of them was the creation of people, of Northlanders. They had arrived, and they were now strangers in a land that may have forgotten of their existence or never known at all.

• • • • •

By unspoken agreement, they set up camp not far away from the strange avalanche site, just past the cairn where a fire pit had been dug into the snow. Ryd helped set up a tent, and he couldn't help but notice how both Carin and Ras moved as gingerly as he did, as if each new thing they touched would somehow stick them tighter to this new land.

No one seemed to want to make a fire in the pit, where only a light dusting of new snow covered the bottom.

Finally, Ryd moved a bit away from the campsite and found some scrubby trees, hunting for fallen branches and pulling some away that the weight of snow had left hanging. The sight reminded him too much of the bit of ear he had lost, and it twinged each time his eyes fell upon such a branch.

When he came back, Carin started the fire, turning away to shelter the tinder in the palm of her hand as she had taken to doing. Even when the wood was wet or green, it burned readily for her. Ryd suspected she had hidden away a vial of pimia oil and didn't want anyone else to know. Just a drop of the stuff would catch even a weak spark. Even the fumes were flammable unless you let it sit for a day.

Sitting around the fire, Ryd allowed himself to look around at the landscape. It didn't seem so different from that of his homeland. The trees were a bit shorter, the colors of the evergreens not as vibrant—though that could have been simply melancholy manifesting through his perception. The path they sat near snaked down the mountainside, and in the afternoon light, Ryd could see where the snow line ended. Near the camp-fire was a large barrel filled with meltwater, a gap of about half an arm's length at the top of it. He tasted it carefully and found it to be good, if a bit woody from the barrel. They refilled their water skins from the barrel and sat around the fire, quietly drinking.

After a while, Ryd got up, doffed his snowshoes, and scrambled up the hill behind the fire, trying to get a good vantage point before the sun set and darkness blanketed them from seeing the strangeness of the new land. Ras and Carin turned over their shoulders to look at him, but didn't follow. He clambered up the steep incline. The top of the hill was free of trees, and it afforded him a view over the avalanche site behind them, as well as down the mountain into the foothills and beyond. The snow reached about halfway down from where they camped, and the foothills wrinkled the land like the creases in Merin's face.

Ryd felt the air leave him as if he'd been jumped on.

He sat down on a rock, almost slipping off it because of its thin sheet of ice.

The land that spread out before him was all like the trees he saw around the campsite. Muted colors, like someone had drained the hue from them. Where in the Hearthland he would have seen rivers—he had once climbed to the top of the Haverford Quarry and saw the blue waters crisscrossing the countryside for miles and miles and miles—here there seemed to be none. Outside of the foothills, where the land began to flat-ten, it grew brown like mud and drab. He could see no signs of life around him. As soon as the thought touched his mind, he almost lost his breath again. From Haverford Quarry, he had been able to see the smoke from Cantoranth's hearths, as well as that of Haveranth. Beyond that, smaller homesteads around the villages were visible, and they had flickered like jewels as dusk fell and the lights of lamps shimmered through the dark. It was as if this land north of the mountains bore only death.

His eyes hungrily searched the horizon, looking for anything to prove him otherwise. To the west was only the curve of the mountains—according to Ras's map, farther west they would find the sea, which Ryd had never seen. To the north were drab plains and no signs of smoke or habitation that his eyes could discern.

When he finally saw a wisp of smoke rising to the northeast, just over the next few hills, his stomach took a tumble in his gut. There it was. Proof they were not alone. He stumbled back down the hill to the campfire to tell the others, who listened with straight lips and lowered eyebrows.

That night, without discussion, they all drank as much water as they could hold and refilled their skins.

When Ryd lay in his bedroll after his stint at watch, he tried to slow his breathing. For the first time, he allowed himself to consider that they may not be welcome here. In the Hearthland, there was no contact with people elsewhere—indeed, even the idea of strangers was so foreign that no one voiced it or pondered it. His chest felt tight beneath his cloak, and he half wanted to crawl under Carin's cloak as they had done in the coldest nights, where at least the three of them had each other and knew that they were all bound by circumstance and kinship. He missed his parents. He had been so eager to move from childhood to adulthood, and now he would have given anything to be back within the shelter of their roundhome, the ignorance that had shrouded him. The thought soured his water-full belly, and for a moment, Ryd was suspended between the fear of his current reality and the knowledge that his life before had been a lie. Carin understood. He wished he could reach out to her.

He stayed alone, though, and when the sun lightened the sky, bringing with it the sharp cold of apprehension, they packed up camp and headed down the mountains, snowshoes strapped to their packs.

The ground gave way from snow to mud at midday, and they came across another pile of stones with a white rock at its top.

"What do you suppose it means?" Ras asked Carin. He rarely spoke to Ryd, which was mostly fine except Ryd thought it was because Ras didn't think he had anything useful to contribute.

Carin shrugged. "Navigation, perhaps. A way to mark trails."

The white rock on this one sat clearly on the south side of the stone pile, almost pointing up the mountain. The one at the top had been centered. He supposed Carin's explanation was as good as any.

As the sun made its way westward, the path spread out before them and they caught the first glimpse of a Northlander village.

It was a strange place to Ryd's eyes. No roundhomes, but single poles that stood out from the ground like trimmed trees in small circles. A few were wrapped in canvas, and plumes of smoke rose from chimneys in the roofs, which were unlike any Ryd had ever seen. Red-brown and dusted with the remnants of snow, each structure wore the tiles like scales of a fish. The chimneys seemed to be made of the same stuff but in blocks at the center of the roof's dome and capped with more of the scales. The pole structures, whether bearing canvas walls or not, all had the roofs. They were small, much smaller than the roundhomes in the Hearthland. They came up on a pole standing alone, and Ryd saw that its surface was carved with runes.

"*Lysraht,*" Carin read. "Crevasses. Is that the name of this place?" She traced her finger past the word and frowned, and Ryd moved closer to peer at it.

"*Basan!*" The yell startled Ryd into stopping.

Carin and Ras did the same, Ras with a sharp intake of breath, and Carin's hand immediately went to her bow.

The yell repeated, and it was followed by a string of words Ryd couldn't fully understand. *Basan* he knew meant stop, though it was spoken with a strange lilt, the emphasis off and the vowels drawn out. A moment of panic clawed at him, and from the way Carin and Ras shifted their feet, he could feel the same in them.

A person emerged from behind a large pole. Sy had long black hair bound back with a leather thong and wore thick furs from head to toe. Hys face was gaunt, cheekbones standing out sharply under bright dark eyes. Confusion lit hyr face as sy looked over the trio, and sy turned over hys shoulder to call out another string of unintelligible words.

"I can't understand them," Ras said, his voice cracking like dry wood.

Carin frowned and shook her head at Ryd.

Several more Northlanders appeared, ducking out of the canvas flaps of their huts. One's eyes widened, and sy pointed at Carin's bow, causing a murmur to go through the crowd.

"Carin," Ryd said. "If we can't understand them..."

She put a hand on his shoulder. "I know. It'll be okay."

"Tell them that," said Ras.

The first Northlander approached them, speaking quickly and loudly. When sy saw the confusion on the faces of the Hearthlanders, sy spoke more slowly and deliberately, and the others behind hyr gave a nervous chuckle.

Sy pointed at the three of them and then motioned northward, turning back with a question in hys eyes.

"I think sy wants to know where we come from," Carin said. "What should we say?"

"Well, it's obvious we're not from here." Ras looked as though he wanted to turn back and run into the mountains.

"The truth," said Ryd.

Carin raised her eyebrows, but he saw that her chest rose and fell faster and that the whites of her eyes showed around the deep blue inner circles. Her hand still rested on his shoulder, and with her other, she gestured behind her, to the south. Toward the mountains.

A hush fell over the Northlanders.

"We're from the south," Carin said, her words as slow and deliberate as the Northlander's had been.

The hush turned to a whisper, then a murmur, and Ryd couldn't tell if it was curiosity or suspicion.

HOW VERY stupid they had been.

Ras gathered with Carin and Ryd around a Northlander fire, sitting close to them but not touching as they were. The entire village—if one could call it that—had come out of their dwellings and encircled them. No one had made a move to touch them or take their weapons, but Ras kept his hand close to his hip just in case. Their words swirled around him as they spoke to each other, eluding him. He could tell the tongue they used was similar to his own; at moments he caught wisps of meaning and familiarity, only to have it slip away and vanish again.

He had never for a moment considered that there were more ways to speak to other people than the words he already knew. A rock was a rock was a rock. If you wanted to tell someone about it, you said rock. Here he wasn't so sure, and the inability to communicate with the Northlanders made his skin feel loose on his bones, as if he were swimming inside himself.

The Northlanders spoke in low voices, as if afraid they were wrong about the Hearthlanders being able to understand them and didn't want to risk being heard for what they were saying. Ryd and Carin sat on a log, their legs touching as if the small comfort of a familiar friend could anchor them in this new world where Ras simply felt adrift. He knew he could probably move closer to them, lean a shoulder against Carin's. He wanted to. The village around them was small and at once the largest place he had ever been. Everything around him made him feel as though he had no bearings on the world anymore.

The ignorance of his youth nearly made him despair.

His stomach churned; they hadn't eaten since midday, and no one had thought to bring them anything to eat. Ras wasn't sure if that meant the Northlanders were poor hosts or simply that Ras and the others were prisoners.

Carin opened her rucksack and pulled out a packet of dried fish, causing a stir among the Northlanders. They made no move to take her food as she divided it between herself, Ryd, and Ras, but their eyes followed it with such burning curiosity that Ras wondered if they had fish in the Northlands at all. Eating with fifteen sets of eyes on him felt uncomfortable, and the murmurs that rose and fell around him didn't help.

The first Northlander to approach them seemed to have taken it into hys hands to make them hys responsibility, and sy sat down on a stump pulled up in front of their log.

Sy pointed to hyrself. "Jen ve Lahgirtan."

The woman's name was the first thing he understood, and Ras was surprised by the prickle of tears in his eyes. He saw the release of breath from both Ryd and Carin and knew he wasn't alone.

"Jen ve Lahgirtan," Ras said. At his speaking, ripples went through the gathered Northlanders. He pointed to himself then. "Ras va Cantoranth."

His name caused a bit of a stir, but it was Carin and Ryd who drew more curiosity, as they both pronounced themselves of Haveranth.

Jen ve Lahgirtan gestured between the two of them and said something Ras couldn't understand. Carin and Ryd looked back and forth between one another, confusion writ across their faces. Jen frowned, then stood from her stump, beckoning another villager toward her.

She pointed to herself again. "Jen ve Lahgirtan." Then to the person beside her. "Tinan vy Lahgirtan." Jen took hys hand and touched the thin skin of hys wrist, then her own, repeating the word she'd said the moment before.

At Carin and Ryd's blank looks, she drew it out, pronouncing each part as clearly as she could.

And Ras understood.

"*Sahla'ahmvar,*" Jen said. *Kin.*

A word Ras knew, but not the one commonly used. Sahthren was what Hearthlanders used, for those born of the same parents and close relations alike.

Ras saw understanding glint through Carin and Ryd like a shiver, and they looked at one another, shaking their heads.

Carin gestured around herself at the village and said, "*Lysraht.*" Crevasses. Then she pointed at Jen and Tinan vi Lahgirtan and said, "Jen and Tinan vi Lyrsaht. Carin and Ryd vi Haveranth."

A chuckle went through the Northlanders, and Jen nodded, though her gaunt face still held murky understanding.

The rest of the evening passed thus, with one side or the other naming things and the rest responding. Ras still felt discomfited, though the curiosity on both sides bore with it a strange camaraderie. When they finally set up their tent on the outside of the village, he couldn't help but notice the Northlanders quietly positioned armed villagers nearby.

• • • • •

The next morning, Ras rose early and tried to hunt. He pointed out into the forest when one of the villagers eyed him nervously, then gestured at his belt knives and short bow and was greeted with more curiosity, but the villager let him go.

For several hours, Ras saw nothing but vermin. The foothills were almost eerily quiet, even for the onset of winter. Back in Cantoranth, the snows would have started in earnest, though now with Foresight waning into a sliver, her sister beside her, always smaller and seemingly plumper. There should have been some sort of game in the hills, either saiga or hares or some creature—any creature larger than a squirrel. But the woods were silent and sounded only the rushing of the wind in the trees.

He killed three squirrels and two fat voles, and that was all he could find. Ras had never before had such an unsuccessful hunt. He thought of the stores of food Carin had kept so carefully rationed. They wouldn't last to see Vigil Moon's fullness.

He returned to the village, which they had learned was called Suonlys, for the white-capped mountain that rose up to the south behind it. At the village's center, Ryd had his snowshoes out and was showing them to the villagers. He spoke slowly as if hoping to be understood, but as Ras approached, he saw that the Northlanders followed more the tracing of Ryd's fingertips across the weaves of gut twine and curves of the doubloon tree branches than they did the words he spoke.

Carin he found near the tent, her bow still slung over her shoulder. She saw him approaching nearly empty-handed, and a frown puckered her face as he came within hearing range. "No luck?"

Ras showed her his kills, and he saw her eyes flick skyward, where the sun was already halfway down to the horizon again. He understood the meaning of that as well as she did; that it had taken him all day to find enough food for one real meal between them was yet another worry to add to their pile.

But it wasn't the food she drew his attention to.

She pulled out one of the waterskins, half empty already. The others, he knew, were in the same state. "I thought for certain we would come across a clear stream or spring, but there haven't been any. We will need water, and we will need it soon."

"Where do they get their water?" Ras asked, motioning at the village of Suonlys. Village. Hardly more than a hunting encampment. Surely farther north there had to be proper settlements.

Carin shook her head. "I haven't asked. I'm not sure how. They seem to be treating us with enough wariness, and I get the feeling that water is not plentiful. I worry they will think we are trying to take their resources."

Her words sunk in after a moment, and Carin met Ras's eyes, stricken at what she had said.

All they had done their entire lives was take resources from the Northlands. While Ras had long since come to terms with it, Carin and Ryd obviously hadn't, or he wouldn't be here right now.

"I'll see what I can do," Carin said, and walked off in the direction of Ryd and his snowshoes.

Ras set about skinning his quarry from the day, and carefully reserved the small skins and tails of the squirrels, not wanting to waste any possible things of value. While the rest of the Hearthland may not have done the same, hunters knew how to use even the smallest bits of a creature for something useful.

A short time later, Carin returned with Ryd and six full waterskins.

Surprised, Ras wiped his bloody hands on dampened bavel cloth. "How did you do that?"

"Traded the snowshoes," Ryd said.

"I guess we won't need them." Ras shook the pot full of carcasses in front of him, watching them slide around, barely covering the bottom of it. With a little of the dried fruit from the ialtag, they should make a hearty enough stew, if bland. But for three people...

The stew tasted well enough once it was done, and the three of them picked tiny bones from their mouths, sipping dingy water from their skins. The water tasted of leather and silt, like licking a dusty rock and about as satisfying.

The villagers occasionally came over and tried to talk, but Ras found his mind drifting. He agreed to take second watch and fell into his bedroll.

He woke partway through the night with stabbing pains tearing apart his stomach.

Lurching from his blankets and kicking Ryd in the process, he stumbled from the tent and managed three steps before falling to his knees in the dirt and retching. He heaved until his stomach felt inside out and his eyes dripped stinging tears into the pool of his bile. Ras felt his stomach drop, twisting and clenching, and his skin slicked with clammy sweat. He shoved against the ground, not caring that his hands slipped in the puddle of his vomit, making it to the edge of the village with a half crawl and falling behind a bush where he yanked down his breeches and had to cling to the bush to keep from tumbling backward into his own shit.

Ras lost track of the time that passed while he was behind the bush, alternatively vomiting and loosing his bowels. He begged death to take him as the sun began to touch the sky with cold, cruel light. His head pounded, and dimly he became aware of Carin's voice, rough with bile, and Ryd's as well not far away.

He lost consciousness as the first rays of dawn touched his face.

CARIN HAD never been in such horrible pain.

Once, as a child, she had been running through her mother's smithery just as Rina removed a piece of glowing metal from the forge with her heavy tongs, and Carin had caught her elbow on the red-hot bronze. She had felt a flash of something indescribable, and she had stopped in bewilderment for the tiniest of moments until her mind caught up with the pain and then she screamed, screamed so loudly half the village came running.

She felt like that hot metal had lodged itself inside her stomach now.

It seemed as though every strip of dried fish, every drink of water, every berry and every piece of fruit had decided to erupt from her body. Carin found herself outside Suonlys, clinging to a scraggly tree with every bit of failing strength she had, and found that strength lacking. She could hear Ryd, and further away, Ras, doing the same.

Was this what illness was? This horrible gutting feeling? Nothing green seemed to come from her nose, so she could not be sure. Had the villagers poisoned them?

Carin finally lay back against the damp forest floor, only half a hand-span from where her bile sank into the ground.

Someone approached on soft feet. Carin forced herself to open her eyes and looked up to meet the eyes of Jen ve Lahgirtan.

The look in the eyes of this Northlander stranger was not spite or malice, but confusion and pity. She knelt next to Carin and gently touched a hand to Carin's forehead, murmuring something under her breath.

When Jen turned over her shoulder to call out, Carin realized she hadn't come alone. A few other villagers stood behind her, Tinan and several more whose names escaped her. After a moment, firm hands took her by the shoulders and feet, lifting her from the ground.

Carin closed her eyes, trying not to allow the swaying of her body in the hands of these strangers to make her ill again. After a short distance that seemed to take as long as crossing the Mad Mountains, they laid her down on a pallet. Someone touched a damp cloth to her face. A loud moan a moment later told her Ryd had been brought in, and she opened her eyes at the sound of shuffling clothing to see him deposited next to her. Ras came next. The air smelled sickly sweet and at once sharp, and Carin's throat convulsed on the urge to throw up again.

The villagers murmured still, or perhaps spoke at normal volumes that simply felt muted to Carin's wool-packed head.

When she opened her eyes again, the light had changed, angling into the small dwelling from a different direction. Jen sat beside her, waterskins lain out around her. Carin tried to roll to one side and failed.

Jen lifted a hand to make her stay her movement, unstoppering one of the waterskins and giving it a sniff. She did the same with each of the others, then took small sips from each. Nodding in satisfaction, she then began mixing the water between the skins, pouring some from one to another, always leaving one of them to the side without combining any of the others with it. It was that skin she brought to Carin's lips after several moments, tilting Carin's head back to help her drink.

Carin tried to shake her head, sending water dribbling down her chin, but Jen made an alarmed sound and she stopped. The woman's eyes were dark and bright, like the chunks of shiny black rock sometimes found in the mountains near Cantoranth. They made arrowheads out of them sometimes.

Jen's eyes met hers, almost pleading, and Carin understood. The taste of the water finally coated her tongue, and she knew. This water was the water they had brought with them out of the pass. The other skins had been partially filled with it, and this was the only remaining full one. She allowed Jen to tip the water down her throat and drank.

It felt like a river's worth, but Carin knew it had to only be a trickle. She fell back on the pallet, her muscles feeling as though they had been pummeled with her mother's hammer against an anvil. Jen did the same for both Ryd and Ras, who barely woke enough to drink. Why Carin was awake and alert, she didn't know. She had drunk as much of the water as either of the others.

Jen said something a moment later, and Carin twitched when she realized Jen was speaking to her. Slowly. Carefully. Taking the time to draw out each word.

Carin closed her eyes and listened.

Jen repeated herself, and Carin motioned with her left hand for the other woman to do it again.

The sounds were different than she was used to, but the words...she had never given much thought to words before, not much at all, but as she listened to Jen repeating herself over and over, Carin remembered a time when, as a child, Rina had taken her to Bemin's Fan. There she had played with other children, and she remembered that they spoke of different things than did her playmates in Haveranth. They had words they used that she did not understand, words of the sea and of beaches and shells and sand. Could the cycles spent on opposite sides of the mountains have slowly changed their words to sound differently? To mean different things? What would Dyava think of this?

For a moment, Carin thought of her distant lover, his curiosity and his constant optimism. He would be forgetting Carin's existence even then, but she could remember his.

She listened with new ears then, hoping for some glimmer of meaning.

"*Lah,*" Jen said insistently. Then a word Carin couldn't quite make out. Then again, "*Lah, lu Lahgirtan. Lu Lahg-irtan.*"

And Carin felt understanding wash over her like the waves of the Bemin. *Lah,* that was water. Jen pronounced it with a wider sound than did the Hearthlanders, her mouth open and the word hovering at the top of it, in the hollow above her tongue. *Lu,* that was in. And *Lahgirtan,* Carin got it. She knew. Jen was saying something about the water in Lahgirtan, which meant...bog? A "wet land"?

Carin pulled her head off the pallet and looked at Jen. "*Lah lu Lahgirtan,*" she repeated back.

Jen sat back on her heels, relief crossing her face. She touched the water in the skin she had just given Carin to drink. "*Lah lu Haverant.*" She pronounced Haveranth just slightly wrong, but Carin felt a flash of triumph in spite of the weakness in her body.

Even though the water in the skin wasn't from Haveranth at all, Carin knew precisely what Jen was trying to say. The water from home was safe for her. Water from here, or from Lahgirtan—it was not. Carin looked at the other skins and then understood why Jen had mixed them so carefully. Following Carin's gaze, Jen touched the second skin and put her hands close together. Then the third and put them farther apart. Then the fourth, then the fifth, until by the sixth her hands spanned the whole of the waterskin.

Sometimes in early planting time in Haveranth, the villagers would go to the Bemin in the pale hours of morning and wade into the water. If one went in all at once, the water could shock the body and cause pain. So a little at a time, they would push their feet into the cold currents, then to the knees, then to the thighs, then hips and gasp as the water touched their sensitive middles, then deeper until finally they would submerge themselves in the water.

The water in the skins, that was like wading in.

She met Jen's eyes with as much gratitude as she could muster, and then Carin let sleep take her.

· · · · ·

Recovery took the next two turns, and there were more bouts of sickness on the way. Jen painstakingly fed Carin from the waterskins, sometimes speaking quickly and quietly even though she knew Carin could not understand the words. Carin didn't need to; she understood the meaning. Without water, Carin would die. Vigil Moon was nearly fat in the sky when Carin finally felt well enough to walk a full circuit around the village. Each day Jen, or Tinan or Tinan's bond-mate, Valyr va Sandyu, would come into the dwelling and speak slowly to the Hearthlanders, and after two turns of it, day in and day out, Carin was starting to be able to understand, though sometimes it felt as though she were walking blindly across a log and stumbled when she least expected it.

She walked with Tinan one day, Tinan's arm supporting her only a little as they made laps around Suonlys. For a while she listened to Tinan, who spoke of growing up with Jen to the north, of meeting Valyr, of falling in love. It made Carin think again of Dyava, and when she fell silent and distant, Tinan seemed to sense it and grew quiet.

Dyava. The thought of him still made Carin's heart feel fragile, like the glass from Bemin's Fan. And Lyah and Jenin. She couldn't bring herself to think of Lyah. Listening to Tinan speak felt a bit like being curled up in a chair near her mother's hearth as a child, listening to adults talk about boring adult things, but only hearing the words through the haze of home and warmth and soft dimness. She now understood the words more often than not, but they felt thick and heavy to her, as if she couldn't quite hear them with clarity.

She needed to find the stones the ialtag had mentioned, and she wasn't sure how to go about it or how they would find help. Having left those enormous white bats behind, if Ryd and Ras had not also remembered them, Carin would have thought she had simply dreamed those turns in the cave with the ialtag far above gazing down and those below alternating curiosity and urgent teaching. She made no mention of the ialtag to the villagers of Suonlys.

The villagers, apart from Jen and Tinan and Valyr, mostly kept their distance from the Hearthlanders, only occasionally coming to speak with them after the initial suspicion and curiosity had been blunted.

When Tinan came to the end of hys sentence and paused, Carin grasped hys arm a little tighter. "Do you know of a soothsayer?" Carin asked the question as she had been learning to, not only slowly and with careful precision, but forming the words in a different part of her mouth. The words felt as thick and heavy in her mouth as they did in her ears.

Tinan looked confused by the question, but repeated back, "Soothsayer?"

Carin tried to explain with the terms she was used to. Midwife. Wise woman. Namekeeper. *Murderer,* Carin's mind added helpfully, though she did not give that word voice. None seemed to bring clarity to Tinan's eyes.

She fumbled through words, feeling like she was speaking under water.

Finally, Tinan looked at her with dubious understanding and said, "Find Culy."

"Culy?"

"Sy knows many things."

"Where does sy live?"

This time Carin was unsure if it was the words of her question or the question itself that muddled Tinan's face with confusion.

"Live?" sy asked.

Carin gestured at Suonlys around them. "You live here. Where does Culy live?"

Tinan slowed hys gait as they passed round a low dwelling. "I do not know where sy is. Sometimes sy is in Crevasses, sometimes sy is in Sands. One cannot know. But one passed through here recently, and she said Culy was in Crevasses now."

Surprise made Carin blink, unsure what kind of answer she had just gotten. "You mean sy moves around?"

Tinan greeted Carin's confusion with a blank look of hys own. "What do you mean?"

The idea that perhaps these Northlanders did not live in one place had not occurred to Carin, but as they rounded the dwelling, she looked again at the canvas that wrapped it. It could be removed, rolled up, easily transported. The empty poles where no one had unrolled their canvas. Pallets instead of beds. She stopped walking and reached out a hand to steady herself on a tree.

"Do you need to sit?" Tinan asked.

Carin shook her head. "You do not stay in one place to make your lives here."

"And you do?" Tinan looked at her curiously, almost in awe. "How do you find food?"

"We grow our food. We plant it and tend it and harvest it." Carin felt her eyes growing wider, and Tinan's did the same. "You do not?"

"We find food where we can," Tinan said. "We make our beds where there is food and water to be found. When we no longer find enough, we move on."

Carin thought of the meager hunting Ras had done and their dwindling supplies.

When she returned to Ryd and Ras, Carin took a deep breath and sat next to Ryd on the log they had dragged over to their tent. "Tinan told me about someone who may be able to help us."

Ryd looked up from the small tiger he was whittling and met her gaze. "You can understand them much better than I can. I'm glad one of us can talk to them."

As much as she agreed, it felt good to allow her speech to relax into the familiar patterns of home with Ryd. Her jaw ached from speaking so slowly and in such a different part of her mouth than she was used to.

"Hys name is Culy," she said.

S ART WISHED she could call down lightning from the sky to blast every rotted rover in Crevasses.

For days she'd been slogging through the mud—or rather, Tahin had—trying to make up lost time, and for days she had been dogged at every step by bands of rovers. There were far more of them than usual for the season. With Vigil and her sister both plump and jolly above her head, Sart had taken to riding at night through the rippled hills of Crevasses, avoiding any glow in the trees that could indicate rovers' fire.

The starlight above was cold and bright, as if competing with Vigil's shine, and the path of the moon lit her way across the hills.

It would snow tomorrow, if not in the darkest hours of the night once Vigil tucked herself away beyond the horizon. Sart could smell it on the wind, the dusty chill that would accompany first flurries, then the larger flakes that would stick. At least she hoped they would stick. Snow water was much better to drink than water potted from some mucky, half-frozen creek.

Tahin whistled quietly in the night, her flanks rippling and bulging with her rolling gait. Sart leaned forward over the ihstal's neck, twining her fingers into the fur of her coat that had begun to grow its winter underlining.

She had to reach Culy before sy moved on. Sart wasn't about to spend the cold months haring about Sands. You couldn't even drink the snow water in Sands if it happened to snow at all. Every bit of it was full of grit, and there wasn't enough tatting in the land to filter all of that out. Boggers and Salters weren't much better.

Sometimes Sart's upbringing showed. Though she'd spent much of her childhood outside of Crevasses, it was Crevasses where she felt most at home. She understood the land there, and it seemed to understand her. Her magic came to her more readily, flowed through her and spindled within her without fighting. Farther north, where the sun baked the vast deserts of Sands and cooked reaches of stagnant water in Boggers—and even farther north, where the kazytya roamed in Taigers—it was like meeting someone you thought you knew only to find out they'd changed while you were away.

When dawn's cold touch lit the land, bringing its icy beams to make the falling snow sparkle, Sart rounded a bend in the road and came finally to light on Alarbahis.

She could have wept for the joy of it. Her feet felt like weeping too, as did her inner thighs and her lower back and most of the rest of her.

Sart slid off Tahin's back and led the ihstal toward the waymake. Most of the huts were taken, which was hardly a surprise given the season. She liked walking into Alarbahis in winter, when the homes were full and the chimneys pumped smoke into the air. Seeing most of the huts occupied also told her that there was food nearby. Perhaps a herd of saiga or halka or fyajir was nearby. A single halka could feed the entire waymake for a day or two. Maybe Sart would go hunting herself. Rule was, you shared the meat but got to keep the rest. She could use with some new bone tools and with winter coming, another layer of hide wouldn't go amiss in her bedroll.

The snow had begun to fall in earnest, as she found an empty hut and began to close it off. Her canvas was stiff for lack of use, but sturdy and waxed to hold tight against winter's winds. She worked quickly, securing Tahin to a post in front of the hut and lashing the canvas to the lower rungs of the roof to close out the snow. It didn't take long before she had her hut secure, inside swept out and bedroll set up, flaps tied tight.

Set up bed first, that was her motto. The last thing she wanted was to get caught up with Culy over breakfast and have no blankets to crash into.

The waymake was just beginning to stir around her, the sounds of flints striking to kindle fires, coughs and grunts and the occasional laugh. Sart strode through the huts, walking toward the northern edge of the waymake where she knew she would find Culy.

Hys hut was always inviting, the canvas painted with red-orange runes of hearth and home and kin. Smoke drifted from the chimney, silvery in the morning light. Sart opened the flap and ducked inside without announcing herself.

Culy sat cross-legged on hys pallet, a woolen cloak around hys shoulders and a plate of baked eggs and what looked like spiced saiga meat on hys lap. Sy smiled as Sart approached. "Took you long enough to get here."

"The world conspired against me. If you hadn't been in such a hurry to leave Salters, I could have caught up with you there."

"I had to be here at a certain time."

Sart plunked herself down next to Culy on the pallet, reaching over to snare one of hys eggs. She peeled it carefully, discarding the shell into a small bowl at the center of the hut. "Where'd you find the clucker?"

"Traded a halm knife for three of them. They're out back."

Sart sat back, impressed. "Three cluckers. All layers?"

"One crower among them."

"Culy." Sart shot a glance over her shoulder in the direction he'd indicated, excitement taking spindly root in her chest. "You mean to say that those layers could hatch chicks? Did you know you were getting a crower with them?"

"They were too young to tell."

"A halm knife for three breeding cluckers. You have an ihstal's luck, my friend." Sart bit into the egg, relishing the give of the white and the silken richness of the yolk that threatened to spill out over her lip. She caught it with her thumb and licked it away.

They sat and ate in silence for a few moments. Sart stole another egg—Culy had started with four—and part of the saiga, and her stomach rumbled, wakened by the touch of fresh food.

"*Tuanye,*" she said. "I missed proper food."

Culy set hys plate down on the floor of the hut and leaned into Sart's shoulder. "Lean times," sy said.

"Is it ever anything else?"

Something flickered in Culy's eyes. They were grey like the sea far to the north, but in them were flecks of green. Hys hair was the same gold-brown as his skin, far lighter than anyone else she knew, though she had known hys parents and hys mother had had the same hair as hyr. The touch of hys shoulder was a comfort, and one Sart had missed as much as the food she had just devoured.

"I found a spring," she said.

Culy's eyes snapped to hers, and sy said only, "Tell me."

So Sart did.

When she finished with the tale of the spring and the avalanche and, finally, the rovers she had temporarily dismantled, Culy's face had grown quiet like a waiting kazytya.

"Wyt will be a problem," Culy said. "She's gathered at least fifty rovers to the north, and another twenty or so who aren't rovers at all. Families."

Sart looked at hyr, aghast. "How can so many people survive in one place?"

"I would very much like to know the answer to that question. I can't get anyone near her, though. I've tried." Culy's eyes grew distant, a look Sart knew all too well. Sy had people throughout the land, and at any given moment, she knew sy could reach out to any of them. If hys attempts to infiltrate Wyt had failed, there must be some reason.

Sart would have to find out how sy did it someday.

"Are you wintering here?" she asked.

Culy leaned back against the piled coverlets, and Sart joined hyr a moment later, their arms still touching. "I had planned to, but if Wyt's people keep making forays into the waymakes, I'll have to do something about it."

The rovers had never really organized before, and for good reason. It took food and water to supply large groups of people, and those two things usually weren't found together in abundance. "Do you know where she's based?"

"Salters, up to the north, just on the northern crest of Boggers. You know where the big ihstal herds used to run?"

Sart nodded.

The light from the fire's embers made Culy's skin glow and flicker. "Strange days we live in, Sart. Sometimes I think—"

Sart didn't get to hear what Culy thought, because someone burst through the tent flap and collapsed on the goatskin rug. Blood smeared across the cream-colored fur in a bright red arc.

L YARI'S SHIRT chafed her neck. Higher upon her chest than she liked it, it barely scooped at all and felt like the nooses Tamat used to wrangle hys goats in the fields. Above it was a beaten bronze necklace that remained cool upon her skin even though she'd been wearing it for the past hour. The soothsayer's cuff still hung loosely at her right wrist, its runes flashing in the firelight, and she wore Merin's on her left now. In remembrance.

To anyone else, it would seem simply traditional.

To Lyari, it meant more.

Her pale green tunic reached only to her elbows in spite of the chill of the day, soft wool from Cantoranth sheep, slit at both sides to allow free movement of her hips and belted at her waist with more beaten bronze. Each scale of her belt shone with a different rune, each of the moons of the cycle. Vigil Moon was high overhead, and its rune on her belt sat just over her right hipbone.

Leggings of wool-lined leather covered her legs, and tall triple-lined boots covered all the way to midthigh, almost meeting her tunic. Her hair flowed loosely down her back, and she sat at her trestle table, strands of pale green vysa with tiny brass clasps laid out on the shining maha tabletop. She took one by the clasp and twisted a small lock of hair between her fingertips, fastening the brass around it near her scalp. She repeated the motion fourteen more times, one for each moon, each tiny clasp bearing runes like her belt. When the last clasp took hold of her dark hair, she laid her hands in her lap to rest.

Carin used to plait her hair for her.

Lyari thought of the day of their Journeying, the day of their departure, the bells tolling across the village to summon everyone to their work. They had missed the first bell, and the second, and Lyari had begun her Journeying much as she had begun anything else in her life, her hair sloppy and escaping its plait, tumbling over one shoulder where it would flop about with every move she made.

With careful hands, she reached up to her scalp, where her hair parted down the center, framed by the clasped strands of vysa. Her fingertips took hold of her hair and began to plait it against her head, ringing from temple around to the back, where she twisted it into a knot and pushed a halm stick through it. Starting again on the other side, she did the same again, meeting it at the back of her head and joining the two plaits. Pulling the ends of the vysa strands from the circle of plaits so they trailed down through the rest of her hair, she shook the lot of it over her shoulders.

Her fingertips trembled when she finished. She took her place on a cushioned chair at the head of her table then and waited.

At sundown, her door opened without warning, but Lyari was not unprepared. One by one, the elders of Haveranth filed in. Rina, dressed all in deep scarlet that bloomed out of her cloak like the petals of a hibiscus. Old Wend in warm gold like turmeric; Ohlry in hys pale blue like the winter sky; Varsu with his folds of indigo robes falling like dusk to his feet.

Rich colors, all adorned with the same belt as Lyari wore. They sat at her table without comment, and Ohlry pulled a bottle of redberry cordial from hys cloak, pouring it into squat glasses that twinkled in the firelight. It was her position to take the first drink, she knew. Doing so would bind her to the elders and the governance of Haveranth.

All seated and still silent, Lyari waited.

Old Wend held his cup to his lips and drank, licking the viscous red liquid from the corner of his mouth before speaking. "Soothsayer," was all he said.

"Soothsayer," the others repeated, stealing glances at one another and at Lyari, who sat shocked in her seat, too surprised to say anything.

Old Wend drained the rest of his glass.

Silence stole over the room, except for the crackling of the fire in the hearth.

No one seemed to know what to do; the soothsayer always drank first, and Old Wend knew that as well as Lyari did. His taking the first drink would have been considered a grievous insult if Merin were there. But Merin was not.

Lyari felt very, very young.

Old Wend had seen as many harvests as Merin, or very near to it. Ohlry and Varsu had each seen over a hundred, and Rina, until now the youngest of the elders, had nearly that herself. With eighty harvests she had birthed Carin, still within her reproductive time, but barely. Merin's notes had told Lyari that in cycles past, no elder with fewer than one hundred and fifty harvests had been accepted.

Lyari had just barely seen eighteen.

She was to have continued working with Merin for scores of cycles to come before this day. In one movement, Wend had made clear his lack of respect for Lyari.

The room, along with all the people in it, seemed to know that as well as she did. Rina and Ohlry lifted their cups and drank, small sips each without meeting Lyari's eyes.

Lyari's cheeks grew warm, and she placed both palms on the smooth maha table, drawing from the coolness of the wood, willing it to spread through her body so her humiliation would not show.

"Some three cycles until the reinvocation," Varsu said then, straightening his robes and leaning forward on the table with both arms. He hadn't touched his cordial.

Touching hers would admit that she had no control over the meeting, and, without looking around at the others, Lyari carefully slid the squat glass of ruby liquid away from her on the table and stood. "Three cycles," she repeated. Her voice held steadier than she expected, and Old Wend had the decency to cough.

She thought she saw a flash of triumph in Rina's eyes, but it was gone so quickly she might have imagined it.

The rest of them were silent, and it was the quiet that Lyari did not like. The quiet meant that they were thinking too hard about whether she deserved this place. In the coming moons, Lyari would have sat alongside Merin at the head of *her* table—a table that had now been burned to ash—and over time, Old Wend and Rina and Ohlry and Varsu would have come to accept and respect her place there.

Time was no longer a luxury Lyari could enjoy. Instead it slipped around her fingers like a sly fish in the river. Flowing always away, toward the sea. Never back again.

"Three cycles," she repeated. "In that time, we will prepare for the reinvocation."

"And how do you expect to do that?" Old Wend demanded. His knees cracked as he stood, placing both gnarled hands on the edge of the table where his knuckles stood out, pale in the dim light. "You're greener than the first planting's sprouts, girl."

Lyari thought of Merin's hair catching fire in her own hearth and bit her tongue, wanting more than anything to say the words, *Do not call me girl.*

Instead she met Old Wend's eyes and pictured Carin and Ryd standing over his shoulders, cold and dead. "I will do what I must."

Varsu's eyes had fallen on Lyari's untouched glass of cordial, and he exchanged a glance with Ohlry. "It seems none of us have all the choices we would like. Wend, if you've a solution to our troubles or have stumbled somehow upon a way to bring Merin back from ashes to guide us, by Vigil above, share."

Ohlry, hys lined face and dark, silver streaked curls framed by the pale blue hood of his cowled tunic, nodded agreement.

"Merin wouldn't have known any better herself. She wasn't there for the last one," Wend said, eyes on his empty cordial glass.

Rina smacked the table with the flat of her hand. "And you were? Shut your mouth, Wend. Varsu's right, but he didn't go far enough. You may be the eldest among us, but you keep yourself well enough away unless it suits you."

Wend's wrinkles seemed to deepen into creases, and he opened his thin-lipped mouth. "Now, see here, smith. This is my village and my homeland too, and if a new-whelped hysmern is the one holding all of us between her fingers, I'm not going to watch her drop us into famine and death."

Hysmern. Child. Lyari felt her face burn, and not from the heat of the fire. Merin had taught her that the old land to the north had gods, wise but aloof. Gods were not only man or woman but both or neither or changing, *hysu.* When the Hearthland's founding families had made their way south through the mountains, they had left behind those gods because they had become their own. But in some words, remnants remained, and in the word hysmern, god-having, Lyari felt the shame of being compared to the Northlanders in their starving ignorance, just like the Hearthlander children in their own.

She thought of Jenin, who was, like Ohlry, hyrsin, which meant god-like, transcending through knowledge.

As if thinking of hyr summoned Jenin, sy appeared by Wend's side, face quiet and eyes shining.

Hys silence spoke more to her than any words could, and Lyari went back to her seat and lowered herself upon it. She had nothing with which she could threaten Wend, no piece of information that would win his trust. She had few tools and little time, but she would do with her position what she could. It would be slow, slow, slow.

She would bide what time she had, and she would bring Wend to heel at her side. She sat straighter and said nothing, but she made eye contact with Wend and held it.

Rina drummed her calloused fingers against the table, drawing Wend's gaze to herself. "Lyari is not hysmern; she is soothsayer, and you would be wise to remember it."

No one else said anything to Lyari's favor or fault.

Lyari's cordial remained untouched in the center of the table, and she watched Old Wend's eyes drift from Rina to look upon it.

CULY, CARIN was told, was something of a legend in the Northlands, though as much as she asked, no one would really tell her why.

Tinan and Jen drew a map on the back of Lyah's scroll, showing the location of other settlements—waymakes, the Northlanders called them—in Crevasses where they might start to look for Culy. The closest was several days away, and with the clouds gathering above, Carin began to doubt the decision to trade the snowshoes for water. Since their illness, the other Northlanders had each helped them find and store potable water without asking for payment, and Carin couldn't help but feel childlike in their kindness. She couldn't tell if their expressions were made of compassion or if within them there was a spark of pity for a reason Carin could not begin to guess at.

They left Suonlys as Vigil waned in the sky and the snows began to fall in earnest across the foothills of the mountains.

The others stayed in the waymake, where Jen said they would winter.

Carin had never considered people using winter as an action.

Carin fell into step with Ryd and Ras as they descended the hilltop where Suonlys lay, quiet in the falling snow. She hoped the snow would stick. To be able to melt snow into drinkable water would save her a significant amount of worry.

She had spent the turn learning what she could of the area, both from the map given to her by the siblings from Boggers and from speaking to the other Northlanders, which was difficult. Carin found that each of them seemed to speak differently, just enough that after spending a day with Jen, trying to have a conversation with one of the others from Sands or farther north, from Taigers, felt like having to relearn everything she had tried to absorb. Carin recalled the effortless ease of the ialtag, how one touch could communicate emotion, information, goals. Ras and Ryd had an even more difficult time.

The humming that had been her constant companion grew somewhat louder and more insistent the farther north they traveled. Carin wished she knew what it was she was supposed to do with it, aside from lighting small fires.

What Jen and Tinan had told her about rovers made her afraid to light a fire at all, though they would have to in order to ward off the chill of the winter night.

Carin wanted to understand the humming in her body, and as they walked, she tried to listen. As always, no answers found her in that stillness. The snow fell in cold, hard flakes at first, then later as the sun warmed the air, in fat clumps. Ryd ate it as they walked, swiping it from branches where it gathered and biting into packed lumpen shapes he made with his hands. After a time, Ras did the same. Carin followed, realizing every cold touch of ice to her lips could be the last clean water she'd find for some time.

She'd expected the Northlands to at least look like home, but where she thought to see doubloon trees and maha, she saw instead scrubby pine and low bushes she couldn't place.

Strangest was the silence.

No red crests flitted from tree to tree, bright against the drabness of winter. No hawks above. No herds of halka had left traces that she could see—not bitten down bushes or scarred tree bark from their antlers.

The first waymake they came to was cold and empty. Carin greeted its stillness with relief, to have no more unknown to face today. At its center was a pile of grey stones topped with a white rock that sat on its eastern edge.

"Do you think we should follow it?" Ras nodded sharply toward the white stone. "On the morning, when we leave?"

"It's the direction we're going anyway." Carin pointed to the northeast. "The next sett—waymake is Alarbahis."

Ras nodded again, and Ryd looked up at the sky.

"A couple hours of daylight left," he said.

"I'll hunt," said Ras.

Carin shouldered her bow, itching to drop her rucksack in one of the waymake's huts and walk free of the extra weight. "I'll do it."

At first she thought Ras would protest, but after staring at her for a moment, he coughed and set about attempting to stretch the canvas of their tent around one of the huts. Ill-fitting and not long enough to go all the way around, it would at least break the force of the wind and keep the snow from drifting in on their heads while they slept.

Carin wandered in widening circles out from the waymake. When a hare scampered across her path, she couldn't believe her luck, shooting it quickly. Tramping through the snow to retrieve the hare and her arrow, she felt a hot flash of triumph, followed quickly by shock that washed over her like a snowball tucked down the back of her shirt. Never in her life had Carin thought she would feel such relief at the sight of a dead hare. Not since she shot her first with her bow had she felt such pride, to be able to feed herself. Haveranth was never so short on hares that killing one was a desirable thing. Here, far away from her homeland, Carin felt as if the ground had tilted beneath her feet.

The real reason she had wanted to get away wasn't just to hunt. Away from Ryd and Ras and the waymake, Carin could let herself breathe. She had a tightness in her chest that wouldn't abate.

She pulled the arrow from the hare's carcass, the hum in her body deepening as she cleaned the arrow in the snow and replaced it in her quiver. She picked the hare up by the ears, aware of how their bellies would, for one night, be full. In spite of the immediate needs for survival, there was something else. She knew Ryd wanted to talk about Haveranth, and as much as Carin knew he needed it, she couldn't. To speak with him about it when they were always in hearing range of Ras—it was too much.

But alone, her hands working at the hare, she could let the work happen and free herself to think.

Dyava would be preparing for the Night of Reflection by now. It was a usual thing for lovers in Haveranth to sneak small trinkets into the reflection vessels for one another, and the cycle before, Dyava had found a white pebble flecked with gold. Fool's gold, most likely, but it had shimmered in the firelight when Carin peered at it through the water. What would it be like, to forget someone you had loved? Would there be a hole there? Something that pushed at the edges of your mind, whispering that something had gone missing? Carin didn't know. The villagers remembered that there were Nameless but never who they were. Only the elders remembered.

Lyah was the soothsayer's apprentice. She would remember, and so would Old Wend, Ohlry, Varsu. Rina. Carin's mouth felt dry at the thought of her mother, the youngest of the elders. Which meant her mother would know every day that it was her daughter who had become Nameless. Rina would be able to see the gaps where Carin and Ryd had existed in the lives of the village. Carin wished she knew if her mother felt the grief of it or if she simply accepted what Merin had done. Carin wondered if her mother thought she was dead. If her mother had truly believed sending Ras and the other hunters to kill her had been justice.

Carin swallowed, her fingers stilling on the animal that would fill their bellies that night.

They still had two turns to walk before they reached the next waymake. This hare would have to last. Thoughts of Haveranth slowly swirled away, lost in the more immediate need of now.

Something caught her eye a short distance away, against the snow.

Dung.

A large pat of it, steaming in the cold air. She hadn't been there long, but she should have seen it sooner. Around the dung were hoof-prints the size of her palm. Carin's heart expanded in her chest, picking up a heavy beat of excitement. An animal had been here. A large one—and very recently.

Carin tied the hare's ears to her belt with gut and followed, the animal's tracks standing out in the snow. Excitement made her giddy, and her fingertips worried at the fletching on her arrows in her hand as she kept one ready to draw. The tracks led down into a gully, and she followed, listening to the woods around her. It wasn't long before she heard the cracking of twigs and the sound of breath that reminded her of her mother's bellows back in Haveranth.

On silent feet, Carin moved from tree to tree, sideways toward the creature. She could see it now, hulking in the late afternoon light. It was easily three times the size of the ihstal she knew, and its hide was covered in thick, curly wool. Such a hide would be a precious thing in the cold months to come.

She circled the beast until she could see its head, its great curling horns twisted back at the sides of its neck. She watched it move, saw when it turned its face toward the east and exposed the tender flesh behind its jaw.

Carin drew and loosed her arrow in one long motion. The bowstring twanged loudly, the sound ricocheting from the trees. And the beast cried out, falling to its knees in the snow.

Letting out a whoop, Carin ran toward it, drawing her belt knife. Such a thing could feed them for nearly the whole winter if they smoked the meat. She fell forward onto her own knees next to the creature, placing her hand on its head and murmuring a thank you for its life, meaning it more than she ever had before. Her hand stayed upon its head as it breathed its last, steam rising from its nostrils in the cold.

When she was sure it was dead, she began to work.

She took the hide first, thankful the beast had fallen forward and collapsed instead of leaning over onto its side. She pulled the hide, watching the steam rise from the body into the air and feeling for the first time in moons that she had done something worthy of pride. She could feed her people with this. They would not go as paupers into Culy's waymake.

Carin heard the chuffing growl behind her only seconds before falling into the snow. Something large and heavy slammed into her.

She rolled out of the way, feet kicking up pine needles and dusty snow. Her eyes grew wide, as wide as the beast she had just killed. A tiger dug its teeth into the carcass of the creature.

Its tail was as long as one of her legs, and its white and black stripes seemed to melt into the snowy forest even from where she stood. The tiger's paws were as large as the hulking creature's hooves. Larger.

For a moment Carin stood in awe of the animal. She had never seen a tiger so close. South of the mountains, they wore orange, and occasionally she had seen one in the foothills of the mountains, but they never came close to people.

This one seemed to not even notice her.

It tore long strips of red, red meat from the animal's haunch, strips that disappeared down its throat almost as quickly as it could pull them off. Their food, disappearing down the throat of a giant cat.

And Carin knew she would have to kill it, and the thought filled her with a bitter twist of despair.

Her hand trembled as she nocked an arrow, her bloodied fingers staining the pure white halm of the shaft with red smears. Red and white, life and death together. She raised the bow once, then let the string slacken again. That kill was hers, and she would need every haunch, every cut, every bone Ryd could fashion into a tool. The horns for drinking or signaling. The thick, wooly hide for warmth.

The humming in her body grew as she raised the bow for a second time, resolution stealing over her like the soft darkness of moonset. The tiger stood out in the clearing like a shimmering star.

Her arrow caught it just where she had shot the beast it was eating, just behind the jaw, straight into the brain.

The tiger made a sound that was more surprise than anything else, and it collapsed atop the creature.

Every tree around her burst into flame.

I T TOOK six trips for Carin, Ryd, and Ras to return to the empty way-make with the meat from Carin's kills.

They had come running upon seeing the smoke, finding Carin ringed by flaming trees with two dead animals at her feet.

She offered no explanation, and neither Ryd nor Ras asked outright, though Carin knew the time was coming where she would have to tell them, and Ras at least gave her a long look before setting about his work.

The humming had lessened.

Together they brought the animal carcasses back to the waymake. Ras set about butchering the lumbering beast—Carin wanted to know the name for it; it seemed wrong to depend on something to live without being able to properly name it—and Ryd took the bones to set in a circle around their hut's fire to dry.

Carin herself set to butchering the tiger. She had killed the magnifi-cent beast, and as much as she hated the necessity of it, she could let no part of it go to waste. As she worked, she could not stop the litany in her mind. *I'm sorry,* she thought, over and over. *I'm sorry, I'm sorry, I'm sorry.*

She always thanked the beasts she killed, for their lives. She had nev-er felt remorse for it before. Uneasy, Carin realized that taking the life of the tiger had felt more like murder than killing the hunters Merin had sent. The tiger had wished her no personal harm; it hunted simply to eat. The hunters, Carin knew, had hated her some small bit. For threatening the lies they lived on, perhaps. She saw it in Ras every day, much as he was part of their group now.

Carin finished after some time, the whole waymake full of the sounds of everyone working.

In the corner of the hut was a makeshift sink, dug into the earth and lined with hardened, fired clay. She filled pot after pot with snow and melted it over the fire until the sink was full. On the rest of the jour-ney, she had managed to tan the smaller hides of rabbits and hares and squirrels, but for the large animals she had slain today, she would need to do more.

While the skins soaked, Carin and Ryd and Ras cooked long steaks of the beast and ate the meat while its insides were still red and as they ate, juice dribbled out over their chins. They ate until their stomachs bulged and their fingernails were caked with grease. And when they were finished, they continued to cut strips of the meat and worked at drying the remainder, leaving a few to sizzle and eat with burned fingers even as the thinner pieces began to dry.

They worked late into the night. After several hours, Carin pulled the skins from the water and scraped them again, cleaning them as best she could. She heated the animal brains in Ryd's biggest pot, held high above the fire to warm it without cooking it, stirring the brains together until they formed a thick sludge, which she smeared over the hides and then rolled up to sit at the edge of the hut. Tomorrow she would clean them again, then hang them over plied gut twine to dry until it was time to soften them.

Breakfast came, and no one was yet tired of meat.

Carin caught Ras grinning at her over the fire, and she returned the smile with a wide one of her own. If he had hated her once, he didn't seem to now. She smiled back, dipping her head in a quick nod at the young man.

Later, he helped her set up the softened hides to smoke.

"Strange," he said.

"What?" Alarmed, Carin's hands froze on the tent of skin she'd made over some smoking embers in one of the empty huts. The wind blew through, but if she tended the coals well enough and kept away their flames, the skins would be proof against water for the journey. Proof enough, anyway. She thought of Ryd's tattered, thin cloak and the way he had shivered his way through the mountains. The thick woolly pelt of the beast would keep him as warm or warmer than the cloak her mother had given her.

Carin felt the memory of her mother like a sore muscle days after High Lights. She shook off the feeling, prodding Ras's foot with her own.

"What?" she asked again.

"To think two pelts and a few bundles of meat can make me feel as fat as a squirrel in spring."

Carin nodded. She didn't have to tell him that things were different.

"How did the trees catch fire?" he asked suddenly. His irises, pale green and clear, stood out against the bloodshot whites. They had gotten little sleep, and a night and morning standing over smoking fires had not helped.

Carin shrugged one shoulder and adjusted the skin over the fire.

"You don't know?"

When she was silent, Ras finished tying a loop of twine around the ceiling beam of the hut, tugging the canopy of fur so it lined up with Carin's over the smoke.

"I know magic when I see it," he said finally. "I know that's how you've been starting fires."

Carin's hand went still on the thick pelt of the tiger, which swayed gently in the wind. "You know nothing."

"I knew Merin."

At that, her eyes met his. Unease filled the pit of her stomach along with the meat she had eaten for the past day. "And I suppose she taught you somewhat of magic."

Ras shook his head. "She did not teach me, but I saw it used. It's how she gave us our orders."

Tingles spread through Carin's hands and up her arms, creeping slowly like ants toward a dead vole. She had never thought of Merin using magic, not really.

"If you don't have anything useful to tell me about it, then leave it be," she said shortly.

Ras shrugged then. "Control it before it controls you."

With that, he left her to arrange the hides.

A short time later, she returned to their shared hut with the two hides. She found only Ryd, bent over a large stone with bones spread out around him, interspersed with his carving tools. To his left, he had already arranged a set of carved bone tools, simple but serviceable. The horns he had set aside.

Carin walked up to him and draped the woolly pelt over his back. The neck and head covered his with ample space, and with a few quick stitches of one of his bone needles, the fur would serve as both bedroll and cloak. He went still when it touched him, then looked up over his shoulder, which made the pelt slide off to the side.

"It's for you," Carin said. "It'll keep you warmer than what you have."

Ryd turned and dug both hands into the thick wool of the pelt. The scent of smoke clung heavily to it. "Thank you."

She sat next to him, her fingers tracing over the tools he had made. "We won't be able to stay here long," she said.

"I know."

Ryd paused, pulling the pelt back over his shoulders and around his body. "The day by the river," he said. "Magic?"

Carin didn't want to talk about that day. Memories of it were as fuzzy as if they had been seen through the smoke of the fire, but she remembered waking to see Ryd's eyes looking into hers and the way the humming had become a part of her every day since. She didn't want to talk about magic, or think about it. The humming itself was now a distant tone, quiet and unobtrusive in the back of her mind. It was as if the fire in the trees had released some of the pressure, like a nut bursting over a glowing coal.

She didn't talk, only nodded. For Ryd, it seemed to be enough.

He reached out to her and took her hand, squeezing it once.

The touch shocked Carin's skin, shocked her for the relief of it. She held his hand for a long moment, drinking in the simple welcome touch of a friend. Out of the corner of her eye, she saw Ryd wipe away a tear with his free hand. Carin squeezed her fingers around his just a bit tighter.

· · · · ·

They set out early the next morning for the next waymake. Their rucksacks, which had grown thin and empty over the turns before, now bulged with bone tools and dried meat. Their waterskins were full, and Carin felt safer with the food on their backs than she did with her bow at her side.

The tiger skin she kept for herself, rolled up tightly in her rucksack. She had seen Ras's eyes on it, but she wanted to keep it. To remember as much as she could that in that moment before her arrow pierced its brain, she and the large cat had been only two creatures trying to survive. Had Carin not just slain the other beast, had she instead come across it after the tiger killed it—she may have then been the dead one.

One turn later, they saw smoke.

Before long, the waymake appeared around the edge of a hillock, right where the land flattened out into plains to the north. Nearly every hut seemed to be occupied. The sight sent Carin's nerves to trembling like the strings on a dulcimer. This was a full community, and they would enter it as strangers again.

By the way Ras and Ryd both adjusted their packs on their back and straightened their shoulders, she could see they felt as ill at ease as she did. Alarbahis was twice as large as Suonlys and bore far fewer empty dwellings. There were people here. Many of them. Each of them a question.

"Do you think Culy is here?" Ryd asked.

Ras grunted. "Either sy is or isn't. Either way we'll have shelter and enough food to last us some time. We should learn what we can of these folk."

Jen and Tinan had told Carin that the waymakes served for everyone—you claimed a dwelling as your own, and while the roof belonged to you, no one would trespass under it. With food as scarce as it was, Carin wasn't sure she wanted to risk leaving theirs unattended.

They drew little notice as they selected a hut at the edge of the waymake, but the moment they began stretching their tent canvas, which barely reached two thirds of the way around this hut, someone in the neighboring dwelling began to watch them.

After a time, a man came over and stared openly, expression blank and eyes curious.

Carin began to dread the moment he would speak, not trusting her ears to recall how these Northlanders formed their words and how she was to pull meaning from them. Her stomach felt stuffed with stones.

He peered more closely at Ryd, and Carin watched out of the corner of her eye as he lifted his hand and pointed. "*Fyajir*," he said. Then a quick string of words Carin could not understand.

She stepped away from their work and warily approached the man. As she drew closer, he seemed to see her more clearly, blinking in surprise.

"Carin ve Haveranth," she said, pointing at herself.

"Ham va Keham," he returned, though his eyebrows had sunk on his forehead as if he were trying to puzzle her out. He said something else, then repeated the first word he had said. "*Fyajir.*"

"Please. Slowly." Carin spoke the words as close to the Northlander style as she could, and the man's eyes widened.

After several breaths, he said, slowly and with great precision, "*Voul fyajir dy harin?*"

Where did you find fyajir?

"Fyajir," Carin said blankly. The man pointed at Ryd's back, at the enormous pelt he wore as a cloak. Understanding burned through her, hot and bright and clear. The beast. Fyajir. She heard the word cleanly then, heard its parts. Pillow skin. Of course.

Carin pointed in the direction from which they had come, to the southwest. The man blanched.

"Tigers," he said. That word Carin understood without issue.

She nodded, bending to pull the tiger skin from her rucksack. At the man's gasp, she jerked her head up to look at him. His gaze fell on her halm bow, and he took a step back.

"I will not hurt you," Carin said slowly.

He took another step back. Another Northlander happened by just then, bumping into the man's shoulder.

"Culy," the first man said, then rattled off a string of words to the other Northlander, too quickly for Carin to comprehend.

The second Northlander took off toward the north at a run.

Ras looked up from where he was lashing the canvas to a pole, pretending not to see Carin's interaction with the Northlander Ham va Keham.

"Looks like we found hyr," he said.

Culy hyrself arrived not long after. Carin, unnerved by the gathering crowd of Northlanders that surrounded their pitiful hut, sat guard in front with her halm bow across her lap and both belt knives unsheathed under the guise of cleaning them.

When sy arrived, Carin saw hyr coming. She knew hyr the way one might know a fabled creature. The Northlanders gathered around their hut moved almost as one when Culy approached. Sy was tall, half a head taller than Carin. Hys hair was the color of Early Bird tree bark, a soft gold brown that matched hys skin almost without varying in shade at all. Carin had never seen hair that color before. Hys eyes were grey, the same grey that cloaked the sky above their heads, and even had sy been alone walking toward Carin in a field, she would have sensed hys importance.

The humming grew almost imperceptibly.

Culy strode up to their hut, eyes flickering back and forth to take everything in. Carin saw that grey gaze light on Ryd's fyajir cloak, then on the tiger pelt that lolled half out of Carin's rucksack like a tongue, then on the canvas that stretched not all the way around the hut. And more, in the angled planes of Culy's cheeks, Carin sensed sy was looking deeper. Ryd came up behind her and stood just at her shoulder. Ras leaned against a pole, one hand picking at a loose splinter of wood.

With Culy looking down at her, Carin could not help but rise to her feet. She sheathed her knives at her belt.

"You are the strangers," Culy said, and Ras twitched behind her because hys voice spoke the words with such confidence and precision— in nearly identical speech to that of the Hearthland.

A murmur rose up behind hyr like a breeze ruffling the fields around Haveranth. Carin wondered if they could understand what Culy said.

"We are," she said quietly. Her hands perched carefully on her belt, not touching the hilts of her knives, but close enough that she could grab them if anything went wrong.

"Ham," Culy said, looking over at the first man who had come over. Hys next words were mellifluous and unintelligible to Carin, and she felt the bones in her spine try to stack themselves atop one another to keep from curling in on herself.

She shifted her weight, and Ryd's hand touched her shoulder.

Culy's eyes were on them, and Carin felt frozen in hys gaze.

"We do not wish to harm you," sy said. "I have asked Ham to fetch proper covering for your hut."

Sure enough, moments later, Ham returned, and with a nod and gesture at Ras, began to pull down the tent canvas to make way for the other.

"I can understand you better than the others," Carin said.

"I am not quite like the others," Culy said, and Carin thought she detected a spark of mirth in those grey eyes.

"Who are you?" Ryd asked the question with uncharacteristic bluntness.

Culy did laugh then, throwing back hys head and turning a bright smile in Ryd's direction. "Culy," said Culy.

"We were told that perhaps you could help us." Carin let the words tumble from her mouth, aware that fifty sets of eyes were watching her, curious and uncomprehending of her words.

"Help you how?"

Carin looked about. "Perhaps we could speak in private."

"Perhaps tomorrow," said Culy. "You have just arrived, and I have many things to attend to. Be welcome here. The snow that falls on your roof is your own and none other. Consider the hut's covering a gift, as I feel you have come a long way to sleep here tonight. Be welcome in Alarbahis, unless you prove yourselves a threat."

With that, sy turned and left, leaving Carin feeling as though something had been snatched directly out of her grasp.

The crowd began to disperse with a murmur, and Carin turned to help Ras and Ham with the canvas covering.

Out of the corner of her eye, she thought she saw a woman with short-cropped black hair hanging back from the crowd watching them.

TWO TURNS had passed, and each day Ras woke to the news that again Culy had said "perhaps tomorrow," leaving Carin to fume and Ryd to compensate by carving bones.

Ras felt as though his strength had been taken from him.

The snow continued to fall, not as heavily as it did in Cantoranth but heavily enough that they were able to gather enough water from the roof of their hut to survive. The meat held, but Ras knew if they didn't find more food soon, they would starve.

Ras had settled into an uneasy rhythm. Each morning, he woke at first light and ventured into the hills to hunt. He returned hours later with a few sluggish squirrels or a hare if he was lucky. He envied Carin her halm bow but never dared ask to borrow it. The villagers always whispered when he returned, but no one came over to speak to him.

In the evenings, he would sit and make arrows while Ryd carved. For all the young man was an undirected thing, his hands took to his tools like a bird finding its wings, and the bone needles and instruments he made became valuable items they traded. Three for a set of tatted woolen cloths—fyajir wool, Ras had found, was a useful thing in every instance—for filtering water. Two for a handful of dried currants.

The days and turns passed thus, and Ras grew anxious. Culy, after that first visit, had not returned. Though they were not told otherwise, Ras often found himself itching at the edge of the waymake, wondering how free they truly were within and without.

With Reflection growing pregnant in the sky and game growing leaner on the ground—indeed Ras himself had watched his body change, grow harder—one morning Ham ran by their hut with a yell.

The man had perhaps fifty harvests, still a young person by any standard, and he called out to Ras even as he buckled his belted sheath across his narrow hips.

"Halka!" he said. He pointed up the hill, where Ras could see the sky slowly beginning to lighten.

It unnerved Ras that the mere prospect of a large animal to hunt filled him with desperation.

"How many?" he asked Ham. His words felt clumsy, and even after the turns—now moons—spent north of the mountains, Northlander speech still often eluded him. Every time he spoke, he was unsure he would understand the answer.

Ras hated it.

"At least fifteen." Ham grinned, showing teeth in desperate need of a cleaning. Ras missed his rilius resin. He had used the last of it in the cave with the ialtag, those strange winged beasts. He missed the ease of their communication, but he did not miss the sense of smallness he had felt in their midst, nor the sense that those who shared so easily were probably best at knowing how to conceal.

Halka he understood. Ras's fingers twitched for his bow. Placing one end against his foot, he restrung it easily.

A woman came over, her own bow dangling from her fingertips. She murmured something to Ham that Ras couldn't quite hear, let alone understand. Her name was Dahin—or maybe Dahym. She sometimes came to sit and ply twine whilst watching Ryd carve in the evenings.

Ras stood watching as a few others trickled over, all speaking in low, excited tones.

For a moment, he thought they would leave him behind, closing shoulders to show that he was not welcome. But then Ham and Dahin turned and beckoned him to follow.

The swell of relief and pride that puffed up Ras's chest felt silly and young, like a child showing hys parents a painted stone and receiving a kiss and praise in return.

The hike up into the hills took half the morning. While they walked, the sun rose, cold and unfeeling, always a reminder that Ras was home no longer.

Night was easier. Soft, gentle darkness could spin webs of comfort.

The day cut through illusion and memory, even short as it was in winter.

It also cut through hope.

They walked for hours, up and down slopes of the foothills, venturing closer and closer to the mountain. Dahin began to click her fingernails together, her hands free of any mitts in spite of the cold. When the sun passed its apex, they had still found no trace of the halka.

"They were here," Ham said.

"They move faster than we do," Ras said, and some of the others looked at him curiously, as if he himself were a halka that had opened its mouth to speak.

One of the others whose name Ras did not know pointed up the hill with two fingers. Ras only caught one word in two, but the word he caught was tiger.

The beast must have spooked the halka into moving more quickly than usual. Ras thought of the tiger skin Carin kept rolled in her rucksack, wishing he had killed the beast and earned its pelt himself. He understood why she had given the fyajir hide to Ryd—the smaller man's previous cloak was as warm as a layer of doubloon leaves. Ras was surprised he'd made it through the mountains with all ten fingers and all ten toes without losing more than that flap of earlobe.

When the sun began to move toward the west and Reflection rose over the hills without either shining light on the missing herd of halka, the group slowly began to return to Alarbahis empty-handed.

Panic was not a word Ras liked to apply to himself. He hated that he depended on his skills without them bearing fruit, and each day that went by reminded him that he had left behind a land of bounty for one of scarcity. That the people were not at each other's throats over the scraps they had boggled him.

Alarbahis's smoke appeared in the distance. A wet thunk sounded behind Ras's shoulder.

Ham yelled, "Rovers!"

Ras felt a jolt go through him, a flash of bright fear.

Spinning to face the attackers, Ras nocked an arrow and fell into a crouch behind a bush. He had always been the hunter, not the hunted.

A person armed with a bronze sword and shield came sprinting toward them, and Ham dropped to one leg and rolled to avoid a second arrow that whistled through the air.

In the back of his mind, Ras scowled at the craftership of the fletching, to make such a sound of warning. He loosed his own ghostly silent arrow at the attacker. It hit its mark, blossoming out of the person's neck and spattering the snow with crimson.

A quick look told him that they were outnumbered in spite of the one Ras had downed. Grim, he nocked another arrow, seeing a group of ten rovers advance over the snow. Half of them had bows drawn, men, women, hyrsin. Each wore darkened leather with a bright white rune on their left shoulders.

Ras aimed for the rune on one of the archers, striking his mark again and dropping the archer to her knees. She fumbled for her arrow, but could not pull back the string. His second arrow went through her heart.

A clash of bronze swords brought his head up sharply. Close. Too close. Ham had out two daggers that glinted as he shifted them in his hands, and he darted in between one of the rovers and a hunter from Alarbahis.

Someone laughed.

The sound was so disconnected to the blood on the snow, that for a moment Ras forgot himself and nearly fumbled his next shot.

A woman's voice cut through the yelling and the clank of metal. "So, southerner. You want to prove you deserve that bow?"

At first Ras thought she was talking to him, but he couldn't turn to look. He responded by landing an arrow between the eyes of a rover, then stopped short. The arrow that pegged the rover's forehead was white, not brown. His own had gone wide and caught a lagging rover in the chest. Spinning around, he saw Carin almost a hundred paces away, face grim and bow held at the ready. The young woman at her side had short black hair and dancing eyes, and she laughed again with approval, clapping Carin on the shoulder before running into the fray, sword spinning.

They were no longer outnumbered.

Within moments of the girl entering the fight, she had downed two rovers. Ras finished the one he had injured, and the other hunters fell upon the remaining attackers until the snow turned to red slush.

The girl sauntered back toward Ras, looking right past him at Carin. "Guess you deserve that bow after all."

SART'S FINGERS pulled at the seams on the dead rover's sleeve. She didn't like the rune that decorated the shoulders of each of the rovers, and she certainly didn't like that they had attacked the band of hunters so close to the edges of Alarbahis.

For the *second* time within the wax and wane of a moon. Talar hadn't made it, after collapsing several turns before, not one stride from where Sart currently sat in Culy's hut.

Culy was also less than amused. Sy sat at the edge of hys hut, watching Sart with a pensive expression painting hys face.

"You say the southerners were there?" Hys tone reflected the expression on hys face, a low and foreboding rumble beneath the words.

Sart nodded, smoothing out the buckskin leather over her knee and scratching lightly at the painted rune. "The girl was already running toward the fight when I heard it begin. Nice shot, that one. Her companion, the bigger one, isn't half bad himself."

"You say companion and not friend."

"I've been watching them. The young woman and the smaller young man, they are close. They often touch one another, sit near one another, speak in low voices. The other stands apart, though they seem to trust him well enough."

Culy tilted hys head to the side. "They come from the other side of the mountains."

"I know."

"They speak our language, or close enough to it."

"I know."

"Why are they here?"

"That I do not know." Sart folded the buckskin garment in her lap and drummed her fingers against the leather with a pat-pat-pat-pat. "I think I am more concerned with why these rovers are wearing this rune."

"Something will need to be done about that, yes."

"If Wyt has found a way to supply large groups of people in her camp, she will soon be unstoppable. She will have enough numbers of able-bodied fighters to attack any waymake, take any of their goods, and be gone with it before anyone can summon so much as a cacklebird to their side." Sart sniffed at the paint on her fingernail. "This is powdered diver beak. That fits with what you said about Wyt's location. Divers love Boggers. They make a half decent stew, too, if you have the patience to catch twenty of them."

Reaching out a hand, Culy took the buckskin from Sart's outstretched arm.

"The girl, the southerner girl, she uses magic," Sart said after a pause. "She's about my age. They all are."

"I know."

Sart thumbed her nose at hyr. "She doesn't know what she's doing though. It seems as though they are not sure why they are here themselves."

"They would not be here without some purpose."

"I meant that they are adrift."

"That much anyone can see." Culy stood, setting the buckskin down on the seat sy vacated. "They are vexed that I have not gone to speak with them. Let them. I very much want to see what they will do when frustrated. They have not volunteered any information to anyone, and until I know more, I will not be comfortable leaving them to their ease here in the waymakes. Outlanders or not, they are ignorant of this place and our people, and that can make them dangerous."

Sart nodded. "What would you have me do?"

"Make friends with them."

She felt a smile tug at her cheeks. "Gladly."

Sart found herself a short time later leaning against the pole of Alarbahis's one empty hut, watching the southerner girl clean her arrows.

The young woman knew she was there; Sart could tell when someone watched her out of the corner of an eye, and she respected that this one did just that without losing focus on her task.

"What is your name?" Sart asked her.

She did not jump or show any other sign of surprise except for her lips coming together where a moment before they had been just slightly open. When she spoke, it was slowly and not without effort. "Carin ve Haveranth."

Haveranth. Haver, Sart knew, was a name. Anth was an old word, a lost word, one Sart only knew because of Culy's obsession with knowledge. It harkened back to a time long past when there had been water—or so Culy insisted—flowing freely throughout their lands, from Salters to Crevasses. Even Sands at that time had held streams and springs at its edges and oases in its center. The word *anth* meant waymake, but a waymake in which people stayed all through the cycle of seasons. Who was Haver, she wondered.

"Sart ve Lahivar," she said, the ve sounding strange to her ears, as no one used it with her anymore. "May I?"

At Carin's nod, Sart moved over to sit near her on the large stone in front of the hut. She could feel tremors of magic around the girl like waves of heat from a fire. They buzzed and hummed like a plucked string, and Sart kept her hands firmly planted on her knees to resist the urge to stretch one arm out into that field of power and taste it.

Magic could be drawn in from the world, like she had done with her hands in the muddy creek to the west while seeking to fool Barit and his band of ridiculous rovers, or it could be collected like dung on the bottom of one's boot.

Carin was caked in the stuff. It stuck to her, eddied around her.

It worried Sart somewhat. Magic worked off emotions, required an emotional catalyst to be accessed at all, and volatile emotions fed volatile magic.

"Your Haveranth," Sart said. "What is it like?"

She asked the question carefully, wanting to convey nothing but the curiosity of someone discovering a new interest.

Carin looked up from her arrow. Her eyes were deepest blue, an uncommon color in Sart's experience. They were also intelligent and clear, holding curiosity and, from the way her brows angled downward and her lower lids angled upward, a touch of suspicion. Somewhere beyond that, far more than a touch of grief. She had lost much, and yet here she was. Continuing on.

Sart liked her already.

The girl began to speak, her voice halting as if she were trying to talk around a large stone on her tongue.

"There are more colors," she said. Her gaze rose to the waymake, full of drab grey and brown and the dingy cream of the huts' canvas. "Hunting yields more food, as does fishing. There are fields of food. Sweet orange yams and nutty grains. Groves of red apples and purple-green cajit and bright yellow persimmon. Conu trees near the sea, some inland, and ice-mint that grows in gardens near our homes. Water flows near our village and up from the ground, clear and sweet and clean."

For as pretty a picture as she painted for Sart, Carin's eyes grew cloud-ier with each word, and by the time she got to the word clean, she looked as if she wanted to snap her halm arrow in half. Sart made a note to relate that to Culy. That Carin was telling the truth she did not doubt.

"Why are you talking to me?" Carin asked suddenly.

Sart felt a change in the air, like the coming of a lightning storm. Her chest felt sharp and inverted, as though something pushed into it at the heavy bone that bound her ribs together in front. The hair on her arms prickled.

Carin dropped the arrow in her hands as if it had cut her, and looking down, Sart saw dual dark marks on either side of the smooth white wood. Sart reached down and picked it up, raising it to her nose to sniff.

Sure enough, the arrow smelled like a smoldering log.

"Because," Sart said, handing the arrow back to Carin with as steady a hand as she could manage, "you need to learn to control that."

Carin took the arrow, her fingers rubbing at the dark spots on it. Her chin turned downward, and she pushed her lips together hard enough that a pale line appeared around them against the brown of her skin.

"Why are you here?" Sart asked. If Carin got to ask blunt questions, so did she.

The other young woman scuffed her right foot in the snow, nudging away the topmost layer of powder to reveal ice compacted by the tread of feet. "I preferred not to die."

"You may still die here."

Carin met her eyes then, and Sart looked long into their blueness, wishing some glimmer would tell her what lay in the stranger's mind.

"At least then, I will die having made a choice of it, and not like a rabbit caught in a snare it did not see." She appeared to bite off the final word in the sentence, and the edge of it felt ragged and raw. Carin took a breath and looked in the direction of Culy's hut, though the dwelling itself was not visible from where they sat. "I need to speak with Culy."

"Tell me why." No one would see Culy until sy wished it, and these strangers would need a better reason than simple desire.

Carin's fingertips dug into her knees. She went quiet, and the sounds of the waymake filled the space. Sart could hear the scraping of Carin's friend working bone into carved tools, could hear the clank of pots two huts down and the waymake's one young babe wailing in the distance.

From the young woman's reticence, Sart supposed that whatever had forced—and she had no doubt it was force—the trio of southerners from beyond the mountains to cross those peaks and end up here was something dangerous or frightening or both. Perhaps they had done something to deserve it, but Sart thought that was not the case. Involuntarily, she looked to the south, where the mountains rose to touch the sky with jagged teeth, frozen and hungry. Nothing but death behind and the chance of life ahead would be enough to make her go stumbling into that icy maw. Somehow these three had come through without being eaten.

Sart waited for Carin to answer, thinking of Culy. Sy knew many things, had gathered scrolls and books and scratchings from stones for the whole of hys life, seeking out the past in the hidden places, where sometimes rotting wooden boxes betrayed the time before with secrets spilled into whoever's hands were there to catch them. Sart had not hys ambition nor hys thoroughness, but over the cycles she had learned from hyr what she could. That there were lands beyond their shores, she knew. That they held people, people whose purple glass sometimes washed onto the beaches of Salters and who may have even once touched their toes to the sand, she did not doubt, though the world she walked through was quite big enough for her without them. But of the lands south of the mountains, she had never heard a whisper.

"We came from here," Carin said after a long, long pause.

Sart had counted fifty breaths waiting for Carin to use hers to speak. And now she used it to tell a lie.

"If you're from here, I'm a fyajir," Sart said, voice drier than Sands on the longest day.

"Not me. My people."

That got Sart's attention.

It would explain how their words were so similar, yet different. The shift in language had come easily to Carin, but less so to her fellows, who still greeted any direct address from the people in Alarbahis with the panicked look of a babe facing down a kazytya. Sart knew from Culy that language was a living thing, and indeed those who spent time more in one part of the land than another tended to sound differently. Culy said that in times past, the language may have been completely different and that those strangers beyond the sea likely used different words.

Sart turned sideways to look directly into Carin's face. "Your people. How did they come to live south of the mountains?"

Carin's mouth opened, then shut again. "You will think I am out of my wits," she muttered.

"Perhaps," said Sart.

A bark broke the sudden silence, and after a beat, Sart realized it was a laugh.

"Well, if you don't try to kill me in the next few beats of my heart, I will try to explain to you what I know," Carin said, then added belatedly, "It's not much."

"I'm listening."

And listen she did. Sart listened as Carin related her quest to find her name—what a silly thing, as if such a thing could be lost!—and of discovering the magic that fed life into her land. With each passing moment, Sart wished it were falsehood, but she felt her insides deflate like a hardened stomach balloon tossed about by children and then stepped on by an ihstal. She felt the hum of magic surrounding Carin as she spoke, the pulse that protruded from the space around her skin and into the space around Sart's, melding with her own. The strength of it, the way magic gathered itself to Carin as if it were cold and she a raging fire—it twisted something inside Sart, and it told a story beyond Carin's words. It had a rhythm, and that rhythm was truth.

Culy had asked her to befriend this woman, and Sart had agreed without thought. But she had not expected this.

When Carin finished, she looked at her feet, then back at Sart. "You said I need to control my magic, which means you know somewhat of it."

Tricks and tapestries of necessity, yes. But for once, Sart's words failed her at the scope of the magic Carin described. To alter an entire land—of that, Sart knew less than nothing.

"Bring the scroll you spoke of," said Sart, and her voice was jagged and harsh in her own ears. "We will go to Culy."

CARIN FOLLOWED Sart across the waymake, her knees feeling like congealed mutton as she walked. She grasped Lyah's scroll against her chest where it was wedged between her breast and her shirt. The snow had stopped, and afternoon light broke through the grey clouds to sparkle upon the snow that had fallen. Around her Northlanders pulled snow from the roofs of their huts to melt. Never had Carin thought she would pay such close attention to water.

Culy's hut bore runes on the outside, painted in red. Sart ducked in first, and Carin paused just outside. Her feet stayed stuck to the ground as if crossing the threshold into Culy's home were the last step to sever her ties to her own. Once she went in, once she told hyr about the stones and what she intended to do, there would be no going back.

She hovered for a moment, heart high in her chest and stomach low in her body, a sick feeling squirming between them. She felt a fool, to be here in this land where every day was a struggle to feed herself, thinking she could change things for them. Make it better. And Carin knew that if she were to change anything, it could hurt the place she had grown up in. It could hurt Lyah, her mother. It could hurt Dyava.

For a moment, hanging there outside the flap of canvas, it wasn't enough that her people had left here and stolen the life from this land. It wasn't enough that merely thinking of Haveranth and the spreads of food, always available, now made her want to smash the hardened clay tiles of the waymake's roofs. It wasn't enough that she wanted to fix things. For a moment, she herself wasn't enough, and pulling back the canvas flap felt like pulling aside a boulder.

Carin pulled back the flap and stepped into the hut.

A fire burned at the center of the hut, and Culy stood in front of it, warming hys hands over the blaze. Carin's face felt hot, and when Culy looked up at her, she wanted nothing more than to spin round and dive back out of the hut. She had managed to get from Haveranth here without starving to death or otherwise dying, but standing in front of the person who had greeted her and then shunned her and her companions for several turns made her feel even more small than she had surrounded on all sides by the Mad Mountains.

"Welcome," Culy said after a beat. Sy gestured to an arrangement of cushions on the rug and motioned for Carin to sit.

She obeyed, unsure of what else to do.

Again she repeated her story, and again she felt certain that either Sart or Culy would laugh or grow angry or simply not believe her. They did none of those things, only sat with still faces and hands crossed in their laps.

When she finished, Culy met her gaze, hys grey eyes almost black in the dim light. "What is it you wish of me?" sy asked.

In Haveranth, Carin had never felt as though the elders were in charge of the village, not really. They made what day-to-day decisions were necessary, arbitrated minor disputes, doled out small punishments when such things were required, but never had she felt like a supplicant in their presence. It had never occurred to her to feel thus, as if she needed to make some reason for her presence, her very existence.

"I need to find the stones and break them," Carin said simply. "That was what the ialtag told us."

"Ah." That was all Culy said, and in that one small sound, Carin felt herself reduced to being a child and being scolded for some small thing, like stealing a conu fruit or sneaking out of bed. "That you encountered ialtag is marvel enough. If they truly spoke to you, something else entirely. Most folk here think them no more than a myth."

Sart did not speak, and Carin wanted to get up and leave. She counted her breaths to measure the time. They could take Lyah's scroll and go farther into the north. There was no need for them to stay here, with Culy and hys people. Because they were, Carin realized, hys people. What power over them sy had, Carin did not know, but in every move Culy made, others responded. If Culy didn't believe her...

She stood on wobbly legs and made for the exit.

Culy's voice stopped her with her hand on the canvas flap.

"If you break these stones, what comes of it? If this magic you say your ancestors created, if it is shattered with the shards of rock, what becomes of us?"

What Carin heard in those questions was, *How can we trust you?* She wanted to say that the land would return to what it once had been, but she didn't know what it once had been. Dim memories and cloudy pictures from the Hidden Vale—that was no real knowledge. For a moment, she considered saying that everything would be fixed, like a snapped bowstring restrung. Instead, she heard herself say to the flap of the hut, "I don't know."

"Do you know why I am able to speak to you so much more easily than the rest of my people?" Culy asked suddenly.

Carin turned and met hys gaze. "No."

"You look like us, so you are not from beyond the sea. Your eyes are blue, and those of your companions are green. Long, long ago, those colors were more common here. Some words you use vanished from speech here many cycles past. Since you could not be from across the sea and some of your words were familiar to me, I supposed that your people had moved elsewhere, perhaps far away, and that your language retained something that ours did not. I have made my life one of study, and the words you use that we do not are words I have known. You are not one of us now, but once your blood was born here. If what you say is true, if your people are the reason mine starve, grow ill, and thirst, I will hold you responsible for making it right."

Hope warred with terror in Carin's chest. "And if I fail?" Something stopped her, and she took a step closer to Culy. Sy remained seated, as did Sart, but in spite of Carin looking down at hyr where sy sat, she had no doubt that Culy was still in control of everything within the walls of the hut. She thought for a moment, heart racing. She had asked the wrong question. Carin tried again. "What will failure mean, to you?"

Something like triumph shone from Culy's face. A slight twitch of hys lips, an almost unnoticeable tightening of hys cheeks—Carin couldn't tell what it was that had caused the change.

"You wish to break the stones your people used to bind the life of our land to their bidding. Whatever comes of that is on your shoulders, for good or ill."

Carin nodded once, her head heavy on her neck. She took a long breath and held it, listening to her heart beat. Letting out the breath, she reached into the folds of her overshirt and pulled out Lyah's scroll. "This is what I know of it. It isn't much."

Culy reached out and took the scroll, and the twitch of hys lips and tightening of hys cheeks grew more pronounced as hys long fingers closed around the rolled, half-smushed parchment.

In Haveranth, sometimes villagers played a game in the village hearth-home, moving painted pieces of glass over a plank of carved maha. To win, you had to remove all of your pieces from the board before your opponent, and doing so required thought and strategy. Carin felt then as if she were playing with a full set of pieces against someone whose own were piled to the side with only one or two left to remove.

But in her mind, she took one of her glass pieces from the board, seeing the hunger in Culy's eyes as sy took the scroll from Carin's hand. She had given hyr something valuable.

If Carin had learned anything since setting her snowshoes down in the Northlands, it was that knowing what a person valued was the most important thing to know about them.

Her shoulders straightened, and she returned to her cushion to sit.

She would do what she must.

THE AIR smelled of salt and fish.

Lyari sat in a seaside roundhome, looking out the window at the estuary that became the place of the Bemin's death. She felt an odd moment of cohesion, knowing that she had seen the river from source to delta, as if she had witnessed the whole of its life cycle.

She would have given much to be out in it, her bare feet in the silty riverbed, her fingers tickling a climber fish that would later warm her belly with its tender orange flesh.

Instead, she waited inside Harag's roundhome in an empty room, the fire banked to embers and the windows spatted with mist from the sea. Oil lamps burned, scenting the air lightly with the pimia, though it did nothing about the other smell. Fish and salt.

She couldn't decide if she liked the smell of the sea. Lyari had come here as a child with her parents to visit a distant cousin, cycles back when she was still hysmern. She remembered playing with many of the local children, but the village of Bemin's Fan did not ring with children's voices now.

Lyari sat in the roundhome of Harag, the soothsayer of Bemin's Fan, a cold soup of clams and lemon in front of her, though she was not hungry and had not yet lifted her spoon to her lips. Outside, snow blew through the village and howled against the chimney and the windows, but it did not stick, melting or blowing away with the warmer winds from the west.

Lyari shifted on her bench, the cuffs of her wrists clanking on the table, which was made of carefully fitted and buffed driftwood. Trees were sparser here. New roundhomes here, Lyari vaguely remembered, were often made with wood cut to the north in the dense forested foothills and rolled down by villagers or pairs of ihstal.

Her food untouched, Lyari wondered what was keeping the soothsayer. Harag had kept her waiting when she arrived in the village, too, leaving

Lyari to sink her heels in the sand for long enough that the sun moved a handspan across the sky before Harag finally appeared to fetch her.

Short and thin, Harag had seen some seventy harvests, and with them her dark hair had found its first strands of grey. The soothsayer wore layers of dusty vysa, rose-colored and salt-crusted, and she wore no cloak, her own soothsayer's cuffs at her wrists inset with small shells. Lyari had had an irrational moment of jealousy over the simple adornment, but it washed itself away on the rational anger of being left to wait.

Now she waited again. Lyari tapped her right cuff against the table.

Harag appeared after a few more moments, strands of pale pearls hanging from her hand. The strand bore pink and black and white pearls, sometimes grouped, sometimes alternating. On closer inspection, there were as many black pearls as pink. At one end, there was hardly any white, but at the end dangling from Harag's left hand, there were no pink pearls at all.

Harag sat, her eyes hard as glass.

She laid the string of pearls out in the center of the table, her fingers tracing across the black and white end with a tightness to her face.

"Every time a child is conceived, I add a black pearl," Harag said. Her voice sounded somehow like the driftwood table, tossed about but buffed into working order. "When the child is born, pink. If the child is lost..." she trailed off.

Harag's hands went to the coil of pearls in the table's center. Mostly black and pink, Lyari reached out and touched the strand. The pearls were cold against her fingertips.

"When the last reinvocation was completed, Tavis ve Beminohna began this strand. At its start, every child conceived found hyr first breath." Harag moved her hand back to the black and white end. "Now every child conceived dies."

The strand ended with a black pearl, followed by a white one. Lyari knew that it had been only recently that whoever carried the child had lost hyr.

Lyari knew that in Haveranth there were only ten children with ten harvests or fewer. Until she saw the pearls, though, the meaning of it had escaped her.

Harag saw her face, and when she spoke, her voice was as bitter as the saltwater sea. "You are not prepared for this," she said. Anger dripped from her words like beeswax from a candle. Lyari felt it pool around her, but she did not let it touch her.

Merin had told her a little of this. That their population suffered and declined, she knew. But what was she to do about it? Nothing.

Instead of helping bring new life into the land, Merin had focused on ending it. Lyari met Harag's eyes. A strand of hair fell into her face, and Lyari pushed it back. "I will find a way to right this."

When Harag scoffed, Lyari pushed on.

"Before the reinvocation, not after."

"That is not possible." Harag's voice wore coldness and sharp mistrust. "You have no magic. You are barely more than hysmern, playing at being grown."

Harag pulled the strand into her hand, draping the coils across her palm.

"You think you will succeed where I have not?" Harag let the strand of pearls slip through her fingers, where they hit the table with a patter like heavy rain. "You think that you, barely named and somehow soothsayer, will manage to right a course Merin herself could not alter? You are a fool."

"I will do it." Lyari's voice sounded distant in her own ears, like listening to the sea through a large shell.

The room seemed to grow dimmer, and Harag stood, her hands in front of her body as if she were cradling a ball of yarn. A sharp crackle sounded behind Lyari, and she jumped, turning to see the fire blazing from embers to flames in an instant. The oil lamps on the kitchen worktop did the same, their flames as long as Lyari's fingers. She heard a sound like a whisper, and the windows began to ice over, spirals of frost twisting across the glass.

"You are nothing," Harag said. "You know nothing. You play at things you do not understand. You are not the one who will right this land."

And you are? Lyari once again felt words pressing hard at her teeth and wanted to voice them, to throw them at Harag like stones, to dash the string of pearls, constructed by soothsayers over five hundred cycles, against the floor of the roundhome. Instead, she looked up at Harag and placed her elbows on the table, hands clasped in front of her face. She thought of Old Wend taking his cup of cordial and licking ruby droplets from his lips, how Rina and Ohlry had done the same, only Varsu waiting for her to begin and never touching his.

Lyari looked at Harag over her hands and did not move.

Now was not the time to push back, not like that.

She noted how quickly the other woman had moved to magic, and as the flames died down behind her and the frost began to melt on the windows with the spray of the sea, Lyari marked it well. Then she took the strand of pearls, sliding it from the table and coiling it over and over around her arm. She tucked the end back against her skin, securing it. Then she got up and walked to the door.

Harag made a strangled sound behind her, but Lyari did not turn.

Harag did not try to stop her.

She pulled her cloak from the hook near the door and sheathed herself in it, unbinding her ihstal mount from the post outside of Harag's roundhome. Mounting the happily whistling beast, she nudged it forward into the town.

A pair of children tossed stones toward the sea as she rode past, and in her mind was a cool whisper as her eyes fell upon them. Hadrit. Lahany. She felt their names swirl into her, take root in her belly where they made a new home.

A small smile danced at the corner of Lyari's mouth and felt sweetness on her tongue. Her untasted soup still sat cold on Harag's table, and Harag had just told her all she needed to know.

Old Wend may have hated it. Harag may have resented it.

But there was only one real soothsayer in the Hearthland, and all names belonged to her.

The pearls warmed to her skin.

THREE DAYS after Carin gave Culy the scroll, sy told her sy knew where one of the stones was.

As much as Carin couldn't shake the feeling that she was being toyed with, she had to go. Sart offered to take her, and within moments, it was decided. Tahin, Sart's ihstal, could easily carry them both, and they would move faster mounted.

Carin packed her rucksack, her clothes clean but smoky from being dried over the fire. The nights they managed to do the washing—winter, according to Sart, was the only time anyone managed to clean their clothes regularly inland—she, Ryd, and Ras would sit nude by the fire, bathing themselves as best they could with the melted snow they set aside. They traded Ryd's carvings and bone tools for soap and other things they could not make themselves. The soap smelled of lye, but Carin would rather smell like that than the underside of a latrine. Ryd learned to emulate the tools the Northlanders used to scrape their skin clean, flat bone paddles with a curved handle they would draw over the whole of their bodies to dry themselves or clear away grime. They had seen no towels.

She heard Ryd come in before she saw him, and she knew it was him by his breathing. Ras always sounded like he had something lodged in his nose, and he snored loudly enough that Carin wondered if Culy could hear him from the opposite side of the waymake.

"You're really leaving." Ryd said it with a finality that proved it wasn't really a question.

"I have to."

"I know." He came to sit on a rock by the fire, poking at the banked embers with a stick to stir it into flames. "I thought I would be with you, though."

"I'm not leaving forever. I'll be back." Carin regretted her words the moment they escaped her mouth, but she didn't try to walk them backward. Instead she smiled wryly at Ryd. "You will be well here. They already value you for what you make."

Ryd looked at his hands. "Who would have thought I would be a carver?"

"Not I," said Carin. She pushed down on the clothing in her rucksack and pulled the leather flap over the top to close it, then met Ryd by the fire. "Do something for me."

"Of course."

"Learn all you can from Culy. About this land, about what sy knows. It's been a long while since our lessons ended in Haveranth, but we know nothing here. And this will be our home, for good or ill." She remembered Culy's words. They echoed a Hearthlander proverb that Carin now figured must have found its footing here.

"Or it will be our grave." Ryd gave her a crooked smile that she never would have seen on his face even one cycle past. His face was thinner, but there was a clarity to him Carin had not seen before, and it wasn't just the newfound muscles of his body making him look sharper. He saw more, watched more, observed more.

"Perhaps." She took his hand in hers and squeezed it. "Do not tell Ras what I asked of you."

"You don't trust him."

"I trust you."

Sart and Carin were on the path to the northeast shortly after, leaving at midday even though they would only have a few hours of light to travel by. It had been moons since Carin had mounted an ihstal, and she knew by the time they reached Boggers that she would regret being out of practice. It felt strange to be propelled over the slowly leveling hills on feet that were not her own, and stranger still to have Sart in front of her, the other girl's back against her chest and Carin's knees fitted behind Sart's.

Sart spoke of magic as they rode, explaining in patient terms what she had meant by control. "All things seek balance," she said. "If you gather magic to you, it must be used or it will find a way to use itself—not always in the way you would hope."

That brought a flash of heat to Carin's face at the memory of the trees she had set fire to after killing the fyajir and tiger. She didn't speak for a long while as they rode.

As the days passed on Tahin's back and the nights with Sart teaching Carin control of her magic by firelight, the land grew flat around them. The snows stopped, and the air grew balmy. While the winter sun occupied its apex in the sky, Carin would feel trickles of perspiration down her back and soon took to riding atop her cloak instead of wearing it. When she asked about the weather, Sart only laughed.

"The farther north, the warmer it will be. We are only a few days from Boggers." Sart stiffened when she said it, as if remembering something, but Carin didn't ask.

They didn't encounter many other people on the way, and those they saw mostly kept their distance. Perhaps it was the halm bow strung across Carin's back or the ihstal they rode, but Carin felt relief enough to be left unmolested.

Sart pulled Tahin to a halt near dusk, over a turn after they'd left Alarbahis. She slid from the ihstal's back and sank into a crouch, motioning to Carin to do the same. "Keep a hand on the halter," Sart said, passing off the leather strap to Carin.

Carin obliged, holding the strap at her side and slinking forward. The ground around them had grown wet and soggy, but it did not yet pass for the bog the region was named for. In the distance, Carin could see a glimmer of light over the next rise.

"Lahglys," Sart said. She looked behind them, then at Carin, her eyes moving from Carin's feet to her head and back. "There's not a lot of time to explain, and I could be wrong. I overheard that there are some rovers at Lahglys who want nothing to do with Wyt and the people she's gathering. While we're here, I might try and speak to them."

"You want to stop and talk to rovers?" Carin had heard folks in Alarbahis talking about Wyt and the rovers she was supposedly gathering to her, and indeed she'd encountered some of them that day Ras had gone hunting with Ham and the others. But Carin didn't feel particularly inclined to stop and talk to people who might kill her before she could reach even the first stone. "Couldn't we come back after we find the stone?"

"We're here now," Sart said. "Besides, they're in our way."

Carin wasn't quite sure what to say to that.

They stayed where they were for a few more moments, then Sart looked over her shoulder at Carin. "You're not the only one with magic, my new friend."

A bright twinkle shone in Sart's eyes, and she led the way forward. When they reached the rise concealing them from the waymake of Lahglys, Sart took Tahin's halter from Carin and stood, murmuring into the ihstal's ear. Tahin whistled happily, then sprinted away to the east.

"What are you doing?" Carin took three steps after Tahin, her hand trailing helplessly after her. "You..."

"Tahin'll wait for us and evade anyone who tries to come near."

Dumbfounded, Carin stared at the other woman. "You must teach me this thing."

"They won't do it for just anyone. Tahin likes me." Sart grinned after the beast, who had left a trail of torn up sod in her wake. "And you. She likes you, too."

"That's reassuring."

"With me, now." Sart led the way forward with painstaking slowness, taking care to stay beneath the crest of the rise that shielded them. She circled around the waymake from the west, and Carin couldn't help but marvel at the way Sart moved with such confidence from one place of concealment to another.

Carin had been able to do that once. For a moment, a sense of longing nearly overwhelmed her, bringing with it the scents of thick loam and wet river rocks and the woody perfume of the maha trees. Then Sart stopped short in front of her, and Carin, still somewhat crouching, ran her nose into Sart's shoulder, which smelled of sweat, ihstal, and leather instead. Sart had stood to her full height and shifted to the side, leaning around a hummock of grasses.

"One thing," Sart said.

"Yes?"

"If they threaten to kill us, shoot one of them. Preferably somewhere painful."

Carin nodded, moving her bow from where she had slung it across her shoulders. The sun was still high in the sky, which didn't leave many shadows to hide in. For all the times she had stalked animals, Carin had never stalked people. She wondered if they could feel her coming. When Ras and his gang of hunters had turned up on her path, she had felt them for days. Knowing what it was like to be on the other end of it made her cautious, and knowing that her goal was far beyond a waymake full of thieves and killers made her fingers tighten around an arrow and pull it from the quiver.

From their approach, Carin could see that only three or four of the huts in Lahglys were occupied. The rest stood like skeletons, barren and empty.

When they reached the western edge of the waymake, Sart stopped next to a hut, stuck two fingers in her mouth, and whistled loudly enough that Carin heard startled clanks from cookpots banged into hooks and surprised voices that sounded like nuts popping on a fire.

"I hope you know what you're doing," she muttered to Sart.

"Remember what I said."

"Visitors!" A man stepped out from behind one of the huts, sword drawn in his hand. "And one brought us a halm bow."

Carin took that moment to nock her arrow, her fingers fitting themselves to the bowstring.

More rovers appeared around them, women and hyrsin and men, all armed with bronze weapons and some, Carin couldn't help but notice, with jagged-edged halm daggers, the kind that hurt more coming out than going in.

"Kill them," the first man said.

Carin put an arrow in his hip.

He jerked back, falling to the ground with a spitting curse tumbling out of his mouth. The other rovers started forward, but Carin drew another arrow and aimed.

Sart's smile was as wide as a frog full of flies.

S ART FELT as though her blood had turned to lightning. She smiled at the rovers, turning a beatific look on the one Carin had shot and stepping forward.

They stepped back, and she liked it.

"Now that we're all acting like civilized folk, why don't you tell me about a fellow rover named Barit and why he wants to help Wyt get you out of here."

One of the rovers spit, his hand clenched tight around the hilt of his sword. "Barit's rotten to the bones."

"Why, yes. I believe I noticed that when I met him," said Sart. "You can tell me what I haven't already figured out for myself, or my friend can use you all as cushions for her lovely halm pins. Start with Wyt."

The rovers exchanged looks, some of them darting glances at Carin and her bow. Sart liked that, too. The more attention they paid to the bow, the less they'd be paying to her.

The hum of magic around her grew, inaudible to everyone but her.

If what Carin said was true about the land she came from and the stones she sought to break, it could change everything about Sart's world. Problem was, Sart had to live in her world as it was for the present, and that meant dealing with Wyt.

Sart concentrated on the hilts of the blades in rover hands, thinking of Carin's halm arrow that still bore twin scorch marks from Carin's own flesh.

With a yell, the rovers dropped their blades with a clatter, flapping their burned hands in the air. The one Carin had shot still groaned, and as Sart watched, he wrenched the halm arrow from his hip and flung it to the side, away from any chance of Carin getting it back without wading through a puddle of rover blood and rovers.

There was a reason she hadn't tried that trick with Barit, and the weariness that stole over her then was a nice reminder of why. She could have disarmed Barit and his band, but it would have left her exhausted and half asleep a league down the road—which would have been worse.

Here, though, these rovers were home, and Tahin was only a call away.

"Wyt," Sart repeated. "Barit seemed to think you all had some sort of disagreement with her, which means I'm inclined to like you."

"You do this with people you like?" The rover on the ground asked the question through clenched teeth, his hand pressing into the hole in his hip.

"I haven't decided whether I actually like you yet, but your chances improve the sooner someone starts talking."

A young man who had been swaying from foot to foot and trying not to stare at Carin's bow blurted out, "It's not we don't like Wyt, no. Not that. She don't like us."

"And why is that?" Sart turned her smile on the young man, flashing her teeth. It didn't have the comforting effect she'd hoped for. She thought the young man might wet himself.

The man on the ground pushed himself to his knees, then pulled himself to an unsteady standing position by pulling on the canvas of the nearby hut. "She don't like me in particular. I tried to kill her."

Carin barked a laugh, and Sart wanted to do the same.

"Sounds like a reasonable excuse for disliking you," Sart agreed.

"It was ten cycles back. She don't forget nothing."

"In her defense, I tend to remember those who try to kill me as well." Sart smiled wider at the man, who swallowed, clearly remembering the two words he'd used to command his rovers. "I could be persuaded to let my memory falter, however."

"Just tell me what you want." The man's voice went surly and pouty like a child denied hys favorite toy.

"I want you to work against Wyt. Find out what she's doing and how she's managing to gather so many people to her."

"I can tell you already she's got something precious. Nobody can seem to agree on what, though."

The rest of the rovers shifted, their stances relaxing, though several still sucked on burned fingers.

"I knew that much myself," Sart said. "Find something specific."

"And just how are we supposed to tell you what we found?"

"I'm wintering in Alarbahis with Culy," Sart said.

The rovers blanched at hys name, which gave Sart a happy glow of surprise. The sun broke through the clouds, lighting the faces of the rovers and casting Sart's shadow against the ground, dark and tall. It reached all the way to the rovers from where she stood.

"And if we don't?" The new speaker was someone with long black hair clubbed over one shoulder. Sy wore heavier leathers than the others, and hys eyes watched Sart with enough heat that Sart was glad she and Carin were the only magic-workers in the crowd.

"If you don't," Sart said, "I'll let my friend practice her archery on you."

The hyrsin snorted.

Sart had stopped paying attention to Carin, but suddenly the hut behind the injured rover caught fire, the flames taking with a loud *whoof* that made the rovers yell and drag their leader away from the blazing canvas. Beyond it, smoke rose from the pole of an empty hut.

At first Sart thought Carin had done it by accident, but when she looked, she saw Carin's face screwed up with concentration and felt the humming buzz of power around her. It wasn't a burst like a wave over a rock, but the funneled water of a cascade.

One of the rovers whispered, "Tuanye," loudly enough for Sart to hear it, and she didn't try to dissuade hyr.

Others tried to smother the flames, but the hut went up faster than they could move, and smoke billowed into the air.

"Are you finished?" Carin asked.

Sart nodded. "Send someone to Alarbahis once you have what I want." She paused with her fingers halfway to her lips to trill a whistle to call Tahin. "And because I'm not wholly unreasonable..."

She walked toward the injured rover, and knelt next to him, touching her hand to his hip just over the wound. The hyrsin who had spoken began to reach for hys sword, but one strum of Carin's bowstring made hyr freeze.

The arrow's point had been smooth and the shaft unbarbed, and the wound was clean, if deep. Sart felt the ground beneath her come alive, and she spun the magic from it into thread that knit the rover's skin back together under her touch. She felt it close and heal, more with her mind than with the touch of her fingers, and though she could not see her, she felt Carin's eyes on her.

When it was finished, she looked at the rover. He looked back, though he swallowed continuously as if he were about to be sick.

"What is your name?" she asked.

"Hylwit," he said. "Hylwit va Sparnihlan."

"Sart Lahivar," she said, then beamed at him when he jumped. Still crouched by his side, she whistled for Tahin.

The ihstal came bounding toward them moments later, and Carin gave Sart a leg up before climbing up behind her.

They rode away at a run for two leagues, then slowed when Tahin finally grew winded.

"Things here are very different," Carin said softly from behind her. Her breath tickled Sart's ear.

"You didn't set things on fire back home?"

"I never shot a person before I left home."

Interesting. Sart looked straight ahead, thinking about what it would be like to live in a land where you only killed things to eat. When she spoke, it was firmly. "Do not speak about your land in the hearing of others. You are no longer from there, but from here. If they learn of a place where food and water flow like you say they do, they will be desperate."

"And they are not desperate now?"

Carin's arms rested around Sart's waist, and for a moment the sensation made Sart feel as though she were trapped in someone's rucksack.

"You see us as desperate because you have never lived as we do. We survive. We do as we must. And we have colors, too."

RYD'S STOMACH growled loudly. Ras looked up from where he sat across the hut, skinning a pair of rabbits he had killed while hunting.

If he resented finding food for the both of them, he didn't show it. Ryd had never been particularly good at hunting, but after the Journeying, he had found it easier.

Ras spitted the rabbits over the fire and turned to leave. "I'll return after first watch. I agreed to take first with Ham."

While the rabbits cooked over the fire, Ryd went through the contents of his rucksack. He'd packed it in Haveranth in such a hurry that he was still discovering things he'd brought. Several packets of seeds—he'd thought for certain they would find a place in the mountains where they could live in peace as Nameless—those he set aside, wondering if they would even grow in the Northlands. He also found a small pot of grease that would have been useful in the mountains when his lips chapped from the wind.

He had the packets of seeds in his hand when someone bumped into him. Seeds scattered over the rug and the packed earth beneath it.

Ryd spun to find Culy—how the hyrsin had entered the hut without a sound, Ryd did not know.

Culy's face was amused, hys grey eyes assessing as always. Whenever Ryd saw hyr, he always got the impression that Culy took everything apart to its layers with one glance.

He dropped to the floor to retrieve the seeds. They may not be useful here, but Ryd didn't want to risk losing them. There were Early Bird seeds scattered about, as well as persimmon and hibiscus and carrot. A few other varieties of apple, some cave chili seeds, and, from the look of it, redberries.

Handling the seeds felt like touching the dead.

To Ryd's surprise, Culy knelt beside him to help. "I am sorry if I startled you," sy said, hys words spoken with exaggerated slowness that made Ryd feel like a child again, even though he knew it was necessary for him to understand. Ryd envied Carin's ease with the Northlander way of speaking.

"It's fine," Ryd lied. He'd gotten most of the seeds already, and he straightened, going to the spit to turn the rabbits.

"With your friend gone, how do you fare?"

The smell of smoke and cooking meat filled Ryd's nose and made his stomach growl again. "I worry for her."

Culy nodded. "That is not a surprise."

"Are you the leader here?" Ryd blurted out.

The amusement returned to Culy's face—though perhaps it had never left. "Here in Alarbahis, at this moment, yes. Though what is true in one place is seldom true in all places."

"I disagree," Ryd said, feeling reckless. "An apple will roll downhill in the Hearthland as much as it will here in the Northlands."

"The Northlands," Culy mused. "Such is the name you give to our home. Creative."

"It's at least as creative as Boggers," Ryd muttered. He knew he ought not to provoke the leader of the waymake in which he was making his home, but his frustration came tumbling out of his mouth.

Culy laughed. Sy had a rich laugh, like thick vysa robes freshly woven. Ryd had never given much thought to his own laugh, but hearing Culy he wondered what he sounded like to others.

"Fair point," Culy said. Sy looked at the seeds Ryd held in his hands. "May I?"

Ryd poured a small spattering of them into Culy's palm. While the rest of Culy's appearance was tidy—polished, even—hys hands were rough from toil, with callouses making their homes across the mounds of his fingers. From what, Ryd didn't know, but something about the sight of hands well-traveled set his mind at ease just a bit.

"In your land, you plant seeds and stay to tend them?" The upturn at the end of Culy's question reminded Ryd of a child asking something sy thought was silly to ask.

Ryd sat on the stone he used as a chair, nodding at Culy and wondering how it was possible for two places to live so differently. "We grow our food and build homes near it. We keep animals from ravaging our crops and tend to them each day. One day in five we feast."

"Feast." Culy made a sound like a snapping branch. "The only feast we have here is a waterfeast on the darkest night, if the snowfall is enough. And only in Crevasses."

"But you know the word."

"I know many words." Culy peered closely at the seeds. "If you plant these here, do you think they will grow?"

It was so close to Ryd's own musings that he couldn't help the grim smile that slid across his face. "I cannot say."

"Shall we try?"

At that moment, Ryd peered into Culy's grey eyes just as sy peered into hys hand at the seeds. For a heavy space of time, Ryd saw what Culy truly held in hys hands: the potential of sustenance, of food, of enough.

When Ryd spoke, it was slowly. Speaking with Culy was easier than with the other Northlanders, perhaps because Culy so clearly tried to emulate the patterns of the Hearthlanders in hys words. "If we plant them, it must be near the Planting Harmonix, when the day and night share equal time, just before the days begin to lengthen. But I cannot say what will come of it. They may sprout and grow or wither and die. They need more water than they are likely to find here."

Culy seemed to accept that, sighing. For three beats of his heart, Ryd thought that the hyrsin would keep the seeds and not hand them back, but then Culy outstretched hys hand and lightly brushed them into Ryd's waiting palm.

"How did you know where the stone was?" Ryd asked suddenly. The moment the words left his mouth, he wished he could catch them in his fingers and stuff them back in. But Carin had asked him to discover what he could, and now the question hung in the air like steam.

"I know this land," Culy said. "Some people live in one or two regions, traveling within them to seek food or water or safety, but I have made a study of it all. I have charted it from Crevasses to Taigers, through the hot deserts of Sands and the thick muck of Boggers—our creatively named regions, as you say. In doing so, I have found remnants of former times and tried to piece together what I could of it."

"And what did you find?"

"It would take more than a simple conversation over spilled seeds to answer that question."

Blushing, Ryd carefully put the seeds away, and in spite of the small smile about Culy's face and the sudden warmth of his own cheeks, Ryd heard between Culy's words something of import. This place belonged to hyr, sy knew it well, and sy put hys mind to understanding it and its people. Ryd thought he would be smart to remember it. He recalled his lessons with the other hysmern, from five harvests to fifteen where he got to learn first who he was—man, woman, or hyrsin—and then to seek inward to prepare for the Journeying to find his name. Merin had always said that knowledge held more power than magic.

After the events of the past cycle, Ryd no longer could find it in himself to doubt it.

Culy paused, as if considering whether or not to continue. Sy moved to sit on an adjacent stone, able then to look Ryd in the eyes. "The stones your friend seeks, there are five of them, yes?"

The memory of the images Ryd had seen in the cave in the Hidden Vale surfaced, tied in with what the ialtag had shown him. "There are five," Ryd said.

"I know of three possible stones," said Culy. "There are places throughout these lands where the memories of our ancestors live on through ruins they left behind. Stones, yes, but also buildings that have since fallen, more permanent than our waymakes. It seems, once, our ancestors lived as your people still do, in one place, dwelling where water and food were easily brought to hand. I sent Sart and Carin to one of them."

At that, Culy's expression took on a sharpness like Ras's did when he hunted an animal and it evaded his arrow or snare.

"What is it you think will happen if your friend succeeds in breaking these stones?" sy asked.

Ryd shook his head. "Whatever my ancestors did will be reversed."

To his shock, Culy held out hys hand again, and in hys palm blossomed a ball of light the size of a blacknut shell. "You believe it will be so simple?" Culy closed hys palm around the light, and though it shone for a moment through hys fingers, when sy opened hys hand again, it had vanished so completely that Ryd couldn't be sure he'd seen it at all.

"I don't know."

"Allow me, then, to give you a brief lesson." Culy made the light reappear, and it spread to each of hys fingertips, five new tiny balls of light, all connected by a golden thread like the midsummer sun. Sy pressed hys finger down over one of the lights, and it snuffed out, though the others seemed to grow brighter.

Sy snuffed out a second, then a third, then a fourth, until all that remained was the ball of light in hys palm and on the tip of hys thumb.

Ryd had never seen magic so closely.

All the lights sprang back into being, then Culy pressed hys fist over the one that hovered on the center of hys palm. They all went dark.

Culy stood, wiped hys palms on hys breeches, and went to the hut's flap to leave.

"If you change one thing, it changes others," is all sy said.

L YARI'S EYES burned. For the past turn since returning from Bemin's Fan, she had shuttered herself in her roundhome with Merin's scrolls and stacks of parchment, reading, organizing, and learning as much as she could about the woman and the legacy she had left behind.

It had taken days of waking before dawn's first fingers of light and staying awake long past dusk pulled the sun beneath the horizon, but she had finally found a pile of parchment that described the spell the founding families had used to create the Hearthland's bounty.

She could not be sure, but she suspected the elders were watching her.

At least one of them found some reason to stop by her roundhome each day. Old Wend wanted her to arbitrate a dispute between two children warring over a plaything. Rina wanted her opinion on what type of etching she should do on the bronze platter for the Night of Reflection. Ohlry stopped by for tea. Varsu asked if she needed help.

On one day, Ohlry and Rina had come in just as Varsu left, and Lyari had very nearly broken under the absurdity of it.

Instead of spreading out the scrolls and notes across her trestle table as she wanted to, Lyari laid them out on her bed. No matter how intrusive the elders were, they would not set foot into her bedroom without her permission, and with them stopping by regularly, she did not want them to see the extent of her studies in plain view.

Jenin had not appeared to her in several days, and Lyari could not explain why. And since Merin's death, Lyari's own parents had not come to see her. That, at least, she understood. It could have been taken as a sign of weakness, and with the elders treating her like she had yet to bear her own appellation, an additional sign of weakness would have been unwelcome. She missed them nonetheless.

This morning, Lyari had found the answer to a question that had been niggling at her like a pebble in her shoe—how none of the Northlanders were able to follow southward on the heels of the founding families.

From what she could tell, the founding families had sealed the passes. She couldn't figure out if the barrier was an actual physical boundary or if they had somehow erected a wall of magic that would simply turn people away somehow, but they had somehow managed to make it so no one from the north could travel southward.

It was a relief to find it, like digging said pebble from its place lodged in her heel. It meant no one from the Northlands could come south, that the mountains were impenetrable.

While Merin lived, she had taught Lyari of all the passes out of the Hearthland. One, in the Mistaken Pass—Merin had thought that the pinnacle of cleverness—Lyari had known about even before her Journeying. That secret she had never told Carin, never hinted at, and before the Journeying, it had seemed only like a banality because no one in their right state of being would attempt to cross the Mad Mountains at all.

After her Journeying, however, the location of the passes was anything but banal.

Their location was how Merin had managed to find Carin and Ryd and kill them. How the hunters knew which parts of the mountains to search for Nameless.

Lyari shuffled through the scrolls, pulling out the next in the line she'd made.

Her eyes fell immediately on the rune of *marhan,* to sacrifice. A sharp vertical angle like an arrowhead, with a smaller inverted inside it. The rune was the verb form, always the verb form. At the top of the scroll there was the now-familiar code of five circles of white wax that marked this parchment as being about the spell.

Merin had told her what she was to do, that she would have to choose five sacrifices from five different families over the coming cycles. That when the time came to reinvoke the spell, it would require blood. It had been done before, and it would be done again.

But as Lyari read the scroll, her blood began to turn to crystals in her veins. Five deaths to bring about countless lives, that she could balance. The scroll required more.

Five families. Not one person from each—the entire family line.

She looked up from the scroll, tears blurring her eyes. The beating of her heart felt hollow in her chest. Her fingers bent the parchment, and one nail punctured it, poking through until it dug into her palm. She forced herself to unclench her hand, to smooth the scroll against the coverlet of her bed. A single drop of saltwater fell to the parchment, but it did nothing to the ink.

"You see now," said Jenin, appearing at the foot of her bed. "You see."

A knock sounded at the door.

Lyari wanted to scream at whomever it was to leave, to go far away and leave her in peace. Instead, she swung her legs over the side of the bed and put her head between her knees. Blood rushed to her head, and she breathed deep, taking in the scent of the fur coverlet and the beeswax candle that burned on the side table. She stood, breathing again, holding her eyes wide so as not to allow more tears to fall.

Did Rina know? Did any of the elders realize what cost this reinvocation bore?

She walked to the front door and pulled it open.

Dyava stood on the other side.

Such relief that filled Lyari to see it was not, for once, one of Haveranth's elders swiftly vanished at the sight of Jenin's brother standing there.

Lyari could not find words to greet him.

"You have not spoken to me since you returned from the Journeying," Dyava said, looking over Lyari's shoulder. "May I come in?"

"Yes," Lyari said, stepping aside. Jenin stood against the far wall, hys eyes on hys brother with an unreadable expression.

Dyava waved her off when Lyari offered tea, instead perching on the ritual stone that sat against Lyari's hearth.

Silence stretched out.

Dyava did not look like Jenin, not really. Only their eyes were truly similar. Dyava was broad where Jenin was slim, taller by half a hand. Before the Journeying, Dyava had been full of smiles and warmth. What little Lyari had heard of him since was that he had sobered, grown withdrawn and reticent.

"I am sorry, Dyava," Lyari said softly. She could give him no comfort where he had lost a member of his family, and she could not speak to him about the loss of Carin. He wouldn't even remember her, even though Lyari knew he had watched Carin raise this very roundhome with her hands and brought her food and conu juice as she worked. The thought built an ache in her chest, and for once, she did not try to stifle it. "I am so very sorry."

He met her gaze, and Lyari went to sit beside him. His body felt warmer than the fire.

"I don't know why I came here," Dyava said. "I haven't been sleeping, and something feels wrong. But out of reach, like I can't touch it."

Jenin came to stand beyond Dyava, frowning at hys brother. Lyari tried not to look at hyr. She instead placed a hand on Dyava's shoulder. "Since Jenin died?"

Dyava looked up, then toward the door. "I can't stay long. Clar said she would be coming here, and I wanted to tell you to please be kind to her."

Confused, Lyari pulled her hand back. "Why would I be anything but kind to Clar?"

"Wend has said that you are in a temper lately."

"Wend said—" Lyari stopped, feeling both brass cuffs on her wrists. She moderated her tone, with some effort. "The elders have seen fit to ensure that my studies are progressing. Several times per day."

A small smile cracked Dyava's lips for a moment. "I can see how that wouldn't improve one's temper."

He rose to leave.

"Dyava," Lyari said as he reached the door. He turned. "Come back sometime. I should not have let so many moons pass without—without speaking to you."

"I understand why you did." Dyava looked for a moment as if he might move toward Lyari, but instead he placed his hand on the door, glancing out the window. "I'll come back sometime soon."

When the door closed behind him, Lyari sat back leaning on her hands against the enormous ritual hearthstone. She didn't have to wait long; the girl knocked within moments.

For an instant, Lyari saw Clar covered in Jenin's blood, and that image blurred and became Clar's own blood trickling down the sides of the hearthstone.

Lyari wanted to be sick. She tried to steady herself as she opened the door. Lyari welcomed Clar into the roundhome, thinking of Dyava's words.

Clar closed the door behind her and shook the snow from her boots. Outside the snow still fell in heavy, fat flakes. It had hardly let up in days, and Lyari's journey home from Bemin's Fan had been a trial, even with a hearty ihstal beneath her that cared little for the snow up to its thighs. She had arrived home with sodden legs and feet like blocks of cold stone. Clar's face was flushed as she removed her cloak, and Lyari didn't think it was from the wind.

When she got her first look at the girl, she saw the redness of her eyes and the wetness beneath her nose. Lyari beckoned to Clar to sit at her hearth, stirring the almost-vanquished embers until they sparked and flamed when she tossed a handful of dried cajit shells upon them.

"What is it, Clar?" Lyari asked, trying to push the thought of Clar's bloodied body from her mind and finding it stubborn.

The girl didn't answer for a moment, her mouth opening and closing like a fish nosing for chum. "Merin," she said finally.

Lyari felt cold even with the fire beginning to rise up in the hearth. *What of her?* she wanted to ask, but she held her tongue tight against her teeth.

"First Jenin died, and now Merin. And you—you had to go on the Journeying alone! How did you survive? I...that cannot be. Every day I wonder if someone else will be next. Every day I wonder if the same will become of me."

Alarmed, Lyari opened her mouth to lie, to say that Jenin had been murdered, but of course Merin was an accident, a tragedy.

Clar beat her to it. "I know Merin mixed up her sparkleaf with ice-mint. I know that it was an accident, but...she was..."

"She was our soothsayer," Lyari said, and the grief in her voice was no lie. Merin had just died to her before her body met its end, is all.

The girl nodded, and without warning, she fell into Lyari's arms. Her bare hand brushed Lyari's, and like the wind over the chimney, Lyari heard it. *Calyria. Calyriacalyriacalyria.* The name wove through her, finding its way to where the children of Bemin's Fan had been named in her, and Lyari knew, by the quiet darkness of the longest night that this was who Clar was. Calyria ve Haveranth, as she would be known one cycle hence.

Clar's words—*you had to go on the Journeying alone*—how they tore at Lyari's heart. *I will hold your memory, Carin, Ryd. I will not let your names vanish from my mind.*

The village bell began to toll.

Clar's head snapped up—for Lyari could not yet call her by her true name—and her eyes were wide and red like the now-glowing embers in the hearth.

Lyari squeezed her hand. "It will all be well," she said, though she didn't even believe it herself.

Jenin stood at the shuttered window, face grim.

Hurriedly, Lyari and Clar threw on their cloaks and laced up their boots and pushed out into the fast-falling snow.

A cry rose from across the village hearth-home, opposite Lyari's roundhome. As they grew closer, Lyari saw why.

Falyr and Reylu's roundhome had collapsed.

The entire dwelling lay crushed, the remaining wall like a jagged tooth of a tiger, the roof caved in. Someone yelled, and Rina pushed her way past the growing crowd of villagers, shouldering them out of the way with arms that every day worked her bellows. A hush descended on the village. Lyari began to run, her feet moving as fast as she could make them through the knee-deep snow. She saw the village elders already there, Ohlry and Varsu and Wend all lifting rubble from the collapsed roof.

The sight stung her—her roundhome stood between Varsu's and the village hearth-home, and yet he had not stopped to collect her on the way. Only the elders could ring the village bell, and it only took one of them. None had thought to alert Lyari.

She hurried forward and slipped between the villagers who blocked her path, her feet sliding on the snow. She stopped just before rushing in to join the elders, looking around at the rest of the village. This was the most snow she had ever seen fall upon Haveranth. Every roundhome wore a heavy cap of white, and to Lyari's eyes, the sight was nothing but a portent of death.

Lyari spun around and gathered her breath, bellowing into the crowd of onlookers. "Go! All of you! Climb onto your roofs and clear the snow before your homes are next!"

For a moment she thought they were going to ignore her, and indeed, many looked past her to Old Wend and Rina, who heaved a large beam out into the road.

But then one person moved—Tamat, Lyari thought—and the others began to follow, their movements slow at first, then quickening with urgency.

Lyari turned back, waded into the wreckage of the roundhome, and got to work.

Hours later, night had fallen across Haveranth, and there were four bodies laid out in front of the collapsed roundhome. Lyari's muscles felt stretched tight like leather that had been dried too quickly to soften properly, and her entire body was slicked inside her clothing, cooling quickly in the frigid air.

Four dead. Two parents, the mother's sahthren, and their child of eight harvests.

In her mind, Lyari saw a white pearl added to a string.

She made her way home to prepare for mourning, and stopped on the threshold, looking up.

Someone had cleared her roof of snow.

When she went inside, she found her fire restored and a pot resting on the embers. A note set on the table read:

Thought you would be hungry. —Dyava

THE STONE was right where Culy had said it would be, half-buried in a boggy hummock. Carin slid off Tahin's back when she saw it, running toward the stone as fast as her unsteady feet would carry her. She felt a thrum of familiarity when she looked at it, a shock like coming around a bend in the river to see a person you knew. Reaching out a hand, Carin touched the stone with careful fingers.

The hum of magic filled her space, her body and the air around it. As her hand lay against it, the hum grew stronger, louder, brighter until Carin felt her skin begin to itch and she jerked her arm back. Even in a bog, she didn't want to accidentally set something ablaze.

Sart tied Tahin to a vine-covered tree and came to join Carin by the stone.

"This is one of them, then?"

Carin nodded, as sure of this as she had ever been of anything. She traced her hands over the face of the stone, and they found deep grooves in the surface, half obscured by slimy moss. Looking around, Carin saw some coarse grasses growing in an uneven plume not far away. She plucked a double handful and began to use them to scrub at the stone face, wiping away the slick green layer and exposing bits of grey underneath, discolored from their long-worn slime.

"Runes," Sart said.

Carin's first finger traced a horizontal groove across the center of the stone. Cut deep, it had endured for hundreds and hundreds of cycles. From it, three lines cut downward, long on either end, shorter in the middle. "*Avarn,*" she said. To revive. *Avarn* also meant to water, and the rune itself was a symbol of rain falling from a cloud.

She looked up to see hunger in Sart's eyes and something else she couldn't quite describe.

"Avarn," said Sart. "This spell your ancestors wove. You said it controlled five things. Water was one of them."

Carin nodded, tracing the rune again. Her flesh seemed to yearn for the stone, to seek something within that it had lost, perhaps. She tried to funnel the humming like Sart had taught her, to spindle it inside her.

As a child, Carin had liked watching Novah ve Haveranth spin bavel into thread, watching her feet work at ingenious pedals and turn a rapidly spinning wheel that took clouds of fluffy bavel and made it into the finest plied thread in the Hearthland.

Trying to spin the hum that buzzed at her bones and skin felt like her feet kept falling off the pedals and the wheel locked up.

She thought of what Culy had said, that anything that happened after the breaking of the stone would be laid upon her shoulders. Looking at Sart, she wondered how much of the woman's camaraderie was true and how much would turn to smoke as soon as something began to go wrong. She liked the short-haired young woman, but Carin was not sure if trust was a value she could afford any longer. The memory of the ialtag came to her mind. Carin missed the easy understanding of their communication, how they were able to impart whatever it was they thought or felt into a single touch. No ambiguity. No confusion. Just an open channel of thought.

"We should try and break it if that's still your plan," Sart said.

Carin jerked her fingers away from the stone as if they had encountered something sharp.

"I need to think," said Carin.

"Forget what Culy said." Sart bent to touch the stone herself, dark eyes shining with hope. She straightened a moment later, digging some green moss from beneath her fingernail. "If you think this will help restore whatever has been lost, it is a chance worth taking."

Carin thought she agreed, but after moons upon moons of trekking across the world, weariness wore her like a cloak. She considered what Sart had said as they rode away from Lahglys on Tahin's back. That there were colors here, that people found a way to survive. Carin could do the same, could adapt. Her body had changed in the past nearly twelve moons. Whatever comfort had clung to her bones before the Journeying had long since gone. Her stomach was flat and rippled with muscle, her breasts smaller but tighter. She had already reshaped herself to fit this new land; surely she could continue to do the same.

For the first time since crossing the mountains, Carin wasn't sure what she had in her to risk.

THE NIGHT of Reflection came to Haveranth.

One cycle past, Lyari had been preparing for the feast with Ryd and Carin and Jenin. Laughing and pelting one another with bits of yam, they had nearly dropped an entire pot of conu and cave chili soup on the village hearth-fire, which would have doused the flames they were sworn for the cycle to tend.

After a moment of silent terror and shame, they had righted the pot, restoked the fire, and clapped one another on the backs before realizing half the village had seen them.

Now Lyari was alone.

Sort of. Jenin stood not far away, seeming to watch as villagers brought their bronze bowls to the hearth-home, arranging them around the fire's ledge. They also brought with them a torch from their own hearths, waiting until Clar built up long sticks of wood in the smoldering pit and until all the village roundhomes were represented. Lyari walked past Jenin with her own torch, lit from her own fire. She could scarcely remember getting there; the preparation of the day had gone by in a blur and left Lyari feeling as though the day had gone through her instead of the other way round.

How many Nights of Reflection had she seen? Eighteen? None had been quite like this one.

The darkest night had fallen like snow from a tree branch, and Lyari nodded at villagers as they approached the hearth-home with their torches, each of them standing in front of their small pool.

Lyari looked into hers, almost able to sense Jenin's censure. The bronze bowls of still water were supposed to be a mirror into the cycle's past. Families placed into them small objects that would reflect the time they had seen. Last winter, Jenin had sneaked a tiny soapstone fish into Lyari's family bowl, and she had slipped a tiger tooth into hys.

This cycle, Lyari's held lies. A stone with a feather etched on it, for Merin. Two interlocked rings of brass to symbolize her soothsayer cuffs. And the fish for Jenin, to remember hyr.

The latter was the only truth in her pool, and as she gazed down into it, the flickering fire from her torch illuminating her reflection, Lyari felt a flash of anger that she could have nothing in the bowl for Carin or Ryd. A stout wind blew through the village hearth-home, bringing with it the sharp mist of snow. Torches guttered in the wind but did not blow out.

As soothsayer, it was Lyari's duty to signal to the villagers when to lower their torches into the hearth-home's pit to light the fire that would burn all through the cycle. She opened her mouth to do so, but a voice cut through the brittle air.

"May the warmth of our village hearth be carried into our homes," Old Wend intoned from across the circle.

Lyari's mouth fell open. A wash of confusion went through the villagers, those who held torches and those who encircled them alike. Slowly they began to lower their torches into the pit.

Body moving jerkily, Lyari let her torch dip downward, trying to keep her breathing steady and her hand from trembling. Shame filled her, and Tamat and Antin on either side of her would not meet her gaze. Across the circle, Dyava did. Lyari met his indignant eyes for one long moment before looking away.

She made herself stare into the hearth of her village, watched the fire from the torches light the sticks Clar had so carefully arranged. When the flames roared high, they dropped their torches into the fire.

Lyari didn't give Wend a chance to cut her off this time. "For all in need of warmth," she said, and to her surprise, her voice boomed out through the circle of villagers.

"For all in need of warmth!" The village cried out in return, and Lyari felt a flash of triumph, as much for the chagrin on Wend's face as for their response to her. She heard Dyava's voice raised even higher than those around him, and out of the corner of her eye, Lyari saw that his eyes narrowed at Old Wend as he said it.

With that, the villagers began to disperse, all staying under the roof of the pavilion. For the day, they had covered the outside walls with large sheets of canvas to keep in the warmth of the fire and shelter themselves from the wind.

Lyari moved with the rest of the villagers, making a circuit of the hearth itself and peering into the pools left by others. She saw everything and nothing, and halfway around the hearth, Jenin fell into step beside her.

"You will need to do something about him," Jenin said.

Lyari's head snapped to the side, and she pretended to be looking for someone to cover the sudden movement. She covered her mouth with her arm, feigning a yawn. "Dyava? Or Wend. Do you think I should—"

"No!" Jenin stopped her before she could finish the thought, and Lyari paused by a villager's pool—Malcam's by the look of the tiny red-stone apple that lay at its bottom. Malcam was Ryd's mother. Anger began to lick at her again, but Jenin went on. "They do not trust that you can lead the village, and they know, perhaps better than you, that it is not just this village you are to lead."

"What would you have me do?" Lyari spoke as softly as she could to avoid notice, but still a child of twelve harvests looked at her sideways. Lyari waved hyr off.

"Prove yourself to them. Take charge. Do not let Wend continue to undermine you."

Lyari passed Tamat, who touched two fingers to her lips. Lyari returned the gesture, nodding her head.

Once Tamat moved on, Lyari spared Jenin a questioning look. Sy returned it with an encouraging smile.

"Call the cycle," Jenin said.

Calling the cycle was the soothsayer's duty, as was signaling the lowering of torches and the declaration of the village hearth-home. Lyari looked into the next pool she came to, and seeing a serpent at its bottom, stopped and raised the bronze bowl above her head.

"Cycle of Serpentine!" She called across the pavilion.

She happened to have Varsu in her gaze as she said it, and Lyari caught a nod of approval from him.

"Today is the Third Bud of Reflection, Cycle of Serpentine!" Lyari's voice rang above the rustle of villagers. The previous cycle had been named for the climber fish. "Today we leave the Cycle of Climber and enter the Cycle of Serpentine. May we learn from the serpent that dwells under cool rocks and guards its home against intruders."

Lyari caught Wend's gaze as she said it, and he looked at her as if he had bitten into an unripe iceberry.

The villagers murmured their approval, and for a time, Lyari wove in and out among them. Jenin vanished between two children, there one moment and gone the next, and Lyari allowed herself to be caught up by her people. The older children, who had reached fifteen harvests and declared their appellation at Harvest Harmonix, laid out the feast in the pavilion.

Lyari imagined what it would look like from the outside, the pavilion's canvas glowing with the warmth of the hearth fire within, scents of curried goat and halka and saiga and fish stewed in conu broth filling the air. She filled a wooden platter with potted persimmon and dates, cajit candied with sugar-tree syrup and tender pieces of mutton and venison. For as much as the night was meant to be one of gaiety and fellowship, the air beneath the pavilion's roof remained uneven and threaded with sadness. Four more should have been there to celebrate with their village, and the return to earth for Falyr and Reylu still felt fresh in the minds of the village.

It was unfair that Falyr and Reylu earned this place of solemnity when Carin and Ryd were no longer remembered.

It had chilled Lyari when she had stumbled again across the spell that erased the Nameless. Such a thing could only be done with the participation of those whose memories were to be altered, and it was a clever thing, using the naming ritual at High Lights to complete it. As Merin had spurred the town to repeat the word *Nameless* over and over, so had the villagers given up their memories of the exiled. They would remember eventually that there had been Nameless one cycle, but if pressed, could not tell anyone which cycle it had been. Only that knowledge that someone had become Nameless, with no memory of who the Nameless had been.

Which left Merin free to have the Nameless killed.

Lyari no longer felt hungry. She tried to swallow a last bite of persimmon and failed.

She instead positioned herself near the hearth, where anyone could come and speak to her. For a long while, no one did, though once her parents walked by her and smiled proudly at her before moving away. She missed them. She knew why they kept their distance—they would for some time to show that she stood on her own feet—but in that moment she wanted nothing more than to be in the comfort of their arms.

For a time, Lyari thought she would be left to sit alone, and she wished Jenin would return so at least she could have some company. Instead, she sat in solitude, surrounded by the folk she had grown up with.

Tilim surprised her by approaching, his plate full of all meat and no fruit or vegetables to be seen. At his side was Lyris, a man Lyari did not know well as he kept mostly to himself and tended a beautiful garden of citrus. Lyari wondered how his crops would do this cycle with the heavy snow. Lyris took Tilim's hand, then beckoned at someone behind him. Anam, a hunter, stepped forward, shyness writ across her face if not in her stature. She stood taller than Lyris and nearly as tall as Tilim.

"Soothsayer," Tilim said. "We wish to bring a child into the village."

Lyari had almost forgotten this ritual, and she felt her face grow warm. She thought of the strand of pearls that she now kept on her side table next to her bed, and of the white pearl at the end. The Night of Reflection marked the return of the sun and the light that would reveal the new cycle. It also marked the early turns of the sowing season for those who wished to have children.

Tilim held Lyris's hand high, and villagers around the pavilion took note. In previous cycles, the men may have drawn little attention, but this one had brought more pain and hardship than the village had expected, and at the sight of their hands raised together to declare to all of Haveranth their desire to have a child, a low murmur of excitement buzzed into being.

"Anam has agreed to bear our child," Lyris said, reaching out to take Anam's hand and drawing her to stand beside him and his bond-mate.

Lyari remembered what she had read. "Anam, do you give your body over to the bearing of a new life for this pair?"

Anam ducked her head and smiled. "I want no children of my own, but I desire to help my friends."

"Haveranth, witness. Tilim and Lyris declare to you that they wish to grow our village with Anam's help." Lyari walked toward them, uncertain of what she was to do next. She took Anam's hand and led her to stand between Tilim and Lyris, then rejoined their hands. "For the coming moons, you will be one until a child is conceived."

Someone pressed a glass of iceberry wine into Lyari's hand, and she took a step backward to hold it to her lips with both hands.

"For your child I wish life," she said simply.

The village cheered, but Lyari heard them only faintly, wondering whether these three would prove Harag wrong or if it would bring only more signs of death.

S ART COULDN'T stop thinking of the spring.

Seeing the rune *avarn* on the stone only strengthened her resolve. Culy might have been willing to take a studious and cautious view on Carin's desire to break the stones, but Culy had earned hys place in the world and was a walking memorial of the Tuanye, one of the few people born hyrsin in body as well as mind. As such, Sart knew Culy walked in their world but also through it. Man and woman and both and neither. Sun and moons. Life and death. Whatever hys people needed hyr to be, so Culy became and was willing to do so. Sart had known hyr long enough to know that sy would continue in that way, whatever came hys way. No one had made hyr into what sy was; Culy had done that hyrself.

Sart saw things a bit more prosaically.

She had to depend on her wits and her muscles and her magic. While Culy had all of those things, sy had the added reverence of hys nature, and that was something Sart would never have.

Carin set up their camp not far from the stone, working quietly with a grey cast to her face. Every so often, she stole a glance at the stone or at Sart as if trying to puzzle out how the two fit together.

The wind that blew over the land from the north felt dry to Sart's skin. Everything felt dry; in her life the one constant was that there was never enough water. Even in Crevasses in winter, though the snow allowed for waterfeasts and the people were able to relax a bit after the hard toil of the rest of the cycle, there was never truly enough. Perhaps the stone could change that.

It didn't take someone very schooled in magic to sense the power of the thing, and Sart was far from ignorant. She had watched Carin's fingers dance across it and felt the magic swirl into the other woman like she was calling it home. What would happen when that power broke?

Sart thought of the spring she had found and wondered what it might be like if such wealth were to be found everywhere from Crevasses to Taigers. What if breaking the stone made springs appear across the land? The memory of the lush blue grasses and fiery orange sugar-tree leaves intruded into her mind. For all she had told Carin that there were colors to be found here, Sart admitted in the recesses of her own mind that she had never seen colors such as those.

They ate a brief meal of dried fyajir and some carrots that had long since gone limp.

"We'll break it," Carin said suddenly.

"What?" Sart hadn't expected Carin to make up her mind as they ate, and she admired that the other woman had managed to surprise her.

"Break it." Carin's voice sounded hoarse, and she bit off a length of carrot, chewed, and swallowed.

They waited until first light, sleeping fitfully in the humid night.

Sart woke feeling clammy and nervous, but excitement threaded through both of the less pleasant feelings.

When they were finally standing in front of the stone, Carin reached out to touch it once more. "I don't know how to do it."

Sart laid her own hand on the stone next to Carin's. "I think I do, but if you would rather be the one to start this, I think you've earned it."

Her proclamation had a queer effect on Carin, who frowned and slowly removed her hand from the face of the stone. "If it's all the same to you, you do it."

Sart felt a rush of buoyant giddiness. Carin took two steps back from the stone, looking over her shoulder at Tahin. The ihstal paid little attention to either women or the stone, grazing on coarse grass and slurping stagnant water from a puddle not far away.

Putting both hands on the stone, Sart closed her eyes.

The hum of magic surrounded her before she'd drawn a single breath. Everything else seemed to dim, even the morning light through her closed eyelids seemed to disappear into the folds of darkness. After a moment, Sart could feel neither the ground beneath her feet nor the breeze against her hair. She felt only the touch of the stone on her hands and mind, heard the whispers of its magic swirl through and around her. For a moment, she marveled at it, at the expanse of it. It seemed to her that she could sense the other stones through this one, far away and latent, but waking as the hum of magic rose around her and the stone before her.

Sart felt as though the stone had accepted her, taken her into itself. She floated in that quiet darkness, listening to its song. Though it was one tone that buzzed through her, a song was what it was. Its melody was the patter of rain and the soft kiss of falling snow. Its rhythm was the thunder and strikes of lightning that cast themselves down from the sky. It rose and fell around her, and yet somehow it stayed constant. Hungry.

Sart almost hated that she had to bring it to an end.

The stone was water, and wasn't. Its rune meant revive, and that was the nature of water, to do exactly that. But water was also powerful and destructive. Sart had sat on the cliffs of East Sands and watched the waves batter their feet. She had seen the swells rise up and overtake the gulls and black emerald birds that made their homes near the sea. And of the canyons and folds of Crevasses, Culy had told her that they were carved out long ago with nothing but the force of water flowing through them, wearing them down.

Sart pulled that force through her, drawing on the stone itself to provide the power for its own destruction. She felt it rise within her like a tide, spilling out in ripples over the ground she could not feel beneath her feet and the stone in front of her she communed with through her hands. She drew upon that water and pictured it rupturing the stone from the center, snapping the stone in two with a screech and a rush of movement.

The magic rose around her until Sart felt as though she stood in a waterspout, that if she were to reach out her arms to either side that they would touch mist, mist swirling so quickly that it would burn like sand. It rose and it rose and it rose, and Sart felt it pull her upward like a wave. She rode it, carried by its power and force.

It was going to break. She felt the tension in the stone, felt the force within it sending fissures throughout like cracks in glass. It was going to break.

Something wrenched inside of her.

The magic that surrounded her crashed over her head and downed her, and Sart flew backward from the stone, her hands dripping water and her body shaking and convulsing. She felt as though she had taken the sea into her lungs.

Dimly, she felt Carin's hands on her shoulders, pulling her up. She heard the other girl calling her name and Tahin's anxious whistle.

Sart couldn't move. Her limbs felt waterlogged and heavy.

Then she was moving, but she wasn't doing it. She felt herself dragged and deposited atop something warm. Tahin. Stomach down, the pressure of the beast against her made her heave, and Sart threw up, seawater gushing from her belly.

Someone yelled in the distance. A deep voice. Not Carin. Sart tried to look up, but her head swam with the current and she could not move it.

She heaved again, more seawater flowing out of her onto the ground.

She felt Carin's body to her side, the other woman's knees digging into her hip and shoulder. Something heavy landed on her back.

Tahin moved beneath her, lurching to her feet and starting to run. The movement made Sart's stomach convulse again. She opened her eyes once, just in time to see a band of rovers descending on their tent. One turned her way, and in the light, Sart caught a glimpse of a white painted rune on hys shoulder.

"Did it break?" Sart spat the words out, her mouth bitter and full of salt.

Tahin ran across the ground, padded hooves quiet but her gait far from gentle.

Carin leaned forward, pressing against Sart to secure her. "No," she said. "We failed."

Tahin leaped over something, and Sart's belly came down hard on the ihstal's back, the weight on her own adding to the impact.

Sart watched the ground speed by her, and then it blurred into nothing.

THIS TIME, the game was real.

Ras followed the trail, Ham at his side, excitement pulsing in his chest. The small round pellets of dung were fresh enough not to have frozen, and their size and quantity told him that they had found a whole herd. Saiga.

Not as large as halka, and it would take more than one or two of the beasts to provide any real sustenance for the people in the waymake, but a whole herd of saiga could be as many as thirty beasts.

Ham's step was light upon the ground, and Darim—Ras had learned that indeed her name was Darim—had clasped Ras's shoulder at the first sign of the animals.

The clouds hung low in the sky, thick and heavy like the last vestiges of sleep when you haven't had enough. The snow had stopped, though the air still kept its cold, and the tracks of the saiga were easy to follow.

Ras's short bow, newly restrung, felt strange in his grasp. He had practiced with it outside the waymake to make sure the string was functional, but it still felt too tight and odd in his hands.

The Northlanders moved almost silently through the hills, and Ras had to admit that they impressed him with their skills. He found himself emulating Darim. She moved like a fish moved in the water, flowing from one place to another.

Slowly, the sun moved a handspan across the sky, and Ras was so concentrated on moving in silence that he almost didn't notice when Ham raised one hand in a fist, signaling them to stop. A rustle in the bushes ahead drew his attention.

There it was. A fair distance away, visible only because its brown hide stood out against the snow. A saiga, its tube-like nose snuffling at the underside of a snow-covered bush as it tried to root out something to eat. Ras looked farther, and there were more, dotting the landscape. Walking food.

Without being told, the hunters from Alarbahis spread out in a line, and they began to advance on the beasts, each holding arrows in their draw hands with one nocked and ready.

Ras counted as he walked forward. Five. Eleven. Seventeen beasts scattered throughout the low trees of the foothills. Beyond them, the mountains rose stark and white, disappearing into a low bank of clouds. He thanked the wind for blowing toward him and not away, concealing the hunters just a bit longer than they would be if upwind of the animals.

Out of the corner of his eye, he saw Darim raise her bow. As if made of one mind, the group drew and fired. Ras lagged only slightly behind, and by the second arrow loosed, he shot in time with the rest. Quickly, one arrow after another, drawn and fired in one fluid motion that sent up a flurry of snow and cries from the saiga. Red splashed the snow, and Ras felt hot pride swell his chest, followed by gratitude that this time the blood against the ground's white backdrop was not from people but beasts.

With a whoop, the hunters ran forward. Some of the saiga had been felled with one shot, and those that hadn't quickly took deathblows from arrow or belt knife, ending their pain with a quick motion.

The rest of the herd scattered southward into the hills, but those they left behind lay dead in the snow, and Ras felt himself triumphant.

He counted the animals as he came to his first kill—he could tell it was his by the arrow through the animal's skull—and the excitement that rose in him felt like he had just seen his fifteenth harvest and had his first successful hunt. Eight saiga lay dead. With six hunters, it would be a task to carry them all back to Alarbahis. Two of the Northlanders whose names Ras still did not know set about cutting a low branch from a nearby tree. One of them began carving notches into each end of it, deep grooves that would hold a length of rope in place so they could string the beasts between them. The other hunter began butchering two of the beasts, and Ras turned to his own.

Ras noticed that the other Northlanders reserved the blood of the saiga in treated belly bags. He had no such tool, and he felt as though he had done something wrong when he began to drain the animal of its blood, watching the red flow splash into the snow as he held the beast upside down. Ham gave him a curious look, but said nothing.

Within another handspan of the sun, they were on their way back to Alarbahis. Two pairs of hunters walked with three saiga each slung between them on bound branches, the long poles resting against their shoulders. As they marched back, Ras would occasionally hear a brief grunted exclamation, punctuated by a word he didn't understand. After the second time, he looked back to see the hunters hefting the pole from one shoulder to the other.

They arrived back in the waymake to the excited buzz of the other inhabitants. Eight saiga would mean food for several days for all who lived there, and a place was cleared of snow near Culy's hut for the hunters to butcher the animals.

It was there Ras learned that a portion of each beast went into a cache, to be smoked and laid aside for days in which there was no game to be had. Small rations would be enough to sustain people when food was scarce, and though Ras at first balked at the idea of sharing his kill, he soon realized that the others did it without thought or resentment.

The language still eluded him, and Ras wished Carin would return. Ryd never seemed to want to talk with him, and indeed for the past days Ryd had been sequestered with Culy, with whom he seemed to have no trouble communicating. Ras never thought he would thirst for conversation the way he thirsted for water. He sat that night with the Northlanders around a fire that reminded him somewhat of the village hearth-home in Cantoranth. The people gathered and ate of the saiga, sharing stories Ras could not follow in word but still managed to enjoy by the rise and fall of the voices and the laughter that accompanied them.

He felt himself a stranger still, but as he watched the Northlanders around him smiling and joking with one another, he thought that perhaps he could come to accept this place if it would accept him in return. Grudgingly, he admired the strength of these folk, to eke out their lives where everything from a bite of meat to the water to wash it down was hard won.

The next morning he woke to the sound of a scream.

Ryd jerked awake on the opposite pallet in their hut, and met Ras's eyes over the cold fire pit.

"What was that?" Ryd asked.

"I don't know." Ras hurried to his feet, dressing as fast as he could manage. He belted on his quiver and slung his bow over his shoulder, just in case, and noticed Ryd loosening his belt knife in its sheath.

They left the hut together, and from across the waymake, a keening sound rose through the air. It was soon joined by another voice, then a third.

Their walk became a run.

Near the fire, where last night Ras had sat with the Northlanders and listened to them speak and laugh and sing, a pool of vomit trickled over the snow. In it was flecks of clotted blood.

Beyond the puddle, three Northlanders backed away from a man on his knees. He clawed at the snow, spitting red into the white.

Another scream rose from behind them, and someone bellowed Culy's name.

"What's happening?" Ras kept close to Ryd, his hands ready at his bow. What if they were somehow blamed for whatever was going on? Would the Northlanders come at them? He looked at Ryd as if to say, *Be ready to run,* but no one seemed to be paying any heed to their presence at all.

Near the fire, the Northlanders began to gather, speaking in low murmurs.

"Can you understand them?" Ras asked. Dread filled him, pulling like the force of a tide.

Ryd shook his head.

Culy appeared, running to the side of the fallen Northlander, who began to vomit again. Ras backed up, turning to look urgently at Ryd.

"This could be bad for us," he said.

Ryd looked at him, confused. "I think it's worse for him."

"We are strangers here. Do you truly think they will trust that we had nothing to do with this?"

"We didn't."

Ras wanted to curse at the young man's foolishness. "We know that. They do not."

Ryd still looked uncomprehending, then looked past Ras and pointed to Ham. "Ask him what is going on."

Ham stood back from the crowd, and he came over when Ras beckoned to him. He only hoped he could manage to communicate.

"What is happening?" Ras asked slowly. He hated the fear that accompanied the question, the anxiety that descended upon him when Ham's eyes met his and the other man opened his mouth.

But the words to come out of it made sense, and Ras almost rejoiced at the relief of it until his mind processed what was said.

"The saiga were diseased."

Ryd understood before Ras did. "The meat caused this?"

Ras could not take his eyes off the pool of vomit and thought of the way he had felt in Suonlys when the water had turned his insides to pain and bile. He had thought he would die. "They will recover, no?"

Ham met Ras's gaze with confusion drawing his eyebrows together. "They have the gut-rot."

Was that not what Ras had had? He looked at Ryd, who seemed to find the statement as foreign as he did. Movement caught his eye, and he turned to see several Northlanders piling saiga meet onto the fire with fresh wood.

"No! What are they doing?" They were taking the meat. All of it. The reserves, the cuts that had been put aside for today, all of it. Ras had left his saiga with the others, and panic rose in him at the sight. Each of the villagers handling the meat wore grim expressions and cloths over their faces.

Ham was watching Ras as if he were the real oddity. "You do not understand. The gut-rot will kill them."

"Kill them?" Ryd asked. "But..."

Ras thought the same as Ryd, that they had had it and lived, but then Ham went on.

The words were still strange in Ras's ears, and he struggled to understand as Ham spoke. It took Ham repeating what he said three times for the meaning to sink in.

"It comes from the meat. We do not know why it doesn't kill the animal, and this is the first I have seen of it in several cycles. Likely it was only one animal." Ham let out a long breath as someone's voice raised in a wail across the waymake. "There is sometimes a way to tell, to see green mucus on the saiga's eyes and nose, but we saw nothing of it on these. We are fortunate this disease does not pass from person to person. It only comes from eating the infected animal."

Culy pulled hys belt knife from its sheath and reached down to touch the top of the vomiting man's head. From where he stood, Ras saw Culy's mouth move, but had no way of knowing what sy said.

The knife came down, plunging into the man's neck.

Ryd yelped and jumped forward as if to run to his aid, but Ham pushed a hand back against Ryd's chest.

"You cannot help him. He will die. This is mercy."

Mercy.

The waymake filled with the sounds of grief and the smell of burning meat.

R YD FELT as though someone had turned his head around and left him to stumble through the waymake without being able to see. That was what this place was like for him. Each time he thought he saw where he was going, his feet seemed to take him in another direction entirely.

This place frightened him, and he didn't want to admit it. In the turns that followed the deaths of the five Northlanders from gut-rot, Ryd tried to learn from Culy all he could about this thing called disease.

When first he had learned about it, he thought it was all the same, that if you got disease, it was one thing and you could live through it. But as he spoke with Culy and the other Northlanders, their speech slowly becoming easier for him to understand, he learned that disease was not simply one thing at all, but a word like a roof that housed many others beneath it. Gut-rot. Wasting sickness. The water-lung. Flesh-rot. Bulber bloat. Those were the ones that could kill a person and would more often than not. Gut-rot was a near-instant death sentence. Flesh-rot could be treated with the right herbs, but finding those herbs was not easy, as they grew only in a few places in Boggers. Whispers stole around Alarbahis sometimes, filled with apprehension about what Wyt's presence in Boggers meant for many things. People who kept to Boggers and Sands would trade those herbs—medicinal herbs, Culy called them—in exchange for rare sugar-tree syrup from Crevasses or other tree resins that could not be found in the wetlands.

With Wyt and her people settled in or around Boggers, the folk in Alarbahis grew more and more anxious as winter went on, for when spring came, many would have to change their plans of where they would go next. Even the word *settled* seemed to unnerve the Northlanders, who were used to traveling across much of the land throughout the turning of the seasons. Many often spent spring in Boggers and Sands. Wyt frightened them.

Ryd's nervousness stemmed from this fact that if the native folk of the Northlands were upset, how much more should he be as a stranger?

Each morning when he rose, he tried to remember the things Culy told him about disease and illness. He had learned that the horrible pain and vomiting and diarrhea he had experienced with his friends in Suonlys was due to the water. Why, he did not understand, but Culy told him with all seriousness that it was not wholly uncommon to struggle to drink water in a new area, though the violence of their illness was more extreme. Culy said the gut could grow used to new water, given time, and indeed on that count Ryd knew sy was right.

There was so much to learn that Ryd felt as though his world could not fit any more information, and he tried to navigate the Northlander people as well as he could. The deaths, for instance. Death in itself was rare in Haveranth, but when someone did die, either through accident or age, the village would set fire to their roundhome, burning away all that remained to return them to the earth and commit them to memory.

When Ryd said so to Culy, the hyrsin had stared at him. It was one of the first times Ryd managed to well and truly surprise hyr. Under the force of that grey stare, Ryd thought about what he had said and how it must sound to Northlanders, that in the Hearthland they would put an entire dwelling to fire. Burning food and tools and clothing and...Ryd had himself reeled under that epiphany, and he could tell Culy saw it.

Waste. That was the word. It was a word that Ryd had learned since coming to the Northlands, and one treated as a curse by the people. To waste was wrong.

He found, in those days, that he and his friends had been fools. In Suonlys, they had traded their snowshoes for a few skins of water. Culy told him bluntly—though also with a touch of wry humor—that they had paid outrageously for the water. One pair of the snowshoes should have supplied them with water and several other additional tools for the whole of a moon. For three, they could have bought medicine, fresh fruit were it available, meltwater instead of potted.

Ryd consoled himself with the reminder that the people of Suonlys had cared for them for two turns while they recovered. The consolation lasted about as long as it took to realize just how quickly the Northlanders in Suonlys could have left them instead to die.

Too much to learn.

One day, Ryd asked Culy why there were no children in Alarbahis except for a single babe.

"Most of them live in Boggers or Salters," Culy told him. "In Salters, the sandsmiths have contraptions that catch water from the air and funnel it into bottles."

Ryd tried to imagine that. "Water from the air?"

"Have you never walked through the mountains when there are low clouds? Have you never seen fog? Those things make the air wet, and in Salters the air is often wet."

Ryd had never thought of it that way, but then in Haveranth their water came from clean, pure wells and springs. He didn't say so, though.

Later that day, Ryd saw Lyah's scroll on a low table in Culy's hut and pointed to it. "May I look at that?"

Culy nodded, and Ryd took it in his hands. While they traveled over the mountains, he had had few chances to look at it, and though much of it was unintelligible to him—Ryd knew nothing of magic—he noticed a diagram of the hearthstones used in the spell. It looked like the plans for a roundhome, he thought, tracing his finger from stone to stone on the parchment. He missed roundhomes, with their central hearths that fun-neled all of the smoke out through the chimney. Here, the roofs of the huts still had chimneys that drew smoke upward, but not enough, and the huts were always smoky.

He missed doors.

"When do you suppose Carin and Sart will return?" Ryd asked, replacing the scroll on the table.

"I cannot say," Culy said, and Ryd understood that to mean sy was unsure whether *when* should have been omitted from Ryd's question.

Ryd massaged his side, where a pain had poked at him. He had been sitting hunched over too long.

He blew his nose on a woolen cloth. It always seemed to drip these days, and at first he had been alarmed at all the talk of disease. Water-lung, he had been told, often began with a dripping nose. Culy had taken one look at him, peering closely, before pronouncing him safe and telling him it was likely something in the air that didn't agree with his nose.

Culy said things like that often, about air and water and the two containing things, which Ryd didn't quite understand.

Outside the hut, someone called Culy's name. Culy set down the scroll sy had been reading and left the dwelling, Ryd following out of curi-osity. The voice called out again, with more urgency.

By now, Ryd could understand most of what the Northlanders said, and his own speech patterns had begun to emulate them in tone and pro-nunciation, though he saw that Ras still struggled. Ras spent most of his days hunting with Ham, and after the deaths of the folk who had gotten gut-rot, Ryd had noticed an increased wariness in Ras. For all the time he spent with Ham and Darim, it seemed they communicated mostly with-out words, learning each other through the time they spent hunting.

The person who had called out to Culy was a woman. She wore two short swords belted at her side, and her hair was plaited over one shoul-der like a long black tail. It reminded Ryd of Lyah, and he looked invol-untarily to the south.

She spoke in a low voice to Culy, pointing to the west. As Ryd moved closer to her, he noticed a smear of blood on her hand, and saw that her sleeve bore a wide gash where it looked like an arrow had nearly caught her in the shoulder and only barely missed.

An ihstal was tethered not far away, and its coat was so lathered that Ryd thought this woman must have almost run him to death on the way into Alarbahis. It took a lot to tire an ihstal, and the animal swayed on his feet, struggling to bend to sip water from a bowl on the ground. His legs wobbled, and when the ihstal pawed at the ground with a padded cloven hoof, Ryd could see the hoof shaking.

"They attacked a caravan," the woman said to Culy. "There were at least twenty of them. Twenty, Culy. Twenty rovers. I've ridden for three days to reach you in time."

"What was the caravan bringing? Do you know?" Culy glanced over hys shoulder at Ryd, opening hys mouth, but then seemed to change hys mind and instead turned back to the woman.

"Blackroot and heartfoil. Whole bundles of them, along with glass-ware from Salters and black sand from north Sands."

Culy's face changed, and hys eyes grew as dark as thunderheads. When sy spoke, hys voice came out deeper, and hys breaths were slow and steady as sy held hys arms carefully at hys side. "Twenty rovers, you said. Were they wearing any sort of marking?"

The woman nodded, and Culy struck hys leg with one fist.

"Wyt," Culy said.

Hys hair was clubbed back from hys face, trailing down hys back and exposing the sides of hys neck. From where Ryd stood, he could see a flush of red appearing on the side of Culy's throat.

"And the caravan drivers? Did you see what happened to them?"

The woman shook her head. "I was too far back, but I heard yelling as I rode away. If I had to guess..."

Culy reached out and clasped the woman's shoulder. "You did well. Thank you for watching the Lahi'alar for me."

Ryd was not sure what Culy meant by Lahi'alar. The words by them-selves made sense, but he couldn't understand them together. Water web? Water way?

The woman nodded. "What will you do?"

"It's time I show Wyt that actions are not without consequences," said Culy.

As mild as hys words were, Ryd did not want to be the one on the other side of them.

TAHIN SEEMED to have a magic of her own. Carin had pushed the ihstal at a grueling pace for days, even after she outpaced Wyt's rovers. Just after Sart had lost consciousness, one of the rovers had almost hit Tahin with an arrow. Had hit, really, but only grazed. The ihstal didn't even seem to notice, and Carin didn't see the blood until after she stopped briefly for a rest when the sun had finally crested the horizon and she felt safe enough to pause. She watered Tahin from her skin and stroked the animal's long neck, murmuring a thank you in her ear. Tahin whistled in response, and Carin felt a pang spread through her chest at the thought of what could have happened had Tahin not been there.

The ihstal had very truly saved her life—and Sart's.

Sart still had not woken up. A few times a day, Carin tilted her head back and poured water down her throat, checking the other woman's breathing and pulse to make sure she was still alive. She was, though Carin had never seen anyone stay unconscious this long. Then again, the only person she'd ever truly seen unconscious was Jenin when sy fell from the loft in hys family's roundhome and knocked hys head on the thankfully rounded edge of a low bench. Sy'd only been out for a few minutes, but Sart had been out for days.

Carin didn't know what to do.

She had fled on Tahin without direction, only aiming the ihstal away from the rovers at her back and chasing a trail she couldn't be sure led anywhere good.

On the third day, once it became mostly clear that she hadn't been followed that far, Carin had turned southward. At least that much she knew, and if she skirted the foothills of the mountains, eventually she knew she could find Suonlys and follow the path she had taken once before to Alarbahis.

She tried not to think of how Sart's attempt to break the stone had failed.

At first, when Sart had both hands upon the stone, Carin had felt it, the magic that rose within the stone and melded with that in Sart. She had been sure it would work, feeling the magic that bound the stone become brittle and start to crack. But something had gone wrong, and what, Carin could not say.

Whatever it was had snapped back on Sart and left her nearly dead and vomiting up saltwater. It was that which Carin found most terrifying, with Tahin carrying them away from the rovers at full tilt. Once she was out of the range of the rover arrows—and they were out of hers after two had fallen to her halm bow—Sart had continued to heave saltwater onto the ground. Carin wasn't sure how she knew so clearly that it was seawater coming from the other woman's belly. Maybe it was the scent of the sea she remembered from that long past visit to Bemin's Fan or the humming magic around her that tasted it and knew, but Carin felt fear, bright and sharp and cold, and she almost collapsed over Sart's back when the woman finally stopped retching.

That night, she dared make a fire for the first time, digging it into the ground and keeping it as small as she could. Carin managed to catch a ground squirrel. She stewed it in a small pot and let the broth cool, then poured that down Sart's throat.

She hoped for some kind of response from the woman, but instead nothing came but the quiet rise and fall of her stomach with her breath.

Having to ride with Sart slung over Tahin's back and her rucksack atop her own was worrying to Carin, so she took some time to work her knuckles into Sart's back along her spine, massaging the muscles as best she could without disrobing her in the cool night air. Even though Sart hadn't vomited in some time, before Carin curled up to sleep, she made sure to position Sart on her side in case she heaved in her sleep. That,

Carin knew to do from home, for sometimes the villagers of Haveranth drank too much iceberry wine or mead and got drunk enough to sick up. If they drank to the point of passing out, Merin or another older villager would make sure to keep them on their side in case their stomachs emptied in sleep so they would not choke.

As she tried to lull herself into dozing off, Carin tried to remember Lyah's scroll about the spell. She wished she had thought of making a copy of it before giving it to Culy, and she felt foolish for not doing so. Perhaps there was something in there that could explain why Sart had failed. She had seemed so close.

A thought took root in Carin's mind, wriggling in until she could not help but toss and turn on her bedroll. She was thankful there had been no rain or snow since losing the tent to the rovers, but the ground was still damp beneath her bedroll, and she could not ease into sleep. Her mind kept returning to the way she had felt with her hands on the stone, how it had seemed to recognize her, know her for what she was.

Perhaps that was why Sart had failed; it was Carin's ancestors who had made the spell. Maybe only one of their descendants could break it. Or maybe no one could. Maybe the ialtag were wrong.

Not for the first time, she thought of Culy's words to her about the stones, and of what that implied about Sart's current condition.

This was supposed to be Carin's task. Sart's near-death was Carin's fault.

Unable to sleep even when the sky began to lighten, even though her eyes felt as though she had poured dust into them, Carin rose before the sun touched the horizon and went to Sart's side. She gave her water and the rest of the squirrel broth and sat back to eat the remainder of the squirrel meat herself.

She wondered if what had happened with the stone could happen in other ways, listening to the hum around her. Inspired by the idea, she knelt at Sart's side, ignoring the damp that immediately soaked through her breeches, and placed her hands on Sart's forehead.

The hum around her did grow stronger, but only just. Sart did not stir. Carin closed her eyes and listened, unsure of what else to do. She tried to remember the things Sart had said about magic and about how Sart could gather it and spindle it, where Carin simply collected it from her surroundings. Carin thought of the branches of magic Lyah had spoken of, of the five forms of it. *Var, Ryh, Pey, Dyupahsy, Abas.* Life, Will, Force, Potential, Energy. All magic fell through one of those. Carin didn't know which of them came most easily to her, and Sart hadn't tried to help her figure it out.

For the first time, she tried to listen intentionally to the hum, to see if she could detect any changes when she directed her thoughts at different aspects of magic. The grass beneath her knees, *Var.* The desire in her to see Sart open her eyes, *Ryh.* The force that made her limbs feel heavy, *Pey.* The stillness of Tahin and how quickly the ihstal's muscles could go from quiet repose to bursts of action, *Dyupahsy.* And the wind that danced through travel-greased strands of Carin's hair, *Abas.*

She repeated herself over and over, going through each of the branches of magic, listening to the hum.

At first she heard nothing, no change at all.

But after the fourth or fifth repetition, as she returned to *Var* and thought of grass and the dead squirrel that had lost its life to feed hers, Carin felt a stir in the hum, a lower tone, deeper and more resonant and as faint as a vibration felt through a table if someone were to set a heavy plate down at the opposite end.

She listened to the hum, learning it and hearing what it had to say. Carin didn't allow herself to feel triumph, not yet, not when Sart's breathing had yet to change. With her fingertips on Sart's temples, she could feel the slow, steady pulse of her blood. There was no change in that to be felt, either.

As long as Carin sat there, nothing seemed to happen. With closed eyes, she listened to the hum and its languid quiet, wishing it were closer, louder, more immediate.

After some time, she gave up. Her fingers tingled where they had sat against Sart's skin for so long, and Carin busied herself cleaning up the camp, finally clucking at Tahin to lie down so she could pull Sart over the ihstal's back again.

Carin tried not to think of the emptiness she felt with Sart still unconscious, how alone she was in a land where any person she met could be a danger.

Thinking back to where she had started, Carin didn't feel like the near-adult the Journeying was supposed to have made her. At first, shame filled her. All her life she had been told that finding her name would make her grown, that it would start the path and bring her into the village as a full participant. She only had known not what participating in the village really meant. With a shock, Carin realized that her Journeying hadn't been a coming of age at all, but a threat. Join the village and keep the secret or die. Her whole life she had thought the Nameless simply went away, but where had she thought they really went? Now, seeing the Northlanders and how they moved to chase food or water, she understood. The Nameless would not have simply turned and left their homes behind. When winter snows came to the mountains or food was scarce, surely they would have turned home to something familiar. To beg or to steal. None of them ever did.

She knew now why that was.

The Journeying was an illusion. Exile was never an option, only lies or death.

E VEN THOUGH Ras's understanding was not yet perfect, he could not miss the unease that filtered through Alarbahis after news of the caravan's takeover by rovers.

From what he could piece together, rovers seldom worked as one. Like most predators, they sought out the weak or perceived vulnerable along the roads—little more than well-trodden paths, really—of the Northlands. That they were now fighting in large groups for a common aim disturbed everyone Ras overheard, and it disturbed him, too.

Life had begun to find a sort of rhythm in this new land for him, and he was not prepared to see that go away.

It seemed right, somehow, when Culy sent for him.

He met the hyrsin in hys hut, where a low fire burned and Culy sat with a deep plate of clucker eggs. Eggs! Ras could not remember when he had last seen an egg. How quickly things that had once been taken for granted became luxuries once lost.

Ras stopped himself from going down that path.

"You wanted to see me?" he asked instead, eyeing the eggs with scarcely disguised longing.

"I wonder if you might consider helping me with something," said Culy. Sy took an egg in hys hand and rolled it against hys knee, cracking the blue-green shell. He peeled it into the bowl, and the smell of the egg made Ras's mouth wet with hunger.

Ras tore his eyes away from the egg and hoped his stomach didn't betray him. "What do you want me to do?"

"The hunters all like you. More than that, they say you are competent." Culy gave Ras a rare smile, which was still only a half upturn of hys lips on one side.

That the hunters spoke well of him made Ras feel prouder than he had in some time, especially because he had admired their skill. More than their skill, but their tenacity, too. He returned Culy's half smile with one of his own. He waited for Culy to continue.

"It seems our lands have come upon some troubled times," said Culy after a long pause.

"Wyt?" Ras had heard the name so many times in the recent turns that he would have been surprised had Culy done anything but nod.

Indeed, Culy nodded immediately. "Wyt is a problem. She has resources; that much is clear by the number of people she has gathered to her side. She must have something that will entice them. I cannot compete with someone who outnumbers me so much."

Ras peered more closely at Culy. Though no one had said it, it was obvious to anyone paying attention that Culy was the leader here. When sy said jump, half the Northlanders would fly if they thought it would bring a pat on the head from the hyrsin. Ras recognized that. It was the way Hearthlanders reacted to Merin. In the Hearthland, each village was governed by the soothsayer and her group of elders, but they were never faced with a threat more dire than a Nameless or two. Ras stopped himself at that, trying to keep himself from grimacing. A Nameless or two was the reason he stood here in front of Culy and wasn't happily ensconced in front of his own hearth, in his own roundhome, where his biggest worry was whether he would hunt halka or saiga.

"What is it you want me to do?" Ras asked.

"I would like for you to go with Ham and Darim to the north, into Sands, and seek out some families I know who usually stick close to the waymakes there this time of cycle. Speak to them. Tell them what happens in the west. Tell them I need good people to be watchful and help control the rovers Wyt is sending out to steal from honest folk."

Ras couldn't help but feel a swell of pride again. He was nodding and agreeing with Culy before he could stop himself. Then he thought of Ryd. Much as Ras thought it was a person's responsibility to take care of hyrself, Carin would stick him full of halm arrows if he so much as set foot more than a day's hunt away from Alarbahis. And Ryd was a dismal hunter. He couldn't kill a rabbit if it hopped onto his lap. With fish, he would have been fine, but fish needed water to exist, and there was fair little enough of that here.

Culy seemed to read his mind. "I will, of course, ensure that Ryd is taken care of. He has been good company and I would not want your friend Carin to take anything amiss."

With that, it was settled.

It took about the space of a turn for Ras, Ham, and Darim to prepare for their trip. They spent most of those days hunting, dividing the meat in half: some for the waymake's use and the rest to be dried and taken along with them. Ras was able to trade a few pelts for a pot of sweet berries that reminded him of home, and he tucked it into his rucksack with everything else.

Ryd didn't seem disturbed by his leaving, and when the day came to go, Ryd got up to wish him well.

The entire waymake saw them off, though without fanfare, their faces as solemn as they had been on the day of the saiga incident.

Culy had also given them leave to ride hys ihstal. Ras hadn't ridden in moons, but the moment he mounted the beast, it seemed to come back to him, and ihstal weren't so twitchy that his mount would throw him for being nervous. Once they were on the backs of their ihstal and ready to leave, Culy handed Ras a small parcel, wrapped loosely in wool, handing it to him as if it were glass.

They left midmorning with Renewal Moon waning overhead, and Ras felt a thrill to see the huts fade into the distance. Ham and Darim joked together—Ras was finally able to mostly understand them. Once the waymake had vanished behind them, Ras opened the small parcel Culy had given him, unfolding the soft wool as he rode. Ham and Darim looked over at him curiously, and Ham raised an eyebrow when he saw what Culy had given Ras.

It was an egg.

R YD WASN'T sure what was stranger: being alone in Alarbahis with neither his childhood friend nor his attempted murderer or the kindness the Northlanders seemed to show him.

Since Ras had departed a turn before, Culy had given Ryd a standing invitation to break his fast with hyr every morning. And so Ryd went, usually bringing with him whatever small carving he'd been working on the day before, and Culy would share baked clucker eggs and a flat bread he was told was made with the stems of the grasses that grew in Crevasses, dried and powdered. It tasted exactly so, though not in an unpleasant way.

Culy liked asking Ryd about Haveranth and the Hearthland, and though Ryd understood that perhaps telling this hyrsin everything about his home was not wise, he shared things instead that he thought would be of little consequence. He told Culy of his childhood, of his grandmother who taught him to whittle, of long walks by the Bemin and listening to the rush of water. He stopped speaking of the river once he realized it sounded...odd to boast of something the people in his new home would find to be a treasure. Ryd understood that, just as he understood that as the days grew slowly longer and the sun returned to the land, the Northlanders grew more anxious, little by little. Soon there would be no snow to melt for drinking, and when he remembered that, he spoke no more of rivers.

But he did tell Culy of being sat on, which at first drew amusement from the hyrsin and then pity.

"I understand why you would choose to go," Culy told him that day. "It is an unpleasant thing to have others treat you as though you do not matter."

From that moment on, Ryd looked a little closer at Culy when sy spoke, because he wasn't sure anyone would say that and truly mean it unless sy had been through it.

Ryd liked to pace Culy's hut on those mornings as they talked, and Culy didn't seem to mind. Sitting lately made Ryd's side cramp up, and he liked moving around.

One day, Ryd brought in a carved tiger that he had spent the last two turns working on. The stripes were carefully cut deeper into the wood, and he had carved it so they moved with the grain. Culy took the wooden animal in hys hands, looked at Ryd as though sy'd never seen him before, and told Ryd to stay where he was.

Ryd waited for what seemed like an entire day—but was probably only a few hundred heartbeats—until Culy returned, and sy was not alone. With hyr was a tall man with dark mustaches that reached all the way past his jaw. He was the first person Ryd had seen with that much facial hair. Few people grew any at all, let alone grew it so long. The man wore a pale brand on his cheek that stood out against his brown skin.

"Ryd, I would like you to meet Aryt va Tirahs," sy said. "Aryt is a halmer, and if you would like, he will train you to be one as well."

All Ryd could think of was Carin's legendary halm bow. He nodded immediately.

Aryt was a soft-spoken man, and he wanted to start Ryd's training that day. Ryd led him to his own hut, where Aryt took Ryd's carvings in his hand one after another, peering at them with little expression on his face. He looked at small animals, carved trees, and sets of bone tools alike until finally he nodded his satisfaction and said, "I've seen these about. Folk are happy with what you've done."

For a moment, Ryd grinned, surprised by the compliment.

Then Aryt returned the smile dryly, his mustaches twitching at the corners of his mouth. "Halm is quite different than regular wood or bone," he said. "We shall see how you do with it."

Aryt knew of a halm grove a two days' walk from the waymake, and they set out the next morning. Ryd had a great deal of questions he wanted to ask, but being with someone new in a strange place left him shy, tongue firmly locked behind his teeth.

If Aryt was curious about where Ryd had come from, he didn't let it show; he led the way in relative silence as they walked. When they arrived at the grove, Ryd stopped the moment he laid eyes on the trees. Their trunks were white and smooth like doubloon trees, but where the bark on the doubloon trees' trunks peeled away in dingy chunks, the halm seemed to grow like rock. It was the first he had seen in the Northlands, and it gave Ryd a strange feeling to see something so familiar from home. Ryd walked to the first tree and laid his hand on it. He knew that halm did not splinter like other woods, nor did it easily burn.

He wondered if the trunk bore rings like maha, or if it was simply pure milky white all the way through. The tree seemed to be made of light and all that light was. Cutting, blinding, able to show any flaw.

The whole way they had walked, Ryd had assumed that the instrument sheathed on Aryt's back was his sword, so when Aryt pulled it from his back and unsheathed it, the sight of a long saw surprised him. But of course, to work with halm, you first had to get it off the tree.

The saw was not just one layer of metal, Ryd saw, but three. The teeth were murderous, and they made him revise his thought that it couldn't also be a weapon.

He expected Aryt to begin sawing off a branch, but instead he sent Ryd off to gather wood and started building a fire.

Ryd came back with armfuls of wood and stacked it in a tidy pile. Aryt piled it all on the fire, almost faster than Ryd could carry it. Soon, the flames reached nearly as high as Ryd was tall, and when he paused for a moment to catch his breath, Aryt sent him to get more with a look.

Four trips later, the sun had dipped below the horizon and the air grew colder, but Ryd's back dripped sweat and his hair was soaked through. He kept carrying wood until Aryt held up a hand to signal him to stop, and only then did Ryd notice that Aryt had placed his saw on the hottest part of the fire.

He felt very foolish when he saw it. Of course it would need something more; halm weapons could fend off bronze. A halm shield—though Ryd had never seen such a thing, only heard tales of them as a child—would stop any arrows but those that were also made of halm. Carin's bow and its arrows would pierce hardened leather and bronze plate alike. Though there were no armies in Haveranth, the villagers all knew old stories of wars fought and won. Until coming north, though, Ryd had thought of them as mere stories. Now, looking at this tree, Ryd wondered how many true things he had thought false. There was no saw by itself that would cut through halm, no matter how many teeth it had.

When the saw glowed pink in the fire, Aryt covered his hands with thick leather gloves, like the ones Ryd used to see Rina use in her smithery. He pulled the saw from the fire and walked toward the nearest halm.

"I'm going to start with this one because it's smaller," he said. Then he pointed up with his spare hand, at the trunk of a halm that bore its first branches above Ryd's head. "For those we would need more preparation."

Ryd couldn't tell if Aryt was trying to make a joke or not.

The branch Aryt began to saw was about as thick as Ryd's leg, and the glowing teeth of the saw still barely cut into the dense wood. Perspiration beaded on Aryt's face from the exertion and the heat of the blade. The smell of hot wood rose through the air. It didn't smell like the smoke from the fire, nor did it smell like any other burning wood Ryd had ever smelled. It had an almost acrid scent, as if it were barely even a living thing.

Less than a quarter of the way through the branch, the saw cooled too much to continue. Ryd fetched more wood, and they continued that way well into the night, reheating the saw and cutting into the branch, then fetching more wood for the fire and doing it all over again.

Sometime past moonset, the branch finally gave way and fell to the ground. Aryt gave it a tired nod and placed the saw carefully propped up on Ryd's woodpile to cool without the shock of the snow. He didn't touch the branch, so Ryd walked over to it and lifted it. It weighed more than he expected, and he almost dropped it.

He bent to get better leverage, and a sharp pain doubled him over.

"It's dense, but it's not that heavy," Aryt said, but Ryd barely heard him.

The pain in his side gnawed at him, like a burrow-bug digging deeper into his flesh.

When Ryd made no answer to Aryt, the man hurried to his side. "Ryd. You are hurt?"

Ryd heaved a breath, and the pain slowly lessened until he could stand almost straight again. He tried to look at Aryt. "I have been getting a cramp in my side. It hurts less now."

Aryt frowned, but he let it lie. Ryd noticed, though, that as soon as the saw was cool enough, Aryt carefully cleaned it and sheathed it and set up their tent for the night without asking for help. Ryd had thought they were staying more than one night, but the next morning, Aryt packed up the tent and shouldered the heavy branch of halm, and without a word, they started back for Alarbahis.

The return trip took three days instead of two, and Ryd had his suspicions of why. Though the pain in his side did not return, Aryt insisted on giving him long lessons each morning and stopping early each night.

They finally reached Alarbahis just after midday on the seventh day after leaving. Rajil, a weaver Ryd had met once or twice, came rushing up to them. Assuming he meant to talk to Aryt, Ryd started to stand aside, but Rajil looked right at him.

"Your friend. She has returned." Rajil looked at Aryt, and this time Ryd immediately knew he was not a part of what passed between them. "Sart is with her. She is...unconscious."

Aryt's entire face sharpened with the pronouncement.

Ryd was already running toward Culy's hut. If Carin was hurt—Ryd couldn't bear to think of what he would do if Carin weren't okay. Had they succeeded in breaking the stone?

He burst into the hut and almost ran into Culy.

Culy sensed the reason for his panic and motioned to Carin, who stood bent over Sart, her hands on Sart's temples.

Ryd almost fell to his knees with gratitude. All he had heard were the words *she is unconscious* and thought Rajil had meant Carin.

"She is unharmed. She saved Sart's life."

"Of course she did." Ryd said it without thinking, but everything in his chest seemed about to burst. Carin was well. Of course she was well.

Sart was not. Far from the vibrant woman Ryd had first met, Sart's body had grown wan and pale, her skin like the thinnest brown leather stretched over a guttering candle. He could almost see her struggle to live. She had lost weight, her muscles dwindling and her skin tight to her body.

"What happened to her?" Ryd whispered the question, horrified.

"She tried to break the stone and failed."

"And Carin saved her?"

"Wyt's rovers found them just as Sart tried to break the stone. Carin got her away and has been sustaining her life."

Ryd thought he saw Carin's shoulders twitch at that, but she didn't look up.

"Culy, I can't tell if it's working." Carin's voice hissed out of her mouth as if she were speaking from between clenched teeth.

Ryd moved closer and saw that was exactly the case. Her deep blue eyes were bloodshot, and she had grown thinner as well, though something had shifted in her.

"It's working," Culy said softly. "You can help her. I cannot."

Ryd wanted to ask why, but he held his tongue.

"Ah," Culy said, and a smile ghosted across hys face.

Carin made a strangled noise, her body tensing and her shoulders shaking.

Sart's eyes opened.

L YARI FELT winter burst like a drumhead stretched too tight.
It happened so suddenly, the coming of spring. One day the snows fell and fell, blanketing all of Haveranth in deadly white, and the next, the sun shone hot and melted away the snow like a war of light. The next day rain fell, and though the village was almost ankle-deep in mud, the villagers of Haveranth all came out of their homes and stood in the rain, the fat spring rain that had come so quickly on the heels of snow and fell in spite of the sun still taking its place in the sky. The rain fell in sparkling drops that glittered rainbows in the air, and the people of Haveranth rejoiced.

Lyari celebrated with them, and when a child of twelve harvests began to dance in the rain, Lyari joined hyr and danced, her feet squelching in the mud that spattered up all over her pale green clothing.

She couldn't muster any care for the mess.

The dancing spread through the village, and someone brought a drum to the village hearth-home, where Clar stood, dutifully tending the fire, looking as though she wanted to smile and join in. In one moon's time, Clar would depart the village on her Journeying. Lyari tried not to think on it. Then someone else brought a flute, and someone a dulcimer, and someone else another drum, and music pounded through the hearth-home, to the beat of dancing feet.

After a time, Dyava appeared through the mud and rain and crowd and tugged Clar from her post to whirl his cousin about in a torrent of droplets. Clar was laughing by the time she stumbled, dizzy, back to her job of tending the fire. Lyari met Dyava's eyes briefly, and she couldn't help the smile that came to her lips.

When the rain finally stopped, the villagers beamed at one another, and Lyari understood them well. One other roundhome had collapsed in the last moon, despite their vigilance in removing the snow. It had taken two more villagers from them. After the grief winter had brought among them, haunting their steps as they climbed their roofs and pulled down the snow like they were fighting off death itself, the new fallen rain brought with it a release Lyari hadn't known they needed.

She didn't see any of the elders at first, and she moved through the village in the mud, smiling and greeting the mud-splattered people until she came across Wend and Varsu speaking quietly down Haver's Road to the west. Their clothes were still clean, if wet, and Lyari felt a fierce sense of pride steal through her at the sight. She looked more like her village than they did.

They saw her, and she met their gaze defiantly until Lyris and Til-im came toward her wearing smiles and mud both, and their happiness wiped away Lyari's worry over the elders who were supposed to be her biggest support.

She returned home a short time later to clean herself off, and she found Jenin waiting for her just inside. Sy gave her a wistful smile at the sight of her, and Lyari's memories whipped back in time to an autumn rainstorm just after they had both reached their fifteenth harvest and declared their appellations to the village. She remembered how Jenin had run to her in the rain and swept her up in hys arms, murmuring in her ear. "Hello, Lyah el Jemil ve Haveranth," to which she had responded, "Hello, Jenin yl Tarwyn vy Haveranth."

Together they had stayed that way, the rain pouring down their faces, rejoicing in this first step to becoming adults, to knowing themselves and one another just a little better than they had in the morning. The rain had been cool, almost cold, but Jenin had warmed her from head to toe, brushing back the always-stray hairs from her plait and kissing her soundly.

They had still been children, then.

Now, Jenin stood in front of her, hys face forever locked as sy had been the morning of their Journeying when hys throat had been opened to bleed, and Lyari had seen another harvest come and go. For a flash, just a flash, Jenin's visage changed, and sy stood before Lyari the way sy had that day, fifteen harvests and soaking wet. And then the flash was gone, and things were as they were now.

"I miss you like this," was all sy said.

Lyari couldn't speak through the water that wet her face, and this time it wasn't from the rain.

The turns passed and spring returned to the Hearthland, bringing with it longer days that began to fight with the night for dominion over the time. As Planting Harmonix grew closer and the village woke to the toil of the cycle, Lyari rode her ihstal south to meet the other soothsayers of the hearthland.

She made sure to arrive first, leaving an entire day before she had told Harag and Reynah she would.

Lyari needed to see the place.

The meadow where the reinvocation was to happen spread out around her in a lush blue pool of grasses that waved like the sea in the breeze. Early wildflowers bloomed against that backdrop in flashes of white and red and orange and yellow, and Lyari set up her tent in the soft grass and then went to lie down in the meadow instead of on her bedroll.

Here, in this place, she could almost forget everything that had happened.

This was the place she would water with blood three harvests hence.

Two. Two harvests now.

Lyari wasn't sure she would ever have enough time.

The next day, Lyari packed up her tent and dressed herself, readying her things to leave as soon as she was ready. And then she waited.

Harag, soothsayer of Bemin's Fan, and Reynah, soothsayer of Cantoranth, both arrived at once, and when they crested the hill from the north, they found Lyari seated on a large red vysa cushion in the middle of the blue grass of the meadow, her back to them and her hair plaited into a neat tail over one shoulder. She had chosen vysa robes of deep gold, woven by Novah and embroidered with white pearls from the strand she had taken from Harag. The robes felt rich like butter, and her skin glowed gold-brown in the sunlight, which bathed her where the robes scooped low over one shoulder. She'd even woven a necklace of red firestones made by someone in Cantoranth.

She did not turn to look at them.

Her ihstal grazed on the grasses nearby, letting out a happy whistle.

She heard the other soothsayers coming, their feet whisking through the grasses, and Lyari smiled to herself. She made them come to her.

Two more ihstal joined Lyari's in grazing, and the snuffles of grass in their snouts and their high-pitched whistles made Lyari envy the simplicity of their lives for a moment.

Just for a moment.

Harag and Reynah came, walking together in a wide circle around her. Lyari looked resplendent, and she knew it.

She looked up at them and did not stand. Harag's gaze fell upon Lyari's robes, met the white pearls that she knew too well symbolized death. Reynah did the same, but her gaze was on the red firestones that were as full of life as the pearls were full of death, and Lyari fought to keep her face still when both soothsayers took a full step backward.

They needed her. She did not need them, unless they were chosen as the sacrifices for the reinvocation, and even in that death they were not necessary, for there were many, many other families in the Hearthland.

Something of it must have come across on Lyari's face, because Harag's composure broke, and a sob shook her shoulders.

Lyari didn't know what Merin had been like with these women, if they had been friends or simply comrades, but she found she didn't care. They were as complicit in the deaths of Carin and Ryd as was Merin.

It would take time, but Lyari did not intend for more Nameless to die at the hands of hunters in the mountains. First, though, she had to get to the reinvocation.

"Please," Lyari said, hearing the dryness in her own voice as she greeted the two soothsayers. "Sit."

They had left their bedrolls in bags that draped over the backs of the ihstal, and they had neither cushions nor blankets to sit upon. Their faces were travel-weary and glistened with perspiration, and because they had arrived half a day early, Lyari assumed they had meant to greet her with fresh faces and clothing.

They had not expected she would beat them here.

Lyari had only met Reynah once before, and not since Lyari herself was still considered hysmern. She remembered the older woman as kind-faced and thoughtful, if a bit flat. Now, Reynah's face betrayed a pinchedness beneath the surface as though her head had swelled with worry and her skin no longer fit.

Harag, by contrast, looked as though she might shred her own clothing out of rage. As Lyari watched her, Harag's eyes sought out the pearls on Lyari's robes.

Lyari knew what breaking up that strand would do to Harag.

After half a cycle of having her station undermined by everyone who was supposed to accept her as their equal, Lyari had finished allowing it.

The invitation—or command, as Lyari knew they knew it was—hung in the air, heavy and ponderous, until the weight of it brought both of the other soothsayers to their knees and then onto their rumps in the grass.

"We had a hard winter in Haveranth," Lyari said conversationally without preamble. "Since we have all arrived early, I would like to get started."

It was likely that both Harag and Reynah had traveled for many days to get here. Bemin's Fan was three days riding from Haveranth, and Cantoranth five, and the meeting place added another two. They would be weary from the journey, their legs bowed and tired from riding, their muscles tight and in need of stretching.

"Two roundhomes collapsed this winter in my village," Lyari said, ignoring all pretense of acknowledging their exhaustion. She looked at Reynah. "What was your situation in Cantoranth?"

"We lost several before your messenger arrived and told us how to prevent it." Reynah looked as though she wanted to say something else, but she kept it to herself.

"I did not ask you for vagaries. How many?"

"Five."

"And how many lives were lost?"

Silence answered Lyari's question, so she repeated it.

"How many lives were lost?"

"Fourteen."

Lyari had already known the answer. The messenger she had sent had returned with that number in exchange. Bemin's Fan had had no such problem with snow. She simply wanted to hear Reynah say it aloud.

"Did it not occur to you to remove the snow?" Lyari asked, already knowing the obvious answer to the question. Had they thought of it, they wouldn't have lost five homes and fourteen villagers from Cantoranth.

Fourteen. Twenty total with Haveranth's deaths, and with no more children born yet this cycle—though it was early and they tended to come into the world in autumn and winter—the loss of so many dwindled the population even faster than it otherwise would have.

"We have never had so much snow," Reynah said slowly.

"Have you then never seen what happens when a simple tree branch is laden with too much of it?"

"Lyari, that is unfair." Harag burst out. "There was no way of knowing what would happen."

"There was a way of making an educated guess." Merin had often said that about magic, and Lyari thought it seemed like common sense in general. "If it is your duty to ensure the safety of your people, it is your duty to think of that which they do not."

"She is correct," Reynah said, as if Lyari were not sitting directly in front of her.

"You will let this child speak to you that way? Merin at least deserved our respect!" Harag had a handful of grasses that rapidly became a flurry of small bits under the flurry of her fingers, and Lyari thought rather calmly that at least Harag hadn't decided to shred her tunic.

Reynah started to speak again, but Lyari got to her feet and took three large steps toward them. To their credit, they did not move backward, nor did they try to stand.

Lyari looked down at them, catching the two older women in her gaze. "I am not a child, and you will remember that in the future."

"You don't even know what your duty entails."

A smile crept across Lyari's face. "Is that so? I do not know that I am to select five bloodlines from the Hearthland, which I will spill across the hearthstone, exactly there?" She pointed behind her to her bright red cushion. "I do not know that neither of you hold the names to your village's children, that Merin is the one who told you their true names when they left for their Journeying and not a moment before?"

Reynah gasped then, but Lyari ignored her.

"I know their names," Lyari said softly. "You are no true soothsayers, whatever magic you may possess. It is my blood that holds the power over the reinvocation, and without it this land will wither and die, and you with it. This grass is watered by blood, and I will do this thing to keep it growing, but you will never again do me the dishonor of forgetting that there is only one soothsayer in the Hearthland, and I am she."

With that, Lyari stood, called to her ihstal, and when the beast knelt for her, she mounted, securing her rucksack in front of her. The vysa robes spread out over the ihstal's pale gold pelt, and Lyari wheeled herself around to look one last time on Harag and Reyna.

"There are twenty white pearls on these robes, Harag, in case you lost count. Such was the cost of winter."

She rode away, leaving the red cushion in a sea of blue grass and the two women trying not to drown in it.

The moment she arrived home, she set the village about reinforcing their roofs.

ALL HIS life, Ras had oriented himself by the simple fact that when he went north, the world grew colder. Now, as he traveled northward with Ham and Darim, the air grew warm and then hot. Ras had never lived in dry heat, and after an entire moon traveling this way and that through Sands, he woke one day in three with a nosebleed from the dry air.

Ham showed him how to hunt lizards, some as small as two fingers together but others as long as his forearm, and at night when they spitted the strange, green little creatures over their meager fires, Ras would rub the grease on the inside of his nose.

He hated the smell, but after a time it stopped the nosebleeds from being so frequent.

It seemed leaving Alarbahis had cursed them with ill luck. Everywhere they traveled in Sands, the people they sought had just moved on. The waymakes Ras had seen here were dug deeper into the sand, where the clay bricks that lined their inside could keep folk cool during the day and warm at night, when the darkness sucked the heat from the air as if to make up for the cruel scorching sun of the day.

Ras's skin darkened in the constant sun, and when he remarked on the heat, Darim laughed at him and told him to wait until summer arrived, when he could spend High Lights toiling in sand that would blister your skin and stick to the sores. Still, that night she brought him two long, spiky leaves of a plant and told him to break them open and spread the inside juice on his face and arms where the sun's warmth lingered even after dark.

He had been surprised that Northlanders observed High Lights, but upon further thought realized that his own people must have brought it with them from the north when they moved through the mountains into the Hearthland.

Now, living here, Ras looked back on High Lights and felt foolish. For all they covered themselves in ashes and toiled throughout the brightest day of the cycle in penance, the Hearthlanders were fed and happy even in their feigned suffering for the plight of those they had handed this poor fortune.

They rode only in the cooler parts of the day, stopping as often as possible where there was a waymake at midday to wait out the hottest sun before riding on. The waymakes were smaller and more frequent here. At one point, Ras wondered aloud who had built them, and Ham laughed.

"They have been here far too long for us to know who put them there, but we all do our part to repair them. We all use them."

Darim nodded. "My family are claymakers. When I was a child, they would find what clay they could and bake the tiles for the roofs. Wherever we went, if there was need of them, we traded them for other goods."

It made Ras think of how the folk in Alarbahis had reserved part of the doomed saiga for the waymake's use, and he nodded, satisfied by their answer but left feeling again as though he were not truly at home. In Cantoranth, people traded goods, but they tended their own homes more often than not. Then again, here in the Northlands, the waymakes were their own homes. They just happened to have different ones depending on the day.

They came up on a larger waymake later that day, just as the sun puddled on the horizon in a lake of gold and orange and pink. Ras had noticed that day and night neared the same lengths, and remembered that, one cycle past, he had been in Cantoranth preparing for the sowing. He remembered the strange quiet of Planting Harmonix when no Journeyers set forth from Cantoranth. They would be doing the same now. He remembered Sahnat telling him as they departed to hunt the Nameless that this cycle there would be six total Journeyers. Ras wondered if any of them would become Nameless and who would be the one to introduce them to their deaths.

Ras looked at the waymake as they approached, and it was with relief that he saw some of the huts occupied, thin tendrils of smoke from folk starting fires to ward off the inevitable chill of the desert night.

Ham and Darim seemed to have been here before. They rode forward ahead of Ras and straight to a hut near the edge of the waymake. He passed the waypost on the path. By now Ras had learned to read them. Each waypost declared the region and the name of the waymake, as well as how many huts it held. Though he hadn't noticed much before, since traveling with Ham and Darim, Ras had learned that some of the huts were different sizes to account for families. Not that Ras had seen any families.

This waymake was called Sansil, red sand.

The name didn't make sense to Ras, as the sand all around him was more of a light yellow, but he wasn't about to argue with a sign.

Since the waymake was inhabited but still far from full, Ras took a hut for his own, a smaller one across from where Ham and Darim set up their own. Though they were not bonded, the pair was close and shared a home, even when given the option of their own space. It made Ras miss the other Hearthlanders, though he also liked not being yelled at for snoring.

He was just setting up his bedroll when Darim came, scratching her fingernails against the canvas to alert him to her presence. He turned and gave her a smile, which she returned.

"Our luck has changed at last," she said. "Dunal is here in Sansil."

Dunal was one of Culy's friends, and one they had been chasing across Sands for what felt like an entire cycle of moons.

Ras stopped what he was doing and followed Darim out of the hut.

They found Dunal at the central hearth, though no fire burned in it, and he sat with an already-cooked lizard the size of two of his hands together, picking meat from the tail and popping it in his mouth.

Seeing lizard now made Ras's nose itch.

When Dunal saw Ham and Darim, he looked up and jumped to his feet, clapping both of them on the back and folding Ham into an embrace.

Ras hung back from the encounter, only speaking when he was introduced and letting Ham and Darim explain the situation. At that, Dunal's face grew troubled, and his fingers slowed their picking at the lizard carcass on his lap.

"I've heard tell of Wyt," he said. "They say she never runs out of water."

Having been in Sands for the past moon, even to Ras that sounded enticing. He had learned to harvest water from the large cactuses that grew abundantly in the parts of Sands they had traveled, though to Ras cactus water was still below snow water and well water on his list of favorite sources.

"She is gathering people to her. Rovers." Ras chimed in then, and Dunal looked at him curiously.

"So I've heard," Dunal said. He pointed across the waymake to a smaller hut where a man shook the sand out of a shirt before hanging it over a stretched line of gut twine. "He came here after being attacked by Wyt's rovers. They took nearly all he had, but they left him with his life."

"Rot," said Darim. Her face grew stormy, and her foot bounced on the sand as Ras had noticed it did when she was angry.

"Culy needs your help," Ham said.

Dunal closed his lips, then he looked to the west. "I don't need to tangle with Wyt," he said.

"I think you've just told us that she isn't leaving people the choice in that," Ras told him.

"There is a difference between knowing you could be struck by lightning and climbing trees in a thunderstorm," said Dunal.

Ras gestured around him and grinned. "I see no trees here."

That got a smile from Dunal, but he didn't respond to Ham.

Ras thought of the waymakes, how all of the Northlanders helped keep them up and how all of the Northlanders shared a portion of their larger hunts with others. In spite of the scarcity in which they lived, they thought of one another. "If Wyt grows strong enough to gather bands of fifty rovers, would any waymake be safe?"

At that question, Dunal looked Ras over once more, intelligent eyes observing, seeking out anything in Ras's appearance that might give him an idea of whether or not Ras truly thought this was a threat.

Ras continued speaking in a low and urgent voice. "If what you have heard is even remotely true and Wyt has so much water, her numbers will only grow. Will you choose to climb that tree now, knowing the risk, or will you wait until you are chased up it?"

When they left Sansil, Dunal came with them.

E VEN RIDING Tahin made Sart remember how much her little bout of near-death had weakened her. Her legs felt too wobbly even on the ihstal's back, and she had lost so much of her body that her breeches sagged and made her legs look like she was a clucker wearing people clothes.

Carin's arms rested about Sart's waist, as usual, and these days it felt a bit more like the other young woman was trying to keep Sart on the ihstal than about ensuring she herself didn't fall off the back.

It had taken two turns to convince Culy that she was well enough to travel, and Sart's brain had muddied enough with her indisposition that she hadn't thought of the best reason until the last day. Once she remarked to Culy that she would be better off in a place where there was abundant water and she could devote the time she usually spent filtering and potting the stuff to resting and improving, sy had agreed almost immediately.

She wished she'd thought of it sooner. Even now, Sart could almost feel the presence of the spring coming closer. If she remembered correctly, it should have been just over the next rise.

Sart was prepared to see it overrun with Wyt's people and their stupid rune-marked shoulders. She was prepared to see it abandoned or never found, if the folk she had sent had not made it.

What she didn't expect was to come upon the spring and see huts had sprung up around it.

And children.

There were children here.

She counted six of them. She had sent only the family with two.

Sart squinted, her eyes not quite able to make out whether any of the faces were familiar.

She heard Carin's gasp behind her, and she understood it well. It had been moons upon moons since either of them had seen a child, with the exception of the babe in Alarbahis, and spring had taken hyr and hys family to other places.

There were five small huts in a semicircle around the spring, and surrounding all of it was lush blue grass. It carpeted the entire clearing, spattered here and there with wildflowers. The sugar-tree had started to bud, and its leaves that showed were the bright blue of new growth that stood out against the tree's pale bark and the darker color of the grass.

As they approached, the sound of the children's laughter grew quiet, and Sart saw that they all were watching her and Carin come toward them.

She thought they would run away, but after a moment, one of the children let out a yell. "Tata! She's here! She's here!"

Well. Sart wasn't quite expecting that either.

The flap on one of the huts twitched, and out came the man Sart had seen in the pass with Geral. He looked older since she had seen him last, and this time he wore a sword alongside his belt knife.

Sart stopped Tahin and slid off the ihstal. Carin followed her lead, looking sideways at Sart with a question in her eyes.

Sart would have answered, but she was pretty sure she had the same question.

The man strode toward them, and when he didn't stop, Sart felt Carin bristle and reach for her bow. Sart stayed her with a small twitch of her hand, and the man enfolded her in an embrace with one swift movement.

He smelled of pine and leather, and for what felt like a hundred breaths, he didn't let go.

When he pulled back, there were tears standing in his eyes. He motioned to the spring. "Please. Drink."

Tahin had already started, and the children all gathered around the ihstal.

The beast didn't seem to care much for the children, as she was more interested in the fresh cold water that flowed from the ground. Sart dropped to her knees beside the spring and drank, her stumbling fall forward more from her own fatigue than thirst.

Carin did the same, and Sart heard her make a startled noise when the water first touched her tongue. They both drank greedily of the water, which to Sart had somehow grown in sweetness and coldness far beyond what her mind could remember.

When they had drunk their fill, they followed the man—who introduced himself as Talnyt—to his hut, where he bid them to sit on cushions and fed them spring's first berries. Berries!

"I will never be able to thank you for what you have done," Talnyt said to Sart. "We came this way as slowly as possible, avoiding the Lahi'alar and following your map as best we could. And on our way, we encountered two other families, each traveling with their children to Pahlys. We couldn't help but share what you had said, and they thought it was worth the risk to see if there was truly a spring of fresh water here."

Sart looked over at Carin, whose mouth was open like she had something to say but didn't know how. Either that or she was as astonished as Sart.

"The spring flowed through the winter," Talnyt continued. He pointed to the west. "I followed it one day, and it leads straight to the sea. There are no waymakes that far south in Salters, so we don't get that many visitors."

Sart couldn't believe what she was hearing. "You have lived here in peace all winter?"

"Not wholly. There have been some...rover troubles."

"Have they found the spring?"

Talnyt shook his head. "No, no. Nowhere near it. There are five bonded families here and six children. We send out people in groups of three to watch the land to the north. To the south, the mountains shelter us. Pahlys is the only waymake to the southeast, and most will stick to the Lahi'alar to travel to it, rather than leaving the roads to explore."

Sart thought about that and the position of the waymake. With the mountains at their back, they were indeed fairly safe, but some defenses wouldn't hurt. She pictured the area surrounding the spring. Not far outside there was a swatch of dead trees that would work. So she told him.

"If you want to keep rovers away, here is my idea." Sart described a nice bit of trickery, of building a hut to the east near a creek where most people would be and surrounding it with simple defenses. Fill a jug or two with water that was half spring and half potted creek water, and any rover would see the hut, rejoice that a defended home would almost certainly have something of value, and then they could take the entire jug of water and leave, feeling as they they'd found something worthwhile.

For this waymake, she suggested they build a simple fence around the homes to keep the children safe.

Some time later, once Talnyt went to discuss Sart's ideas with the others, she and Carin set up their tent. It took longer than usual, because Carin kept stopping to look around.

"What is it?" Sart asked her.

"This place," Carin said softly. "It reminds me of the Hearthland."

She pointed off a ways to the west, where the new creek was lined on either side in blue grass. "This is what a river looks like, though quite a bit larger."

Sart tried to imagine the creek larger, and she found she could do it, but she would never have a way of knowing whether or not what she imagined was true.

Carin's face grew pensive. "This is what it is like in Haveranth. If this is what it is supposed to be like here, then we need to find a way to do that."

Sart felt a chill go through her, though she knew what Carin meant. Her body was still relearning itself after being unconscious for whole turns.

"You want to try to break the stone again."

"I do."

"But we failed."

Carin looked at her, then came closer and squeezed her hand. "I'm sorry to say this, but you failed."

After trying to be angry about that for a few moments, Sart gave up and shrugged. "That's fair."

The smile that graced Carin's face was a bit rueful, but she didn't apologize. Instead, she kept talking. "When I touched the stone, I felt it. It was as if it matched me, knew me. It wanted whatever magic I have, but it wanted to give back, too. You were close to breaking it. I could feel it beginning to rise up in you, but then something got stuck and it...realized it didn't know you."

Sart thought about that. It wasn't nonsensical; magic behaved strangely, and like magic called to itself. If Carin was the product of the spell that had changed the land in the first place, maybe it was her touch that could break it.

That night, Sart asked Talnyt about the news from Boggers, knowing that anything to come out of there was almost certainly related to Wyt. Sure enough, Wyt's numbers were growing steadily and she had set up a second outpost south of her first, for those who wanted to join up but had yet to prove themselves worthy. Sart snorted at that, but it troubled her.

It seemed to do the same for Carin. They both knew enough to think that Wyt would have her people sit on an old, moss and algae covered stone simply because someone else wanted it.

Nonetheless, it was troubling.

The next morning, Sart and Carin walked the perimeter of the lush area around the spring together. There was a buzz in the air, and it wasn't magic. Looking down at a patch of wildflowers, Sart stared at the sight of a bee, happily bumbling its rump around in a flower. When was the last time she had seen a bee? Where had it come from? Where did it live?

For the space of a few heartbeats, Sart imagined herself following that bee to its hive just to see where it made its honey. But then she saw another bee, and around her the world seemed to come alive with sound. A fluttering movement above her head caught her notice, and two birds flitted by, calling at one another.

Sart's breath came faster at the loudness of this place, looking around her and taking in what she really saw. Bees. Flies. Birds. That morning, in the earliest hours, they had seen a halka downstream, its antlers bearing many points and its mouth full of blue grasses. Sart had said nothing, because she couldn't bring herself to kill it for enjoying this strange oasis of bounty.

Carin seemed to be feeling as uncomfortable as Sart, and she kept giving her head little shakes that made Sart feel like the other woman was trying to brush something off.

"This is familiar to you, is it not?" Sart asked. They walked close together these days, as much out of habit as anything, but with her body still deciding if it were going to give out on her, Sart took comfort in the warm presence of Carin's shoulder next to hers and the knowledge that if she were to pitch forward into the stream, Carin would probably catch her before she drowned.

"It is." Carin's eyes were as blue as the grasses, and again Sart found herself marveling at the color.

"You seem unhappy."

"It is painful for me to," Carin trailed off, looking around them. "It is painful for me to see this place as it is now, and know that the wonder of it for you and your people is because this is not something you have seen before. Because of me. And my people."

"You did not do this thing, my friend. If you keep taking credit for past wrongs, you will forget to enjoy the sights of these bees. You should enjoy the bees."

A small smile spread across Carin's face at that, but it faded in a moment. "Perhaps I did not do this, but it doesn't change how I feel."

Sart looked around them. She wanted to see through Carin's memories for a time, to learn what it was that was so different about Carin's home to make her so regretful. It couldn't just be food and water, powerful as those things were.

She allowed herself to think on what it could be like if a whole land were like this. Since she had last seen this place when it was on the cusp of winter, that simple spring had reached out tendrils around it, expanding its circle. Already the trees Sart had seen were larger. One sapling she had seen had nearly tripled in size. The animals returned—though they would leave if they began getting hunted too much; Sart would have to speak with Talnyt about that—and there were children who played here.

"We can do something," Sart said finally. "You can."

Carin knew immediately of what Sart spoke. "But Wyt—"

"But Wyt nothing. If you want to break that stone, we will find a way to fight Wyt away from it and trade our lives for the time you need, if that is what you want." Sart thought for a moment. "It's what I want."

Carin blanched, and for a long moment they stood in silence, watching the wind sing its song and the insects lend their harmony. Sart didn't say it aloud, but she willed Carin to say yes. To help her spread this throughout the lands, this song. What could the world look like if they didn't have to spend their days just trying to make it to the next one?

The other woman didn't speak, but after a time, she took Sart's hand and swallowed and nodded.

THE MOON Revive floated high in the sky with her sister. Carin couldn't have found it more appropriate as she and Sart rode north on Tahin to Silirtahn. Culy had someone there, Sart had said, and this person would likely be able to help them scout out the part of Boggers where the stone sat, growing more moss to replace what they had scrubbed away from it.

By now, the rolling gait of Tahin, coupled with the warmth of Sart's back, lulled Carin enough that she found she could doze on the journeys. Never had she thought it would be possible for her to sleep while riding an ihstal, but Carin had learned in the past cycle that people could adapt to just about anything.

They reached Silirtahn on a cloudy day after the sun had peaked in the sky, and Carin still marveled at the sight of the sea. Her first glimpse had come one turn back as they rode Tahin from the east, and she wasn't sure she would ever adapt to seeing so much water at once. When she had visited Bemin's Fan as a child, she had been too busy playing with other children in the village to give much attention to the clear blue waves that crashed on white sand. Making bowls from conu shells had been more exciting at the time, and now as an adult grown, Carin greeted the sight of the sea with the awe it deserved.

The expanse of it had chilled her at first, and on the heels of that thought came one that made her shift her weight on Tahin's back. How frustrating it must be for the Northlanders, to have so much water and be able to drink none of it? It went on and on to the horizon, that water, and at first Carin had thought it was like the Bemin, which flowed wide and deep—or so she thought—and you could stand at the very center of it and only have an arm's length of water above your head.

Sart had laughed at that, laughed so hard that Carin felt her torso shake and quiver. It had taken some time for Sart's chuckles to fade, and then she explained that yes, the sea was wide and deep, but farther than fifty paces from shore—and sometimes fewer—you could not stand with your head above water, and that farther out the sand dropped away and the water went down and down and down and down and no one really knew how deep it went. When Sart said that, Carin's mind stuck on the down and down and down and down until she felt as though she were falling into the center of the world, where it was cold and blue and dark.

From then on, each sight of the sea loomed in Carin's mind, this ever-present vastness.

It didn't help that Sart also told her stories and legends about there being people on the other side of it, though hearing that there was another side and that even such vastness had its own boundaries did fill Carin with some small sense of relief.

Silirtahn sat a little way back from the shore, and from the moment Carin's feet touched the sand, she noticed that there was more a sense of permanence about this waymake than the others. Huts were covered and sand-spattered, their canvas dug down into the ground instead of sitting atop it. A few had small decorations outside, baubles of green and blue glass, hollow reeds cut diagonally in varying lengths so that when the wind blew, they both sang and bumped against one another with a pleasant sound.

They found an empty hut and began to set it up, together pulling the canvas tight around the poles and securing it under the roof. Sart didn't tuck the bottom into the sand, but weighed it down with rocks instead.

Carin looked to the west, far into the horizon. A distant flash lit the sky, and as she watched, another. "Is it going to storm?"

At first Sart looked confused, but then she followed Carin's gaze out over the sea and shook her head. "That is always there. It never comes much closer than that. When storms come, they will come from the north." She motioned up the beach where the sand curved out to the west into a headland, steep cliffs dropping into the sea. Carin suddenly wanted to go there, out onto that point, and feel what it might be like to have the sea surrounding her on three sides. It would be a reckless feeling, a free feeling.

Instead, she helped Sart build a fire.

They had brought as many skins of spring water as they could carry, and while Carin tended to the fire, Sart went into the center of the waymake to trade for food. She came back with three fish, a sack of strange jagged shells, a pot of thick grease, a plucked gull, a length of rope, and a woman.

The woman was clearly not part of the trade.

Tall and muscular, she carried with her a long staff that was inset with some of the same jagged shells in the sack Sart set on a low table in the hut. She looked at Carin with interest, setting her staff to lean against the canvas wall of the hut.

"I see what you mean about her eyes," the woman said, grinning at Carin and raising two fingers to her lips in greeting. "I wouldn't mind looking into the eyes of a woman like that."

Carin's face turned hot, but she returned the gesture. Woman. It had been so long since someone had applied the words woman or girl to her that Carin had forgotten the way they felt too tight, too small. And her eyes besides—she had noticed that most of the Northlanders had eyes that were dark brown or grey or nearly black, but she hadn't given much thought to her own standing out. Carin suddenly felt too much for where she was and unsure if she fit anywhere, even in her own skin.

"Valon ve Avarsahla," the woman said.

"Carin," said Carin simply, and Sart gave her a strange look.

"Valon is going to take you to scout out the stone," Sart told her.

That made Carin stand up straighter. "You're not coming?" Her alarm came as much from being with someone actively flirtatious as the impending lack of Sart's presence, but the moment the words left her mouth, Carin felt foolish. The last time Sart had been near the stone, it had almost killed her. And as much as her personality had sprung back like hearty spring grass, Carin knew she tired easily. In the mornings, Sart began the day by setting her hands and toes on the ground and trying to use her arms and back to push her weight away from the ground over and over. While she was up to about twenty repetitions, she had confessed to Carin that before the stone, she had been able to do one hundred without stopping.

Carin had begun to join Sart in her exercises, at first to encourage her and then to keep up with her, but having a run-in with Wyt's rovers would push Sart's returning strength too far.

So the next morning, Carin found herself atop Tahin once more, riding southeast with Valon ve Avarsahla behind her. It felt strange and wrong and uncomfortable to have a stranger at her back with a weapon, but if Sart and Culy trusted this woman, Carin would find a way to do the same.

Valon's company was not unpleasant, once Carin got used to someone speaking in her ear. At the very least, Valon seemed to sense Carin's discomfort with flirting and desisted. Carin felt relief like a cool breeze at that. She found she liked Valon well enough, as they rode. Valon had been born in Salters, though like all the Northlanders, called no place home. She stayed in Silirtahn now only at Culy's behest, preferring the cool ridges of Crevasses to the constant mist of the sea. She told Carin of the cycles she had spent bouncing back and forth between Sands and Taigers, and how she had learned to find water by following baszyt, which she would never kill. Carin had to ask what a baszyt was, and was told that it was a grey animal about the size of a saiga with thick, almost hairless skin and a long horn on its snout that it used to break open cactuses in Sands.

Carin also didn't know what a cactus was, but according to Valon, they were spiky plants that held water in their middles.

It occurred to her that the Northlanders could tell her just about anything about animals or plants and she would have no real choice but to believe them. She hoped they wouldn't think of spinning tales just to make a fool of her, and for a moment the thought filled her with such helpless panic that she almost laughed aloud. She decided that if she ever found that to be the case, she would simply start telling real stories, true stories of the Hearthland, because the people there lived in such a foreign way that anything she said would sound a lie.

Soon the landscape began to look familiar to Carin, even though, the last time she had been here, she had been fleeing with an unconscious Sart and not paying much heed to the ground that churned beneath Tahin's feet.

This time, they approached at a wary pace, and even Tahin seemed to sense that they wanted to stay concealed. The ihstal's whistles grew quieter, almost as if she were talking to herself, and Carin wondered if the beast was as nervous to return here as she was.

They tethered Tahin about a league away from the stone, and the smoke from rover fires was already visible in the distance.

Valon and Carin approached slowly and cautiously, staying as low to the ground as they could. Carin kept her halm bow slung across her back, as the bright white of the wood would stand out against the dark green-brown of the edge of the bogs.

There was a small copse of scraggly bushes not far from the stone, and they sheltered in it from a pattering of rain that began to fall through a hazy sky. Carin peered between branches in the direction of the stone, straining her eyes to see what she could.

The land dipped down a bit, and while she couldn't get a clear view of the stone's location, she saw something that disturbed her. The smoke wasn't just one plume but several clustered together. In the moons since Carin had been here before, something had changed. Valon saw it almost as Carin did.

"They've built a waymake."

Carin supposed it only made sense, that if the rovers wanted to stay near the stone for whatever reason, they would build shelter. It didn't, however, make her task any easier.

"We ought to go closer," Valon said. "We need to see how many are there. Do you think they could have moved the stone?"

Carin hadn't even thought of that. She closed her eyes and imagined what the stone had looked like, then she paced out a rough shape in the ground, dragging her boot along the earth to show the size. "It's about that wide and as tall as I am. It would take a great deal of strength to move such a thing." She thought about Haverford Quarry northwest of Cantoranth, where the folk of Cantoranth cut away stone for the hearths of their people. They rolled the stones on logs, teams of ihstal yoked to the stone and people ready to move logs from the rear to the front. Carin had only seen this a few times, but she knew the toil that went into moving such a stone. And the one they sought here was larger than those that formed the hearthstones of her homeland.

"It's unlikely, then, that they have taken it away," said Valon.

With a terse nod, Carin peered out again.

"You circle around from the east." Valon pointed to the same small hillock Carin and Sart had used for cover when they first ventured up in search of the stone. "I'll do the same from the northwest. Stay out of sight. Don't go any closer than you have to. See if you can get an idea of how many rovers are in the waymake, and I'll do the same. Meet back where we left Tahin when the sun is one handspan from the horizon."

They left the copse, and Carin moved as quickly and silently across the soggy land as she could. The rain stopped, but the air remained hazy, and a fine mist clung to her hair and eyelashes.

Her path took her downwind of the waymake, and soon she smelled the smoke from their fires. There was a different scent to the smoke than simple wood or the coal that folk in Bemin's Fan gathered and traded to people in Haveranth, but Carin could not place it. It smelled warm and rich like fresh-tilled earth.

She crept closer, apprehension making her slow. Last time she had encountered these rovers—though she knew the people down there now may not be the same as the last time she was here—they had very nearly killed both her and Tahin.

Her boots sank into the soft earth, squelching. Soon she was in sight of the waymake, and her heart fell. There were eight occupied huts and at least another four she could see standing empty. A waypost had even been erected to the west where Valon would be. She was about to turn away when she heard a loud whoop from the waymake. Rovers poured out of huts at the sound, some with bows slung over their shoulders and others wearing swords at their hips, short swords and longswords and sickleswords and daggers.

Carin edged to her right, trying to see between the huts at the cause of the commotion.

Someone had come in from the west.

Even before they came around the side of one of the huts, Carin knew, and her stomach felt like it was full of rot.

Two rovers had Valon by the scruff of the neck, blades trained on her. Her staff had been sliced in half, and one of the rovers threw it on the waymake's central fire where blue flames licked up from it, eerie and strange.

Carin quickly counted rovers again, fingering the arrows at her belt quiver. Eleven rovers she counted, and she had at least thirty arrows, twenty halm and another ten of a wood she could not name. Ras had made those for her.

She warred with herself. Even if she could shoot all eleven rovers full of arrows from where she stood—and that would be a feat in itself—she could not shoot them all before they started to move and hide and shoot back. She was fast with her bow, and she could shoot three arrows in quick succession with arrows held in her draw hand, but more than that would take time, and by then she would be dodging arrows herself.

She was vastly outnumbered.

Carin could see the stone now, just an edge, peeking out from behind a hut.

She was the only person who could break it, and she couldn't do that if rovers killed her.

Staring into the waymake, Carin tried to will Valon to give her some sort of sign. A movement, a gesture, a mouthed *go*, anything that would make her feel free to leave.

But Valon simply hung her head, watching her staff burn in the fire.

Carin turned away. She hated herself all the way back to Tahin, and it wasn't until she was mounted alone on the ihstal's back that she gave herself leave to stop.

If the rovers were going to kill Valon, she'd likely already be dead. That they took her alive meant they thought she would be of some use, whether that use was information or anything else. Carin and Sart would find a way to get her back.

Still, Carin had thought the older girl capable enough not to get caught.

LYARI THOUGHT on Merin's hawk and what a useful thing it would be to have such a creature flying above the heads of the Journeyers as they trod northward into the mountains. Quicken Moon had already begun to wane, and the six Journeyers had been gone nearly two moons already. It worried Lyari to not know, though perhaps had she not seen Lin and gleaned Merin's uses for the animal, she would not have thought to worry more than any of the other villagers fretted over the Journeyers.

Clar had gone with them, and she would return new-named before long.

Two young villagers of sixteen harvests had taken over the tending of the hearth-home fire, and in that Lyari felt more the continuity of the cycles than anything else. What would she do when a cycle came where no Journeyers would depart on Planting Harmonix? Who would tend the fire for the cycle? Lyari had begun a record of all the villagers, going from roundhome to roundhome for purported visits, sharing curried mutton with them and drinking their conu juice and sweet icemint tea, but at each shared meal with them she asked details of their families, piecing together a full ledger of all who resided in her village and their ages, and from it she began to see the pattern of pictures emerge.

At the time the reinvocation came, there would be no Journeyers that cycle at all. Within seven cycles, there would be no Journeyers for two summers together. After that only one.

The single bright spot in these grim facts was that Anam had conceived a child with Lyris and Tillim. Lyari sent the news to Cantoranth and Bemin's Fan, along with baskets of Early Bird apples and bundles of the spring's first herbs, and she knew that to Harag and Reynah, the joyous tidings would feel like more threat than celebration.

That was exactly how Lyari wanted it.

She spent her days learning everything she could from Merin's scrolls. Spells, theory of magic, and anything she could find about fertility and the spell her ancestors had cast. To make a group of people fertile would have taken a great deal of magic and energy, and it stood to reason that the people of the Hearthland struggled to conceive and carry children to term because they were in the waning cycles of the spell. The child-bearers had scores of cycles where their bodies were capable of producing a babe, but Lyari knew not every attempt was successful and that it was not so simple as for, say, the rabbits that mated and birthed whole litters of kittens. People were different, and their bodies responded to more than simple desire or need.

All in all, the spring progressed in peace, and the people of Haveranth allowed themselves to rejoice and relax at Anam's news. Lyris and Tillim were so full of joy that you couldn't walk by them without catching a grin, and after the death of the winter, the villagers of Haveranth clung to those smiles as if they could keep them in a jar. More than once, she saw Anam seated at the hearth-home fire, a crowd of children asking permission to touch her swelling belly, wonder in their eyes.

Everything for Lyari moved with the smoothness of the Bemin's flow until the sliver of Quicken vanished into the dark sky that would birth the new moon, Bide, and she heard a commotion in the village hearth-home.

The noise of it was loud enough that Lyari could hear it from her bedroom, and she hurried to dress herself and attend to it, not knowing the cause.

Old Wend was the cause.

He stood in the center of the village hearth-home, and his words boomed through the gathered villagers. "We must prepare ourselves for the winter!" He bellowed into the crowd, and Lyari saw a few nods. "When I counseled our soothsayer that she should encourage you to reinforce your roofs, she thought I was only a mad old man, but thankfully, she listened to the wisdom of age."

Lyari stopped on the edge of the hearth-home, then quickly retreated back several steps until the nearest roundhome concealed her. What was he saying? The idea to reinforce the roundhomes' roofs was hers, only hers, and she had neither consulted with the elders nor asked their opinion, because not only was it the sensical thing to do, but no one would logically oppose such a thing.

"The winters will only grow harsher," Wend went on. "The way we have gone about things must change. We must adapt and be ready."

Peering around the edge of the roundhome, Lyari saw hysmern in the crowd, children who had not yet declared appellation and older ones who had but not yet made the Journeying. Wend's words skirted far too close to the reason for the Journeying itself, and though he was not wrong, this was not his place to sow fear in those too young to know the reason for it. This was not a burden to be shared by the children of Haveranth. White anger filled her, clear and hot under the sun. Lyari could not stay to listen, knowing even as she turned her back that Dyava and other adults were also in the crowd behind it.

The thought added shame to her rage.

She found Jenin in her roundhome when she returned, and hys face was sober.

"You heard that, did you not?" she asked hyr.

Sy nodded, looking seemingly through the wall in the direction of the hearth-home. "It is time to do something, Lyari. He cannot be allowed to take your legs out from under you."

Lyari agreed, and late that night in the peak dark of the new moon, she and Jenin walked north to the river, where Old Wend's roundhome sat on the banks of the Bemin just by the bridge.

She pushed the door open and entered, then closed it behind her and struck her flint to light a small oil lamp in the palm of her hand.

Wend's room was right next to the kitchen, and Lyari walked in without any attempt of quiet. She had brought no weapons, and she had no intention of killing him or harming him, but Wend had no way of knowing that, and indeed, he thought her so young and silly that it wouldn't even occur to him to consider she might be dangerous. It struck her that Wend had respected Merin, listened to her, but knew not to fear the woman who had killed her.

Holding the lamp in front of her, Lyari kicked Wend's bed as hard as she could.

The old man made a strangled grunt and sat straight up in bed, fumbling for something on his side table.

"Stop, Wend."

He squinted at her, his eyes adjusting to the dim lamplight. "Lyari. What are you doing here?"

"I thought it was time you and I had a bit of a talk."

"There are better times for such things," he said.

"I think you'll find I don't care what time would be convenient for you."

"Insolence does not become you."

"And lies do not become you." Lyari leaned over the foot of the bed. "Good idea, reinforcing the roofs of the roundhomes. I'm so glad you brought me this wise thing, so that in my youth and ignorance I could see your wisdom and tremble at its strength. You have taught me much, Old Wend, but not the things you think."

Wend fell silent and still, his fingers frozen to the hem of his coverlet. "Perhaps I have underestimated you."

Lyari was past the point of believing such words from him. She thought yet again of the way he had drank his redberry cordial before given leave, and knew full well that he never would have so much as laid his fingers on the glass had she been Merin at the head of that table.

"Fewer than three harvests hence, and I will reinvoke the spell that keeps your redberry cordial in your pantry and on your lips. This is the duty I have agreed to do, and if you think those harvests between now and then give you leave to make a mockery of me in front of the villagers I protect, then I will find a way to silence you."

The light was dim and flickering, but Lyari thought she saw Wend scoot back on his bed just a bit.

She let her voice fall into quiet tones. "There have been enough deaths this cycle, and there will be still more before the sacrifices."

She let the word *sacrifice* be its own threat, and she saw in the glint of lamplight across Wend's eyes that he knew it.

"You have lost much," he said finally.

Lyari didn't answer that, but she felt Jenin beside her, hys presence stronger support than her spine that held her body upright.

And Wend gasped. This time Lyari didn't have to wonder if she had seen him move, because he scrambled back against the headboard of his bed, his feet scrabbling for purchase on his bedlinens.

"Jenin?" Eyes wild, Wend fumbled again at his bedside table and found his candle. He lit it with a touch, just a flicker that barely caused a weak spark, but the candle flame grew.

So Wend had magic, some small bit of it.

Beside her, Jenin said nothing, only stood. Wend continued to suck in large gulps of air, and finally he closed his eyes and leaned back as if denying what he saw with his body as if it could take the specter of Jenin's face away.

Lyari left, but before she went she set the lamp on the coffer at the foot of Wend's bed.

He needed to know it wasn't a dream.

The next morning, Lyari woke to Rina pounding at her door.

"Wend is dead," she said.

Lyari's heart nearly leaped from her body. She followed Rina at a run up the road to Wend's roundhome, and there he was, sprawled in his kitchen, a broken mug of conu juice spilling out from his hand in a puddle.

No blood. No marks. Just the stench of voided bowels melding with burned flatbread.

Lyari met Rina's gaze, shock taking her body and making it immobile.

She had not done this. Had Wend been found in his bed huddled against the headboard, perhaps Lyari would have taken grim credit. But when she looked through the door into Wend's chamber, the lamp she had sat at the foot of his bed was gone, and his coverlets were pulled neatly up to his pillows.

As much as Lyari found she couldn't regret this development, she knew she would have to find what had happened. Not for Wend's sake, but for her own.

Death had found Haveranth once again, and as Lyari looked over the scene, remembering that Wend had seen Jenin's face just before she left, a great many questions swirled in her mind.

THE SMOKE from half a hundred fires filled the air. Summer was well in swing, and only a few turns stood between Ras and High Lights. His pride at what he had accomplished smelled like the smoke on the breeze.

The waymake of Lysytant was situated just over the hills from Boggers and Sands alike, nestled in the creases of the land. There was little water to be found, only weeds covering the ground with their fibrous stalks and bursts of small purple flowers. There were goats, though, and Ham told Ras that only goats would eat the weeds. Ihstal wouldn't touch them.

Some of the people who had gathered with Ras wove the stalks of the weeds into coarse mats, because they were sturdy and lightweight and good for cleaning mud off your boots. Knapweed, they called it. Or stalk-weed or any number of other variations Ras heard used.

Ras spent his days now moving within the waymake and without, where people had put up tents in the lack of available huts. Over the past three moons, he had managed to find people from Sands to Taigers, and though he would likely never know this land as well as Culy did, his travels had given him some of his old reassurance back. He could find water in the hot desert where the sun beat down upon him. He could hunt baszyt, and he had even spotted a kazytya from afar, the ihstal-sized feline moving quickly away as soon as it sensed the presence of hunters.

And this, the waymake full of people who were ready to disrupt Wyt's plan to bring the whole of the Northlands under her fist.

At the edge of the camp, one of Ras's scouts rode back, his ihstal in a lather. She didn't dismount when she approached him, only pointed over the next hill. "Rovers," she said. "Marked ones. At least eight."

Ras whistled sharply, and over a dozen people came hurrying his way, those who were on duty for the later spans of daylight. Making their way to the ihstal herd at the center of the waymake, Ras mounted his favorite, a lively beast called Bas that someone had insisted he ride because their names were so similar. Ras thought the idea was absurd, but the ihstal was fast and fearless and Ras couldn't find fault in the animal, whose name meant *hammer*.

They rode out into the hills, following Ahn, the scout, as she led them to the others she had left to keep eyes on the coming rovers.

It wasn't the first time rovers had ventured so close, but Ras had no intention of allowing them to see the size of his band. He had received some few messages from Carin, who split her time mostly between some waymake on the edge of Crevasses and Silirtahn in Salters, and until the moment Wyt's rovers saw Ras's own face, he wanted them left in ignorance of the numbers he held behind him.

He rode next to Ahn at the head of the group, kneeing Bas to walk closely with Ahn's ihstal. "Did they see you?"

She shook her head. "We don't think they have any idea we're here. They seem to be just passing through."

"You're sure they're wearing Wyt's rune?"

Ahn scowled at him. "Does a turd stink?"

Ras liked Ahn as much for her choices of words as he did for the woman's sheer competence. "Spread out," he said. "Make sure everyone knows I want to catch at least one of them alive."

She gave him a curt nod and edged her ihstal away.

The group fanned out around the hillside where the rovers were camped. Sure enough, when Ras caught his first look at them, their shoulders were marked with the same rune Wyt had all her people use. He wasn't sure what she hoped to accomplish with it; perhaps it was a mark of arrogance.

The rovers spotted them when Ras's mount crested the hill. They sprang into a flurry of motion, grabbing for swords they had let sit next to them on the ground and hastily stretching bowstrings back into place.

Ras yelled at the top of his voice, "Put down your weapons and you may come with us alive!"

He didn't expect them to heed him, but one sword fell to the ground immediately.

A moment later it was picked back up by another of the rovers, whose grim face betrayed her anger as she shoved it back into the hand of the one who had dropped it.

The fight didn't last long, and Ras's arrows found their marks with such speed that the rest of his people scarcely had time to move forward with their swords before all that was left was the sound of dying.

And cursing. The woman who had shoved the sword back into the grasp of her comrade had taken an arrow to the shoulder but was very much alive and spitting rage at Ras, his family, and whatever gods had given him life's breath.

Ras walked up to her, smiling. "Looks like we get to bring you back with us alive after all."

For some reason, she didn't find that comforting.

Ras had her brought to his hut, where she was left, bound and gagged with a strip of leather on a small pile of the weed-stalk mats. He ate his evening meal quietly, sipping water from his waterskin and wiping the juice from the salted baszyt steak from his chin. He'd even choked down the grilled cactus the rotted sanders ate. They said it helped you keep your body watered, but Ras wasn't sure it was worth the slime.

When he was finished and had cleaned his plate with a damp cloth, he knelt beside the woman and pulled the leather gag from her mouth.

She spat at him.

She missed, so Ras chose to ignore it. "I hadn't really planned to kill you, but if you insist on being rude, I might change my mind."

"Wyt will kill you."

Ras smiled. "Interesting thought," he said. "Tell me, what does she mean to do with the world once she's killed everyone who doesn't wear that mark?"

He flicked his fingernail against the white rune on her left shoulder, and she stared at him with hard eyes. Even lying on her side with legs and arms bound, she managed to hold herself in an air of confidence and defiance. Ras could respect that, even if it didn't serve his ends just now.

"Wyt isn't trying to kill everyone," the woman said. "She is trying to help us."

That was unexpected. Ras raised an eyebrow, settling back to sit on the floor next to her. "Exactly how does sending her rovers out into the world to kill people help? Or perhaps she's helping by stealing caravans of blackroot, never mind if children die of flesh-rot besides? Or is she only trying to help the people who steal to make their meals?"

The woman's face grew tight, and her lips made a vertical line that almost touched the floor, as her head was on its side. "It might have started that way, but it's different now."

"Imagine that."

"It's true!" The woman wet her lips. "You don't know what you're talking about."

"I know that Wyt won't be allowed to terrorize good people any longer."

When the woman tried to protest, he gagged her again. Then Ras left his hut and found Ham and Darim. They were working with a group of young archers, teaching them how to shoot faster and more accurately and how to keep their arrows easily accessible.

He turned to Darim. "I need you to get a message to Carin," he said.

"Of course." Darim patted one of the archers on the shoulder and strode toward Ras. "Do you know where she is?"

"Go to Silirtahn," he said. "If she's not there, someone will know where to find her."

"And tell her what?"

"Tell her we will move as soon as she is ready for us."

R YD'S SIDE throbbed, but he ignored it and helped Culy organize hys scrolls.

Culy sat across the hut, a blade on hys lap, eyes closed and concentrating. Several turns back, Ryd had been whittling outside at the central fire of Alarbahis, watching the sunset turn the sky colors he couldn't name, and Culy had stormed by, cursing wildly. When Ryd asked what happened, Culy told him that sy had people all over the Northlands and that each of them had a weapon sy had touched with magic to inform hyr if any ill came to hys people. Someone had broken the staff of one of these folk, a woman from Salters, Culy had said. Aside from that knowledge, Culy had no way of knowing whether she was alive or dead.

Ryd felt disconcerted by the magic he now saw in his daily life. He had become so accustomed to seeing Culy as sy currently was, eyes closed and a strange feel to the air around hyr, that it no longer struck him as remarkable. Instead, Ryd continued to sort scrolls into piles on the small table. Culy, unlike many of the other people in the Northlands, often traveled with a cart. Though families had wagons and carts to be able to shelter children from rain or snow or wind, most folks who had no offspring traveled by foot or ihstal, their only real belongings in a rucksack or sling across their mount's back. One of the scrolls caught Ryd's eye, and he smoothed it out.

It was Lyah's.

Ryd had looked at it before, but not closely enough to really study it. That would take time he did not have, and though Culy allowed him to read the scrolls on occasion, Ryd knew without asking that there was no way he would be given leave to take the scroll from the hut to study it in depth.

He sighed and rolled it back up, placing it in the wooden grid of cubbies that housed all of Culy's scrolls. When he was finished, Ryd tidied the rest of the table, moving two pots of ink to the side.

Ryd sat down to whittle. He had no idea how long Culy would be busy with whatever it was sy did with that blade, but Ryd knew he likely had enough time to finish something small. He worked for a while until the embers of the fire lost some of their glow and he had to stop to stoke it. When he returned to his seat, he frowned at his work. This time he tried to make a baszyt, but as he had never seen one, felt rather sure it looked ridiculous.

Someone scratched at the tent flap, and Culy's eyes opened. "Come in."

The person who entered was Abhil, a hyrsin who often left Alarbahis for two to three turns before coming back with news. This time seemed no different.

Travel-stained and perspiring, Abhil went to Culy and raised hys two forefingers to hys lips in greeting. "You will not believe why I have come."

Culy quirked an eyebrow, and Ryd perked up his ears to listen, fairly sure that Culy would lend credence to just about anything Abhil had to say.

"Wyt would like to meet with you."

Ryd dropped his whittled baszyt on the floor. Neither Culy nor Abhil seemed to notice. While Ryd found that information far from incredible—all told, he was surprised Wyt hadn't said so sooner—the moons had passed and seasons had changed and this was the first anyone Ryd knew had heard directly from Wyt herself.

"That is a bit of a surprise," Culy said. "How is it you came to know this?"

"One of her people found me near Suonlys. He was looking for you and heard you might be in Crevasses still. He is half a day's ride from here, camped just barely in the flats." Abhil looked over and started at the sight of Ryd, then belatedly greeted him with the same touch sy had shown Culy.

Ryd returned it, picked up his baszyt, and began to whittle again.

"Why did he not come to Alarbahis?" Culy's voice held amusement, and Ryd couldn't tell if it was due to Abhil's reaction to his presence or the fact that this rover of Wyt's had given the waymake such wide berth.

"He seemed to think he'd be killed on sight," Abhil said dryly. "He asked for you to come to him there, in good faith, for him to tell you in person about what Wyt wants from you."

"Curious." Culy stood, placing the blade sy had been working on back in its sheath and tossing it on hys bed pallet. "What are the chances that this is a trap?"

Abhil shrugged. "Little to none. I already sent a few folks back that direction to scout it out. If you go, one of them will wait for us to let us know if it is safe."

"Very well," said Culy. Sy straightened and started to gather hys things. "We will depart shortly."

Abril nodded and ducked out of the hut, leaving Ryd and Culy alone once more.

Culy seemed to be pondering something, and sy looked at Ryd for a long moment. "I think it is probably best if you stay here," sy said.

Ryd felt a pang at that, and not the now-usual pain in his side, but he chose not to argue. "I will meet with Aryt while you are gone and continue work on my halming."

That brought him a nod of approval from Culy, who then strode from the hut. Ryd watched hyr ride away, then returned to Culy's hut.

Half a day's ride, Abhil had said. That gave Ryd an entire day and likely more to do something he had wanted to do for several turns.

He pulled a fresh length of parchment from Culy's tightly bound roll and pulled up a stool to sit at the table. His fingers easily found Lyah's scroll where he had put it a short time ago, and he took out a well-worn reed pen from a sack at the back of the table. Dipping the pen in a pot of ink, he began to copy the scroll. Carin hadn't thought to do this earlier, and that had been a mistake. Now Ryd had a chance, and he would take it.

It wasn't that he expected Culy to deny permission. Ryd simply could not take that risk. Culy had become a mentor, but Ryd was not certain he could extend the trust of their relationship to friendship. For all his seeming acceptance, Ryd knew his place in Alarbahis was fragile. And he was separated from Carin.

Lyah's scroll was long, and she had written small. It would take most of the inkpot and much of the night to copy. When he was finally finished and the oil lamp guttered and burned low, Ryd set the copied scroll on the floor of the hut, carefully laid out to finish drying. He weighed it down with his carving tools. From his belt, he pulled a cloth. Then he upended the pot, dumping a puddle of ink on the table. He wiped it up with the cloth, but left a few small smears.

Rubbing the drips from the pot itself, he stoppered it and replaced it at the back of the desk. For good measure, Ryd smeared a swatch of ink across his belt and pushed some under the fingernails of his right hand.

If Culy asked about the depleted inkpot, Ryd would simply say he spilled it on the roll of parchment.

CARIN REREAD Ras's message four times before showing it to Sart. "Soon, then," was all Sart said.

They had spent the past moon trying to come up with a way to rescue Valon from Wyt, but the more time passed, the more anxious Carin felt. Wyt's numbers were too strong, and as much guilt as Carin felt for not trying to rescue her when she was first captured, she knew they would likely have to wait until Ras moved and she had had her chance to break the stone.

More pressingly—and indeed, Carin hardened herself to think of this as more pressing—Culy was on hys way to join them at the spring.

Sy arrived two days later with a group of others, but it wasn't the hyr-sin who drew Carin's attention.

Ryd was with hyr.

Carin hardly recognized the sound that came from her throat, and she flung herself at Ryd, nearly knocking him to the ground. His arms enfolded her, bonier than she remembered, but his pale green eyes were the same, and she pulled back enough to look into them. He pressed his forehead to hers. The warmth of his skin and the familiarity of his pres-ence—Carin's shoulders shook with a sob she could not contain.

For the past moons, she had gone about her business and done what she had to, running to and fro with Sart from Silirtahn to the still-name-less waymake at the spring and back again. She had heard from Ras at least once every other turn, but she had heard nothing from Ryd, only the news from Culy's messages that Ryd was training as a halmer and had a quick mind and nimble fingers both.

Carin could have told Culy that. Now, seeing him in front of her, he looked older. Gone was the scrawny young man from Haveranth. He had grown a little, and now looked Carin right in the eye at a level with her. His muscles were tighter, his shoulders grown broad even with his slen-der frame.

"Halming, eh?" Carin said to him, wiping tears from her cheeks. He gave her a bashful smile.

"Turns out I am good at something," Ryd said, reaching into his rucksack. He held out a sheathed halm knife, then pulled it out careful-ly. It was not only barbarously hooked on the end, but the hilt was tooled with a set of runes that twisted all the way around it.

Carin took it from him, running her fingertips over the runes and testing the edge of the blade on her hand. "Ryd, this is a marvel."

"I had help from Aryt," he said. "But the rune work is mine."

She tried to hand it back to him, but he pushed the knife back at her. "It's for you."

Though she partly wanted to protest such a gift, Carin hugged the knife to her chest. Having something made by Ryd's hands somehow teth-ered a part of her to the earth that she hadn't realized felt adrift.

"Thank you," she said finally.

Carin turned to Culy, who had been greeting Sart, but Carin was also somehow sure sy had been watching this exchange between her and Ryd out of the corner of hys eye.

She greeted hyr with a polite nod and touch of her fingers to her lips, and Culy responded in kind. The next thing sy said was simply, "Show me the spring."

Watching Northlanders discover the spring was like watching a child see hys first rainbow.

In the relatively short time she had known Culy, she had not seen hyr as someone to show ready emotion, but when the first cup of spring water passed over hys lips, tears filled hys eyes and spilled over, and in the passing of the day that followed, there were many more tears of wonder and relief and the simple awe of coming across a treasure they didn't know existed.

Summer had settled over the land, and the persimmon Carin had planted had blossomed and now bore a few small fruits. She had managed to make a small garden near the hut she shared with Sart, and she taught Talnyt's children to tend it when she was away.

The children had abundant food and water, and one of them even had begun to tend toward plumpness. Carin hadn't thought she would ever see a plump anyone ever again, and though part of her wanted to caution the others in the waymake to show care not to become too used to this place and its sustenance, she couldn't bring herself to tell any of them to be careful.

And yet wariness lay at the pit of all Carin did, whether it was planting vegetables in her garden or discussing tactics with Sart. Through all of it was the knowledge that this place, this lush place, could any day be overrun with Wyt's people, the children turned out and their parents hurt or killed.

Talnyt understood that, Carin knew, but he seemed determined to keep it from his children. From all the children in the waymake, to be sure. Now there were ten, three more families having come to the spring after one of the Northlanders went to fetch them. Some had come from Sands where water, standing or running or otherwise, was only seen in the case of the rare rainstorm that would more often flood the desert and rush away than not, the hungry sand slurping it up and ravening once more with dust and rock and wind.

That night, when the fire burned low and the sleepiness of darkness cloaked them, Culy told them about the message from Wyt.

"She wants to meet with you? Now? Are you going to go?" Sart sounded as if someone had suggested she build a hut from ihstal dung.

"I think the timing of it is likely significant," said Culy, nodding. "I'm far from unknown. If she wanted to speak with me, there have been moons upon moons for her to do so. Instead, she waits until now, and I would like to know why. I am not inclined to meet with her, not before we make an attempt on the stone."

Ryd and Carin exchanged a look, but Carin couldn't think of anything to say about that, so instead she brought up Valon. "We have tried to figure out a way to rescue her," Carin finished, and for a moment she feared that Culy would be angry that she and Sart had not succeeded.

"No, do not." Culy looked at Carin with what could only be called relief. "That you say she was taken alive tells me they want her alive for some reason. I was most happy to hear that she was not killed immediately."

That time, Ryd and Culy looked at one another, and Carin watched the understanding pass between them. Strange that Ryd had been so fully taken into Culy's circle, though she supposed it was no stranger than her own situation. Ryd looked tired, Carin thought. Looking more closely at him it seemed even the water had not been enough to perk him up after the journey they had made to get to the spring.

Culy went on a moment later, interrupting Carin's thoughts.

"I think you are also correct in assuming that Wyt has made her camp around another spring. What I see here convinces me of that. I wonder what it is she expects to get from meeting with me," Culy mused.

Sart had been quiet throughout the entire conversation, which Carin found odd, but she spoke up now. "Then you agree? The best chance we have is to break the stone?"

Sart held Culy's gaze, her own face impassive, though by now Carin had spent enough time with her to know that the slight crease at the top of her forehead meant she was waiting to breathe until she got her answer.

Culy turned to Carin. "I do. And I think I have managed to figure out why you can succeed where Sart did not."

Carin didn't get a chance to hear what that reason was, because at that moment, Ryd buckled over and screamed in pain.

Dimly, Carin realized that the bustle of the waymake had come to a sharp halt, but she was already on her knees beside Ryd, holding his head back from hitting the leg of a table. "What's wrong with him?" she demanded.

"I don't know." Culy joined her on the floor, hands going to Ryd's abdomen.

Ryd made a sharp growling sound through gritted teeth, and a moment later repeated it with a voice like needles stabbing into Carin's heart. "My side."

Culy blanched, and the sight frightened Carin almost more than the tears of pain that ran down Ryd's cheeks.

Her eyes sought out Sart, and what she saw on Sart's face did not reassure her. Alarmed, she looked at Culy, whose attention was still locked on Ryd's stomach.

"Culy," said Carin. "Please."

"I can't be sure just yet, but if I am right, this is very dire. I will not lie to you."

"Sart?" Carin met the girl's gaze and felt the urge to beg her to say something. "Someone tell me!"

Sart looked back and forth between Carin and Culy, and when Culy sighed and nodded, Sart let out a long breath.

"It's called bulber-bloat," she said. "It's a disease, like we talked about."

It had been a long time since that conversation, and much of it ran together in Carin's memory. "Tell me what that means, Sart."

"It means there is something growing within him."

"What?" Carin's mind filled with the image of a tree's roots digging their way into the earth, twining around rocks and through rabbit warrens, but bringing pain instead of life.

"Help me move him to the pallet," Culy said, and Carin lifted Ryd's shoulders while sy got his legs.

They laid him out on the pallet, and he finally gasped a breath, heaving one after another until the tears stopped flowing from his eyes and the perspiration that had beaded on his forehead began to dry in the heat of the hut.

"I was right then," Ryd said, and they all looked at him.

"What did you say?" Carin felt every muscle in her face go slack.

"They told me, a while back. About diseases. It's not like what we got in Suonlys," Ryd said, giving Carin a wan smile. "I've been learning all I could about them, about the ones that you can live through, like water-lung and the drips—and the ones that you can't. Flesh-rot and gut-rot and bulber-bloat. I learned what the signs were. I was pretty sure when the pains started."

"You foolish boy," Culy said, and Carin almost hit hyr until sy went on. "Had you told me sooner, I could have helped ease the pain."

"But not save my life."

Culy shook hys head. "No, I cannot do that."

"There has to be something to do," said Carin. She looked at Ryd. "How long?"

"Before I die?"

"No! How long has this been going on?" She thought back to the past cycle. There was no disease in the Hearthland, no...rot of any kind when it came to people. This very land had poisoned him.

She wanted to tear up the ground, but that would not save her friend.

If someone had told her merely one cycle before that Ryd would supplant Lyah as her best and closest friend, she would have thought they had had too much iceberry wine. But when Carin had left home behind, it was Ryd who stayed by her side. Maybe for his own reasons at first, but now he was here with her, his own person, and no one in their lives here would even think to sit on him.

Ignoring the confusion on Sart's and Culy's faces, Carin climbed over Ryd and curled herself up against his back, wrapping her arms around him. His hands found her arms with the strength of someone who did heavy work, and as her new halm belt knife dug into the side of her leg, she did not doubt that he did heavy work.

After a few bemused moments, both Sart and Culy retreated from the hut, fastening the canvas flap in place and leaving Carin and Ryd alone.

They lay in silence for some time.

"How are you doing here, Carin?" Ryd asked. "I have thought of you so often."

"I am—" Carin bit off the end of the sentence. She had been about to say, *I am of no importance,* but she realized that, to Ryd, she was. She thought for a moment, then took a shaking breath. "I think when I declared my appellation, I chose wrong."

Ryd was quiet. He did not turn his head to look at her, and for a long moment, Carin simply felt him breathe against her chest. "Were you planning to change your appellation at High Harvest, back in Haveranth?"

She noticed he did not say *back home.* "Yes. No. I don't know. I had spoken to Dyava about it—" saying her lover's name still felt like the slicing of a halm blade into her heart, "—but I was not sure."

"But you are now."

"I don't know," Carin said. "All I know is that *woman* and *girl* do not feel like me. I'm not certain *hyrsin* or *man* or *boy* do either."

Ryd did turn then, his lips forming a sweet smile as he met Carin's eyes. "Be you," he said.

Dyava's words from so long ago.

Carin held her friend closer, knowing he could feel her tears through the fabric of his tunic. A moment later, they both wept, their shoulders shaking in unharmonious rhythm, curled tightly together in a still-strange land.

Finally, Carin could take it no longer.

"Tell me, Ryd. Please. Tell me how I save you."

"You don't always have to rescue me." The quiet smile in his voice, harkening back to the eve of their Journeying when she had pried Stil's squeak and six others off him, made Carin's heart feel as though it were about to shatter.

"Yes, I do," she said. "Please, Ryd. Tell me how I save you."

She felt the quiet rise and fall of his breathing against her stomach and the renewed grip of his hands on her arms at his middle. She smelled the sweat on him, its scent somehow acrid and tinny. And she heard the cracks in his words as she squeezed her arms tightly against him and he said, "You don't."

THE NEXT morning, Culy entered the hut to find Carin and Ryd still huddled together on the pallet, and sy had woken them brusquely to insist on looking at Ryd's stomach.

Carin made herself watch.

She sat aside as Ryd disrobed to his breeches and lay down on the pallet. His torso was smooth and flat, with the planes of muscles clear across every inch of it. Nothing looked amiss to her.

Culy moved hys hands across the whole of Ryd's stomach, fingers probing at the skin below his ribs. Hys face showed little, and Carin watched for any twitch of lips or eyes that might give her some clue into what sy was thinking. Finally, sy sighed and nodded to Carin.

Sy looked down at Ryd and said, "You're right. I wish you had told me sooner. Does Aryt know?"

Ryd nodded, and Carin frowned until she remembered that Aryt was the halmer teaching Ryd the craft.

"I asked him not to say anything," Ryd said. "He agreed. He lost a child to bulber-bloat a ten-cycle back."

"I remember," said Culy. "I treated hyr."

With a shift of hys shoulders, Culy told Ryd to breathe all the way in and then all the way out. On the out, sy pointed to Ryd's side, halfway between his bottom rib and his hip. And Carin saw it, the slightest bulge that was in the wrong place for a muscle. When Culy placed two fingers on the bulge and pushed, Ryd yelled.

Culy stopped. "This is why you are always pacing in my hut, isn't it?"

"Sitting hurts sometimes."

When Culy drew a breath, Carin was surprised to hear it quaver.

"Well?" Ryd said. "Aren't you going to tell me?"

"Tell you what?" Carin asked, then regretted it.

"How long I have before I go back to the earth."

"Three cycles, maybe four," said Culy without hesitation.

Three cycles. Maybe four.

Carin thought of Merin and her nearly two hundred harvests.

Ryd might not see his twenty-second.

"Can I get up now?" At Culy's nod, Ryd sat up with no hint of pain—though Carin noticed that his movement was jerky, as if he had learned to avoid positions that would cause it—and pulled his tunic over his head.

With that, he left the hut, leaving Carin with Culy.

"Before you ask, no, there is no way."

Carin expected that, but she pushed on anyway. "The stones."

"What about the stones?" She had caught Culy by surprise, and hys gaze turned inquisitive.

"There is no disease in the Hearthland, Culy," Carin said. "None. If we get the drips it's because of cold, not because of disease. We cough because of smoke or because we gulped down food too quickly or because we don't swim as well as we should and go under. We sick up only if we drink too much iceberry wine. There is no flesh-rot or bulber-bloat or any of the others. One of the stones in the spell made it so. If I break that stone—"

Culy cut her off. "What would that do except bring disease to your homeland?"

Flummoxed, Carin made a fist and hit her own leg as hard as she could. "I don't know. It's the only thing I can think of."

"You should try, but this is not something in which you should place your hope."

"You don't believe that breaking the stones will help your land."

"I believe that all actions have consequences and reactions, and I believe that, as I once told you, that while some good may come of this thing you wish to do, you must be prepared that ill will come as well." Culy met her gaze, then walked to her and gently took her hands. "Though just because some ill may come does not mean that it is not worth doing."

Carin clung to hys hands for a moment, and then they both let their arms drop.

Culy barked a laugh a moment later. "I'd be lying if I said I don't want you to succeed at least partly because it will force your people to feel what they have made for us."

At first, Carin felt her hackles begin to rise, and she opened her mouth as if to say that was wrong, but then she remembered High Lights and the banality of their so-called remembrance, and she couldn't help but nod.

"Ryd should stay here from now on," she said. "At least there is ample water, and he can plant a garden and carve. There is a halm grove three days' walk from here, too."

She half-expected Culy to fight her, but instead sy agreed with a tight smile.

"If there is a way to save Ryd, I will find it," said Carin.

The smile vanished from Culy's lips, and sy inclined hys head. "If there is a way to save Ryd, I think you are the only one who could find such a thing. But many others have tried, with magic and without, and they have all failed."

Carin left the hut and went straight to Mari, a short woman with a matching temper and eyes almost the same grey as Culy's. She had seen over eighty harvests and her black hair wore a bright band of silver at the front, which she had cut shorter to hang partially over her face. She was fast, she was smart, and Carin knew where to send her.

"Go to Ras," she said. "Tell him we will make for the stone on High Lights."

Mari's ihstal was almost white, and Carin watched as Mari leaped onto the animal's back and rode off to the north.

Bide already waned in the sky, her sister beside her, the two crescents curled against each other like Carin and Ryd had been the night before. Bide. The moon was as appropriate as anything for what Carin was about to do. Bide she would, until Toil waxed heavy in the sky and the sun sapped their strength with the force of its heat. On that day, Carin would bring water back to the Northlands.

That night a hush came over the waymake, with only the quiet murmur of voices and the rushing of the water from the stream filling their ears.

Carin sat with Ryd outside in the blue grasses, arm in arm, as they had been the night before their Journeying.

"What do you think Lyah's doing?" Carin asked suddenly. "Do you think she has passed through her apprenticeship yet?"

"She probably has," said Ryd. Something passed over his face. "Do you think she's ever seen Jenin again?"

Carin's arm tightened on Ryd's, remembering those nights on their Journeying, seeing the face of their dead friend. "I don't know," she said after a long pause.

"She probably thinks we're dead." Ryd barked a laugh. "Who could make it through those mountains?"

He paused for a moment, and Carin knew he was thinking the same thing as she even before he said it.

"Do you think she knows Merin sent hunters after us?"

Carin couldn't bring herself to answer. Someday, Lyah would know. She would have to know. She would be the new Merin once Merin was gone. She would be the one to send the hunters.

"Sometimes I wish we had stayed with the ialtag," she said suddenly. "They lead simpler lives."

Ryd nodded, though Carin couldn't tell which part he was agreeing with. Maybe both.

"Funny, isn't it?" he said. "You'd think that sharing your direct thoughts and emotions with everyone you know would make things more complicated, not less."

They were quiet again for a long while, then Carin spoke again. "Do you really think Lyah thinks we're dead?"

"I think so," Ryd said slowly. Then he gave Carin a wide grin that didn't reach his eyes. "Sooner or later it'll be true anyway."

He pulled something from his overshirt and tucked it into Carin's hand.

"I made a copy of Lyah's scroll for you. Don't tell Culy. I told hyr I spilled the inkpot."

Carin hid the scroll away, her heart beating faster with the relief of having the scroll again. No matter what happened here, she had Ryd. When she said so, he gave a little laugh.

"I'll stay as long as I can."

Above them, the clouds had parted to show the stars, and Carin, unable to respond to Ryd joking about his own death, lay back on the grass and pointed up. Together they named off constellations they knew and created new ones they didn't, and the stars burned bright, bright in the sky, even with Bide and her sister dancing across it in crescent form.

Carin knew the time would soon come when she would not have Ryd by her side, either because she had to leave or because he was gone, stolen by this bulber-bloat that grew inside him, and she clung to that moment there under the sky, feeling younger and more vulnerable than she had since she was a child. It seemed that the light from the stars could shine into her very heart, and like all light, it showed every flaw and crack in her confidence.

She wondered if Ryd felt the same way, if he was frightened. He seemed to face his own death with a kind of matter-of-fact aplomb, and Carin couldn't quite understand it, just as she couldn't quite understand disease. What made these illnesses happen? How did they choose their victims? She wanted to ask Ryd how long it had taken him to look death in the eye, even across the wide-but-ever-shrinking chasm of the cycles between him and it, but when she turned over to ask him, the words sticking to her tongue, she found that he had fallen asleep.

She didn't wake him, only lay her head on his shoulder and looked up at the stars.

93

RAS HAD begun the trek westward with relief.

When Mari had arrived at his camp with word from Carin that he was to meet her at the stone at High Lights, it had sent a breath of excitement through the people gathered there. Some of it was the prospect of finally getting to move, finally getting to do something at long last, but Ras knew—everyone knew, really—that just as vital to their excitement was the fact that water and food were ever scarcer.

When he had first come to the Northlands, Ras had found it unendingly strange that these people moved around so constantly, that they didn't simply stay in one place and live. But now, having been here for nearly a half cycle, he understood. Each day he remained at the camp, a person or two left and did not return. Ras could not begrudge them that. Each day he remained at the camp, Ras himself felt the itch to leave just a little stronger. He watched the scrubby weeds around the camp get trodden into the dirt under feet—ihstal and goat and human alike. He found himself wishing the cycle would wheel itself faster, that the moons would wax and wane quicker, and that Toil would come quickly so he could deliver these people back into the life they knew, where they could find their food and water where they would. Each day he remained at the camp, Ras felt himself to be just a little more of a Northlander than he had been the day before.

He had heard from Culy that Wyt likely had access to a supply of fresh water, either a spring or some other means, and he agreed. Having even one hundred people in his camp without such a thing would have left most people dying of thirst, had Sart and Carin not sent regular barrels of water from their own spring.

Still, as they began the trek through the hills toward Boggers with Toil waxing in the sky above their heads, they were hungry, and they were thirsty, and there weren't enough squirrels and rabbits between them to feed hungry mouths.

They pushed forward hard, the ihstal ranging ahead with riders to alert the rest of the group of any possible rovers of Wyt's, and when the morning of High Lights dawned, Ras had his people in place a league away from the stone.

He had sent Mari ahead to coordinate with Carin, and she came back midmorning with the news that the rovers had a few scouts out but that some of Culy's people had captured them. The path to the waymake, she said, was clear.

They moved as soon as the sun hit its peak in the sky, though the heat and sticky humidity of the air were a miserable combination.

No one would expect them to attack on the longest day in the hot summer sun with no water or food.

The rovers at the waymake saw them coming over the hills and a bell began to ring.

Ras gave a grim smile and signaled his people forward. A bell. A quick glance at the waymake and the people running around it to arm themselves told him that no such simple thing as a tolling bell could save them, not when they were outnumbered almost three to one.

There were barrels of water around the waymake, two per hut, and the sight not only confirmed what Culy had said about Wyt's supply of fresh water, but spurred Ras's people forward, their thirst for water far dwarfing their thirst for blood.

The fight began with one of Ras's arrows through a rover's throat, and the sight of spurting blood sent a roaring yell erupting from the people behind him. Darim leaped from the back of her ihstal, arrows in her draw hand, shooting them so quickly that her every movement blurred. She caught his eye, and together they advanced, her on foot and him on Bas's back, the ihstal whistling high and keen with the excitement he sensed in the air. Over the moons together, Ras and Darim had learned to watch each other in their peripheral vision, and now they each drew three arrows from their hip quivers in tandem, firing them into the waymake. One of each of their arrows caught a rover, and he fell, both heart and forehead punctured.

With a grim smile, they moved on.

Where swords clashed, Ras's swords won there, too. He saw a rover miss a clear killing strike and slice one of Ras's people's arms instead of taking the obvious hit to the heart.

It all seemed easy. Too easy. Ugly.

Within what felt like ten breaths, the rovers were dead, and Ras's people fell upon the water barrels, drinking and laughing with relief.

Ras joined them, but he kept his mind alert as he drank slowly, allowing his belly to adjust to the water. He had had only sips at a time for the past several turns, making sure always that his people got to drink first. The sun beat down upon them, drying the blood on the ground.

The air was heavy with moisture, and Ras hated it. Breathing felt as though he might drown, and he knew he would be happy to return to Crevasses when this was over. Or perhaps Taigers. He hadn't spent any time in Salters yet. Perhaps he would go there.

Ras heard a whistle behind him and turned to see Mari riding toward him. Behind her was Culy—and with hyr, Sart and Carin.

He felt his face spread into a grin at the sight of her, and she smiled back, though it seemed to him her eyes fell on the carnage around him with sadness that kept the smile from touching her eyes. She slid from the ihstal she rode upon with Sart, her halm bow slung over her shoulder and what looked like a new halm knife at her belt.

Her face had changed, grown thinner and sharper with the passing moons, but her sleeveless tunic showed strong brown muscles, deeply bronzed by the sun. Her eyes, always striking, stood out, bold and blue. Her black hair was longer by a handspan and now reached halfway down her back in a cascade of waves.

She came to him and embraced him, and Ras felt a surge of happiness to see a familiar face, even one so much changed by this place they now lived. He wondered what he looked like to her.

Culy and Sart dismounted as well, and they exchanged a long look.

"The stone," Culy said slowly. "Something doesn't sit well with me about this."

Together they walked through the waymake, stepping around the bodies of the fallen. Ras felt a deep satisfaction that none of his people were among them. Some casualties, yes, but no deaths. He saw Ham bandaging the arm of the woman who had escaped death by her attacker's incompetence, and around them people still drank their fill of water and rummaged about in the waymake huts for food. Ras would not begrudge them of giving to the rovers what the rovers gave everyone else in kind.

The stone stood just beyond the edge of the waymake.

Sart muttered as they approached, "There are more huts than last time."

Carin nodded in agreement. "When Valon was taken, there were perhaps ten people here. They almost doubled their population."

This brought Culy's head up, and sy called for Mari. When she came over, he murmured something to her, low and urgent, and Ras could not hear. To Ras, all sy said was, "Be alert, and tell your people to do the same."

Ras turned and called to Dunal, who had found a leg of clucker roasting on a fire and was pulling long strips of meat from the bone. "Dunal! Go round and tell everyone to stay wary!"

To his credit, Dunal trotted off, but he took the clucker leg with him.

Something bright flew through the air.

Twisting around, Ras yelled, "Fire arrow!"

The arrow hit one of the huts, and the canvas began to burn. He couldn't see where Mari had gone at first, but he didn't have to look far. She had mounted an ihstal and started to ride away, but as Ras watched, she took an arrow to the side. She circled back toward the waymake, managing to stay on the ihstal.

People poured over the crest of the hill.

"The stone, Carin! Now!" Sart nearly pushed Carin toward it, but Carin shook her head.

"I'm not leaving you all to fight alone!"

Culy's hands touched in front of hyr, and Ras blinked at what he saw. Something pale and silvery crackled between hys palms, and Ras felt the cold touch of fear at his heart.

"You're not leaving us helpless," Culy said to Carin. "Go now, or you may not get another chance for this stone or any other."

Ras wheeled to the waymake, where his people had already formed up in defensive positions. Between the hill and the waymake, they were cornered.

He hadn't come this far not to leave alive.

SART FELT her nerves jangle when she saw Culy begin to pull on hys magic. What sy did was something she had never been able to manage, but there were plenty of things Sart Lahivar could do that Culy couldn't.

When sy loosed a current of silvery energy straight at a line of incoming rovers, Sart turned to the rovers who were trying to flank Ras's people to her left.

The hot summer sun was pure energy, and she opened herself to it. She felt her sweat dry on her skin, coolness spreading over her as she took the heat of the blazing longest day and spindled it deep within her. The hum rose around her, rising, rising, rising until her teeth buzzed in her mouth and her hair prickled all over her body from head to toes. Sart took the heat and the light from the sun on its day of dominance over the land, and she pulled it into herself. She targeted a group of ten rovers coming into the waymake, and she made her mind tug on the spindling light and heat, drawing it away from them.

One of them cried out, "I can't see!"

Several of the others stumbled. Sart pulled harder, knowing that to them, the day grew dimmer and colder until they would shiver blindly and fall to their knees.

A quick look behind her told her that Carin was staring at the stone without touching it. She started to yell at the other girl to hurry up, but the very sight of the stone almost made Sart lose her concentration on the rovers.

She turned her thoughts back to keeping Wyt's band of thieves and murderers away from Carin.

Sart split off the pull she had put on the first set of rovers, like someone might use two hands separately to guide a partner in a dance. With her left, she kept those first rovers cold and blind, and with her right, she drew down more of the sun to her task.

Her eyes scanned the whole of the waymake, taking in the scene as best she could. Wyt's people all wore that ridiculous white rune across their shoulders, which Sart thought wasn't the smartest thing to do in a battle. The runes on their chests made exceptionally good targets, and when she looked for Ras, she saw he and Darim were hitting those targets more often than not.

She found her own next target on the opposite side of the waymake's huts, riding out of the west. Mounted on ihstal, the rovers covered the ground quickly. Too quickly for Sart's liking.

This time she didn't aim for the rovers themselves; she aimed for the ihstal.

She didn't want to hurt the animals; on the contrary, she would rather they live over their riders. Sart thought of Tahin running in the sand at Salters, of the excited whistles she had made there. Sart filled the ihstal's ears with that whistle, with that pure joy and elation. She saw them perk up, their long necks rising, their gait slowing as they looked around for their happy herd mate. The riders kneed the animals hard, but the ihstal started to prance, moving back and forth instead of forward, short tails raised and waving.

Next to her, Culy had a small smirk on hys face, and Sart returned it. It had been some time since they had worked together in a fight, and she knew sy remembered it as well as she did. Sy flung another sheet of silver crackles out over the incoming rovers. Like Sart, Culy aimed to stop and to slow rather than to kill. Killing with magic was not something to trifle with, and they both knew it.

Sart couldn't tell if Carin had yet started, and by now the rovers were too close to the waymake for her to turn and look. She couldn't afford to lose her focus on the threads of magic she had set in motion.

Another wave of rovers crested the hill.

She saw Culy start, and she felt the same. A sick feeling twisted through her gut, and a grim set pulled itself to her lips.

Where was Wyt finding all these people? From their clothing and weapons, they were from everywhere. That she could gather so many to her if she had found a spring like the one on the border of Crevasses, Sart didn't doubt, but this many people armed and willing to fight? What had she given them? Were they fighting only for the stone, or were they fighting Culy?

Culy had not met with Wyt; neither of them had thought it wise, and now with a battle raging across a strip of almost-bog over a large rock, Sart wasn't entirely sure they would be on speaking terms afterward anyway.

The coolness she had captured with the spindled sun magic began to lift, and a sheen of sweat formed on Sart's face. She tried to count the rovers coming over the hill and failed. Scores of people, all armed and wearing Wyt's rune.

With a bleak, tight smile, Sart saw that she and Culy and all of Ras's people were outnumbered.

Magic wouldn't stay very useful for long.

Sart unsheathed her sword while she still had time, and she pulled from the sun and the earth around her, spindling magic as fast as she could. She grew weary, her limbs feeling heavy and her breathing slowing. But Carin had not yet broken the stone, and because of that Sart would keep going. Carin had fought off rovers and kept Sart alive in this very spot, and Sart would be burnt to a crisp before she let anything stop that woman from her work.

She saw Ras not far away, jerking arrows from fallen bodies as fast as he could. One, two, three, all in his draw hand and fired with blinding speed. He leaped from place to place, quiver empty but always finding new arrows in the bodies of the slain, and Sart couldn't help but admire his grim efficiency.

She couldn't help but notice every one of his shots was aimed to kill.

"Culy," she said, her eyes falling on rovers not far away. They had seen her and Culy, and they began to run in their direction.

"I see them," sy said.

"I'm going to go meet them."

"Go. I'll stay with Carin."

Sart didn't look back, only held her sword low and ran at the rovers. There were five of them and only one of her, but she had the sun in her blade, and when she raised it to the sky, the light burst forth from its bronze length, dazzling in its intensity even to her, and it wasn't aimed at her. The rovers slowed, but did not stop, their eyes blinking in the face of the sun's light drawn down and wielded against them.

She struck, darting in with her sword flashing out, still blazing bright in her hand. One of the rovers stumbled back, and she felt her sword make contact with hys arm, slicing through flesh and muscle until she felt the unmistakable jar of hitting bone.

Twisting, she stabbed out with the blade and hit another rover in the belly. Sart tried to leap backward, but one of the rovers struck not with his sword but with his foot, aiming a kick into her hip.

Sart sprawled backward, keeping her grip firm on her sword. The impact knocked the air from her lungs with a whoosh, and she coughed into the dirt, holding up her sword and yanking on the threads of power she had tied to the sun.

The sword flared up so brightly, it lit the entire waymake. Red blood left jagged, spattery green imprints on the insides of Sart's eyelids, and for a moment she thought she'd blinded herself. But then a foot stomped down on her leg, and she struck out with the blade itself, slicing into the tendon at the back of the owner's knee.

Sart rolled away and jumped to her feet. Movement behind her and to her right drew her gaze, and she let out a gasp as a pair of rovers descended on Culy. Sart spun, swinging her sword in a wide arc and lunging forward even as she made the sword flash once more, and she felt the blade make contact with rover bodies. Before they could recover, she darted toward Culy.

She caught one of the rovers in the back, and this time she did aim to kill. Her sword plunged between his shoulder blades, and she twisted and kicked at him at the same time, stabbing him through the heart and shoving him off her blade in two quick motions. Culy hit the other square in the chest with that silvery energy, and when the rover stumbled backward, Sart put her sword through the rover's throat.

Around her, Culy's magic rose like the wind, crackles of silver threading through the air. Hys eyes burned silver with it, distant as if seeing far beyond the waymake, beyond the battle, beyond the earth itself.

The rovers faltered in their attack for only a moment, fear drawing their faces tight and making their steps falter. But only for a moment. One of them yelled something Sart could not hear, and they ran forward into the field of Culy's magic.

Carin's hands were on the stone; Sart could see that now.

"Break it, Carin!" Sart screamed.

But she didn't know if the girl could even hear her.

CARIN'S FINGERS touched the stone, and everything behind her ceased to exist.

There was no Ras shooting arrows into rovers, no Culy and Sart wielding magic, no hordes of Wyt's people cascading over hills to kill them all.

No.

There was only Carin, and only the stone, and when her hands touched it, she felt the stone welcome her home.

It knew her. She understood that now.

When her hands touched the stone, Carin could see deep into its soul, where it held the memories of thousands of cycles. It had watched as the land changed, soaking up the water like a ball of bavel fibers dipped in the river. This stone had seen a massive forest with trees the size of twenty people stacked atop one another wither and fade and burn away into nothingness. This stone had seen the small sandy desert grow and spread and take over the land like that bulb in Ryd's belly would do to his body.

This stone had seen death and disease and thirst, so much thirst.

It wasn't the stone's fault, for a stone wants nothing more than to be a stone. A stone does not seek out any purpose that will require it to be something it is not, but this stone had had purpose thrust upon it by magic, and this stone behaved as just about anything will when forced into something unexpected; the stone adapted.

And so the stone sucked water from the Northlands and gave that water away by pushing it to the south. The stone changed the way the mountains sent their runoff, pushing it southward instead of allowing any to come north.

When Carin's hands touched the stone, she felt it know her, and she felt it welcome her, and at the same time she felt it wish for its own end.

A stone that wanted nothing more than to return to being simply a stone.

Carin felt the hum of magic surround her, or maybe she just listened again, for that hum had become so much a part of her life each day that she now barely ever noticed it.

She noticed it now.

It spread over her like the sea, and like plunging into the sea, Carin went down and down and down and down, and it was cool and blue and dark there. Blue like her eyes and blue like the grasses and blue like the sky.

The hum surrounded her, and she floated.

While she floated, she thought of home, of that place she had left behind. She understood the stone better then, because all Carin had wanted was to go on her Journeying and find her name. She had wanted to return to her village and live in peace in the roundhome she had made with her hands. She had wanted to work maha into window frames and help her mother with her forge and drink iceberry wine and end the day with Lyah crawling through her window even though she was allowed to use the door. She had wanted to greet Haveranth at High Harvest and tell the villagers who she truly was, not woman, not man, maybe not hyrsin either. She had wanted to kiss Dyava's lips until they were swollen and spend nights upon nights exploring his body.

But instead of all that, Carin had learned that it was all a lie. There was no home, no gentle work, no peace to be had for her. Perhaps no self, either.

She felt the stone sing then, a song of stones and sleep and time that lulled Carin where she floated, content in the knowledge that for once, for the impossible, inexplicable now, she was understood.

She told the stone stories, about those days before the Journeying. She told the stone of Ryd and how his friendship had transcended everything she was supposed to want and turned her into someone she truly wanted to be. She told the stone of Sart and the way they rode Tahin together from place to place and how feeling Sart's breathing against her chest had become another form of home. She told the stone of the magic in her, and how she let it be quiet deep inside of her.

The stone told her stories too, about the days before it had been made into more than a stone. It showed her a land where crops were just beginning to flourish and where birds flew back and forth across the sky. It told her stories of people who came and sat in the shade of it, back when it was whole. And it told her stories of the day people came and broke it apart into smaller pieces, and forced each of those pieces into a role they didn't seek.

For a long time, Carin floated and shared herself with the stone. And when she was done, and it was done, they hung there in that cool, blue, dark place, and Carin knew it was time.

From the deep within the stone, Carin rose.

The stone bore her up, and around her was the hum that grew louder and louder and louder.

Carin had long since lost her body in the stone, and she felt as though she became the stone, as though the stone became her and they were one and the same. The stone showed her herself, not man or woman or hyrsin but simply self, and Carin thirsted to *be*.

She became thirsty, so very thirsty. She ached like mud left to dry and crack in the sun or like lips in the cold winter wind. She longed for the cool, blue, dark place and found herself baked dry and brittle. A scream tore through her, tore her apart, rent her from top to bottom and from side to side. She had no top or bottom or sides, but she shattered and cracked into pieces as innumerable as the stars.

From around her—or maybe within her—a noise broke the air.

It shredded every sound that had ever been, from the low rumble you feel in your gut to the highest screech that pierces your eardrums. It was all sounds and none, and it did not stop.

Slowly.

Slowly.

Slowly.

Slowly.

Slowly.

Slowly.

A heartbeat.

Carin's hands flew off the face of the stone, and like water rushing from a lake into a funnel, she spiraled back into the being of body.

The tang of blood filled her nose, and the clash of swords and twang of bowstrings filled her ears, and her skin dripped sweat from every pore. Salt water. Sea water. The perspiration of a stone, of that stone.

Her body.

She had a body.

Around her, a battle raged, and Carin could not look away from the stone.

She felt the shift like someone had kicked the world, and she looked wildly around to see if anyone had fallen to the ground. No one had, and still she stood, and no one at all seemed to notice her.

The din of the battle dimmed around her, and in her ears and mind and body the hum rose until she could not breathe and the only thing she felt was the thub-thub, thub-thub, thub-thub of her heart in her chest.

The stone cracked in half.

Carin had a single breath to see it happen before something hit her and her feet left the earth.

She fell unconscious before hitting the ground.

SOMEHOW, SHE woke.

Carin's eyes opened, but she could not move.

Something wet trickled down her lip and into her mouth. She opened her mouth to gasp a breath and tasted blood, like licking bronze.

The sun had moved away from its apex in the sky and now sank toward the horizon, and for a while Carin simply watched it, trying not to look directly at it for too long, but feeling as though it were watching her, seeing her.

She moved, finally, after a lifetime.

Her muscles screamed at her, and as she lurched to her feet, steadying herself on a barrel—how had she gotten near a barrel?—Carin brought her head up and looked around.

Her first thought was, *Everyone is dead.*

Her second was, *Dead people don't move.*

Her third was, *I'm moving. I'm not dead.*

Carin tried to take a single step and nearly collapsed. She sat hard on the barrel, which was on its side, surrounded by mud.

Mud. The barrel had held water, and something had knocked it over. The stone.

Carin swung her head around and found it, right where she had left it. Split down the middle.

The crack had fissured at the central line of the rune for water, and the inside of the stone looked somehow fresh and clean, where its outside still wore thousands of cycles of muck and moss.

Looking down, she saw her bow. The shaft was unharmed—halm was awfully hard to harm—but the string was snapped. Carin picked it up, hoping she wouldn't need to use it, because even had the string not snapped, she wouldn't have been able to draw it.

Her arrows were somehow still mostly in her hip quiver.

Her fingers found her belt and Ryd's halm knife, which was also unharmed, though the hilt and sheath were caked in mud.

Slowly, Carin came back to herself.

And then she remembered the others. She leaped to her feet and nearly fell again. She was surrounded by bodies, some of them groaning or moving slightly, but no one was yet sitting up. She couldn't tell by looking at them what had made them fall, whether it was the breaking of the stone or an arrow in the chest or a stab wound.

Sart.

There was Sart.

Carin stumbled forward on legs that felt as though her bones had been removed through her feet. She tumbled to the ground at Sart's side and pushed at Sart's shoulder until she rolled over.

At first Carin thought she was dead, but then she saw the rise and fall of Sart's stomach and the trickle of flowing blood from her nose and thought that she had never in her life been so happy to see someone bleeding.

Culy lay a short distance away, hys hair flown loose from its normal club, several strands stuck into blood under hys own nose.

Sy stirred, and Carin turned her attention back to Sart. She patted softly at Sart's cheek, and Sart's eyes flew open.

The whites were dotted with red, which made Carin jump, but then Sart's lips curled into a smile.

Right then, that was the only thing in the world Carin needed to see.

IT WAS Ryd's idea to name the waymake at the spring Lahivar, after Sart, since she discovered it.

He didn't really give her a chance to object, because he decided on it and asked the other folk there, and by the time Sart returned with Carin and Culy and a whole herd of others, they'd already made the waypost and stuck it in the ground. There wasn't much she could say against it after that, unless she decided to set the waypost on fire, and Ryd really hoped she wouldn't do that.

He had been afraid, deeply afraid, when Tahin the ihstal came sprinting back into the waymake alone, three days after High Lights. But then Mari had followed in her wake not half a day after, nose caked in dried blood and clutching a broken-off arrow in her gut. It was Mari who told them what had happened, and she'd managed to get out most of the story before she passed out.

Together with Talnyt, Ryd managed to get the arrow out and clean the wound as best they could with fresh water from the spring.

The next morning, Ryd woke early to the sound of people crashing through the woods, and he hurried outside, half terrified it would be Wyt's rovers. But it wasn't.

Carin and Sart each rode their own ihstal, and Culy was not far behind. With them were...people. Lots of people.

Ryd immediately looked around at the huts of Lahivar and wondered how many more they could fit along the stream.

He wanted to be the first to greet them, but Tahin beat him to it, her whistle piercing the air as soon as she saw Sart and Carin from her grazing spot. Both Sart and Carin cried out with the shock of seeing her, and they both launched themselves from the back of their ihstal to meet Tahin and reassure her that they lived. As soon as Tahin realized they were staying, she pranced away as if to say she'd known all along.

Ryd had never known ihstal could be liars.

Sart saw the waypost first, and for a moment she stared at it with a blank face, then she looked at Ryd. "Did you do this?"

He shook his head. "We all did."

"You've all gone and done this the wrong way around," she muttered, and that was all she would say on the matter, but Carin took one look at the waypost herself, and her face spread into a grin.

While they had all been gone, Ryd, not wanting to feel useless, had come up with a plan, and that night he showed it to Culy. It was a simple sketch of a roundhome. Five poles and a central hearth, similar to the huts of the waymakes, but built to be permanent. Insulated with mud-packed grasses and fitted with windows. He had heard there were sand-smiths in Silirtahn, and he showed Culy how it could all be done.

It was only then, looking again at the plan for the roundhome, that Ryd remembered the errant thought he had had while reading over Lyah's scroll and seeing the structure of the spell stones.

They looked like a plan for a roundhome.

Five poles, five stones.

Culy immediately pulled out one of hys maps of the Northlands, and Ryd pointed to the spot where Carin had broken the first stone. With his finger, he traced a circle from that stone around the entire center of the landmass. Not once did it go over the sea, and when he finished, he tapped his hand on the map.

"It's at least a place to start," he said.

Culy was silent for a moment, pointing at two other places on the circle. Then sy nodded. "It is at that."

Ryd didn't think Culy only meant the stones.

WHEN TOIL finally waned, taking with it the bulk of Carin's apprehension, she and Sart followed the spring's stream down to the sea, both mounted on Tahin's back. They were both quiet as they rode, and Carin neither questioned it nor tried to break the silence.

The sea was the same as their stillness, and it filled Carin with unease.

Sart noticed and gave her a wry smile. "It's not always stormy, you know."

Carin pointed out to the horizon, where no flashes of lightning lit the sky, and indeed the clouds had gone. "You said there was always a storm there."

At that, Sart looked quickly, eyes following the horizon line where the storms should have been. Carin noticed the small crease at the top of her forehead again and her own unease grew.

"Culy said all actions have consequences," said Carin, and she didn't just think it was true because Culy had said it.

"One storm fewer likely would be a boon to the fish," Sart said.

Both of them knew that part wasn't true.

Since Carin had broken the stone, she had felt a vast openness inside her, and she wasn't sure what it was. It paired with the hum of magic she felt, and when she wondered if it were related, she felt it both was and wasn't. Of the five branches of magic that could be plied together, one was *dyupahsy*, potential.

Maybe that was it. Potential was a neutral thing, neither good nor ill of itself.

But looking out over that strangely still sea, Carin felt fear take hold, for she wasn't sure what that potential would bring.

The lure of the sea quickly lost its pull, and Carin and Sart got back on Tahin and rode back to Lahivar.

It felt strange, calling a waymake by the name of someone she knew, but, Carin supposed, calling the village of her birth Haveranth must have been strange to anyone who knew Haver.

Back in Lahivar, life settled into a small set of routines. Carin tended her garden, and she taught Sart how to do so as well. Over the next turn, she showed Sart how to properly plant different kinds of seeds and how to make sure they got enough water and sunlight to grow. Which needed shade, and which needed space. The days were still long and the nights stayed warm, and around the new village of Lahivar, there was new life.

The waymakes of these lands had central hearths, and together, Carin laid the stones for a new kind of hearth-home, where life-giving fire would burn. Together, they built a tentative new peace.

She knew, perhaps too well, that it could not last. Not when there were more stones, and not when Wyt still held most of Boggers. One day, one of the scouts reported that a rider was approaching, wearing Wyt's rune and bearing no visible weapons.

After a quick discussion, Culy, Sart, and Carin decided not to let this messenger into the village. Instead, they mounted their ihstal and rode to meet her.

It was Valon.

The sight of the older girl Carin had seen captured sent zigzags of chills across her flesh, and Sart froze in front of her on Tahin. Culy, at least, pretended to be unfazed.

"It cheers me to see that you live, Valon," sy said, and Valon flinched. To Carin's eyes, however, her flinching came an instant too late.

"I did not betray you," she said.

"I said nothing of the sort, only that I'm glad you're not dead."

There was silence, and Carin felt an apology try to come out of her mouth, but she held it back, wanting to hear what Valon would say. For someone who had been captured and held against her will, she looked remarkably well.

"Wyt wants to speak with you, still. With all of you, and the man, Ras. She regrets what happened at the stone."

"Regrets." Sart's voice was neutral, but her back was so tense that Carin thought it would stop an arrow.

Nearly all of the rovers Wyt had sent were dead.

"Where does she want to meet?" Culy asked. "I'm not inclined to pay her any visits."

"She would meet you in a neutral place. She wanted me to assure you that she means no harm to you or your new waymakes." Valon's voice broke. "Culy, she means it. She did not send me to fight against you at the stone, for she did not wish us to harm one another. She is harming no one, only providing us with fresh water. Real fresh water, Culy. From a spring. The clearest and coldest water you've ever tasted."

"I see," was all Culy said. "And what does she expect to gain?"

Valon's mouth opened, but no sound came out. Finally, she said only, "Will you come?"

"I will send a message when I decide. Until then, tell her to keep her rovers under her control, or what happened at the stone will look like a fist-fight." Something passed between them that Carin could not quite catch, like a fluff from a bavel stalk she used to chase in vain as a child.

As they rode back, Carin said, "There is too much that we do not know."

"Consequences," was how Culy responded.

New people arrived each turn from elsewhere, bringing with them gifts of smoked fish or dried meat, fresh berries or crafted items, and most of them had heard of what happened at the stone and wanted to meet Carin.

The problem was, she didn't know what to call herself anymore.

The first few times, she told them that she was Carin vy Haveranth, and it sounded as wrong to her ears as the female *ve Haveranth,* as did simply calling herself Carin, mostly because those she told her name in that case waited as if she'd forgotten half of it.

Summer went on, and in the afternoons now, a storm often rolled out of the mountains, fat drops of rain falling over Lahivar.

The days came and went, and Carin and Sart tended the gardens daily until the heavy dark clouds began to roll in, casting their pregnant shadows of rain over fresh green shoots of new life in rich black soil.

One day, a new group of travelers arrived at the village, bringing a small herd of goats and a stack of cut halm. They wanted to meet Carin, and when they asked for her by name, they asked for Carin Lysiu.

When Carin heard what they called her, she froze, her hands dug into the soil of her garden.

For that moment, the life blooming under her hands meant nothing, and the future broke away from the contentment of her new home and garden, for as she drew in breath, with it came the knowledge that this would truly not last, and that each successive breath she took brought her closer to its end.

That knowledge came, for she heard that name and understood it as her own, and it found its home inside of her just as she had heard it echo through the cave in the Hidden Vale a lifetime before.

Resolutely, she stood, brushed the damp earth from her hands, ignoring the dark crescents beneath her nails, and went to greet the people who had named her.

Carin Lysiu.

Carin Stonebreaker.

HARAG VE Beminohna sat in her bedroom and watched sand creep across the face of her mirror.

The sight made her skin shift like the surface of the sea, and her breath came short and fast in her chest. She had not seen this in moons, many of them, and she should not have been seeing it now.

In the sand's grains that crept across the glass of her mirror, words began to form, as delicate and as light as a spider's silk. *Follow Lyari.*

Harag felt a coldness rise up in her chest, and she felt as though she were trying to stand on the waves. As a child ran by, Harag's stomach was a mass of bile, for she did not know hys name. Only Lyari ever would, and if Harag wanted her village to continue believing that she was their sooth-sayer, she would have to go on as she ever had and ask the soothsayer of Haveranth to tell her.

By Harag's side was a long strand of three-ply vysa, almost empty except for the single black pearl at the knotted end.

• • • • •

A hawk winged north from the Mistaken Pass, where it had spent the winter among the herds of ihstal that lived there. Hard feathers fought the air over the mountains, and the winds were rough and harsh, but still it flew on.

The hawk flew straight and sure over the peaks, unfettered by all it had left behind and undeterred by the winds that buffeted its wings. Its goal ahead, the past behind.

The hawk flew into the north.

• • • • •

In the north, something burst in a mountain, and water sprayed out, out, out and down over the face of the mountain as if it had erupted in tears of joy. Across the land, beneath the feet of the people and animals who trod upon it, far under the soil and clay and rock, water began to flow and surge. It burbled up from the ground, free, always seeking lower ground. The water moved as it would, released from its tiring uphill flow.

Where there once was a muddy creek, soon a gush of water would find its way down from high in the mountains, weaving around hills and washing away silt and clay. It spread and spread across the land without thought or purpose beyond doing as water does, and it would not stop for beasts nor people, roads nor waymakes.

The water was free, and it would not be caged again.

• • • • •

Valon ve Avarsahla sat alone in her hut.

That they left her alone was good. It meant they had begun to trust her. Valon's fingers danced over the blade Culy had slipped to her. A small bronze knife, meant for her belt. This they could not break and throw in a fire to burn.

When her fingers touched the hilt, she felt Culy's presence like a grey wind, and though it was not the first time—nor the hundredth—that she had felt it, she felt hot tears well behind her eyes, sharp like relief. It cut through the turns and moons of worry, and her fingers grasped the hilt tight against her palm.

What she had told Culy was only the truth; Wyt kept her people watered and fed, for around the spring grew grasses and trees, and the animals had begun to come their way. She had given hyr the message she had held for moons, and she had seen in hys eyes that sy understood.

Now all that was left to do was bide her time.

She hated waiting.

Almost as much as she'd hated letting herself get captured.

• • • • •

A bright fire blazed in the hearth, crackling and hot, sending light in a golden pool around it.

Calyria fought back tears.

Everything she had thought, everything she had suspected since she had held her cousin as sy bled out and felt hyr die in her arms—it was all true.

And now, with Jenin beside her, present, hys eyes full of concern and hys neck no longer crusted with dried blood, she finally understood. What she had been told. What she had done. What she would now do.

Jenin watched as Calyria sat in silence, offering nothing but hys presence.

The blood had faded with Calyria's growing knowledge, healing like a cut on a finger.

"You see me as you expect to see me," Jenin had told her, very much dead to the villagers but every inch truly alive.

Now, beside hyr, Calyria felt the warmth of her cousin's skin.

The night was cool for midsummer, and the fire's heat did little to ward it off. This was her roundhome now, this small place where she could leave her village behind. She understood now. The frantic whispers, the secrecy, the knowing looks exchanged when others thought she could not see. She looked into the fire, thinking of the blaze at the village hearthhome she had spent the past cycle tending, never allowing it to go out.

In her roundhome, her solitude felt safe, and around her she built a bubble of it.

She remembered leaving the other Journeyers at Cantor's Road, saw their meld of joy and relief to finally be allowed to go home. She remembered returning, one foot dragged out in front of the other, following the Bemin to Haveranth and finding how the village ignored her. And she remembered those few remaining days, spent in her new roundhome in peace with only an occasional visit from Lyari, who was ready to listen, but Calyria would not speak.

Not of what she had seen in the cave, not of the Journeying there and back with five near-strangers to whom she was now both bound and unbound, not of her return.

Calyria kept all things folded deep inside her chest now. She had made her choice, and as the days spread out before her in their inexorable march, she knew it was the right one, even as she wished with everything in her being that it could have been otherwise.

Could she have done as others had? Fled the village and become Nameless?

Calyria didn't know, and she didn't think so.

It wasn't just what she'd been told, in urgent low tones and hastily given warnings with eyes and ears turned outward in case the wrong person happened by, that the hunters would now be ever more vigilant against any Nameless trying to escape the Hearthland. It wasn't just that to find the passes she now could name in her sleep would require more moons of walking, many, many more. It wasn't even that she would have had to do that walking with a target rune painted on her back.

For those reasons and more, she didn't think so.

There was a space of breath in her chest, and in that space she kept her name. Not the one she had found in the cave, but the name that felt hers. Clar. Just Clar. No necessary appellation. She kept her name in that space of breath, and there it would remain.

Tonight, she would sit alone with her belt knife, scraping the remainder of High Lights's ashes from under her fingernails with Jenin at her side, silent and understanding.

Tomorrow, she would leave her bubble of safety as someone else, but she made sure she had a home where she could simply be.

For cycles to come, however many it took, she would face her village as Calyria.

She let her fire gutter and die, and she sat ready in the comfort of the dark.

• • • • •

Far to the west, past the edge of the world in a small boat just off the shore, a dark-skinned man pulled a silver-scaled fish in from the sea. The fish was large, and it would feed his family for several days, but the fish was also wrong. The man frowned at the fish, at its wide jaw and bulging eyes that belonged much farther out to sea than he was.

The man turned to the east, then looked at the fish, and then his head turned to the sea once more, so quickly it hurt his neck. The horizon had changed.

When he looked back to the shore, he saw that the sea had pulled itself back like a curtain, exposing sand that should not have been seen except during a neap tide. The sight filled the man with terror, and, dropping the silver-scaled fish into the floor of the boat, he took up his oars and rowed.

He rowed and he rowed and he rowed, and he continued to row until his boat scraped bottom on the sand. He grabbed his pole and his fish and his rucksack and ran. He did not look behind him, for he had no need of it. He knew what was coming. The almanac had held no such thing, and yet it came. The almanac was never wrong, and yet it was. He ran.

The man yelled for his lover and their child, loudly enough that she came bursting from their stout little house with wild eyes and the child grabbing at her short hair. She froze when she saw him, the child's pudgy hand clinging to her ear, and she did not look at his face, for she saw behind him, down the hill, to the sea, where it was coming for them.

She turned and ran, and he ran with her.

Up the hill farther, there was a large, large cypress that grew in spite of its location—or maybe because of it; a spring came from the hill that fed the tree—and the man reached it moments after his lover and launched himself at the lowest branch. Dropping his rucksack and pole in the cleft of a branch, fish on top of it, he reached down. He took the child from his lover, ignoring the child's screeches and pulling hyr up into the branches. He did not wait for his lover, but instead climbed higher, telling his child in a low, urgent murmur to cling to his back, to hold on tight and not let go.

He heard his lover scrambling up the tree behind him.

Sweat dripped from his face, down his back, under his arms. The child wailed in his ear but clung tight like a loris. Up and up and up he climbed until the branches grew small and would no longer support their weight. He turned and straddled the branch, looking down to his lover, who climbed with his rucksack slung over her shoulder and the fish and pole in one hand.

High in the tree on a hill, they watched the sea live.

Though it seemed like only moments before he had pulled the fish from the water, he watched the sea approach with a strange sense of lassitude.

Over the next hill, he heard the gong bellow out in the village. He met his lover's eyes, so warm and dark, and he knew her thoughts. He hoped the gong had sounded in time and that it was not too late.

Through the branches of the cypress, he saw the ever-present bank of clouds to the east, the stormline that kept ships from traveling much farther than his island. He lived with them always there, the flashes of lightning against dark clouds the constant backdrop of his daily fishing.

He closed his eyes and felt the sea meet the land.

He heard it too, and he heard himself, speaking comfort to his child, telling hyr not to fear, that they were safe and that today was not the day they would join the sea.

He heard his lover doing the same, and he heard her begin to sing and joined her, singing a song about the gentler waves, the ones that lapped the beach and sang them to sleep at night. The child calmed, and the man breathed deeply, and his lover reached over and took his hand.

The sea raged inland, moving fast, the crashing of its frantic race loud, so loud he could hardly think.

He opened his eyes, knowing what he would see.

His home was gone, though homes could be rebuilt.

The conu trees near the shore were gone as well, though in time they would regrow.

His boat was gone, though he could make another.

He looked at the fish high up in the tree, perched on a branch—the wrong, wrong fish that had saved his life, and he laughed and laughed and laughed.

He looked to his lover, squeezed her hand, feeling the child's sweaty little arms tight around his neck, and he told those two people that he loved them, for they were not boats or trees or houses, and they could not be remade.

What he didn't see through his tears of joy was that past the living, roiling sea, the line of storms was gone.

Selected Glossary
of Hearthland/Northlands Words
and Phrases

A—*adverb*, constant, ongoing

Abas—*noun*, energy (ongoing hammer, constant force)

Ahiu—*noun*, friend

Ahmiu—*noun*, lover

Ahmn—*verb*, to love

Al—*prepositional pronoun*, son of

Alar—*noun*, road, web, way

An—*verb*, to be

Avarn—*verb*, to revive

Bahis—*noun*, branch

Bas—*noun*, hammer/cudgel

Basan—*verb*, to stop

Bavel—*noun or adjective*, cotton-like fiber or fabric

Cajit—*noun*, nut similar to a pistachio

Carn—*verb*, to change/evolve

Dy—*noun*, cold

Dyng—*adjective*, cold

Dyosu—*noun/adjective/adverb*, all.
(Literal: dark-light.)

Dyu—*noun*, dark/night

Dyung—*adjective*, dark

Dyupahsy—*noun*, potential

El—*prepositional pronoun*, daughter of

Fya—*noun*, pillow/comfort

Fyahiul—*noun*, "pillowfriends," a term used to describe emotionally intimate relationships or asexual life partnerships

Hahn—*verb*, to survive

Halm—type of tree (Literal: survivor.)

Harin—*verb*, to find

High Lights—Annual summer solstice ceremony of forgiveness and toil. Villagers work under the longest day whilst fasting, and at sundown, ask forgiveness of other villagers for any wrongs they have committed. Those asked to forgive a wrong mark the shoulders and arms of the one who wronged them with ashes. Marking someone over the heart is considered to be a sign of deeply felt forgiveness. At daybreak, the villagers wash the ashes in the river.

Hyr—*pronoun*, gender neutral (direct object). See also: Sy

Hyrsin—*noun*, genderless adult (used like "woman" or "man") See also: Hysmern

Hys—*pronoun*, gender neutral (possessive). See also: Sy

Hysmern—*noun*, genderless term for children, lit. god-having

Irtan—*noun*, earth, land, soil

Jen—*verb*, to be born

Journeying—Rite of passage undertaken by the youth of the Hearthland in order to find their names and join their villages as adults

Lah—*noun*, water/flow

Lahg—*adjective*, wet

Lahgirtan—*noun*, bog (Literal: wet earth)

Lahi—*noun*, water

Lahi'alar—road webs of the Northlands

Lahivar—water of life

Lahm—noun, fire

Lahmn—verb, to burn

Lahn—verb, to flow

Lys—noun, stone/mountain

Marhan—verb, to sacrifice

Mern—verb, to keep/to have

Night of Reflection—Annual winter solstice ceremony of meditation and reflecting upon the year past and the year to come

Ol—*prepositional pronoun*, of, shows causal origin

Pahn—*verb*, to birth/create

Pey—*noun*, gravity/weight

Rahn—*verb*, to fold

Raht—*noun*, fold, glen, valley

Rin—*verb*, to craft

Rover—bandits in the Northlands

Ryd—*noun*, toughness, strength

Ryhad—*noun*, support

Ryhn—*verb*, to strengthen

Sahla—*noun*, flesh

Sahla'ahmvar—*noun*, family/clan

Sang—*adjective*, red

Sandyu—*noun*, eclipse

Sahan—*noun*, blood

Sahn—*verb*, to bleed

Siun—*verb*, to break

Suhng—*adjective*, yellow

Suo—*noun*, light/sun/day

Suon—*verb*, to show/to light/to reveal/to convict

Suong—*adjective*, white

Sy—*pronoun*, third person singular pronoun declines to *hys* (possessive), *hyr* (direct object), *hyrself* (reflexive). All children (hysmern) use this pronoun until the age of fifteen, when they declare their appellation to their village and their gender (man, woman, hyrsin) and the village switches to their new pronouns or continues with the *sy/hys/hyr/hyrself* if the child is a hyrsin. This is a gender neutral pronoun also used with strangers until the stranger gives a different pronoun as a matter of politeness.

Tahn—*verb*, to dance

Tuan—*verb*, to give

Tuanyen—*noun*, (alt. Spelling [archaic], Tuunya) Pantheon of ancient gods (Literal: givers)

V—*prepositional pronoun*, from. Variations: va (male), ve (female), vy (non-gendered, human only), vo (any singular non-human noun, shows non-causal origin or ownership, ie: *bahis vo Rina*, "Rina's branch," as it belongs to Rina and she did not grow it on her body), vi (plural, used with any nouns.)

Var—*noun*, life

Varn—*verb*, to live

Yl—*prepositional pronoun*, child of (non-gendered, see also hyrsin, hysmern)

Yn—*verb*, to go

Pronunciation and Language Guide

Pronunciation (American English phonetics):

A is always ah
E is somewhere between eh and ay
I is always short ih
O is always long oh
U is short like book
Y is always ee

Adding an h after a vowel elongates its sound.

R is lightly trilled
Th is a lighter th sound
C is always a hard C
S followed by I lenites into a soft sh, but preceding vowels do not cause lenition (Example: Silirtahn)
D, G, and B are voiced at the beginning of words, but the voice drops to aspiration in the middle of words (Thus Ryd's name is pronounced somewhat like Reet.)
J is pronounced like an English J

The language also has diminutive and augmentative forms:

Kat—blade
Kasyt—little knife (like a dirk or a Scottish sgian dubh, etc.)
Kaht—sword

Lys—stone/mountain
Lysyt—pebble/hill
Lyhst—boulder/mountain range

CPSIA information can be obtained
at www.ICGtesting.com
Printed in the USA
LVHW02*1551260718
585038LV00007B/70/P